TIMBERLAND REGIONAL LIBRARY

A20006 926579

SO-AAC-618

SHELTON

JUN 4 1987

What's Bred
in the Bone

Timberland Regional Library
Service Center
415 Airdustrial Way S.W.
Olympia, WA 98501

Robertson Davies

WHAT'S BRED IN THE BONE

G.K.HALL & CO.
Boston, Massachusetts
1987

Copyright © 1985 by Robertson Davies.

All rights reserved.

Published in Large Print by arrangement with
Viking Penguin Inc.

All the characters in this book are fictitious, and any
resemblance to actual persons living or dead is coincidental.

British Commonwealth rights courtesy of
Penguin Books Ltd.

Canadian rights courtesy of
The Colbert Agency Inc.

G. K. Hall Large Print Book Series.

Set in 16 pt Plantin.

Library of Congress Cataloging in Publication Data

Davies, Robertson, 1913-
    What's bred in the bone.

    (G.K. Hall large print book series)
    1. Large type books.   I. Title.
[PR9199.3.D3W5   1987]   813'.54   86-22908
ISBN 0-8161-4133-9 (lg. print)

"What's bred in the bone
will not out of the flesh."

ENGLISH PROVERB FROM THE LATIN, 1290

PART ONE

Who Asked
the Question?

"The book must be dropped."

"No, Arthur!"

"Perhaps only for a time. But for the present, it must be dropped. I need time to think."

The three trustees in the big penthouse drawing-room were beginning to shout, which destroyed all atmosphere of a business meeting—not that such an atmosphere had ever been strong. Yet this was a business meeting, and these three were the sole members of the newly founded Cornish Foundation for Promotion of the Arts and Humane Scholarship. Arthur Cornish, who was pacing up and down the room, was unquestionably a business man; a Chairman of the Board to his business associates, but a man with interests that might have surprised them if he had not kept his life in tidy compartments. The Reverend Simon Darcourt, pink, plump, and a little drunk, looked precisely what he was: a priest-academic pushed into a tight corner. But the figure least like a trustee of anything was Arthur's wife Maria, barefoot in gypsy style, and dressed in a housecoat

3

that would have been gaudy if it had not been made by the best couturier of the best materials.

There is an ill justified notion that women are peacemakers. Maria tried that role now.

"What about all the work Simon's done?"

"We acted too quickly. Commissioning the book, I mean. We should have waited to see what would turn up."

"What's turned up may not be as bad as you think. Need it, Simon?"

"I haven't any idea. It would take experts to decide, and they could be years doing it. All I have is suspicions. I'm sorry I ever mentioned them."

"But you suspect Uncle Frank faked some Old Master drawings he left to the National Gallery. Isn't that bad enough?"

"It could be embarrassing."

"Embarrassing! I admire your coolness. A member of a leading Canadian financial family may be a picture-faker!"

"You're neurotic about the business, Arthur."

"Yes, Maria, I am, and for the best of reasons. There is no business so neurotic, fanciful, scared of its own shadow, and downright loony as the money business. If one member of the Cornish family is shown to be a crook, the financial world will be sure that the whole Cornish family is shady. There'll be cartoons of me in the papers: 'Would You Buy an Old Master from This Man?' That kind of thing."

"But Uncle Frank was never associated with the business."

"Doesn't matter. He was a Cornish."

"The best of the lot."

"Perhaps. But if he's a crook, all his banking relations will suffer for it. Sorry: no book."

"Arthur, you're being tyrannous."

"All right; I'm being tyrannous."

"Because you're scared."

"I have good reason to be scared. Haven't you been listening? Haven't you heard what Simon has been telling us?"

"I'm afraid I've been clumsy about this whole thing," said Simon Darcourt. He looked miserable; his face was almost as white as his clerical collar. "I shouldn't have told you my suspicions—because that's all they are, you know—the very first thing. Will you listen while I tell you what is really bothering me? It isn't just your Uncle Frank's cleverness with his pencil. It's the whole book.

"I'm a disciplined worker. I don't mess about, waiting for inspiration, and all that nonsense. I sit down at my desk and wire in and make prose out of my copious notes. But this book has twisted and turned under my hands like a dowser's hazel twig. Does the spirit of Francis Cornish not want his life to be written? He was the most private man I've ever known. Nobody ever got much out of him that was personal—except two or three, of whom Aylwin Ross was the last. You know, of

5

course, that Francis and Ross were thought to be homosexual lovers?"

"Oh my God!" said Arthur Cornish. "First you suspect he was a picture-faker and now you tell me he was a poofter. Any other little surprises, Simon?"

"Arthur, don't be silly and coarse," said Maria; "you know that homosexuality is an O.K. kink nowadays."

"Not in the money-market."

"Oh, to hell with the money-market."

"Please, my dears," said Darcourt. "Don't quarrel, and if I may say so, don't quarrel foolishly about trivialities. I've been busy on this biography for eighteen months and I'm not getting anywhere. You don't frighten me by threatening to quash it, Arthur. I've a good mind to quash it myself. I tell you I can't go on. I simply can't get enough facts."

Arthur Cornish had his full share of the human instinct to urge people to do what they do not want to do. Now he said, "That's not like you, Simon; you're not a man to throw in the towel."

"No, please don't think of it, Simon," said Maria. "Waste eighteen months of research? You're just depressed. Have a drink and let us cheer you up."

"I'll gladly have a drink, but I want to tell you what my position is. It's more than just author's cold feet. Please listen to my problem. It's serious."

Arthur was already getting drinks for the three

of them. He set a glass that was chiefly Scotch with a mere breathing of soda in front of Darcourt, and sat down on the sofa beside his wife.

"Shoot," he said.

Darcourt took a long and encouraging swig.

"You two married about six months after Francis Cornish died," said he. "When at last his estate was settled, it became apparent that he had a lot more money than anybody had supposed—"

"Well, of course," said Arthur. "We didn't think he had anything but his chunk of his grandfather's estate, and what his father left, which could have been considerable. He was never interested in the family business; most of us thought of him as an eccentric—a man who would rather mess around with his collections of art than be a banker. I was the only member of the family who had an inkling of what made him feel that way. Banking isn't much of a life if you have no enthusiasm for it—which fortunately I have, which is why I'm now Chairman of the Board. He had a comfortable amount of money; a few millions. But ever since he died, money has been turning up in substantial chunks from unexpected places. Three really big wads in numbered accounts in Switzerland, for instance. Where did he get it? We know he got big fees for authenticating Old Masters for dealers and private collectors, but even big fees don't add up to additional millions. What was he up to?"

"Arthur, shut up," said Maria. "You promised to let Simon tell us his problem."

7

"Oh, sorry. Go ahead, Simon. Do you know where the extra money came from?"

"No, but that's not the most important thing I don't know. I simply don't know who he was."

"But you must. I mean, there are verifiable facts."

"Indeed, there are, but they don't add up to the man we knew."

"I never knew him at all. Never saw him," said Maria.

"I didn't really know him," said Arthur. "I saw him a few times when I was a boy, at family affairs. He didn't usually come to those, and didn't seem at ease with the family. He always gave me money. Not like an uncle tipping a nephew, with a ten-dollar bill; he would slip me an envelope on the sly, often with as much as a hundred dollars in it. A fortune to a schoolboy, who was being brought up to respect money and look at both sides of a dollar bill. And I remember another thing; he never shook hands."

"I knew him much better than either of you, and he never shook hands with me," said Darcourt. "We became friends because we shared some artistic enthusiasms—music, and manuscripts, and calligraphy, and that sort of thing—and of course he made me one of his executors. But as for shaking hands—not Frank. He did once tell me that he hated shaking hands. Said he could smell mortality on his hand when it had touched somebody's else's. When he absolutely had to shake hands with some fellow who didn't

8

get his clear signals, he would shoot off to the washroom as soon as he could and wash his hands. Compulsive behaviour."

"That's odd," said Arthur. "He always looked rather dirty to me."

"He didn't bathe much. When we cleared out his stuff he had three apartments, with six bathrooms among them, and every bathtub was piled high with bundles of pictures and sketches and books and manuscripts and whatnot. After so many years of disuse I wonder if the taps worked. But he had preserved one tiny washroom—just a cupboard off an entry—and there he did his endless hand-washing. His hands were always snowy white, though otherwise he smelled a bit."

"Are you going to put that in?"

"Of course. He hadn't a bad smell. He smelled like an old, leather-bound book."

"He sounds rather a dear," said Maria; "a crook who smells like an old book. A Renaissance man, without all the boozing and sword-fighting."

"Certainly no boozing," said Darcourt. "He didn't drink—at least not in his own place. He would take a drink, and even several drinks, if somebody else was paying. He was a miser, you know."

"This is getting better and better," said Maria. "A booky-smelling, tight-fisted crook. You can surely make a wonderful biography, Simon."

"Shut up, Maria; control your romantic passion for crooks. It's her gypsy background coming out," said Arthur to Darcourt.

"Would you two *both* shut up and let me get on with what I have to say?" said Darcourt. "I am not trying to write a sensational book; I am trying to do what you asked me to do nearly two years ago, which is to prepare a solid, scholarly, preferably not deadly-dull biography of the late Francis Cornish, as the first act of the newly founded Cornish Foundation for Promotion of the Arts and Humane Scholarship, of which you two and I are at present the sole directors. And don't say you 'commissioned' it, Arthur. Not a penny changed hands and not a word was written in agreement. It was a friendly thing, not a money thing. You thought a nice book about Uncle Frank would be a nice thing with which to lead off a laudable Foundation devoted to the nice things that you thought Uncle Frank stood for. This was a typically Canadian act of smiling niceness. But I can't get the facts I want for my book, and some of the things I have not quite uncovered would make a book which—as Arthur so justifiably fears—would cause a scandal."

"And make the Foundation and the Cornish name stink," said Arthur.

"I don't know about the Cornish name, but if the Foundation had money to give away I don't think you'd find artists or scholars fussing about where it came from," said Darcourt. "Scholars and artists have no morals whatever about grants of money. They'd take it from a house of child prostitution, as you two innocents will discover."

"Simon, that must have been an awfully strong

10

drink," said Maria. "You're beginning to bully us. That's good."

"It was a strong drink, and I'd like another just like it, and I'd like to have the talk to myself to tell you what I know and what I don't know."

"One strong Scotch for the Reverend Professor," said Arthur, moving to prepare it. "Go on, Simon. What have you actually got?"

"We might as well begin with the obituary that appeared in the London *Times,* on the Monday after Francis died. It's a pretty good summing up of what the world thinks, up to now, about your deceased relative, and the source is above suspicion."

"Is it?" said Maria.

"For a Canadian to be guaranteed dead by *The Times* shows that he was really somebody who could cut the mustard. Important on a world level."

"You talk as if the obituary columns of the London *Times* were the Court Circular of the Kingdom of Heaven, prepared by the Recording Angel."

"Well, that's not a bad way of putting it. *The New York Times* had a much longer piece, but it isn't really the same thing, The British have some odd talents, and writing obituaries is one of them. Brief, stylish, no punches pulled—so far as they possessed punches. But either they didn't know or didn't choose to say a few things that are public knowledge. Now listen: I'll assume a *Times* voice:

On Sunday, September 12, his seventy-second birthday, Francis Chegwidden Cornish, internationally known art expert and collector, died at his home in Toronto, Canada. He was alone at the time of his death.

Francis Cornish, whose career as an art expert, especially in the realms of sixteenth-century and Mannerist painting, extended over forty years and was marked by a series of discoveries, reversals of previously held opinions, and quarrels, was known as a dissenter and frequently a scoffer in matters of taste. His authority was rooted in an uncommon knowledge of painting techniques and a mastery of the comparatively recent critical approach called iconology. He seemed also to owe much to a remarkable intuition, which he displayed without modesty, to the chagrin of a number of celebrated experts, with whom he disputed tirelessly.

Born in 1909 in Blairlogie, a remote Ontario settlement, he enjoyed all his life the freedom which comes with ample means. His father came of an old and distinguished family in Cornwall; his mother (née McRory) came of a Canadian family that acquired substantial wealth first in timber, and later in finance. Cornish never engaged in the family business, but derived a fortune from it, and he was able to back his intuitions with a long purse. The disposition of his remarkable collections is as yet unknown.

He received his schooling in Canada and was

educated at Corpus Christi College, Oxford, after which he travelled extensively, and was for many years a colleague and pupil of Tancred Saraceni of Rome, some of whose eccentricities he was thought to have incorporated in his own rebarbative personality. But in spite of his eccentricities it might always have been said of Francis Cornish that for him art possessed all the wisdom of poetry.

During and after the 1939-45 war he was a valuable member of the group of Allied experts who traced and recovered works of art which had been displaced during the hostilities.

In his later years he made generous gifts of pictures to the National Gallery of Canada.

He never married and leaves no direct heirs. It is authoritatively stated that there was no foul play in the manner of his death.

"I'm not mad about that," said Maria. "It has a snotty undertone."

"You don't know how snotty a *Times* obit can be. I suspect most of that piece was written by Aylwin Ross, who thought he would outlive Francis, and have a chuckle over the last sentence. In fact, that obit is Ross's patronizing estimate of a man who was greatly his superior. There's a question in it that is almost Ross's trade mark. It's quite decent, really, all things considered."

"What things considered?" said Arthur. "What

do they mean, 'no foul play'? Did anybody suggest there was?"

"Not here," said Darcourt, "but some of the people on the Continent who knew him might have wondered. Don't find fault with it; obviously Ross chose to suppress a few things the *Times* certainly has in its files."

"Like—?"

"Well, not a word about the stinking scandal that killed Jean-Paul Letztpfennig, and made Francis notorious in the art world. Reputations fell all over the place. Even Berenson was just the teeniest bit diminished."

"Obviously you know all about it, though," said Arthur, "and if Uncle Frank came out on top, that's all to the good. Who was Tancred Saraceni?"

"Queer fish. A collector, but known chiefly as a magnificent restorer of Old Masters; all the big galleries used him, or consulted him, at one time or another. But some very rum things went through his hands to other collectors. Like your Uncle Frank, he was rumoured to be altogether too clever with his paintbox; Ross hated him."

"And that *Times* piece is the best that was said about Francis?" said Maria.

"Do you notice they say he went to school in Canada but was *educated* at Oxford?" said Arthur. "God, the English!"

"*The Times* was generous in its own terms," said Darcourt. "They printed the piece I sent to them as soon as I saw their obit. Listen to this: published in their issue of September 26:

FRANCIS CORNISH

Professor the Rev. Simon Darcourt writes:

Your obituary of my friend Francis Cornish (Sept. 13) is correct in all its facts, but gives a dour impression of a man who was sometimes crusty and difficult, but also generous and kind in countless personal relationships. I have met no one who knew him who thought for an instant that his death might have been from other than natural causes.

Many leading figures in the art world regarded him as a knowledgeable and co-operative colleague. His work with Saraceni may have gained him the mistrust of some who had felt the scorn of that ambiguous figure, but his authority, based on unquestioned scholarship, was all his own, and it is known that on several occasions his opinion was sought by the late Lord Clark. In a quarrel it was rarely Cornish who struck the first blow, although he was not quick to resolve a dispute or forget an injury.

His fame as an authority on painting overshadowed his substantial achievements in the study and scientific examination of illumination and calligraphy, an area not much favoured by critics of painting and sculpture, but which seemed to him to be significant, as providing clues to work on a larger scale. He was also a discriminating collector of music MSS.

15

During his years in Canada after 1957 he did much to encourage Canadian painters, though his scorn for what he regarded as psychological fakery in certain modern movements generated a good deal of heat. His own aesthetic approach was carefully considered and philosophically founded.

An eccentric, undoubtedly, but a man of remarkable gifts who shunned publicity. When his collections have been examined it may emerge that he was a more significant figure in the art world of his time than is at present understood.

"That's a lot better, Simon," said Maria, "but it's still a long way from being a rave."

"It's not my business to write raves, but to speak the truth, as a friend who is also a scholar and a man with his eyes open."

"Well, can't you do that in the biography?"

"Not if it means exposing Uncle Frank as a picture-faker," said Arthur.

"Listen, Arthur, you're going too far. The most you can say is that my book won't have any Cornish money behind it unless it presents a whitewashed portrait of Francis. You forget that I could find a commercial publisher. I don't write bad books, and a book you would think scandalous might appeal to them as a good commercial proposition."

"Simon—you wouldn't!"

"If you bully me, I might."

"I don't mean to bully you."

"But that's what you're doing. You rich people think you have unlimited power. If I decided to write this book entirely on my own responsibility you couldn't do a thing to stop me."

"We could withhold information."

"You could if you had any, but you haven't and you know it."

"We could sue you for defamation."

"I'd take care not to defame the living Cornishes, and surely you know the law doesn't care about defamation of the dead."

"Please, will you men stop being silly and threatening one another," said Maria. "If I understand Simon rightly, it's this very lack of information and creeping suspicion that's holding him up. But you must have some stuff, Simon. Anybody's life can be dug up to some extent."

"Yes, and used by cheap writers with lots of spicy innuendo to make a trumpery book. But I'm not that kind of writer. I have my pride; I even have my tiny reputation. If I can't do a first-rate job on old Frank I won't do anything."

"But all this stuff about Saraceni, and what *The Times* doesn't say about this other fellow—the one who died or was killed or whatever happened— surely can be tracked down, and fleshed out. Though if it means a book that suggests Francis Cornish was a crook, I hope you'll do what you can about that." Arthur seemed to be climbing down.

"Oh, that—I can get that right enough. But

what I want is what lies behind it. How did Francis get into such company? What was it in his character that disposed him to that part of the art world, instead of keeping his skirts clear like Berenson, or Clark? How did a rich amateur—which is what he was, to begin with—get mixed up with such shabby types?"

"Just luck, probably," said Arthur. "What happens to people is so often nothing but the luck of the game."

"I don't believe that," said Darcourt. "What we call luck is the inner man externalized. We make things happen to us. I know that sounds horrible and cruel, considering what happens to a lot of people, and it can't be the whole explanation. But it's a considerable part of it."

"How can you say that?" said Arthur. "We are all dealt a hand of cards at birth; if somebody gets a rotten hand, full of twos and threes and nothing above a five, what chance has he against the fellow with a full flush? And don't tell me it's how he plays the game. You're not a poker-player or a bridge-player, Simon, and you just don't know."

"Not a card-player, I admit, but I am a theologian, and rather a good one. Consequently I have a different idea of the stakes that are being played for than you have, you banker. Of course everybody is dealt a hand, but now and then he has a chance to draw another card, and it's the card he draws when the chance comes that can make all the difference. And what decides the card he

18

draws? Francis was given a good, safe hand at birth, but two or three times he had a chance to draw, and every time he seems to have drawn the joker. Do you know why?"

"No, and neither do you."

"I think I do. Among your uncle's papers I found a little sheaf of horoscopes he had prepared for him at various points in his life. He was superstitious, you know, if you call astrology superstition."

"Don't you?"

"I reserve judgement. What is important is that he obviously believed in it to some extent. Now—your uncle's birthday fell at a moment when Mercury was the ruling sign of his chart, and Mercury at the uttermost of his power."

"So?"

"Well? Maria understands. Isn't her mother a gifted card-reader? Mercury: patron of crooks, the joker, the highest of whatever is trumps, the mischief-maker, who upsets all calculations."

"Not just that, Simon," said Maria; "he is also Hermes, the reconciler of opposites—something out of the scope of conventional morality."

"Just so. And if ever there was a true son of Hermes, it was Francis Cornish."

"When you begin to talk like that, I must leave you," said Arthur. "Not in disgust, but in bafflement. Life with Maria has given me a hint of what you are talking about, but just at this moment I can't continue with you. I have to catch a plane at seven tomorrow, and that means getting up at five and being at the airport not much after six—such is the amenity and charm of modern travel. So I'll give you another drink, Simon, and bid you good-night."

Which Arthur did, kissing his wife affectionately and telling her not to dare to wake early to see him off.

"Arthur pours a very heavy drink," said Darcourt.

"Only because he thinks you need it," said Maria. "He's wonderfully kind and observant, even if he does make noises like a banker about this book. You know why, don't you? Anything that challenges the perfect respectability of the Cornishes stirs him up, because he has secret doubts of his own. Oh, they're unimpeachable so far as money-dealers go, but banking is like religion: you have to accept certain rather dicey things simply on faith, and then everything else follows in marvellous logic. If Francis was a bit of a crook, he was the shadow of a great banking family, and they aren't supposed to cast shadows. But was Francis a crook? Come on, Simon, what's really troubling you?"

"The early years. Blairlogie."

"Where exactly *is* Blairlogie?"

"Now you're beginning to sound like *The Times*. I can tell you a little about the place as it is now. Like a good biographer I've made my pilgrimage there. It's in the Ottawa Valley, about sixty miles or so north-west of Ottawa. Rough country. Perfectly accessible by car now, but when Francis was born it was thought by a lot of people to be the Jumping-Off Place, because you couldn't get there except by a rather primitive train. It was a town of about five thousand people, predominantly Scots.

"But as I stood on the main street, looking for evidence and hoping for intuitions, I knew I wasn't seeing anything at all like what little Francis saw at the beginning of the century. His grandfather's house, St. Kilda, is cut up into apartments. His parents' house, Chegwidden Lodge, is now the Devine Funeral Parlours—yes, Devine, and nobody thinks it funny. All the timber business that was the foundation of the Cornish money is totally changed. The McRory Opera House is gone, and nothing remains of the McRorys except some unilluminating stuff in local histories written by untalented amateurs. Nobody in modern Blairlogie has any recollection of Francis, and they weren't impressed when I said he had become quite famous. There were some pictures that had come from his grandfather's house that had passed into the possession of the public library, but they had stored them in the cellar, and they were perished almost beyond recognition. Just tenth-rate Victorian junk. I drew almost a total blank."

"But are the childhood years so important?"

"Maria, you astonish me! Weren't your childhood years important? They are the matrix from which a life grows."

"And that's all gone?"

"Gone beyond recovery."

21

"Unless you can wangle a chat with the Recording Angel."

"I don't think I believe in a Recording Angel. We are all our own Recording Angels."

"Then I am more orthodox than you. I believe in a Recording Angel. I even know his name."

"Pooh, you medievalists have a name for everything. Just somebody's invention."

"Why not somebody's revelation? Don't be so hidebound, Simon. The name of the Recording Angel was Radueriel, and he wasn't just a bookkeeper; he was the Angel of Poetry, and Master of the Muses. He also had a staff."

"Wound with serpents, like the caduceus of Hermes, I suppose."

"Not that kind of staff; a civil service staff. One of its important members was the Angel of Biography, and his name was the Lesser Zadkiel. He was the angel who interfered when Abraham was about to sacrifice Isaac, so he is an angel of mercy, though a lot of biographers aren't. The Lesser Zadkiel could give you the lowdown on Francis Cornish."

Darcourt by now was unquestionably drunk. He became lyrical.

"Maria—dear Maria—forgive me for being stupid about the Recording Angel. Of course he exists—exists as a metaphor for all that illimitable history of humanity and inhumanity and inanimate life and everything that has ever been, which must exist some place or else the whole of life is reduced to a stupid file with no beginning and no

22

possible ending. It's wonderful to talk to you, my dearest, because you think medievally. You have a personification or a symbol for everything. You don't talk about ethics: you talk about saints and their protective spheres and their influences. You don't use lettuce juice words like 'extra-terrestrial'; you talk frankly about Heaven and Hell. You don't blether about neuroses; you just say demons."

"Certainly I haven't a scientific vocabulary," said Maria.

"Well, science is the theology of our time, and like the old theology it's a muddle of conflicting assertions. What gripes my gut is that it has such a miserable vocabulary and such a pallid pack of images to offer to us—to the humble laity—for our edification and our faith. The old priest in his black robe gave us things that seemed to have concrete existence; you prayed to the Mother of God and somebody had given you an image that looked just right for the Mother of God. The new priest in his whitish lab-coat gives you nothing at all except a constantly changing vocabulary which he—because he usually doesn't know any Greek—can't pronounce, and you are expected to trust him implicitly because he knows what you are too dumb to comprehend. It's the most overweening, pompous priesthood mankind has ever endured in all its recorded history, and its lack of symbol and metaphor and its zeal for abstraction drive mankind to a barren land of starved imagination. But you, Maria, speak the old language that strikes upon the heart. You talk about the Recording Angel and you talk about his lesser angels, and we both know exactly what you mean. You give comprehensible and attractive names to psychological facts, and God—another effectively named psychological fact—bless you for it."

"You're raving ever so slightly, darling, and it's time you went home."

"Yes, yes, yes. Of course. This instant. Can I stand up? Ooooh!"

"No, wait a minute, I'll see you out. But before you go, tell me what it is about Francis you want and can't discover?"

"Childhood! That's the key. Not the only key, but the first key to the mystery of a human creature. Who brought him up, and what were they and what did they believe that stamped the child so that those beliefs stuck in his mind long after he thought he had rejected them? Schools— schools, Maria! Look what Colborne has done to Arthur! Not bad—or not all of it—but it clings to him still, in the way he ties his tie, and polishes his shoes, and writes amusing little thankees to people who have had him to dinner. And a thousand things that lurk below the surface, like the conventionality he showed when he heard Francis might be rather a crook. Well—what were the schools of Blairlogie? Francis was never out of the place until he was fifteen. Those were the schools that marked him. Of course, I could fake it. Oh, I wish I had the indecency of so many biographers and dared to fake it! Not crude faking, of course, but a kind of fiction, the sort of fiction that rises to the level of art! And it would be true, you know, in its way. You remember what Browning says:

> . . . *Art remains the one way possible*
> *Of speaking truth, to mouths like mine, at least.*

I could serve Francis so much better if I had the freedom of fiction."

"Oh, Simon, you don't have to tell me that you are an artist at heart."

"But an artist chained to biography, which ought to bear some resemblance to fact."

"A matter of moral conscience."

"And a matter of social conscience, as well. But what about artistic conscience, which people don't usually pay much attention to? I want to write a really good book. Not just a trustworthy book, but a book people will like to read. Everybody has a dominant kind of conscience, and in me the artistic conscience seems to be pushing the other two aside. Do you know what I really think?"

"No, but you obviously want to tell me."

"I think that probably Francis had a daimon. As a man so much under the influence of Mercury, or Hermes, it would be quite likely. You know what a daimon is?"

"Yes, but go on."

"Oh, of course you'd know. I keep forgetting what a knowing girl you are. Since you became the wife of a very rich man, it somehow seems

25

unlikely that you should know anything really interesting. But of course you're your mother's child, splendid old crook and sibyl that she is! Of course you know what Hesiod calls daimons: spirits of the Golden Age, who act as guardians to mortals. Not tedious manifestations of the moral conscience, like Guardian Angels, always pulling for Sunday-school rightness and goodiness. No, manifestations of the artistic conscience, who supply you with extra energy when it is needed, and tip you off when things aren't going as they should. Not wedded to what Christians think of as what is right, but to what is your destiny. Your joker in the pack. Your Top Trump that subdues all others!"

"You could call that intuition."

"Bugger intuition! That's a psychological word, grey and dowdy. I prefer the notion of a daimon. Know the names of any good daimons, Maria?"

"I've only come across the name of one, engraved on an old gem. It was Maimas. D'you know, Simon, I think I'm getting a little drunk too. Now, if you could just get the ear of the Lesser Zadkiel and—well, call him Maimas— you'd have all you want about Francis Cornish."

"Wouldn't I, by God! I'd have what I want. I'd know what was bred in the bone of old Francis. Because what's bred in the bone will come out in the flesh, and we should never forget it.—Oh, I really must go."

Darcourt gulped the remainder of his drink,

kissed Maria impressionistically—in the region of the nose—and stumbled toward the door.

Not too steadily, Maria rose and took him by the arm. Should she offer to drive him home? No, that might make things worse than if he made it himself, refreshed by the cool night air. But she went with him to the hallway of the penthouse on top of the condominium where she and Arthur lived, and steered him toward the elevator.

The doors closed, but as he descended, she could hear him shouting, "What's bred in the bone! Oh, what was bred in bone?"

The Lesser Zadkiel and the Daimon Maimas, who had been drawn by the sound of their own names to listen to what was going on, found it diverting.

—Poor Darcourt, said the Angel of Biography. Of course he'll never know the whole truth about Francis Cornish.

—Even we do not know the entire truth, brother, said the Daimon Maimas. Indeed, I've already forgotten much of what I did know when Francis was my entire concern.

—Would it amuse you to be reminded of the story, so far as you and I can know it? said the Angel.

—Indeed it would. Very generous of you, brother. You have the record, or the film, or the tape or whatever it must be called. Could you be bothered to set it going?

—Nothing simpler, said the Angel.

What Was Bred
in the Bone?

To begin, when Francis was born there, Blairlogie was not the Jumping-Off Place, and would have strongly resented any such suggestion. It thought of itself as a thriving town, and for its inhabitants the navel of the universe. It knew itself to be moving forward confidently into the twentieth century, which Canada's great Prime Minister, Sir Wilfrid Laurier, had declared to be peculiarly Canada's. What might have appeared to an outsider to be flaws or restrictions were seen by Blairlogie as advantages. The roads around it were certainly bad, but they had always been bad so long as they had been roads, and the people who used them accepted them as facts of their existence. If the greater world wished to approach Blairlogie, it could very well do so by the train which made the sixty-mile journey from Ottawa over a rough line, much of it cut through the hardest granite of the Laurentian Shield, a land mass of mythic antiquity. Blairlogie saw no reason to be easily accessible.

The best of the town's money and business was

firmly in the hands of the Scots, as was right and proper. Below the Scots, in a ranking that was decreed by money, came a larger population of Canadians of French descent, some of whom were substantial merchants. At the bottom of the financial and social heap were the Poles, a body of labourers and small farmers from which the upper ranks drew their domestic servants. Altogether the town numbered about five thousand carefully differentiated souls.

The Scots were Presbyterian, and as this was Canada at the turn of the century their religious belief and their political loyalty were the important conditioning factors in their lives. These Presbyterians might have had some trouble in formulating the doctrine of predestination or foreordination which lay deep in their belief, but they had no practical difficulty in knowing who was of the elect, and who belonged to a creation with a less certain future in Eternity.

The French and the Poles were Roman Catholics, and they too knew precisely where they stood in relation to God, and were by no means displeased with their situation. There were a few Irish, also Catholics, and some odds and ends of other racial strains—mongrels of one sort and another—who had mean churches suited to their eccentricities, dwindling toward a vacant-store temple that changed hands from one rampaging evangelist to another, in whose windows hung gaudy banners displaying the Beasts of the Apocalypse, in horrendous detail. There were no Jews, blacks, or other incalculable elements.

The town could have been represented as a wedding-cake, with the Poles as the large foundation layer, bearing the heaviest weight; the French, the middle layer, were smaller but central; the Scots were the topmost, smallest, most richly ornamented layer of all.

No town is simple in every respect. People who liked perfection and tidiness of structure were puzzled by the quirk of fate which decreed that the Senator, by far the richest and most influential man in Blairlogie, cut right across accepted ideas: though a Scot, he was an R.C., and though rich he was a Liberal, and his wife was French.

The Senator was the person to begin with, for he was Francis Chegwidden Cornish's grandfather, and the origin of the wealth that supported Francis's life until he gained a mysterious fortune of his own.

The Senator was the Honourable James Ignatius McRory, born on the Isle of Barra in the Hebrides in 1855, who had been brought to Canada in 1857 by parents who were, like so many of their kind, starving in their beautiful homeland. They never succeeded in getting the ache of starvation and bitter poverty out of their bones, though they did better in the New World than they could have done at home. But their son James—called Hamish by them, because that was his name in the Gaelic they customarily spoke between themselves—hated starvation and resolved as a child to put poverty well behind him, and did so. Necessity sent him early to work in the forests which were a part of the wealth of Canada, and ambition and daring, combined with an inborn long-headedness (to say nothing of his skill with his fists, and his feet when fists were not enough), made him a forest boss very young, and a contractor for lumber companies shortly after, and the owner of a lumber company of his own before he was thirty, by which time he was already a rich man.

A common enough story, but, like everything else connected with Hamish, not without its individual touches. He did not marry into a lumbering family, to advance himself, but made a love-match with Marie-Louise Thibodeau when he was twenty-seven and she was twenty, and he never desired any other woman afterward. Nor did the life in the camps make him hard and remorseless; he treated his men fairly when he was an employer, and when he came to have money he gave generously to charity and to the Liberal Party.

Indeed, the Liberal Party was, after Marie-Louise and one other, the great love of his life. He never stood for Parliament, but he supported and financed men who did so; in so far as there was a party machine in Blairlogie, where he settled as soon as he no longer had to live near the forests, Hamish McRory was the brains behind the machine; thus nobody was surprised when Sir Wilfrid Laurier appointed him to the Senate when he was not yet forty-five, making him the youngest man, and demonstrably one of the ablest, in the Upper House.

A Canadian senator was, in those days, appointed for life, and some senators were known to give up all political effort once they felt their feet on the red carpet of the Upper Chamber. But Hamish had no intention of relaxing his party zeal because of his new honour, and as a senator he was more Sir Wilfrid's man in an important area of the Ottawa Valley than ever before.

When are we going to get to my man? said the Daimon Maimas, who was eager to make his contribution to the story.

—In due season, said the Lesser Zadkiel. Francis must be seen against his background, and if we are not to start at the very beginning of all things, we must not neglect the Senator. That's the biographical way.

—I see, you want to do it on the nature and nurture principle, said Maimas, and the Senator is both.

—Nature and nurture are inextricable; only scientists and psychologists could think otherwise, and we know all about them, don't we?

—We should. We've watched them since they were tribal wizards, yelping around the campfire. Go on. But I'm waiting for my chance.

—Be patient, Maimas. Time is for those who exist within its yoke. We are not time-bound, you and I.

—I know but I like to talk.

32

Apart from Marie-Louise, and of a different order, the Senator's deep love was his elder daughter, Mary-Jacobine. Why so named? Because Marie-Louise had hoped for a son, and Jacobine was a fancy derivation from Jacobus, which is James, which is also Hamish. It suggested also a devotion to the Stuart cause, and called up that sad prince James II and his even sadder son, Bonnie Prince Charlie. The name was suggested with implacable modesty by the Senator's sister, Miss Mary-Benedetta McRory, who lived with him and his wife. Miss McRory, known always as Mary-Ben, was a formidable spirit concealed in a little, wincing spinster. It was her romantic notion that her forebears, as Highland Scots, must necessarily have been supporters of the Stuarts, and none of the books she read on that subject suggested that James II and his son, as well as being handsome and romantic, were a couple of pig-headed losers. So Mary-Jacobine it was, affectionately shortened to Mary-Jim.

There was a second daughter, Mary-Teresa—Mary-Tess inevitably—but Mary-Jim was first by birth and first in her father's heart, and she lived the life of a small-town princess, without too much harm to her character. She was taught at home by a governess of unimpeachable Catholicism and gentility, and by Miss McRory; when she was old enough she went to a first-rate convent school in Montreal, the Superior of which was yet another McRory, Mother Mary-Basil. The McRorys were

33

strong for education; Aunt Mary-Ben had gone to the same convent school as the one over which Mother Mary-Basil now ruled. Education and gentility must go hand in hand with money, and even the Senator, whose schooling had been brief, read consistently and well all his life.

The McRorys had offered their full due to the church, for as well as Mother Mary-Basil there was an uncle, Michael McRory, a certainty for a bishopric, probably in the West, as soon as some veteran vacated a likely see. The other men of the family had not done so well; the whereabouts of Alphonsus were unknown since last he had been heard of in San Francisco, Lewis was a drunk, somewhere in the Northern Territories, and Paul had died, in no distinguished way, in the Boer War. It was in the Senator's daughters that the future of the family resided, and Mary-Jim could not help knowing it.

If she thought about the matter at all, it caused her no misgiving, for she was clever at school, possessed some measure of charm, and, because she was prettier than most girls, was thought of— by herself as well as by the rest of the family—as a beauty. Oh, it is a fine thing to be a beauty!

The Senator had great plans for Mary-Jim. Not for her the life of Blairlogie. She must marry well, and marry a Catholic, so she must know a wider circle of suitable young men than Blairlogie could ever afford.

Money makes the mill turn. With his money

behind her, Mary-Jim could certainly marry not merely well, but brilliantly.

On January 22, 1901, when Mary-Jim was sixteen, Queen Victoria died, and King Edward VII ascended the throne. This pleasure-loving prince made no secret of his intention to change the social structure of the Court, decreeing that in future young ladies of good family should be presented to their Sovereign not at subdued afternoon receptions, as in his mother's day, but at evening Courts, which were in effect balls, and that the doors of the Court should open to people who were not of the old, assured aristocracy, but who had some "go" in them, as His Majesty phrased it. Even the daughters of magnates from the Dominions, if possessed of sufficient "go", might aspire to this honour.

The Senator had made his fortune by seizing opportunities while lesser people failed to see what was before their eyes. Mary-Jim should be presented at Court. Gently, methodically, and implacably, the Senator set to work.

In the beginning, luck was with him. The King-Emperor's Coronation had to wait until a year of mourning for the Old Queen had been observed; a royal illness intervened, so there were no Courts until the royal household moved into Buckingham Palace in the spring of 1903, and initiated a splendid season of Court Balls. Mary-Jim was presented then, but it was a close thing, and it took the Senator all the time at his disposal to manage it.

He began, logically, by writing to the secretary of the Governor-General of Canada, Lord Minto, asking for advice and, if possible, help. The answer, when it came, said that the matter was a delicate one, and the secretary would put it before His Excellency when a propitious moment turned up. The moment must have been elusive, and several weeks later the Senator wrote again. It had not been possible to put the matter before His Excellency, who was understandably much involved in the ceremonies preceding and following the Coronation. By this time it was August. The secretary suggested that the matter was not one of great urgency, as the young lady was still of an age to wait. The Senator began to wonder if Government House was still shy of the McRorys, remembering that awkward affair of more than twenty years ago. He also came to understand the nature of courtiers in some degree. He decided to go elsewhere. He asked for a few minutes of the Prime Minister's time, on a personal matter.

Sir Wilfrid Laurier was always ready to make time to see Hamish McRory, and when he heard that the personal matter was a request that he should politely speed up affairs at Government House, he was all smiles. The two men spoke together in French, for the Senator had always spoken in Canada's other tongue with his wife. The two men were staunch Catholics, and, without putting too much stress on it, felt themselves other than the very English group at Government House, and were determined not to be slighted.

Sir Wilfrid, like many men who have no children, dearly loved a family, and was warmed by a father's desire to launch his daughter into the world with every advantage.

"Be sure that I shall do my very best, my dear old friend," said he, and his leave-taking of Hamish was in his most gracious style.

It was less than a week later that Hamish received a message that he should call again on Sir Wilfrid. The great man's advice was brief.

"I don't think we shall get far with His Excellency," said he. "You should write to our representative in London, and tell him what you want. I shall write also; I shall write today. If the presentation can be managed, it will certainly be done."

It was done, but not quickly or easily.

The representative in London was the resoundingly titled Baron Strathcona and Mount Royal, but the Senator's letter began "Dear Donald", because they knew each other well through the Bank of Montreal, of which the Baron, as plain Donald Smith, was president. He was well aware of Hamish McRory through the freemasonry of the rich, which overrides even politics. A letter from the Baron came as soon as a mailboat could carry it; the thing would be done, and his wife would be pleased to present Mary-Jim at Court. But he warned that it would take time and diplomacy, and possibly even a little arm-twisting, for the desire to appear at Court was by no means confined to the McRorys.

Reports followed over several months. Things were going well; the Baron had dropped a word to a Secretary. Things were hanging fire: the Baron hoped to meet the Secretary at his club, and would jog his memory. Things were rather clouded, for the Secretary said there were people with prior claims, and the list of debutantes must not be too long. A stroke of luck: a New Zealand magnate had choked to death on a fishbone and his daughter had reluctantly been forced into mourning. The thing was virtually assured, but it would be premature to make any moves until official invitations had been received; meanwhile Lady Strathcona was doing some backstairs haggling, for which, as the daughter of a former Hudson's Bay official, she had an inherited aptitude.

At last, in December of 1902, the impressive cards arrived, and the Senator, who had bottled the matter up inside himself for more than a year, was able to reveal his triumph to Marie-Louise and Mary-Jim. Their response was not entirely what he had foreseen. Marie-Louise was in an immediate fuss about clothes, and Mary-Jim thought it nice, but did not seem greatly impressed. Neither understood the immensity of his triumph.

As letters began to arrive from Lady Strathcona, they learned better. The matter of clothes was carefully explained, and as these included garments not only for the Court Ball, but for the London Season it initiated, mother and daughter should lose no time in getting to London and into the dressmakers' salons. A suitable place to live would have to be found, and already the rentable houses in appropriate parts of London were being snapped up. What jewels had Marie-Louise? Mary-Jacobine must undergo a rigorous training in Court etiquette, and Lady Strathcona had booked her into a class being conducted by a decayed Countess who would, for a substantial fee, explain these rites. The curtsy was all-important. There must be no toppling.

Lord Strathcona was even more direct. Bring a large cheque-book and get here in time to have some knee-breeches made, were his principal pieces of advice to the Senator.

The McRorys did as they were bid, and set out for London early in January with a mass of luggage, including two of those huge trunks with rounded lids that used to be called Noah's Arks.

It had been impossible to get them a London house of the right kind, and a house outside the West End was unthinkable, so Lord Strathcona had booked them into the best suite at the Cecil Hotel, in the Strand. If the Court were grander than the Cecil, the McRorys wondered if they would be worthy of it. At the time the hotel outfitted its male staff with three liveries: sleeve-waistcoats and white stocks for morning, blue liveries with brass buttons and white ties for afternoon, and in the evening the full grandeur of plush breeches, plum-coloured coats with cut-steel buttons, and powdered wigs. It was sumptuous in a manner undreamed of in Blairlogie, where a housemaid marked the pinnacle of domestic service; but the McRorys, being naturally thrivers and intelligent, determined not to play the farcical role of colonial cousins any more than they could help, and behaved themselves unassumingly, until they got the hang of things.

The sessions with the decayed Countess presented some difficulty at the beginning, for she showed a tendency to behave as if Mary-Jim's inelegant Canadian speech gave her pain. Snotty old bitch, thought Mary-Jim, who was a convent girl and knew how to deal with tedious instructresses. "Would you prefer that I speak in French, Your Grace?" she asked, and continued for some time, very rapidly, in that language, which the decayed Countess spoke slowly and indifferently. The decayed Countess understood that she had a Tartar in the McRory child, and mended her ways. When she had recovered herself she dropped a remark about the difficulty of understanding a patois, but nobody was deceived.

At last, in May of 1903, the great night came. Marie-Louise, still a pretty woman, was resplendent in pale-blue chiffon and cloth of silver, embroidered with stripes of brilliants, the swathed bodice (over a repressive new corset) fastened with diamonds, which had been hired from a discreet jeweller, who did a large trade in such rentals. Mary-Jim was modestly done up in tulle and mousseline-de-soie. The Senator wore his accustomed tailcoat and white waistcoat above, and his unaccustomed corded-silk knee-breeches and double black-silk stockings below. They were photographed in the drawing-room of their suite at four o'clock in the afternoon, in their grandeur; the ladies had been put to rights by the hairdresser between one and half past two, and had then been forced to bathe with the uttermost care, so as not to wet or tumble their careful head-arrangements. An expert maid from the hotel had encased them in their splendid gowns. After the photographer had gone they ate a light meal in their suite, and then had nothing to do but sit and fret inwardly until half past nine, when the carriage arrived to take them to the Palace. They could have walked there in fifteen minutes, but with the crush of people going to Court, it took a full three-quarters of an hour to make the journey, during which they were inspected, at every stop, by crowds who had gathered to have a look at the toffs.

They had been fretting because they were sure they would know no one at Court—how could they? They would hang dejectedly around the walls, pretending that they were solitary from choice. In their panicky moments they were sure they would bump into things, break ornaments, spill food. The Lord Chamberlain would strike the floor with his wand, crying, "Throw those colonial rubes out!" But that was not the way the King-Emperor entertained.

As soon as they had arrived, and given up their cloaks, a smiling aide swooped upon them, saying, "Ah, there you are, Senator! Madame! Mademoi-

selle! The High Commissioner and Lady Strathcona are upstairs; I'll take you to them at once.
Awful crush, isn't it"—and much more genial,
meaningless, but reassuring chatter until they were
safe under the wing of the Strathconas, and Mary-
Jim had been hived off into a group, not too
obviously defined, of the girls who were to be
presented.

There were thrones on a dais at the end of the
room but—what, no trumpets? No, just a quiet
entry—or as quiet as a royal entry can ever be—
of a very stout, shortish man in uniform and a
blaze of orders, and a lady of great beauty, wearing enough jewels, thought the Senator, to finance
a railway. Ladies curtsied; gentlemen bowed. The
King and Queen were seated.

Without preamble the ladies in the special group
began to lead forward their protégées. An aide
with a list in his hand murmured to the blue-eyed
man and the smiling, beautiful, deaf woman. The
moment came: taking Mary-Jim's hand, Lady
Strathcona led her forward to the steps of the
dais, and together they curtsied; the aide murmured, "Miss Mary-Jacobine McRory." It was
over. The campaign which had taken twenty-two
months was complete.

The Senator, from the crowd, had watched
intently. Had the royal eyes lightened at Mary-
Jim's beauty? This was a king who admired
beauty—had he been impressed? Impossible to
tell, but at least the prominent blue eyes had not
been veiled. The child looked so lovely it gripped

his heart. Dark, high-coloured from her Highland ancestry, Mary-Jim was unquestionably a beauty.

The presentations were quickly over, and the royal couple left their thrones. The aide swooped upon the McRorys again.

"Must introduce you to some people. May I present Major Francis Cornish? He's going to help me in seeing that you get everything you want."

Major Francis Cornish was not very young, not very old. Not very handsome, but not precisely plain. If he were called distinguished, it would be because of the eyeglass he wore in his right eye, and his fine moustache, which defied all laws of facial hair by growing sidewise instead of straight down, and turning up at the ends. He wore the dress uniform of an excellent regiment, but not a Guards regiment. He bowed to the ladies, extended the forefinger of his right hand to the Senator, and said, almost inaudibly, "Howjahdo"? But he stayed with the McRorys, whereas the other aide, murmuring that he had some people to see to, vanished.

The music began: a Guards band, but with string players turning it into a splendid orchestra. Dancing, and Major Cornish saw that Mary-Jacobine had as many suitable partners as she needed. He himself waltzed with her, and with Marie-Louise. Time passed without the McRorys ever feeling out of things or overlooked. And, astonishingly soon to Mary-Jacobine, it was time for supper.

Royalty was supping in an inner room with a

few personal friends, but something of their magic lingered in the large supper-room, where Marie-Louise exclaimed over *Blanchailles à la Diable, Poulardes à la Norvégienne, Jambon d'Espagne à la Basque, Ortolans rôtis sur Canapés*, and ate them all, following with a great many patisseries and two ices. The splendour of the meal quite overcame any lingering coldness she, as a French Canadian, might feel about British royalty. They knew what food was, these people! As she ate, and under the influence of an 1837 sherry, an 1892 champagne, an 1874 Château Langoa, and—"Oh, I shouldn't, Major, but this is my weakness, you know?"—some 1800 brandy, she confided to the Major more than once that his Sovereign really knew how to do things properly. She ate until the new corset began to take its vengeance, for Marie-Louise had not the fashionable lady's art of picking at the splendid supper.

Mary-Jacobine ate very little; she had suddenly become aware of what being presented at Court meant; until then she had only known that it was another step in her life, with lessons to be learned, that meant a great deal to her father. But here she was, suddenly awakened in a real palace, among such people as she had never seen, dancing to such a band as she had never heard. That lady with the splendid diamonds, making her way to the inner room, was the Marchioness of Lansdowne. The lady in black satin? The Countess of Dundonald. That was the Countess of Powis in blue satin, diamond-embroidered; one of

44

the great Fox beauties; known to be a daring gambler. Major Cornish was ready with all information, and when she became accustomed to his murmuring manner of speech she engaged him in what might almost pass as conversation, though on her side it was almost entirely questions, and on his almost telegraphic answers. But he was unquestionably attentive, securing more and more food for the mother, and showing the most respectful, but never slavish, admiration for the daughter.

A stir in the room. The King and Queen were withdrawing. More bowing and curtsying. "Shall I see you to your carriage?" That must be the way courtiers got rid of guests. Marie-Louise, a little overcome with food and wine, pats the front of her bodice indulgently, and her daughter wishes she might sink through the floor. Could any of the countesses have noticed? At last, after some waiting that the aides make as agreeable as possible, the carriage comes and the Senator's name is shouted very loudly by a footman. The Major hands them into the carriage. He leans toward Marie-Louise when she is safely seated and murmurs something that sounds like "Permission to call?" Sure, Major, whatever you please. Then back to the Cecil Hotel.

Marie-Louise kicks off her tight shoes. The maid comes and delivers her from the cruel constriction of her corset. The Senator is melancholy, but exalted. His darling is launched into the world where she truly belongs. In future he will cut his beard in the fashion of the King-Emperor, though the Senator's beard is black, and his physique, developed in his youth in the forests where he had plied the axe and the saw, would make two of the King-Emperor, fat though that monarch undoubtedly is. He kissed his daughter an affectionate good-night.

She retired to her room. Like her father she was melancholy, but exalted, but she was also very young. A Court Ball, her presentation, countesses, splendidly uniformed young men—and now it was over, forever! The maid appeared. "Shall I help you to undress, miss?"

"Yes. Then tell somebody to bring me a bottle of champagne."

Of course, it was the mother stuffing herself that did the mischief, said the Daimon Maimas.

—I fear so, said the Lesser Zadkiel, The McRorys held up very well, otherwise. They were not less accustomed to court than many other people who were there. They had a certain native gumption that kept them in good order, except for the eating and drinking. Do you think it is time now for us to take a look at Major Francis Cornish?

Francis Cornish was a man of fashion, in terms of his era, and within the rules governing an officer of a good regiment. In consequence he was something outside the experience of the McRorys, who found his quiet, drawling voice, his reticence, his eyeglass, and his air of not being wholly alive quite unlike anything they had met with. He was a man with his way to make, for he was a younger son of a good family, without much money except his Army pay, and that would shortly cease. The Major had served well, but not conspicuously, in the Boer War, and had been wounded seriously enough to cause him to be invalided back to England, and he knew that the Army had not much in store for him in the future. He had decided to retire from his regiment, therefore, and he must do something, must find his place in the world, for the next portion of his life. It took him no time at all to decide that marriage was his aim and his hope.

Marriage could be a career for a man like the Major. Englishmen without money had for some time been establishing themselves in the world by marrying rich American girls, and everybody knew about the most significant marriages that had taken place. It was not unknown for fortunes of two million pounds, and even more, to cross the Atlantic through such matches, where the daughter of an American railway king or steel monarch was united with an English nobleman. It was a fair enough exchange, in the eyes of the great world: aristocracy on the one hand, and great wealth on the other, seemed to have been ordained for each other in Heaven. There are Heavens for all kinds of people, including those who think chiefly in terms of aristocracy and wealth. Major Cornish thought there might be a modest place in the world of wealth for himself.

The Major was no fool. He knew what he had to offer: unimpeachable family descent, but without title; a good Army career and the knowledge of how to behave in the world of fashion as well as when confronting Boers who had no notion of how to fight like gentlemen; a reasonable person, though not much in the way of wit or learning, beyond what it took to be a decent chap and an efficient soldier. Therefore, it would be foolish for him to aspire to one of the great American fortunes. But a lesser fortune, though still a substantial one, might be discovered among the young ladies from the Colonies. He had friends at Court, brother officers who would let him know what was coming up, so to speak. The McRory girl, with a large, though not clearly estimated, timber fortune behind her, and herself a beauty—though not yet in the duchess category—would do him nicely. It was as simple as that.

The Court had, of course, its aides, its gentlemen-in-waiting, its special group who might be called upon to look after guests when the Court entertained; it was known as "doing the agreeable". But there was always room for another presentable man who knew the ropes and would do his duty by some of the waifs and strays who always had to be looked after on great occasions. The Major spoke to a friend who was an aide; the aide spoke to a chamberlain; the Major was given the nod for the right Court occasion and gained his introduction to the McRorys. The Senator was not the only man who knew how to plan and contrive.

The London Season that followed the McRorys' appearance at Court was brilliant as no season had been for decades, and although they certainly were not in the thick of it, they managed to appear, somehow, at the principal events. Lady Strathcona was helpful; guided by her husband, who knew which English magnates might like to meet a Canadian magnate who was knowledgeable about investments in that rich colony, they were invited here and there, spent weekends at country houses, and managed to get themselves to Henley and Ascot under good auspices. Marie-Louise's talent for bridge gained her a place in a world that was mad for bridge, and the French-Canadian intonation of her speech, so embarrassing to her daughter, seemed to her hostesses provincial but not disagreeable. The Senator could talk to anybody about money in any of its multifarious aspects without sounding too much like a banker, and his fine looks and Highland gallantry made him acceptable to the ladies. They did not move in the very highest society, but they did pretty well.

As for Mary-Jacobine, her prettiness became something very like beauty in the sunshine of this unfamiliar world. She gained a new bloom. Impressionable as the young are, she moderated her own speech considerably to meet English expectations, and learned to call pleasing things "deevie" and unpleasing things "diskie" like the girls she

49

met. Doubtless it was the unaccustomed rich food and unaccustomed wine that disturbed her convent-bred digestion, for sometimes she was unwell in the mornings, but she learned how to be a delightful companion (it is not a natural accomplishment) and she was a very good dancer. She acquired admirers.

Of these Major Francis Cornish was the most persistent though he was far from being her favourite. She made fun of him to some of her more lively dancing partners, and they, with the disloyalty of flirtatious young men, took up her name for him, which was the Wooden Soldier. He did not manage to appear everywhere the McRorys went, and that did not trouble him, for to be too pervasive would not have suited his plan of campaign. But he had what was needed to be a man modestly in the fashion: he had a small flat near Jermyn Street, and he was a member of three good clubs, to which he was able to introduce the Senator. It was in one of these, after luncheon, that he asked the Senator for permission to put the decisive question to Mary-Jacobine.

The Senator was surprised, and demurred, and said he would like to think about it. That meant talking with Marie-Louise, who thought her daughter might do much, much better. He mentioned the matter to Mary-Jacobine, who laughed, and said she would marry for love, and did Papa really suppose anybody could love the Wooden Soldier? Papa thought it unlikely, and told Major Cornish that the time was not yet ripe for his daughter to marry, and perhaps they should defer the question for a while. His daughter, in spite of her blooming appearance, was not as well as he wished her to be. Could they talk of it later?

August came, and of course it was out of the question for the fashionable world to remain in London. It dispersed toward Scotland, and the McRorys went with it to two or three northern estates. But they were back in London, at the Cecil, by the end of September, and Major Cornish happened to be in town as well, and as attentive as good manners permitted.

So frequent had Mary-Jim's digestive difficulties become that Marie-Louise thought they had gone beyond what Blairlogie called "bilious attacks" and the simple remedies Blairlogie used in such cases, so she summoned a doctor. A fashionable one, of course. His examination was swift and decisive, and his diagnosis was the worst possible.

Marie-Louise broke the news to her husband in bed, which was their accustomed place for conferences on the highest level. She spoke in French, which was another indication of high seriousness.

"Hamish, I have something awful to tell you. Now don't shout, or do anything stupid. Just listen."

Some hired jewels lost, thought the Senator. Insurance would take care of it. Marie-Louise had never understood insurance.

"Mary-Jim is pregnant."

The Senator turned cold, then heaved himself up on his elbow and looked at his wife in horror.

"She can't be."

"She is. The doctor says so."

"Who was it?"

"She vows she doesn't know."

"That's ridiculous! She must know."

"Well then, you talk to her. I can't get any sense out of her."

"I'll talk to her right now!"

"Hamish, don't you dare. She's miserable. She is an innocent, sweet girl. She knows nothing about such things. You would put shame on her."

"What has she put on us?"

"Calm down. Leave things to me. Now go to sleep."

The Senator could as well have slept on hot ploughshares, but though he tossed and turned and gave his wife a night like nothing she had experienced except at sea, he said no more.

After breakfast the next morning his wife left him with Mary-Jacobine. The Senator made the worst possible beginning.

"What's this your mother tells me?" he said.

Tears. The more he demanded that she dry her eyes and speak up, the harder they flowed. So there had to be a great deal of paternal petting and plying of the handkerchief (for Mary-Jim had not so far left the convent that she could be depended on to have one with her) and at last something like a story emerged.

After the Presentation at Court she had felt

both elevated and depressed. The Senator understood that, for he had felt precisely the same. Never before in her life had she drunk champagne, and she had fallen in love with it. Understandable, thought the Senator, if dangerous. She felt very flat, going to bed after all the gaiety, the splendour of Court, the attention of the aides, the presence of high-born beauties, and so—she had told the maid to get her some champagne. But when it arrived, it was not the maid but one of the splendidly liveried footmen of the Cecil Hotel. He seemed a nice fellow, and she was so lonely that she asked him to take a glass himself. One thing led to another, and—more tears.

The Senator was reassured, if not comforted. His daughter was not a wanton, but a child who had got herself into a situation that was beyond her. He had been sure that Mary-Jacobine was the wronged party, and now he was in a position to do something about it. He went to the manager of the hotel, told him that on the night of the Ball his daughter had suffered grave affront from one of the hotel's employees, and demanded to see the man. What sort of place was it that sent a footman, late at night, to a young lady's room? And much more, in a high strain. The manager promised to look into the matter at once.

It was not until late in the afternoon that the manager had anything to report. It was a most unfortunate business, said he, but the man could not be found. It was the custom of the hotel on particularly busy evenings—and the occasion of a

53

Court Ball meant a very busy evening with people who were attending and the much greater number who were not but who wished somehow to have a special celebration—to engage extra men, usually soldiers who were supplied by a Regimental Sergeant-Major who had a sideline in such things, to wear livery and adorn the corridors and public rooms, but not to perform any duty as servants. Through some inexplicable muddle—the Senator could not believe how difficult it was to keep perfect discipline everywhere on a great night—one of these had been charged to take the champagne to Mary-Jacobine, and as the men had been paid off when they left the hotel at three o'clock, it was now impossible to trace the culprit. Precisely what was it he had said or done which had given such offence? If the manager had known earlier he might have traced the man, but now, three months later, he greatly feared it was out of the question. He did not know what to suggest in the way of amends, but he would certainly apologize to the young lady on behalf of his hotel. He had indeed already ventured to send some flowers to her room.

The Senator did not wish to be explicit about the insult. He had been defeated, and as men who are defeated often do, he made a great tale about it to his wife.

Marie-Louise was not a weeper, but a woman of sterling common sense, so far as her beliefs and experience allowed.

"We mustn't lose our heads," said she. "Perhaps nothing will come of it after all."

She set to work to see what could be done to secure a satisfactory outcome. The notion of abortion never entered her head, for it was utterly repugnant to her faith, but in rural Quebec it was not unknown for a pregnancy to fail to reach its term. In any case, a pregnant girl should be in robust health. She adjusted her mind accordingly. Her daughter had been suffering from digestive troubles, and obviously it was too rich a diet that had disturbed her. A good dose of castor oil would put that right. She gave the protesting Mary-Jacobine, who was not now in a position to make too much trouble about anything, a dose that would have astonished a lumberjack. It took the girl a week to recover, but the only effect was to leave her with a look resembling that favourite picture of the period called *The Soul's Awakening*, in which a pale maiden gazes to Heaven with glowing eyes.

Very well. A stubborn case. Next, for her own good, Marie-Louise demanded that her daughter jump to the floor from a table, several times. The only result was exhaustion and despair in the victim. But Marie-Louise had not finished her schemes to give nature a necessary nudge. This time it was not champagne, but a substantial glass of gin—as much as the mother considered to be safe—and a very hot bath.

Mary-Jacobine was even more unwell than after the castor oil, but the tedious little intruder did

55

not budge. All the natural aids Marie-Louise knew were now exhausted, and she confessed to her husband that she was beaten, and something would have to be done.

For a miserable week, the parents argued about the possibilities. They could take their daughter to the Continent, wait out the pregnancy, and put the infant in a foundling hospital. They did not like the idea, and after talking with Mary-Jacobine they liked it even less. Everything that lay deep in their composition—the convent, the brother and sister in religious orders, a simple sense of decency—spoke powerfully against it.

There was, of course, marriage.

They thought highly of marriage and it was the only means possible of salvaging morality as they understood it. Could a marriage be achieved?

The Senator was a man for direct action and he knew something of how the world wagged. This time it was he who asked Major Cornish to luncheon, at the Savoy.

Luncheon in a fashionable dining-room, even outside the Season, when really there is not a soul in London, is not the best place for such delicate negotiations, but the Senator said what he had to say, and asked Major Cornish if, under the circumstances, he was still of the same mind? The Major, coolly eating an ice, said that he would like to think about it, and arranged another luncheon with the Senator for a week from that day.

When the meeting came, the Major looked as if he had grown a few inches. He said that yes, he was prepared to maintain his offer of marriage, but the Senator would understand that things were not altogether as they had been. It was distasteful to talk of one's people, said he, but the Senator should be aware that the Cornishes were an old county family of, understandably, Cornwall. The family seat, Chegwidden (he pronounced it Cheggin, and explained that it meant, in the old Cornish tongue, the White House), was close to Tintagel, the birthplace of King Arthur, and Cornishes had lived there (the memory of man going not to the contrary) so long that they had probably counted King Arthur as a neighbour. When Cornwall had become a royal duchy, several Cornishes at various times served the Dukes of Cornwall as Vice-Warden of the Stannaries. It was a proud record, and an association with such a family might be accounted an honour.

The Major was, however, a younger son, and the family was not a rich one, so it was unlikely that he would ever live at Chegwidden himself, as its master. But he was a Cornish of Chegwidden, all the same. He had served his country honourably as a soldier, but now that he was about to leave the Army, he was undeniably hard up.

The Senator was not utterly unprepared for this, and hastened to say that an alliance with his daughter would certainly include a settlement that would put her husband's mind at ease about the future.

Very generously put, said the Major, but he wanted it to be clear that his suit to Mary-Jacobine was not prompted by any mercenary motive. The Senator would understand that the personal detail he had confided when last they talked could not be a matter of total indifference. Nevertheless he loved her dearly, and over the week past he had come to love her even more, because she had suffered the gravest misfortune that could befall an innocent girl. The Major touched lightly and tactfully upon Our Lord's behaviour toward the woman taken in adultery, and the Senator could not repress a tear or two at this show of fine religious feeling, though he had never thought of Christ as an Englishman with a monocle and an improbable moustache. Here was chivalry, and from the Wooden Soldier! Oh, God be praised!

It would be as well, said the Major, for them to understand one another thoroughly. This surprised the Senator, who thought an understanding had been reached. But at this point the Major drew from an inner pocket two pieces of paper which he handed across the table, saying: "These few matters should be understood between us, and if you will be good enough to sign both copies of this agreement I shall ask Mary-Jacobine to marry me tomorrow morning at eleven o'clock. Take your time in reading it over. It is not complicated, but I assure you I have thought carefully about what would best work toward our married happiness, and I should not like to abridge that memorandum in any way."

He's as cool as a cucumber, thought the Senator, but he did not find himself particularly cool after he had read what was written, in a very fine hand, on the document—for it could not be otherwise described.

(1) It will be clear that I do not wish to enter upon marriage burdened with debt, and I have some outstanding obligations of the sort that accrue to my position in the Army and in Society. Therefore immediately upon my acceptance by Mary-Jacobine, I should be obliged to receive a draft for ten thousand pounds (£10,000).

(2) I estimate that the expenses of marriage, wedding-tour, and subsequent travel to Canada will not be less than twenty-five thousand pounds (£25,000) for which I should be pleased to accept a draft before the wedding ceremony.

(3) My experience with men, and also with finance, as Adjutant of my regiment, appears to me to fit me for a position in industry in the New World, to which I propose that my wife and myself should emigrate after our wedding tour and the birth of the first child. As we must live in a manner congruous with your position and my own, and not below that to which Mary-Jacobine has been accustomed, I propose a settlement upon her of one hundred and twenty-five thousand pounds (£125,000) to be invested or otherwise disposed on my sole authority. In addition, we shall require a dwelling suitable for

your daughter and son-in-law and any family we may have, and I think it best that this be a newly-built house, the construction and planning of which I shall be glad to oversee, submitting all bills for building and furnishing to you for settlement. I shall be ready to discuss the position I shall take in your business enterprises and the salary attaching thereto at your convenience.

(4)   I undertake to bring up and show every proper care for any children attaching to the union, with the proviso that they be reared in the Protestant faith as evinced in the Church of England.

(signed)

FRANCIS CHEGWIDDEN CORNISH

(agreed)

....

For a time the Senator breathed deeply and audibly through his nose. Should he tear the agreement up and hit the Wooden Soldier on the head with a bottle? He had expected to be generous, but to have his generosity prescribed for him, and in such figures, hit him very hard in his Highland pride. To be tied down to a deal! The Wooden Soldier was sipping a glass of claret with total self-composure; the light falling on his eyeglass gave him the air of a miniature Cyclops, about to eat a sheep.

"There are two copies, of course," he murmured; "one for you and one for me."

Still the Senator glared. He could afford the money, though it had never occurred to him that he might pay his son-in-law's debts acquired before marriage. It was Number Four that stuck in his craw. Protestants! His grandchildren Protestants! He had no quarrel with Protestants so long as religion did not become an issue; let them be wrong, let them even be damned, if that was their perverse desire. But his grandchildren—and then he bethought himself of that small, obstinate grandchild who had precipitated this whole hateful affair. If Mary-Jacobine did not marry the Wooden Soldier, then who? Where in the time could he find a Catholic who would take her—a Catholic as outwardly suitable, if not really desirable, as Major Cornish?

"Anything troubling you?" said the Major. "I worked out the financial terms as exactly as I could, and I don't think I could bring any of the figures down."

The figures! How crass these English could be! To hell with the figures! But Number Four—

"This fourth item," said the Senator in a voice that trembled a little; "it will not be easy to persuade my wife or my daughter that it is desirable or necessary."

"Not negotiable, I'm afraid," said the Major.

"All the Cornishes have been C. of E. since Reformation times."

Like his daughter, the Senator was subject to sudden changes of mood. His fury left him naked and weak. What use to struggle? He was beaten.

He took out his fountain pen and signed the prettily written paper—both copies—in his bold, poorly formed hand.

"Thank you," said the Major; "I'm glad we understand each other. If you would ask Mary-Jacobine to be at home tomorrow at eleven o'clock, I shall have the honour of calling upon the ladies."

Surely the Senator might have argued a little more, said the Daimon Maimas. He buckled under very quickly, wouldn't you say?

—No, I wouldn't say that, said the Lesser Zadkiel. It was the temperament of the man, you see, as it was of his daughter. They were so good when they were cool but quite out of their element when they were overcome with feeling. Not that they didn't feel, or couldn't feel; not a bit. The trouble was that they felt so powerfully it utterly overset them and brought them sometimes near to panic. A Celtic temperament; a difficult heritage. Often they made terrible mistakes when an intelligent approach to feeling was called for. You know what happened? In later life the Senator became something of a philosopher, which is a great escape from feeling, and Mary-Jim acquired the trick of banishing or trivializing anything that was troublesome.

—*What about the scene in the Cecil Hotel? said the Daimon.*

—*Oh, that was a real Celtic hullabaloo. Mary-Jacobine wept and vowed that she'd rather die than marry the Wooden Soldier, and after half an hour of that she caved in and said yes, she'd do it. Her parents didn't browbeat her; it was the situation itself that overwhelmed her. It was panic and despair.*

—*Yes, indeed, said the Daimon. I had to deal with the same temperament in Francis, and sometimes it was hard work. He never became either a philosopher or a trivializer; he faced his troubles head-on. It was a lucky thing for him that he had me at his elbow, more than once.*

—*Yes, that's what they call it; luck. It's interesting, isn't it, to observe the parents. It would be quite wrong to say that they sold their daughter to preserve their respectability; they wouldn't have done that. But you have to understand what respectability meant to those people. It was much more than just What will the neighbours think? It was How will the poor child face the world with such a clouded beginning in life? It was What can I do to save my darling from hurt? It was emotion, disguising itself as reason, that governed the Senator. Marie-Louise had a good hard Norman head on her shoulders, but the Church had relieved her of any necessity to use it for thinking. She had done the best she knew and failed. They faced real wretchedness in their terms. It wasn't worry about London, which wouldn't have cared even if it knew. It was Blairlogie. How Blairlogie would have gloried in the fall of a virgin McRory! How she would have felt the whip, all her life!*

In Blairlogie, Aunt Mary-Ben McRory was, in her own phrase, "holding the fort" while her brother and his wife and dear Mary-Jim disported themselves in the fashionable world. She did not mind. She knew she had been born to serve, and she was willing to serve, and if any hint of longing or jealousy entered her mind she prayed it away at once. She was a mighty prayer. In her bedroom she had a little prie-dieu—padded but not overpadded on the kneeling portion—before a fine oleograph of a Murillo Virgin, and the worn upholstery on the kneeler showed how much it was used.

When she was not much older than Mary-Jim was now, God had made it plain to her that her portion was to serve. Dr. J.A. and many other people had referred to it as a freak accident, but she knew it was God's way of defining her role in life.

It had happened at a Garden Party in Government House—or Rideau Hall as it was familiarly called—in Ottawa. That was during Lord Dufferin's last months as Governor-General and Hamish had been asked, as a rising young man and already a political figure, to a Garden Party in late July. Being still unmarried he had taken his sister Mary-Ben, and for the occasion she had bought a splendid hat covered with black and white plumes. How romantic it had been! Delighting in the romanticism, she had wandered into the shrubbery, her mind on the romantic figure of Vergile Tisserant, who had been increasingly attentive, when suddenly—

It is now part of ornithological history, and even has its footnote in medical history, that at that time the Great Horned Owl—a species referred to by the Canadian naturalist Ernest Thompson Seton as "winged tigers among the most pronounced and savage birds of prey"—had been making occasional forays into the more inhabited parts of the country, and now and then had swooped upon humans, and especially upon ladies who were wearing those fashionable black and white hats; for to the owls they looked like skunks. As Mary-Ben strolled musing in the vice-regal shrubbery, an owl swooped, seized the hat, and soared away with it—and with a considerable portion of the wearer's scalp in its terrible talons.

For weeks she had lain in hospital, her head swathed in bandages and her spirit in ruins. How had those girls in mythology survived the fearful, birdlike descents of Jove? But of course they had been singled out for a special destiny, hadn't they? Had she been so chosen by the God of her own faith, and if so, for what? She found out when, little by little, the bandages were removed and her ravaged skull, with only a few locks of hair still remaining, was revealed. A wig was out of the question, for her scalp was now too tender to endure it. She had to make do with little caps, like turbans, of the softest materials. She never made any attempt to ornament the little caps, for she knew what they were. They were the head-dress of servitude, and she had been marked to serve. So—serve she did, in her brother's household, with the little caps protecting her little skull. Not even Dr. J.A. had been so harsh as to mention that the swooping god had mistaken her for a skunk.

She had been keeper of her brother's household for three years before his marriage to Marie-Louise Thibodeau and there was never any question that she should make way for the wife; no, indeed, she served her, and kept tedious duties from her, and when the first child was born she was invaluable, even suggesting the romantic name by which she was known. Marie-Louise, who found the social obligations of a rising man's wife wholly agreeable, was glad enough to let Mary-Ben—who was known even more often as Aunt, as soon as Mary-Jim began to speak—see to the household.

Besides, Aunt had Taste, which can be a form of power in those who possess it.

Aunt's taste and Aunt's judgement came into full sway when Hamish decided to build a fine house, and move up to the hill which dominated the southern horizon of Blairlogie. Marie-Louise had no ideas about houses, but Aunt had enough for three, and it was she who told the builder what was wanted, and drew little pictures, and gently domineered over the workmen. It was a brick house, of course, and not just your common brick but a finely surfaced rosy brick, as impenetrable as tile. Because Hamish was in lumber, the interior finish had all the latest things in turned wood, matched wood, wooden lace worked on the band-saw, and, in the room called the library, wooden panelling, not as it is generally known, but in octagons of what looked like hardwood flooring, set on the bias. Hideous, but of course very hard for the workmen to do, said Dr. J.A., who always had an opinion, and usually a disagreeable one.

Aunt furnished. Aunt chose wallpapers, showing a fondness for flock papers in which a pattern stood out from the background in a substance rather like velvet. Aunt chose pictures, spending money in a way that astonished her brother, in the shops of art dealers in Montreal. Aunt selected the subject for the stained-glass window that did not really light the landing on the staircase; it was Landseer's *The Monarch of the Glen*, a very choice thing. All of this choosing Aunt called "helping wherever she could, without interfering".

Aunt's desire not to interfere influenced the shape of the house, which had a substantial sun parlour attached to the north side that was rarely warmed by any sun. Above the sun parlour was a suite of rooms that was Aunt's alone. She could go in there and shut the door, she said, and be totally out of the way in her little sitting-room—it was quite big, really—and her bedroom with the little prayer-alcove off it, and her bathroom where she could do things she had to do—by which she implied difficult attentions to her destroyed scalp.

Hamish and Marie-Louise need never know she was in the house when they were entertaining, or wanted to be by themselves, as married folk very properly should do.

Busy as a bee, nodding and smiling sweetly, deferring to everybody, Aunt built the house and even chose its name; 26 Scott Street simply would not do, and Aunt proposed St. Kilda, as a lovely name, and a link with Barra. As neither Marie-Louise nor Hamish had any alternative, that was what appeared in the stained-glass fanlight over the front door.

Aunt's mind, busy as it was, never strayed toward introspection or the making of significant connections. If it had done so she might have wondered why one of her evening prayers was so particularly dear to her—that which ran:

God, who ordainest the services of angels and men in a wonderful order, be pleased to grant our life on earth may be guarded by those who stand always ready to serve thee in heaven. . . . God, who in thy transcendent providence delightest to send thy holy angels to watch over us, grant our humble petition that we may be safe under their protection, and may rejoice in their companionship through all eternity.

Did Aunt think of herself as one of those divinely appointed guardians and servers? God forbid that she should be guilty of such pride! But beneath what the mind chooses to admit to itself lie convictions that shape our lives.

There had never been any suggestion that Aunt might go with the family on the great expedition to launch Mary-Jacobine upon the world. Aunt did not repine. She knew she was unsightly. Yes, yes, she insisted upon it, and when Marie-Louise or Mary-Jacobine or the Senator protested that it was not so, she would smile sweetly and say, Now dear, you don't have to be kind. I know what I look like, and I have offered it up.

This business of "offering up" figured largely in Aunt's religious life. After that terrible affair at Rideau Hall, she had offered up her attachment to Vergile Tisserant, as a sacrifice she hoped would be acceptable at the Heavenly Throne. Before Vergile there had been Joseph Crone, who had decided that he would rather be a Jesuit than Aunt's husband, and she had offered him up, too. She offered up her ugliness, as an act of acceptance and humility. Oh, Aunt had plenty of gifts for God, and perhaps God was grateful, for He had given her quite a lot of power in her small sphere.

Letters from Marie-Louise and less often from Mary-Jacobine kept her aware of how things were going in England. Neither of the ladies had much gift for writing but—the mother in French, the daughter in English—they tried for as long as they could to keep Aunt informed. But a new kind of life, and new people, so far removed from anything Aunt had known, were not in their power to describe, and the letters grew fewer and briefer.

Aunt accepted this without complaint. She had much to do, maintaining St. Kilda in good order, and keeping the servants up to the mark. These were a Polish housemaid, Anna Lemenchick, who was so short as to be almost a dwarf, but broad beyond the ordinary, and a cook, Victoria Cameron, who was always on the verge of being dismissed because she had a fiery Highland temper and was apt, in the phrase Aunt used, to "kick right over the traces" if she were crossed. Everything was against Victoria; to begin, she was a Protestant, and there were plenty of Catholic cooks to be had; as well as a temper she had a rough tongue in her head, and gave saucy answers; she was also astonishingly bow-legged, and could be heard all over the house, tramping around the kitchen like a great horse. With these disadvantages it was not surprising that nobody noticed that she had a beautiful dark face, like one of the Spanish Madonnas Aunt admired so wholeheartedly. But who ever heard of a beautiful cook? Victoria's trump card was that she was by many lengths the best cook in Blairlogie, a natural genius, and the Senator would not hear of letting her go. These, with visits twice a week from Mrs. August, a Pole who did the rough cleaning, made up the indoor staff.

The outdoor staff was all embodied in a drunken detrimental called Old Billy, who cared for and drove the horses, shovelled snow, cut grass, exterminated the flowers, and was supposed to do heavy lifting and any odd jobs that turned up. But Old Billy was a devout Catholic and a noisy repenter of his misdeeds and frequent toots, so it was impossible to get rid of him, grave trial that he was.

It was Aunt who looked after young Mary-Tess when she was home on holiday from the convent. That was easy, for Mary-Tess was a cheerful girl, and skating and tobogganing were her great pleasures. Aunt had little pleasures of her own. There was her music; she played and sang. And there was a weekly visit from the Senator's mother-in-law, old Madame Thibodeau, a stately lady far gone in fat, who spoke no English but enjoyed a gossip in French, in which Aunt was as fluent as her brother. Old Billy was sent with the barouche, or in winter with the elegant scarlet cutter, to haul her up the hill every Thursday at four, and haul her back again, substantially heavier because of the great tea she had eaten, at half past five. Each month there was a visit from Father Devlin and Father Beaudry, of St. Bonaventura's; as a guarantee of total chastity, they visited the old maid together, and devoured huge meals in gloomy silence, occasionally punctuated by the more edifying bits of parish news. Irregular and unforeseeable were visits from Dr. J.A.—Dr. Joseph Ambrosius Jerome, the leading Catholic physician of Blairlogie, who kept an eye on Aunt because she was supposed to be frail.

He was by far her liveliest visitor. A little,

spare, very dark, grinning man, saturnine in his appearance and alarming in his opinions, he was locally believed to have powers of healing verging on the miraculous. He "brought back" lumbermen who had chopped themselves in the foot with one of their terrible axes and were in danger of blood-poisoning. He sewed up Poles who had decided some obscure point of honour with knives. He saw people through double pneumonia with poultices and inhalations and sheer exercise of his healing power. He told women to have no more babies, and threatened their husbands with dreadful reprisals if this were not so. He blasted out the constipated and salved their angry haemorrhoids with ointments of opium. He could diagnose worms at a glance, and drag a tapeworm from its lair with horrible potions.

If not actually an atheist, the Doctor was known to have dark beliefs nobody wanted to explore. He was rumoured to know more theology than Father Devlin and Father Beaudry clapped together. He read books that were on the Index, some of them in German. But he was trusted, and nobody trusted him more than Aunt.

He understood her case, you see. He knew her nerves as nobody else knew them. He hinted darkly that to be a maiden lady at her age was not altogether a safe thing, and to her terrible embarrassment he sometimes demanded to squeeze her pallid little breasts, and peep up her most secret passage, assisted by a flashlight and a cold tube called a speculum. A man who has done that has a very special place in a virgin's life. And he teased her. Teased her and taunted her and refused to take her at all seriously; if she had known anything intimate about herself, she would have realized that she loved him. As it was, she knew him as a close, terrifying friend, upon whom she placed the uttermost reliance. He was almost more than a priest—a priest with a strong whiff of the Devil about him.

It was to the Doctor that she first confided the news, contained in a letter that had come from Marie-Louise, that Mary-Jim was to be married! Yes, married to an Englishman, a Major Francis Cornish, very much a swell, it appeared. Well, wouldn't you know that Mary-Jim wouldn't be long without a husband. Such a lovely girl! And it looked as if they would be coming to Blairlogie to live. We shall have to polish up our manners for the English swell, won't we? Whatever would he think of such an old auntie as herself—such a figure of fun!

"I dare say it won't be long before he'll want to know what's under that cap," said the Doctor. "What'll you tell him, then, Mary-Ben? If he's a soldier as you say, I suppose he's seen worse things." And the Doctor departed, laughing and scooping the remains of the cake-tray into his pocket. It was for some children in the Polish section, but he took care to make it look like greed.

At a later visit, Aunt was bursting with news. They'd been married! Somewhere in Switzerland, apparently. A place called Montreux. And they were going to stay there for a while, on a honeymoon, before coming home. Madame Thibodeau had been delighted; a honeymoon in a French-speaking land seemed somehow to mitigate the Major's terrible Englishness.

The Senator and Marie-Louise returned to Blairlogie late in the autumn, and were less communicative than Aunt had expected. Very soon, of course, it had to come out—some of it, anyhow. Mary-Jacobine and the Major had been married by the English chaplain in Montreux, in the English Church. Now it's no good taking it like that, Mary-Ben; the thing's done, and we can't change it. We can pray, of course, that he may see the light at last, though I don't think he's much of a man for changes. Now, put a good face on it, and stop weeping, because I'll have to tell Father Devlin, and he'll tell Father Beaudry, and only God knows what the town will make of it. Yes, I did all I could, and I might as well have saved my breath. I'll have to tell Mary-Tess, too, what her sister's done, and believe me I'll make her understand that there's to be no more of that sort of thing in this family. Oh, Mother of God, there'll be Mother Mary-Basil to tell, and that won't be an easy letter to write; you'll have to help me. Hamish just takes it like a mule; there's no getting anything out of him.

The regrettable baby was not brought into the conversation at this point, or later, till at last a telegram came: "My wife delivered of a boy last

74

night. Regards, Cornish." The telegram came sufficiently late in the year following to still the counting fingers, Aunt's among them, with which Blairlogie greeted all first children.

Of course the town knew all about it, and supposed much that nobody had told. The local paper, *The Clarion*, had announced the wedding in a brief piece, without saying anything about the Protestant aspect of the marriage, but as the name of the officiating clergyman was the Rev. Canon White, it was not necessary. There was the spite of that Tory rag for you! They knew that everybody would understand at once. Thank God the proviso number four was still a secret, but how long would that last! Later *The Clarion* announced the good news of the birth of Francis Chegwidden Cornish, son of Major and Mrs. Francis Chegwidden Cornish; grandson of our popular Senator, the Hon. James Ignatius McRory and Mrs. McRory; and great-grandson of Madame Jean Telesphore Thibodeau. But these were bare bones; rumour supplied ample flesh. The Tory-Scots talked.

You'd have thought the girl could have found a Canadian now, wouldn't you?—Oh, but nobody'd be good enough. The Senator has made a proper fool of that girl.—What foot d'you suppose he digs with?—Oh, sure to be an R.C. with all that raft of priests and nuns in the family and old Mary-Ben with her holy pictures all over the house (some of them right in the sitting-room, wouldn't it give you the creeps!)—he couldn't be anything

but an R.C. Not that I ever heard of an Englishman that was.—Anglicans, so far as they're anything. But somebody told me she met this fella at
the Court.—Yes, and more than that, the King
himself had a hand in the match—sort of hinted,
you know, but that's just like an order—Well, no
doubt we'll find out soon enough. Not that they'll
be telling *me*, a Tory through and through. Would
you believe it, I've lived in Blairlogie for sixty-
seven years, and generations before me, and a
McRory has never so much as given me a good-
day?—They smell the Protestant blood in you,
that's what it is.—Yes, the black drop, they call
it.

But at last, more than a year later, Major and
Mrs. Cornish and their infant son arrived in
Blairlogie on the afternoon train from Ottawa. If
ever the town looked well, it did so in autumn,
when the maples were blazing, and close watchers
said Mary-Jim wept a little as she stepped into the
barouche in which Old Billy drove them to St.
Kilda. The child was in her arms, in a long shawl.
The Major, without hesitation, took the two seats
facing forward for himself and his wife, leaving
the seats with their backs to Old Billy for the
Senator and Marie-Louise. Watchers did not fail
to notice that. There was a mass of luggage on the
station platform for Old Billy to pick up later—
military trunks, metal boxes, and queer-shaped
leather cases that might be guns.

When they retired that night, the Major had
some questions to ask.

"Precisely who is the old party in the little cap?"

"I've told you times without number. She's my aunt, my father's sister, and she lives here. It's her home."

"Rum old soul, isn't she? Wants to call me Frank. Well, no harm in that, I suppose. What did you say her name was?"

"Mary-Benedetta, but you'd better call her Mary-Ben. Everybody does."

"You're all Mary-Something, aren't you? Jolly rum!"

"Family Catholic custom. And listen—you're not the one to talk about caps."

The Major was applying the special mixture, which smelled like walnuts, to his hair, before he put on the woollen cap that supposedly hugged the dressing to his head and delayed baldness, of which he had a dread.

"Eats a lot for a little 'un, doesn't she?"

"I've never noticed. She has terrible indigestion. A martyr to gas."

"I'm not surprised. Let's hope she doesn't go the way of Jesse Welch."

"Who was he?"

"I only know his epitaph:

Here lies the body of Jesse Welch
Who died of holding back a belch:
The belch did in his pipes expand
And blew him to the Promised Land."

"Ah, but Mary-Ben couldn't belch to save her life. Too much a lady."

"Well, it had better go somewhere, or— BANG!"

"Don't be diskie, Frank. Come to bed."

The Major now did what he always did last thing before going to bed. He removed his monocle, for the first time in the day, polished it carefully, and laid it in a little velvet box. Then he tied on a strap of pink netting which held his moustache in place overnight and enabled it to defy its natural instinct. He climbed into the high bed and took his wife in his arms.

"The sooner we build our own house, the better, wouldn't you say, old girl?"

"My very thought," said Mary-Jim, and kissed him. She regarded the moustache-strap as no detriment. It was a conjugal rather than a romantic kiss.

Contrary to probability, during the year past they had become fond of one another. But neither was fond of the child that lay silent in the crib at the foot of the bed.

There was no use delaying the matter, and the next day Dr. J. A. Jerome was asked to take a look at the baby. Dr. Jerome investigating a case was not the jokey, chattering man he was in social meetings, and he did a number of things without speaking. Clapped his hands near the baby's ear, passed a lighted match before its eyes, poked it here and there and even pinched it, then pinched it again, to make sure he had heard its curious cry. He measured its scalp and probed the fontanelle with a long finger.

"The Swiss man was right," he said at last. "Now we must see what we can do."

To the Senator, upon whom he dropped in that night for a dram, he was more communicative.

"They'll never raise that one," said he. "No point in sparing you, Hamish; the child's an idjit, and the mercy is it won't live long."

The Cornishes lost no time in building their house on a piece of land that was visible from St. Kilda, being beyond the big house's garden and across a road. It was not as large as the Senator's mansion, but it was a large house all the same, and Blairlogie people joked that perhaps the Major intended to take boarders. What did two young people, with one child, want with a house the like of that? It was modern, too, in the manner that passed as modern at the time, and word got around that several of the rooms weren't meant to have wall-paper, and were plastered in a gritty way that must be intended to take paint. There were a great many windows, too, as if it wasn't hard enough to heat a house in that climate without having so much glass. It had steam-heating, ex-pensive though it was, and so many bathrooms that the thing was a perfect scandal—bathrooms right off the bedrooms, and a washroom with a toilet in it on the ground floor, so that you couldn't decently conceal where you were going when you went. Snoopers were not encouraged, though it was the local custom to visit any house during its building, just to see what was going on.

The scandal of the house, however, was minor compared to the scandal of seeing the Major and his wife walking to the Anglican church, most Sunday mornings. That was a slap in the eye for the McRorys, now wasn't it? A mixed marriage! Just wait till the boy grows up a little. He'll be an R.C. right enough. The Papists would never let him go.

But the boy was not seen. He was never taken out in his baby-carriage, and when Mary-Jim was asked about him directly, she said he was delicate and needed special care. Probably born with one glass eye, like his father, said the ribald. Maybe he was a cripple, said the people who failed to add that in Blairlogie there were more cripples than he. They would find out, in time.

They did not find out when the house was completed, and furnished. (Did you see the carloads of furniture coming into the station, from Ottawa and as far away as Montreal?) Mary-Jim knew what had to be done, and in due time a small notice appeared in *The Clarion* announcing that on a certain day in June Mrs. Francis Cornish would be At Home at Chegwidden Lodge.

This meant, according to local custom, that anyone not positively Polish was free to come, drink a cup of tea, and look around. They came in hundreds, trudged all over the house, rubbed fabrics between their fingers, covertly looked in drawers and cupboards, sucked in their lips, and murmured jealously among themselves. Didn't it beat the band! The money that must have been poured out! Well, it was nice for them that had it. And Chegwidden Lodge—what were you to make of that? The postmaster's wife said that her husband had half a mind to insist that letters be addressed to 17 Walter Street, which is what the vacant lot had been before this mansion was set up. Everybody agreed, out of her earshot, that the postmaster had only half a mind at the best of times, and nothing of the sort happened. The postmaster's wife reported that letters were posted with Chegwidden Lodge plainly printed on the envelopes. Their own stationery! And Mary-Jim correcting everybody about the way to say it, and wanting them to say Cheggin, as if they couldn't read plain English—if that word was English, mind you.

The day Mary-Jim received Blairlogie was also the last day she did anything of the sort; she had only agreed to a single occasion because of her father's political position. There was no sign of the baby. It was usual for babies to hold court, and be exclaimed over, as the wonders they were.

The baby had a nurse, a starched, grim-faced woman from Ottawa, who made no friends. A rumour went around that when the baby cried, its cry was queer—the queerest thing you ever heard. Victoria Cameron made it her business to track down the source of this rumour, and, as she suspected, it was Dominique Tremblay, the maid at Chegwidden Lodge. Victoria descended upon

Dominique and told her that if she ever dared to open her mouth about family matters again, she, Victoria Cameron, would rip the soul-case out of her. Dominique, terrified, said no more. But when she was questioned, she rolled her eyes dramatically, and laid her finger to her lips; this made rumour worse.

Rumour whispered that the ailing child was the victim of some fault in the father (you know what those old English families are) or—hush!—one of those diseases soldiers pick up from foreign harlots. That would be why Mary-Jim had no more children. Was it choice or inability? Rumour knew of women whose insides were simply a mass of corruption from diseases communicated to them by their husbands. Such speculation kept Rumour pleasantly engaged in dispute for some time.

Rumour was checked after February 1909 when Dr. Jerome told Mary-Jim that she was pregnant again. This was both good and bad news to the Cornishes. The Major was delighted that there was to be a child of his loins—a son, he was certain—and so was Mary-Jim. Although they would not have passed as a loving couple, they were congenial, and invariably as polite to one another as if they weren't married at all, Blairlogie said. But with the caprice of domestics, the starched, grim woman from Ottawa chose this moment to leave. People who discharge employees have to give reasons; employees are under no obligation to explain why they leave. Still, the starched, grim woman volunteered the opinion that another year in Blairlogie would be the death of her, and added insultingly that she had always heard it was the Jumping-Off Place, and now she knew it. So Mary-Jim was pregnant, and had the care of the sick child, except for such help as Victoria Cameron could give her. Victoria showed every sign of becoming a family retainer and champion, although she was still not much more than thirty. Dominique Tremblay was not to be trusted, and was kept out of the nursery.

This was inconvenient, for the Senator wanted his cook in his own kitchen. The Major fussed over his wife like a bridegroom, and was angry with fate when she was tired and in low spirits. Dr. Jerome said something had to be done, and, having said it to the Cornishes and to Marie-Louise and Aunt Mary-Ben, he said it with special emphasis to the Senator, once again as they sat in the uniquely panelled library, over a dram.

"I won't make strange on you, Hamish, it would be far better for everybody if that child had not lived. It's a burden, and it will always be a burden, and it'll be a burden to the new child, because a dooley elder brother is a weight to carry."

"You said it wouldn't live when first they brought it home."

"I know I did, and I was right. It's the child that's wrong. It has no business to be going on living, the way it is. Five years! It's utterly unscientific."

"And of course there's nothing in the world to be done about it."

The Doctor paused: "I'm not so sure of that."

"Joe—you don't suggest—?"

"No, I don't. I'm a Catholic like yourself, Hamish, and a pillar of the Church, even if I'm an external pillar. A life is sacred, whatever its quality may be. But if that Swiss man had had any sense he wouldn't have been such a busybody when it was born. The first five minutes, you know—you don't invite death, but you let nature make its choice. I've done it myself scores of times, and never a twinge of conscience. Some of these fellows, you know, are too anxious to show their skill to have any discretion or humanity. But I tell you plump and plain, I wish that boy were out of the way. He's bad for Mary-Jim, and he's bad for all of you!"

"Well, but what did you mean, Joe, when you said you weren't sure. What weren't you sure of?"

"The child isn't what it was a few months ago. We may be quit of it yet—and the sooner the better."

Apparently Dr. Jerome's suspicions were well founded, for a few days later, after a blazing row with the Major, Marie-Louise summoned Father Devlin in a hurry, and the sick child was baptized for the second time, as a Catholic. And it was only a day or two later that one of the top workmen at the Senator's planing-mill made a small coffin—made it beautifully. And at night a little procession of two carriages took its way to the

Catholic cemetery—a bleak, wind-swept, treeless place and in March dreadfully cold. It was as private as such an affair can be. Old Billy had dug the little grave with pick and shovel breaking the frost-bound soil, and he it was who stood in the background as the Senator and Marie-Louise, Aunt Mary-Ben, and Major Cornish heard Father Devlin read the burial service. The Senator and the Major carried coal-oil lamps to light the scene. There were no tears as the Senator's first grandchild was buried in the otherwise empty McRory plot.

When the spring came, it was Aunt Mary-Ben who saw to the placing of a little white marble marker—it was only a foot wide, and lifted itself above the earth no more than three inches—on which raised letters said FRANCIS.

Mary-Jim's pregnancy went splendidly after that, and on September 12 the subject of Simon Darcourt's biography was born, and christened, in the Anglican Church, Francis Chegwidden Cornish.

So your man makes his appearance on the scene at last, said the Lesser Zadkiel. You were at the birth, of course?

—Where else would I be, said the Daimon Maimas. I'd been on the job, so to speak, since the boy was conceived on December the tenth, 1908, at 11:37 p.m.

—What precisely was it you needed to do? said the Biographical Angel.

—Obey orders, of course. When Francis was con-

ceived—at the very moment of the Major's fortunate orgasm, They summoned me and said This is yours; do well by him but don't show off.

—Had you been showing off?

—I never think that a few flourishes do any harm to a life and perhaps I have overdone it, once or twice. But They take a very different view. When They gave me Francis They said, don't show off, and I tried my best not to show off. That family needed an influence like me.

—You found them dull?

—My dear Zadkiel, we haven't even touched on Blairlogie. There was dullness for you! But it's been my experience, over several aeons, that a good dull beginning does no harm to an interesting life. Your man runs so hard to get away from the dullness he was born to that you can do very interesting things with him. Put them into his head to do himself that's to say. Without me, Francis would just have been a good, solid citizen like the rest of them. Of course, I knew all there was to know about the burial of the first Francis. There was a rum thing, as the Major said at the time.

—You haven't any pity, Maimas.

—Neither have you, Zadkiel, and don't pretend you have. Long, long ago—if we must talk as though time had any meaning for us—I learned that when a tutelary spirit like myself is given a life to watch over, pity merely makes a mess of things. Far better to put your man over the hurdles and scrape him through the hedges, and toughen him up. It is not my work to protect softies.

—Well, shall we get on with the story, now that we have reached Francis? It was necessary to tell about his immediate forebears in some detail, because they were what was bred in his bone, which poor Darcourt wants to find out.

—Yes, but now I am on the job—I, Maimas the Daimon, the Tutelary Spirit, the Indwelling Essence. Though he was a McRory, and a Cornish, and all that goes with such a mixture, I also was what was bred in his bone, right from the instant of his conception. And that made all the difference.

PART TWO

It was in a garden that Francis Cornish first became truly aware of himself as a creature observing a world apart from himself. He was almost three years old, and he was looking deep into a splendid red peony. He was greatly alive to himself (though he had not yet learned to think of himself as Francis) and the peony, in its fashion, was also greatly alive to itself, and the two looked at each other from their very different egotisms with solemn self-confidence. The little boy nodded at the peony and the peony seemed to nod back. The little boy was neat, clean, and pretty. The peony was unchaste, dishevelled as peonies must be, and at the height of its beauty. It was a significant moment, for it was Francis's first conscious encounter with beauty—beauty that was to be the delight, the torment, and the bitterness of his life—but except for Francis himself, and perhaps the peony, nobody knew of it, or would have heeded if they had known. Every hour is filled with such moments, big with significance for someone.

It was his mother's garden, but it would be foolish to pretend that it was Mary-Jim's creation. She cared little for gardens, and had one only because it was the sort of thing a young matron in her position was expected to possess. Her husband would have protested if she had not had a garden, for he had determined ideas about what women liked. Women liked flowers; on certain occasions one gave them flowers; on certain occasions one told them they were like flowers—though it would not have done to tell a woman she looked like a peony, a beautiful but whorish flower. The garden was the work of Mr. Maidment, and it reflected the dull, geometrical character of Mr. Maidment's mind.

It was uncommon for Francis to be in the garden unattended. Mr. Maidment did not like boys, whom he knew to be plant-tramplers and bloom-snatchers, but at this magical moment Bella-Mae had left him to himself because she had to go indoors for a moment. Francis knew she had gone to pee, which she did frequently, having inherited the weak bladder of her family, the Elphinstones. Bella-Mae did not know that Francis knew, because one of her jobs was to protect Francis from bruising contacts with reality, and in her confused and grubby mind, little boys ought not to know that adults had such creatural needs. But Francis did know, even though he was not fully aware who Francis was, and he felt a minute guilt at his knowledge. He was not yet such a close reasoner as to suspect that if Bella-Mae were thus burdened with the common needs of life, his parents might also share them. The life of his parents was god-like and remote. Their clothes did not come off, obviously, though they changed several times a day; but he had seen Bella-Mae take off her clothes, or at least shrug and struggle them off under her nightdress, because she slept in the nursery with him. She also brushed her coarse rusty hair a hundred times every night, for he had heard her counting, and was usually fast asleep before she had reached the century stroke.

Bella-Mae was called Nanny, because that was what the Major insisted she be called. But Bella-Mae, who was Blairlogie to the core of her being, thought it a silly thing to call her by a name that was not hers. She thought Major and Mrs. Cornish stuck-up and she took no pride in being a child's nurse. It was a job, and she did it as well as she could, but she had her own ideas, and sometimes smacked Francis when he had not been very bad, as a personal protest against the whole Cornish manner of life, so out of tune with Blairlogie ideas.

Within the time between his meeting and recognition of the peony and his fourth year, Francis came to know that Bella-Mae was Awful. She was plain, if not downright ugly, and grown women ought to be beautiful, like his mother, and smell of expensive scent, not starch. Bella-Mae frequently made him clean his teeth with brown soap, as she did herself, and declared it to be wholesome; she took no stock in the tooth-powder

93

with which the nursery was supplied. This was Awful. More Awful still was her lack of respect for the holy ikons which hung on the nursery wall. These were two vividly coloured pictures of King Edward VII and Queen Alexandra, and once a month she scrubbed their glass with BonAmi, saying under her breath: "Come on, you two, and get your faces washed." If the Major had known that, he would have given Bella-Mae whatfor. But of course he did not know, because Francis was not a squealer, a kind of person Bella-Mae held in abhorrence. But if he was not a squealer, Francis was a noticer, and he kept a mental dossier on Bella-Mae which would certainly have led to her dismissal if his parents had known what it contained.

There was, for instance, her contumelious attitude, expressed physically but not verbally, toward the other picture in the nursery, which was of A Certain Person. Bella-Mae did not hold with images or idols; she belonged to the small assembly of the Salvation Army in Blairlogie, and she knew what was right, and a picture of A Certain Person, in a room like the nursery, was not right.

To remove the picture, or alter its position, was out of the question. It had been hung beside Francis's bed by Aunt, Miss Mary-Benedetta McRory, who ought by rights to be called Great-Aunt. Bella-Mae was not the only one to have reservations about pictures of A Certain Person; the Major was not happy about it, but rather than have a row with Aunt he tolerated it, on the ground that women and children had soft heads about religion, and when the boy grew older he would put an end to all that nonsense. So there it hung, a brightly coloured picture of Jesus, smiling sadly as though a little pained by what his large brown eyes beheld, and with his lovely long white hands extended from his blue robe in the familiar Come-unto-me gesture. Behind him were a good many stars, and he seemed to be floating.

From time to time Aunt Mary-Ben had a secret little whisper with Francis. "When you say your prayers, dear, look first at the picture of Jesus, then close your eyes but keep the picture in your mind. Because that's Who you're praying to, isn't it? And He knows all about little boys and loves them dearly."

Bella-Mae was sure that Jesus didn't like to see little boys naked, and she hustled Francis out of his clothes and into them with great speed and certain modest precautions. "You don't think he wants to look at your bare B.T.M. with his big eyes, do you?" she said, managing to include both Francis and the picture in her displeasure. For her displeasure was immense. The faith of the Salvation Army expressed itself in her through a repertoire of disapprovals; she lived strongly in the faith of the Army, and from time to time she murmured the Army war cry, "Blood and Fire", with the vigour usually reserved for an oath.

She saw that the Army figured in Francis's life as much as possible, though she would not have dared to take him to the Temple; the Major would not have stood for that. But at least twice a week he beheld her in the splendour of her uniform, and he was the first to see her in the glory of the Chapeau.

The Army uniform cost a good deal of money, and Bella-Mae bought hers garment by garment, as she could afford it. The sensible shoes, the black stockings, the skirt, and the tunic with its wonderful buttons, were achieved one by one, and then the great decision had to be made. Should she buy the bonnet, which was the familiar headgear of the Salvation Lassies, or should she opt for the Chapeau, a flat-crowned, broad-brimmed hat of blue fur felt, glorious with its red-and-gold ribbon, and strongly resembling (though Bella-Mae did not know this) the hats worn by Catholic priests in nearby Quebec. After deep inward searching, and prayer for guidance, she chose the Chapeau.

In full Salvation fig at last, she marched around the nursery, for Francis, singing in a style of her own, which included noises indicative of the band's contribution:

> *At the Cross, at the Cross*
> *Where I first saw the light*
> *And my heart's great burden roll'd away*
> *(pom, pom)*
> *It was there through Blessed Jesus*
> *That I turned to the Right*
> *And now I am happy all the day!*
> *(Pish! scolded the cymbal)*

At the Cro—s—s—s!
At the Cro—o—o—s!
At the Cross where I first saw the light
(boomty-boom)
It was there through His mercy
That I turned toward the Right
And now I am happy all the day!
(Boom, boom!)

It was irresistible. Francis hopped off his bed and paraded behind Bella-Mae, and under her guidance was able to shout, "Thine the glory!" and "Blest Redeemer!" ecstatically at the right intervals. He was elevated. He was free of the repressive influence of A Certain Person, whose sad eyes he ignored. He did not know what he was singing about, but he sang from a happy heart.

The nursery door opened. It was Aunt Mary-Ben, tiny and smiling, her little soft cap nodding pleasantly, for she was not a bit disapproving. Oh, not she! She motioned Francis back to his bed, and drew Bella-Mae toward the window, where she spoke very softly for a few minutes, after which Bella-Mae ran out of the room, crying.

Then Aunt said, "Shall we say our prayers, Frankie? Or I'll tell you what—you shall hear me say mine." And Aunt knelt by the bed with the little boy, and brought out of her pocket a sort of necklace he had never seen before, made of black beads of different sizes, strung together with silver chain, and as Aunt passed the beads through her fingers she murmured what sounded like poetry. When she had finished she reverently kissed the cross that hung on the necklace and, with a sweet smile, held it out to Francis, who kissed it, too. Liked kissing it, liked the reverential quietness, liked the effect of poetry. This was every bit as good as Bella-Mae's march, in an entirely different way. He held the cross in his hand, reluctant to let it go.

"Would you like it for your very own, Frankie?" said Aunt. "I'm afraid you can't have it right now, dear, but perhaps after a little while I shall be able to give you one of these. It's called a rosary, dear, because it's a rose-garden of prayer. It's the garden of Jesus' dear Mother, and when we say our prayers with it, we are very near Her, and we may even see Her sweet face. But this is our secret, dear. Don't say anything to Daddy."

No fear of that. Conversation between Francis and the Major was in a very different mode. "Come here and I'll show you my gun, Frank. Look down the barrel. See? Clean as a whistle. Always keep your gun clean and oiled. It deserves it. A fine gun deserves decent care. When you're older I'll get you one, and show you how to use it. Must learn to shoot like a sportsman, not like a killer." Or it might be, "Come with me, Frank, and I'll show you how to tie a trout-fly." Or, "Look at my boots, Frank. Bright, what? I never let the girls do my boots. You'd never think these were eleven years old, would you? That's what proper care does. You can always judge a man by his boots. Always get 'em from the best maker. Only cads wear dirty boots." Or, in passing, "Stand straight, Frank. Never slump, however tired you are. Arch your back a bit, too—looks smart on parade. Come tomorrow after breakfast and I'll show you my sword."

A good father, determined that his son should be a good man. Not entirely what might have been expected of the Wooden Soldier. There were depths of affection in the Major. Affection, and pride. No poetry.

Mother was entirely different. Affectionate, but perhaps she turned it on at will. She did not see a great deal of Francis except by accident, for she had so much to do. Amusing Father, and taking care that there were no unfortunate encounters when the Cornishes set out for St. Alban's church on Sunday morning, and the McRorys' carriage might be making toward St. Bonaventura; reading a succession of novels with pretty pictures on the covers; and playing the phonograph, which gave out with *Gems from The Wizard of the Nile*, and a piece Francis loved, the words of which were:

> *Everybody's doing it*
> *Doing it, doing it*
> *Everybody's doing it*
> *Doing what? The turkey-trot;*
> *See that rag-time couple over there,*
> *See them throw their feet in the air—*
> *It's a bear, it's a bear, it's a BEAR!*

It was wonderful—better than anything. Just as good as Father's sword, or Aunt's mysterious beads, and far better than Bella-Mae in her uniform, which he never saw now, anyway. Mother took his hands and they danced the turkey-trot round and round her pretty drawing-room. All wonderful!

As wonderful, in their own way, as the ecstatic first moment with the peony, but perhaps not quite, because that was all his own, and he could repeat it in summer and remember it in winter without anybody else being involved.

All wonderful, until the shattering September morning in 1914 when he was led away by Bella-Mae to school.

This would have figured more prominently in the life of Chegwidden Lodge if the household had not been in disorder because of the many absences, which extended from days to weeks and then to months, of the Major and his wife in Ottawa, where they were increasingly favourites at Government House. In addition there were mysterious colloquies with military authorities; the Major acted as a go-between for the Governor-General, the Duke of Connaught, who was a field marshal and knew rather more about military affairs than most of the Canadian regulars. As the representative of the Crown, the Duke could not make himself too prominent, or cause the Canadians to lose face, and it was somebody's job to carry information to and advice from Rideau Hall without being tactless. That somebody was Major Cornish, who was tact personified. And when, at last, war was officially declared against Germany and what were called the Central Powers, the Major became something which was slow to be named, but was, in fact, Chief of Military Intelligence, in so far as Canada had such an organization, and he moved himself and Mary-Jim to Ottawa. They would not be in Blairlogie, he told the Senator, for the duration, which was not expected to be long.

The business of arranging for Francis's education had not been much considered. Ottawa and the pleasures and intrigues of the Vice-regal world were foremost in Mary-Jacobine's mind, and she was the sort of mother who is certain that if she is happy, all must certainly be well with her child. Francis was too small to be sent to boarding-school, and, besides, he tended to have heavy colds and bronchial troubles. "Local schools for a while," said the Major, but not to Francis. Indeed, nobody said anything to Francis until the evening before school opened, when Bella-Mae said, "Up in good time tomorrow; you're starting school." Francis, who knew every tone of her voice, caught the ring of malice in what she said.

The next morning Francis threw up his breakfast, and was assured by Bella-Mae that there was to be none of that, because they had no time to spare. With her hand holding his firmly—more firmly than usual—he was marched off to Blairlogie's Central School, to be entered in the kindergarten.

It was by no means a bad school, but it was not a school to which children were escorted by nurse-maids, or where boys were dressed in white sailor suits and crowned with a sailor cap with H.M.S. *Renown* on the ribbon. The kindergarten was housed in an old-fashioned schoolhouse, to which a large, much newer school had been joined. It stank, in a perfectly reasonable way, of floor oil, chalk powder, and many generations of imperfectly continent Blairlogie children. The teacher, Miss Wade, was a smiling, friendly woman, but a stranger, and there was not a child in the thirty or more present whom Francis had ever seen before.

"His name's Francis Cornish," said Bella-Mae, and went home.

Some of the children were crying, and Francis was of a mind to join this group, but he knew his father would disapprove, so he bit his lip and held in. Obedient to Miss Wade, and a student teacher who acted as her assistant, the children sat in small chairs, arranged in a circle marked out on the floor in red paint.

To put things on a friendly footing at once, Miss Wade said that everybody would stand up, as his turn came, and say his name and tell where he lived, so that she could prepare something mysteriously called the Nominal Roll. The children complied, some shouting out their names boldly, some sure of their names but in the dark as to their addresses; the third child in order, a little girl, lost her composure and wet the floor. Most of the other children laughed, held their noses, and enjoyed the fun, as the student teacher rushed forward with a damp rag for the floor and a hanky for the eyes. When Francis's turn came, he announced, in a low voice: Francis Chegwidden Cornish, Chegwidden Lodge.

"What's your second name, Francis?" said Miss Wade.

"Chegwidden," said Francis, using the pronunciation he had been taught.

Miss Wade, kindly but puzzled, said, "Did you say Chicken, Francis?"

"Cheggin," said Francis, much too low to be heard above the roar of the thirty others, who began to shout, "Chicken, Chicken!" in delight. This was something they could understand and get their teeth into. The kid in the funny suit was called Chicken! Oh, this was rich! Far better than the kid who had peed.

Miss Wade restored order, but at recess it was Chicken, Chicken! for the full fifteen minutes, and a very happy playtime it made. Kindergarten assembled only during the mornings, and as soon as school was dismissed, Francis ran home as fast as he could, followed by derisive shouts.

Francis announced next morning that he was not going to school. Oh yes you are, said Bella-Mae. I won't, said Francis. Do you want me to march you right over to Miss McRory? said Bella-Mae, for in the absence of his parents, Aunt Mary-Ben had been given full authority to bind and loose if anything went beyond the nurse-maid's power. So off to school he went, in Bella-

Mae's jailer's grip, and the second day was worse than the first.

Children from the upper school had got wind of something extraordinary and at recess Francis was surrounded by older boys, anxious to look into the matter.

"It's not Chicken, it's Cheggin," said Francis, trying hard not to cry.

"See—he says his name's Chicken," shouted one boy, already a leader of men, and later to do well in politics.

"Aw, come on," said a philosophical boy, anxious to probe deeper. "Nobody's called Chicken. Say it again, kid."

"Cheggin," said Francis.

"Sounds like Chicken, all right," said the philosophical boy. "Kind of mumbled, but Chicken. Gosh!"

If the boys were derisive, the girls were worse. The girls had a playground of their own, on which no boy was allowed to set foot, but there were places where the boundary, like the equator, was an imaginary line. The boys decided that it was great fun to harry Francis across this line, because anybody called Chicken was probably a girl anyway. When this happened, girls surrounded him and talked not to but at him.

"His name's Chicken," some would say, whooping with joy. These girls belonged to what psychologists would later define as the Hetaera, or Harlot, classification of womanhood.

"Aw, let him alone. His parents must be crazy.

Look, he's nearly bawling. It's mean to holler on him if his parents are crazy. Is your name really Chicken, kid?" These were what the psychologists would classify as the Maternal, fostering order of womankind. Their pity was almost more hateful than outright jeering.

Teachers patrolled both playgrounds, carrying a bell by its clapper, and usually intent on studying the sky. Ostensibly guardians of order, they were like policemen in their avoidance of anything short of arson or murder. Questioned, they would probably have said that the Cornish child seemed to be popular; he was always in the centre of some game or another.

Life must be lived, and sometimes living means enduring. Francis endured, and the torment let up a little, though it broke out anew every two or three weeks. He no longer had to go to school in the care of Bella-Mae. Kindergarten was hateful. There was stupid, babyish paper-cutting, which was far beneath his notice, and which he did easily. There was sewing crudely punched cards, so that they formed a picture, usually of an animal. There was learning to tell the time, which he knew anyway. There was getting the Twenty-third Psalm by heart, and singing a tedious hymn that began

Can a little child like me
Thank the Father fittingly?

and dragged on to a droning refrain (for Miss Wade had no skill as a choral director) of

Father, we thank Thee: (twice repeated)
Father in Heaven, we thank Thee!

Francis, who had a precocious theological bent, wondered why he was thanking the Father, whoever He might be, for this misery and this tedium.

It was in kindergarten that the foundations for Francis Cornish's lifelong misanthropy were firmly established. The sampling of mankind into which he had been cast badgered and mocked him, excluded him from secrets and all but the most inclusive games, sneered at his clothes, and in one instance wrote PRICK in indelible pencil on the collar of his sailor middy (for which Bella-Mae gave him a furious scolding).

He could say nothing of this at home. When, infrequently, his parents came back to Blairlogie for a weekend, he was told by his mother that he must be a particularly good boy, because Daddy was busy with some very important things in Ottawa, and was not to be worried. Now: how was school going?

"All right, I guess."

"Don't say 'I guess' unless you really do guess, Frankie. It's stupid."

Love the Lord and do your part:
Learn to say with all your heart,
Father, we thank Thee!

106

And so Francis left the garden of childhood for the kindergarten, said the Lesser Zadkiel.

—It was his second experience of the Fall of Man, said the Daimon Maimas. The first, of course, is birth, when he is thrust out of the paradise of his mother's body; the second is when he leaves his happy home—if he is lucky enough to have such a thing —and finds himself in the world of his contemporaries.

—Surely it was stupid to send him to school in white, with a nursemaid?

—Nobody thought about it. The Major and his wife thought of nothing but the Major's work in Ottawa, which of course was never defined for the child. But the Major was no fool, and had smelled a war in the air, long before more important people did.

—You sound rather pleased with what happened to Francis.

—I had a rough idea of the direction in which I was going to push him, and I always like to begin tempering my steel early. A happy childhood has spoiled many a promising life. And it wasn't all unhappy. Go on with the story, and you'll see.

As Christmas drew near it seemed that the War was going to last longer than had been expected, so the Major thought he had better close Chegwidden Lodge and move to Ottawa. It would be foolish to take Francis, for both parents were busy. Mary-Jim was deep in women's committee work, and looked adorable in the severe clothes she thought appropriate to her role. It was arranged that Francis should move the short distance from the Lodge to St. Kilda, and live under the guidance of his grandparents and Aunt Mary-Ben.

This meant a great improvement in his lot, for Aunt immediately bought him clothes that were more what other children in Blairlogie wore, and he was happy in his corduroy knickerbockers and a mackinaw coat, and the tuque that replaced his little velvet hat with earflaps. He was happy, too, in his room, not a nursery but full of grown-up furniture. Best of all, Bella-Mae was left at the Lodge as a caretaker, and Aunt made it gently clear that there was no need for her to bother her head about Francis. That suited Bella-Mae, as she said to herself, down to the ground, because it gave her more time to devote to advancement in her own particular Army.

There were some great changes. Francis now ate at the table with the adults, and the manners he had learned while eating with Bella-Mae needed amendment. No grunting, to begin with; Bella-Mae had been a hearty eater and a great grunter as she ate, and as Francis never sat at his parents' table his grunting had passed unnoticed. He had to learn to murmur grace and cross himself before and after meals. He learned to be neat with his knife and fork, and was forbidden to hound morsels of food around his plate. Most significant change of all, he had to learn to speak French.

This had been a matter of some debate. Grand-père and Grand'mère thought it would be useful if they could speak together at table without being understood by the boy. But, said Aunt, he would certainly learn anyhow, and had best learn properly. So he sat beside her at meals, and learned to ask for things in polite form, and finally to make a few remarks of his own, in the pleasing, clear French that Aunt had learned in her convent days; but he also learned the patois (called by Aunt woods-French) into which his grandparents retreated when they had secrets to discuss.

The whole business of French opened a new world to Francis. Of course, he had noticed that a lot of people in Blairlogie spoke this language, with varying degrees of elegance, but he now discovered that the hardware store kept by somebody called Dejordo was, in reality, the property of Emile Desjardins, and that the Legarry family were, to those who spoke French, Legaré. Some tact had to be exercised here, because it was a point of honour among the English-speaking populace to mispronounce any French name, as a rebuke to those who were so foolish, and probably sneaky and disloyal as well, as to speak a private lingo. But Francis was a quick boy— "gleg in the uptake" as his Scots grandfather put it—and he learned not only two kinds of French, but two kinds of English as well. In the schoolyard a substantial quantity of anything whatever was always described as "a big bunch", and any distance beyond what could be covered on foot was "a fur piece of a ways". When adults greeted one another with "Fine day, eh?", the proper reply was "Fine day altogether". He mastered all these niceties with the same ease with which he digested his food and grew, and by the time he was nine he was not merely bilingual, but multilingual, and could talk to anybody he met in their own language, be it French, patois, Canadian-Scots English, or the speech of the Upper Ottawa Valley. He learned manners, too, and would never be so gross as to *tutoyer* Madame Thibodeau, whose social magnificence grew with her fat.

As he had hitherto been chiefly the creation of Bella-Mae, he was now moulded and spiritually surrounded by Aunt. This caused the good lady many anxious hours, for the Major, when it was arranged that Francis should stay for a while at St. Kilda, had said, hastily and with obvious discomfort, that Frank was, of course, a Protestant, and furthermore C. of E., and he had asked Canon Tremaine to look in now and then to see that the boy was alright. But Canon Tremaine, who was a lazy man and not anxious to antagonize anyone so important as the Senator, had called at St. Kilda only once, to the astonishment of Marie-Louise, who had said that of course the little boy was very well, and of course he was going to the Protestant school, and of course he said his prayers, and would the Canon like another piece of cake? Which the Canon ate with pleasure, and forgot that he had meant to ask why Frank never ap-

110

peared at St. Alban's. But upon Aunt fell the burden of caring for the child's soul.

Aunt knew all about souls. A neglected soul was an invitation for the Evil One to take it over, and, once in, he was almost impossible to banish. Francis knew a prayer—*Now I lay me down to sleep*—and of course he knew who Jesus was, because that picture of A Certain Person had been in the nursery for as long as he could remember. But just why Jesus was important, and that He was always present, watching you, and that although He had died long ago, He was still lurking, unseen, he did not know. As for the Holy Mother, friend and guardian of children, Francis had never heard of her. Such neglect of a child filled Aunt with pity; she could not understand how dear Mary-Jim had been so utterly consumed by her Protestant husband as to permit such a thing. What was she to do?

Little use to seek advice from Marie-Louise, whose comfortable, practical mind, when it could be said to be active at all, was now devoted to bridge. Bridge parties and vast Progressive Euchre parties at the church, devoted to raising money for war charities, possessed her. Not easy work, for so many of the Blairlogie Catholics were also French Canadians, and their zeal for a war against the enemies of England was wavering at best. But Marie-Louise had eaten the splendid cuisine of the English King, and was an ardent royalist. Madame Thibodeau was even less useful in the campaign to rescue Francis; the child had been baptized a Protestant, and was damned, and what was all the fuss about? The Senator was more helpful, but he was a man of honour and he had signed the Wooden Soldier's hateful paper guaranteeing that Francis should be a Protestant, and he would not go back on his word; but neither would he interfere if Mary-Ben moved on her own authority. She had better talk to Dr. J.A., who had a long head on him. Don't go to the priests till you've had a word with Dr. J.A.

Excellent advice! Dr. J. A. Jerome knew just what to do. "Frank's a clever lad," he said; "reads a great deal for a boy of his years. Lead him gently, Mary-Ben. Have you ever talked to him about his patron saint, for instance?"

Because he was born on September 12, Francis's only possible patron was the grubby Guy of Anderlecht, a Belgian who had lost all his money in a bad speculation and turned to God in his bankruptcy. Nothing there to light the flame of devotion in a boy of nine. But it was also the day devoted to the Holy Name of Mary, a feast not much heeded, having lost out to the Feast of the Holy Name of Jesus, but it would do for a beginning. So one day Francis found a large oleograph of Mary hanging in his room; it was a reproduction of a Murillo, and, contrary to what might have been expected, he liked it very much. Its soft beauty reminded him of his own mother, whom he saw so rarely, and he listened with interest as Aunt explained how tender and kind the Mother of God was, and how watchful of the fate of little boys. Dr. J.A. was right, as always.

"Not that I approve of what you're doing, Mary-Ben," said he. "But I have to give a lot of advice that I wouldn't think of taking myself. Far better the Blessed Mother than that Son of hers. I never knew a boy yet that I'd trust who really took to that searching, seeking fella."

"Oh, Joe, you just say that to make me shudder."

"Maybe I do; maybe I don't. Half the time I don't know what I mean. But you seem to be on the right track."

Francis had never heard of anybody's mother at St. Alban's, when he went there with his parents. But he was open to stories about someone who pitied those who were in distress, and increasingly he was in distress.

This was because he had been summarily moved from the Central School, which was not far from St. Kilda, to Carlyle Rural School, which was almost two miles distant, but which included St. Kilda in the outermost reaches of its domain. His transfer was an act of covert spite directed at the Senator by the local school board; the secretary of that board, checking the lists, had discovered that Francis Cornish, by moving a hundred yards from his father's house to his grandfather's, had moved into the Carlyle school district, and one September morning when he was was in the third grade he and two other children were told at ten o'clock to bundle up their books and report to Miss

113

Helen McGladdery at their new school. Within an hour Francis, for all purposes sufficient to his age and stage of life, descended into Hell, and stayed there for what seemed to him an eternity.

Carlyle Rural School was not, at that time, particularly rural, for it was on the outskirts of Blairlogie in an area inhabited by workers in the Senator's various mills and factories; it was with their children, and the children of farmers who worked the stony, wretched soil just outside the town, that Francis pursued his academic education and his vastly more significant social, ethical, and economic education.

Having now gained some measure of craftiness, he told Miss McGladdery that his name was Francis Cornish, but she had foreknowledge of his coming, and demanded to know what the C. on the secretary's message stood for, and the misery of Chicken began all over again with new and ingenious tormentors.

At the first recess a large boy approached him, hit him hard in the face, and said, "Come on, Chicken, let's see if you can fight." They fought, and Francis was beaten disastrously.

After that he had to fight twice a day for three weeks, and he was beaten every time. Small boys are not skilled fighters, and though he was hurt and shaken, he suffered no serious damage. But after recess he sat at his desk, wretched and aching, and Miss McGladdery was angry with him because he was inattentive. Miss McGladdery was fifty-nine, and she was soldiering through her teaching career until, at sixty-five, she would be able to retire and, with God's help, never see any of her former pupils again.

A strong Scots background, and thirty years at Carlyle Rural, had made her an expert disciplinarian. A short, fat, implacable woman, she ruled her three groups—for Carlyle Rural had only two rooms and she took the most advanced classes—not with a rod of iron, but with the leather strap that was issued by the school board as the ultimate instrument of justice. She did not use it often; she had only to take it from a drawer and lay it across her desk to quell any ordinary disobedience. When she did use it, she displayed a strength that even the biggest, most loutish boy dreaded, for not only did she flail his hands until they swelled to red, aching paws, but she tongue-lashed him with a virtuosity that threw her classes into an ecstasy of silent delight.

"Gordon McNab, you're a true chip off the McNab block. (*Slash!*) I've given the strap to your father (*Slash!*), and both your uncles (*Slash!*), and I once gave it to your mother (*Slash!*), and I'm here to tell the world that you are the stupidest, most ignorant, no-account ruffian of the whole caboodle. (*Slash!*) And that's saying something. (*Slash!*) Now go to your seat, and if I hear a peep out of you except in answer to a question, you'll get it again and get it worse, because I've got it right here in my desk, all ready for you. Do you hear me?"

"Bluh."

"What? Speak up. What do you say?"

"Yes, Miss McGladdery."

McNab would slink to his seat, as boys held hands in front of their mouths, and girls, greatly daring, sharpened their fingers at him in disdain. It was useless for McNab to snarl in the schoolyard that Miss McGladdery was a dirty old bitch and her pants stank. He had lost face. Miss McGladdery had the total authority of the captain of a pirate ship.

She knew what happened in the schoolyard, but she did not interfere. Young Cornish's grandfather was the leading Grit—the hated Liberal Party—and Miss McGladdery was an unwavering Conservative, or Tory. If the boy had so much grit in him, let him show it; she would do nothing until he complained, in which case she would take steps, but she would despise him as a complainer.

He did not complain, but one day a boy hit him in the eye hard enough to blacken it, and he went home knowing that there would be trouble.

It was not the kind of trouble he expected.

Aunt Mary-Ben, horrified, took him at once to Dr. J. A. Jerome. A black eye was nothing, said the doctor; no great harm at all. But then—

"They're giving you a rough time, Frank? You don't have to tell me. I know. I know everything that goes on in this town. Did you know that? They're a rough lot at Carlyle Rural. Do you know the Queensberry Rules?"

Francis had heard something of this code from his father. You didn't hit below the belt.

"Do you not? Well, Frank, the Queensberry Rules are all very fine in the ring but they've never heard of them at Carlyle Rural, or anywhere in Blairlogie, so far as I know. Did you never see the lumbermen fighting on a Saturday night? No, I don't suppose you have. Those French boys know something about rough fighting. Now look here: you have two fists, and they wouldn't dent a pound of butter. But you've two feet and good strong boots. So the trick is to let your man get close, then you rear back and let him have your right boot slap in his wind. Don't kick him in the groin; that's for later. But get his wind. He'll probably fall down, if you do it right. Then jump on him and beat the stuffing out of him. Give it all you've got. He'll be too busy trying to get his breath to do much. Don't kill him, but get as near it as you dare. Get him by the ears and bang his head on the ground; you can't hurt their heads."

"Oh, Joe, you'll make a tough of the boy," said Mary-Ben, in distress.

"Just so, my dear. That's the whole idea. If you've got any brains at Carlyle Rural you have to be a tough in order to keep them for yourself. In fact, Frank, it's a good principle of life to let people understand that you're really a terrible tough; then they'll let you alone and you can be as delicate as you please, so long as they don't find you out. Now, here's some arnica to paint on the eye. Twice a day is enough. And keep him at home for the rest of the week, Mary-Ben, just to give Miss McGladdery a fright. Let her think she's gone too far."

And it all came to pass very much as Dr. J.A. expected. When Frank did not appear at school, Miss McGladdery was worried, and when she was worried her haemorrhoids tormented her. Of course she would not dream of consulting a Catholic doctor, but when Dr. J.A. buttonholed her on the steps of the Post Office on Saturday she could not escape.

"I hear Carlyle Rural is just as rough as it's always been. Did you ever think you might have an ugly situation there one of these days, Miss McGladdery? It'd be a sad thing if anybody was seriously injured."

A nod was as good as a wink to Miss McGladdery, and on Monday morning she announced that there had been too much fighting in the schoolyard, and if there were any more of it, she would strap the fighters.

Of course Frank was blamed; he had squealed. But obviously he wielded some power, and he had no more trouble with fighting. He was no better liked, and when the great spring game began, he watched from the sidelines.

Most of the boys were watchers, but unlike Frank they enjoyed what they saw. It fed something deep in them.

There was a pond in a field across the road from Carlyle Rural, and in spring it was full of frogs. The game was to catch a frog, stick a straw up its cloaca, and blow it up to enormous size. As the frog swelled, there was a delightful apprehension that it might burst. There was an even more splendid hope that the boy who was blowing might, if enough funny things were said to him, stop blowing for a moment and suck and then— why, he might even die, which would richly crown the fun.

Frank's eyes were upon the frog, whose contortions and wildly waving legs pierced his heart with a vivid sense of the sufferings of Jesus, which Aunt had begun to describe to him. When His Name was used as an oath, Jesus suffered, and when boys were naughty Jesus' wounds were opened and bled afresh. How Jesus must have been agonized by the tortures of the frogs! And— horror!—what must Jesus have felt the day some boys caught a tomcat and cut off its testicles, and let it loose to rush away, howling and bleeding! Francis was dimly becoming aware of his own testicles, which were somehow associated with something Awful about which he could not get any exact information.

Animals did it, as you hurried past with blushes and shame. But surely the boys could not be right who said that people did it, too? That your own parents—but that did not bear thinking of; it was horrible and wholly incredible. Frank's mind was becoming a horror of sick speculation. And, young as he was, his body seemed to be in the conspiracy against him.

Aunt was not his only source of information about the mysteries of life. He found great solace

119

in the company of Victoria Cameron, his grandfather's cook. Aunt did not like him to talk too much to Victoria, who was not simply a Protestant but a Presbyterian of the darkest hue. She knew what was going on in the Senator's house, and she knew it was wrong. Miss McRory was trying to suck that poor boy into the abyss of Catholicism and, although Victoria, as a great artist of the kitchen, was glad enough of the high wages—a resounding thirty-seven dollars a month, and board!—that the Senator paid her, she called her soul her own, and resisted Rome as stoutly as she could without provoking a row. She knew enough about the McRorys to hang them, she told herself, but she held her tongue. Judge not that ye be not judged. Of course, you can't be a Calvinist without judging, but as a Calvinist you know what God's ordinances are, so it isn't really judging. It is just knowing right from wrong.

As is so often the case with people who hold their tongues, Victoria had a vast accretion of bottled-up disapproval, and it could be sensed from the darkness of her gaze, and spells of breathing deeply through her nose that could be heard at a considerable distance.

All she could properly do, as a loyal servant, eating the Senator's bread, was to befriend that boy, and befriend him she did, in her own stern fashion.

He asked her outright about the great mystery: did people do what animals did? Her reply was that there was an awful lot of Bad in the world, and the less you knew about it the luckier you were, and he was not to ask that question again.

Aunt Mary-Ben, dimly aware but not well informed about the opposition in the kitchen, told Frank many a wondrous story about the mercy of God's Mother, as she had seen it evinced in the visible world. Oh, you could always go to Her, Frankie, when you were troubled. Aunt kept her promise, and during the trouble of the black eye she gave him a pretty little rosary, which she told him had been blessed by the Bishop in Ottawa; he was to keep it under his pillow, and soon she would teach him the poetry that went with it.

Frank was deeply troubled, but it would never do to ask her the question he had put to Victoria. She wouldn't know about such things, or if she did she would be sorrowful because he knew about them. And there was always the risk of opening the wounds of Jesus afresh.

The question plagued and puzzled. There was the time that a travelling company came to the theatre his grandfather owned—the McRory Opera House and Blairlogie's principal centre of culture—offering a play tantalizingly called *The Unwanted Child*. There were special matinees for Women Only, at which a Well-Known Authority would lecture on the theme of the play, which was of concern to everyone. Francis knew that Victoria had attended one of these matinees, and he pestered her without mercy to know what the play had been about.

At last she yielded. "Frankie," she said with

great solemnity, "it was about a girl who Went The Limit." No more would she say.

The Limit? Oh, what was the Limit?

Poor wretch, said the Lesser Zadkiel, breaking off in his narrative; don't you pity him?

—No, no, no, said the Daimon Maimas. Pity is a human feeling, and I have nothing whatever to do with it. Your work is so much taken up with human creatures, brother, that you are infected by their weaknesses. Those children at Carlyle Rural, for instance; they were simply what they were. But you tell the tale of Francis as if to condemn them. I never condemn. My job was to make something of Francis with the materials I had at hand. If those materials were rough, they were good enough to grind his spirit down to a surface that showed up several veins of gold. Fine polishing will come later.

—But it made the boy thin and pale and sad.

—Now, now—that's another of your pitying judgements. Put aside pity, Zadkiel. But I forget—you can't; it's not in your welkin. But I can, and indeed I must, if I am to be the grinder, the shaper, the refiner. We work like the classical Greek sculptors, you and I. I must hew the creature out of my own intractable piece of rock and put a fine surface on it. Then you apply the rich colours, of which Pity and Charity are very popular pigments. They seem to give my creation a life that human beings understand and love, but when the colours are washed away by time, the reality is revealed, and I know that the reality has been there since the beginning.

—But this struggle for the boy's soul, as they call it. Pull Devil, pull Baker.

—I hope you use the phrase metaphorically. It would be unjust to call Aunt Mary-Ben a devil; she was about as honest and well-intentioned as human beings generally are, and she wanted her own way because she thought it was the best way. You may call Victoria Cameron a baker, if you choose. There is some justice in that.

Justice, indeed, for Victoria sprang from a long line of bakers, and her father and her brothers Hugh and Dougal ran the best bakery in Blairlogie. One Friday night Victoria got permission from Aunt to rouse Francis at two o'clock in the morning and take him to the bakery to see the Cameron men knead their dough.

The dough was an immense mass in a large round wooden trough that was built with a huge pole at its centre to which were attached three long bands of linen. The three Camerons were sitting with their trouser legs rolled up to the knee, scrubbing their feet in a low sink. Scrub, scrub, scrub till you might think the skin would come off. Then they dried their feet on fresh towels, powdered their feet with flour, leapt from the sink into the dough-trough, seized a linen band each, and began what looked like a wild dance in the dough. Round and round, until the linen bands were as close to the pole as they could be; then they turned and danced the other way, as the bands unfolded, shouting Heigh, heigh, heigh, as they danced.

"D'ye want to scrub up, young master, and dance with us?" shouted Old Cameron. And, quick as a wink, Victoria had his shoes and stockings off, washed his feet and floured them, and popped him into the trough with the men, where he danced as well as he could, for the dough was resistant, like treading on some sort of flesh; but that added to the fun. Francis never forgot that night, or the heat of the ovens, into which had been thrown many bundles of fern, which burned down to a fine white ash. After the dancing, the dough was cut with paddles into what would be pound loaves, and set out to rise again, before they went into the fiercely hot, sweet-smelling brick ovens.

At breakfast the next day, Victoria assured him that he was eating bread he had helped to bake himself.

The boy's life was not at all dark; he was not clever at school, but he attracted Miss McGladdery's attention by the seriousness with which he applied himself in the weekly half-hour that was given to Art. Miss McGladdery taught Art, as she taught everything, and she instructed all three classes at once in the mysteries of drawing a pyramid and shading one side of it so that it appeared to have a third dimension—or as she put it the shaded side "went back" and the unshaded part "stuck out". A pyramid and a circle which shading made into a ball, and, as the culmination

124

of Art, an apple. Shading was done by scuffling down one side of the object with the flat of the pencil's point. But Frank did not think that good enough; he had learned a craft at home in which shading was done with tiny parallel lines, achieved with great patience, and even by cross-hatching.

"If you take the time to do all that tick-tack-toe on your apple you won't be finished by four, and you'll have to stay in till it's done," said Miss McGladdery. So he did "stay in" with half a dozen other culprits who had work to finish before they were released for the weekend, and when he showed Miss McGladdery his apple at half past four she admitted reluctantly that it was "all right", for she did not want to encourage the boy to be "fancy" and try to go beyond what the class demanded and what she herself knew. Frank could draw, which was something not required in Art, and Miss McGladdery had come upon a caricature of herself done in the back of his arithmetic workbook. Miss McGladdery, who was a fair-minded woman, except about religion and politics, and had no vanity, admitted to herself that it was good, so she said nothing about it. Frank was an oddity, and, like a true Scot, Miss McGladdery had a place in her approval for "a chiel o' pairts", so long as he did not go too far.

Almost every Saturday Frank could escape into a world of imagination by going to the matinee at the McRory Opera House, where movies were shown. He got in for nothing, because the girl at the ticket office recognized him, and as he pushed

125

his ten-cent piece across the little counter she winked and quietly pushed it back again.

Then inside, and into his favourite seat, which was on the aisle at the back; he did not crowd into the front rows, as did the other children. Riches unfolded. An episode—locally pronounced "esipode"—of a serial, in which, every week, a noble cowboy was brought to the point of a horrible death by remorseless villains who sought to rob him of the equally noble girl he loved. Of course, it all came out right at the end of Esipode Twelve, and then another great adventure was announced for the weeks to follow. After the serial, a hilarious comedy, sometimes about the Keystone Komedy Kops, who were as incapable of dealing with disaster as the girl in the serial. Occasionally Charlie Chaplin appeared, but Francis did not like him. He was a loser, and Francis knew too much about being a loser to make a pet of one. Then the feature, in several reels; the ones Francis most enjoyed were not usually those that appealed to the other children. *Lorna Doone,* which came from England, was certain proof that the nasty mystery about what animals did and really good people surely didn't was a lie; the image of the beautiful Lorna, who looked exactly like the Holy Mother, but was attainable by a truly good man, who might then kiss her chastely and adore her forever, did more to shape his ideas about womanhood than Aunt's pious confidences. Certainly Lorna was a girl who would never venture within miles of the Limit, whatever the Limit might be. A companion picture in this special group was *The Passing of the Third Floor Back*, in which the great English tragedian Forbes-Robertson (much was made of his eminence in the advertisements and prices were slightly raised) played the role of a man who showed a group of shabby people that they didn't have to be shabby, and who looked so noble, so distinguished, so totally incapable of laughter or any other lively emotion, that he was plainly intended to be A Certain Person, but wearing a fine cloak and a broad-brimmed hat, instead of those sappy robes in which A Certain Person usually appeared. Frank had not yet been taken to Mass, and he had forgotten St. Alban's, but at the movies he fed upon these things in his heart, and was thankful.

Francis had an eye for the movies that took in more than the action; he saw backgrounds, landscapes (many of them painted, if you looked carefully), and angles; he even saw light. It was to his grandfather, the Senator, that he owed this extension of his understanding, for the Senator was an amateur photographer. His techniques were not sophisticated in terms of the Great War period when Francis was so often his companion; he worked with a large box-camera and a tripod. With this load he trudged happily around Blairlogie, taking pictures of the town, and such of its more picturesque citizens as he could persuade to stand or sit still for the necessary number of seconds, and he drove out to the lumber camps from which his growing fortune flowed, and took pictures of the men at work, or standing by giant trees lying on their sides. He took pictures in his mills. He took pictures of young Blairlogie men who were going off to war, with their rifles and kit, and gave copies to their families. The Senator never thought of himself as an artist, but he had an eye for a picture and he was an enthusiastic pursuer of all the many sorts of light the Canadian seasons afford. He talked to Francis about it as if the boy were of his own age. His senatorial and grandpaternal aloofness quite disappeared on these expeditions in search of what he called "sun-pictures".

"It's all a question of the light, Frank," he said repeatedly; "the light does it all." And he explained that all that painstaking shading in Art was related to light—something which certainly had never occurred to Miss McGladdery.

His detestation was pictures that had been taken by artificial light, and he particularly liked to take portraits in a shelter he caused to be made in the garden, to which furniture and draperies and other decorations could be laboriously lugged, and in which—apparently indoors but in fact in some version of the sun's light—he took countless pictures of Madame Thibodeau, of Marie-Louise, of the children of his second daughter, Mary-Teresa, and of his son-in-law, Gerald Vincent O'Gorman, the rising man in the McRory industrial empire. Aunt resolutely refused to be photographed. "Oh, Hamish, I'd break the camera," she laughed. But at her insistence he photographed Father Devlin and Father Beaudry, each leaning over a table in scholarly abstraction, apparently reading a leather-bound book, one forefinger supporting a brow plainly crammed with edifying knowledge. He even persuaded Dr. Jerome to pose for him, his hand resting on a skull which was a prized possession.

Taking pictures was great fun, but it was not so entrancing as what followed, when Francis and Grand-père were locked in a bathroom with no light save that from a dim red lamp, swishing and sloshing the film in smelly liquids in the washbasin and the bathtub, watching for each sun-picture to declare itself, with just the right quality to satisfy the Senator's careful eye. And then—

What followed was best of all, for then Grand-père set to work with an exquisitely pointed pencil to improve on his work by retouching the negative, emphasizing shadows, or giving richness to special aspects of the picture with an intricate shading done sometimes in tiny dots, sometimes in little spiral squiggles, sometimes in cross-hatching, so that the appearance of the sitter was enhanced in a flattering way.

Or, it might be, in a way that was not wholly flattering. Gerald Vincent O'Gorman had a dark beard, and when the Senator was finished with him, his close-shaven jaw had a faintly criminal shadow on it. And Father Beaudry's fleshy wen— not large but emphatic—on the left side of his nose was given a prominence which startled the priest when he received the print that was to be sent to his mother in Trois Rivières. Not even the dignity of soutane and biretta could diminish the prominence of that wen. But Mary-Teresa, who already had a perceptible double chin, lost it in the retouching process. The Senator never commented on these alterations to Francis, but he could be seen to smile as he brought them into being with his delicate pencil, and Francis learned, without knowing that he was learning, that a portrait is, among other things, a statement of opinion by the artist, as well as a "likeness", which was what everybody wanted it to be.

Francis was allowed to do some retouching himself, and he longed to transform the sitters with squints and lumps and deforming wrinkles. This was not permitted, but when Grandfather was momentarily absent he did, on one occasion, manage to sharpen one of Father Devlin's front teeth in a way that seemed to him more expressive of Father Devlin's personality than the unaided truth. Whether Grandfather saw what had been done was never known to Francis. But Grandfather did indeed notice, and a spirit of mischief to which he could not often give rein, and a pride in the psychological perception shown by his grandson, made him hold his peace, and he printed the improved portrait. Father Devlin never understood it, and although repeated examination in the mirror, and exploratory licking, told him that his dog-tooth was not really that of a vampire, he was of that simple group of mankind that believes the camera cannot lie, and besides, he did not like to criticize the Senator.

So, in one way and another, Francis managed to get some joy in life despite the shadow of school and the harassment of virtually all other children. Without being aware of it, he took into his mind and spirit forever a world that was passing away, a world of isolated communities like Blairlogie, which knew little of the world outside that they did not learn from *The Clarion* or, in one or two hundred uncharacteristic households, from the Ottawa papers. There was no entertainment from outside save the films and occasional road-shows at the McRory Opera House; entertainment was provided by church groups, by fraternal orders, by innumerable card parties, and of course by gossip, often cruel and bizarre in nature.

At the top of the class structure were a few families who kept "maids", an order of being who paradoxically conferred distinction, but were themselves held in disdain as underlings. When a maid bought a coat at Thomson and Howat, for instance, Archie Thomson always telephoned her employer (there were about two hundred telephones in the town) to ask if the girl was "good" for it, and to find out if he could what she was paid monthly. If a maid was so audacious as to attract a suitor, her mistress never failed to pop into the kitchen suddenly, to find out if they were up to anything. To employ a maid was splendid: to be a maid was to be sneered at, especially by those ladies who did not have a servant themselves. Protestant ministers were insistent that employers should release their maids on Sunday evenings, so that they could attend late services, but they gave the maids warmed-over sermons.

It was a world in which the horse played a crucial part. Few of these horses were of the noble breed with arching neck and flashing eye; most were miserable screws, rackers, the broken-winded, the spavined, often far gone with the botts, or with nostrils dribbling from the glanders. Even the splendid Percherons that drew the Senator's great sleighs laden with treetrunks were not objects of pride to their drivers, for they were seldom washed or combed, and the accusation that somebody smelled like a horse had a pungency now forgotten. But all of these creatures were hearty producers of manure, and in spring, when the unploughed roads gradually lost their layers of snow, the droppings of November perfumed the air of April, appearing with the lost overshoes and the copious spittings of the tobacco-chewers that had accumulated during the long months of frost.

Where there are horses there must be smiths. Francis spent many a happy hour, of which Aunt would have disapproved, hanging around Donoghue's, where the big horses that pulled the lumber-sleighs were shod with pointed shoes that would strike into the icy roads. There, warmed by the horses and the fire of the forge, he learned rich blasphemy and objurgation from Vincent Donoghue, learned the stench that rises when the hot shoe is placed on the horse's hoof, and the sharper stench when a spark landed on the blacksmith's apron. But he learned no obscenity. Donoghue was puritanical and his horse-vocabulary was for talking to horses as he understood them; he would permit no smutty stories in his forge.

The taxicab was yet to come, and people who needed a carriage for a funeral, or a visit to the hospital, rode in lurching vehicles like droshkys; for winter their wheels were removed and they were mounted on runners; inside they stank of old leather, and of the mangy buffalo-robes that were drawn over the knees of the passengers; the drivers sat on a box in front, wrapped in fur coats of incalculable age.

There were a few horses of the better, proud sort, and of these the Senator's were the best: a team of good bays, and a dancing pony or two to pull the governess-cart in which Marie-Louise and frequently Madame Thibodeau went shopping. Undertakers also had good horses, for that was part of the panoply of death, and of these Devinney's black team were the most admired.

Good horses need good keeping, and when Old Billy finally drank himself into the grave, the Senator made one of the loose arrangements that were common in Blairlogie to have Devinney's driver and groom take care of his horses as well, and it was not long before this man, whose name was Zadok Hoyle, spent more time at St. Kilda than he did at Devinney's Furniture and Undertaking Parlours.

Zadok Hoyle presented a fine figure on the box

of carriage or hearse, for he was a large, muscular man of upright bearing, black-haired and dark-skinned, possessed of a moustache that swept from under his nose in two fine ebony curls. On closer inspection it could be seen that he was cock-eyed, that his nose was of a rich red, and that his snowy collar and stock were washed less often than they were touched up with chalk. The seams of the frock coat he wore when driving the hearse would have been white if he had not painted them with ink. His top hat was glossy, but its nap was kept smooth with vaseline. His voice was deep and caressing. The story was that he was an old soldier, a veteran of the Boer War, and that he had learned about horses in the army.

He became Francis's hero, second only to Grandfather. Zadok Hoyle was a Cornishman by birth, and had never lost his Cornish turn of speech; he usually called Francis "me little dear", which did not sound odd from him, and sometimes he called him "poor worm", which was meant in an affectionate and not a derogatory way. He spoke to the horses in the same terms, and they loved him, in so far as a horse can love anybody. Best of all, he had lived near to Chegwidden Hall in Cornwall when he was a boy, and did not have to be told how to pronounce the name in the proper style. When Francis confided to him the shame of being called Chicken, Zadok said: "Pity their ignorance, me liddle dear; pity their ignorance and despise 'em."

On November 11, not long after Francis's ninth birthday, the First World War, which for so long was called the Great War, ended, but that did not mean that Major Cornish and Mary-Jacobine returned to Blairlogie. Everyone understands that when a war is over, the cleaning-up and the arranging, and the vengeance toward the vanquished, take just as much time and clashing of brains as the conflict itself. The Major had a very good war; he remained a major, because it gave him a certain protective colouring. There were plenty of majors, and the fact that this one was apparently an unusually clever major, attached to the Canadian forces but a familiar figure in the War Office in London, was better concealed from curious people. "High up in Intelligence" was the phrase people used about him, and that was much better than being a lieutenant-colonel, for instance. Such a man could not be spared when there was so much to do, and he and his wife, that popular beauty, had to go to London almost at once, and for an indefinite time.

The fighting had finished, but disease was busily at work. Spreading, unquestionably, from the putrefying dead lying on the battlefields—Blairlogie, knew this to be a fact—the Influenza walked the earth, and killed an additional twenty millions before it subsided. But in Blairlogie, as well as the influenza there was whooping-cough, and that had hardly subsided before there was a rush of what

135

was then called infantile paralysis, the terrible inflammation of the spinal marrow that left so many children on crutches with legs cased in cruel cages, or confined to wheelchairs, if it did not kill them. But Francis, who was not an unusually robust or sickly child, somehow managed to avoid all of these epidemics. Indeed, his first encounter with a severe illness was with whooping cough four years later. At thirteen this encounter left him whooping, as Dr. J.A. put it, like an Indian on the warpath.

"No school for this young man at least until after Christmas, Mary-Ben," he said to Aunt, who was of course the family nurse. "Perhaps not then. We'll see. He's badly run down and he'll be marked for we-both-know-what if he goes among other children too soon. Keep him in bed as much as you can, and load him up with egg-nogs. Doesn't matter if they come up when he whoops; quite a bit of it will stay."

So Francis settled to a long, reflective holiday, as soon as Miss McGladdery had been convinced that there was no point in sending him sheets of arithmetic problems to be solved; she was determined that the sick body should not beget the idle mind, and arithmetic was just the thing for a boy who was too weak to sit up in bed. Francis was very ill, and the injections Dr. J.A. gave him every three days, just above the kidneys, did nothing to make him placid. Indeed, on one very bad day, Aunt got into a panic and sent for Father Devlin, who murmured and sprinkled some drops

136

of water on him. Francis was in delirium, and did not understand what had happened, but Aunt was greatly comforted. When at last he seemed a little better, the Doctor said that he was greatly "run down", and gentle steps must be taken to "build him up".

I suppose that was your doing, said the Lesser Zadkiel.

—Certainly, said the Daimon Maimas, though of course I take no responsibility for the epidemics. It gave me a chance to put our young friend out of the world of action for a while and introduce him to the world of thought and feeling. He had been bullied too much for any good it might do, and the insults to his mother and nasty talk about his family were beginning to wear on him. So I took the means that came to hand to put him out of action for a while. We do that often, you know, with our special people; they need leisure of the sort a bustling, active holiday can never provide. A good long illness can be a blessing. Go on with your chronicle, and you'll see.

—You are a fierce spirit, brother.

—So it may seem, if you take a purely human point of view.

Between bouts of whooping Francis had plenty of time to reflect. He was glad to be secure from the torments of Alexander Dagg, who was a psychological rather than a physical bully.

"D'you know what I'm goin' to tell yuh?" he

137

would demand. "There's bad blood in your family. Your old aunt has a bielding head. Did yuh know that? My Maw says so. D'you know what that comes from? Rotting brains. You'll likely end up with a bielding head yourself."

A bielding head? It was a Blairlogie word, used not in the kindly Scots sense of sheltering, but meaning scabby, overgrown with suppurating outbreaks. Children often had bielding fingers, and displayed them with pride; they were neglected whitlows. But a bielding head? Aunt's head was never discussed, and Francis had never seen her without one of her little caps. He loved Aunt, and hated such talk, but he could not escape it.

"D'you know what I'm goin' to tell yuh? Yer Maw's riding for a fall. My Maw says so. Pride riding for a fall. When she come here last time she was lallygagging around and piling on the agony as if she was better than anybody else. That's what my Maw says: she piles on the agony!"

Piling on the agony? To Francis it seemed that his beautiful, distant mother had an air of distinction unequalled by anyone else he knew. Of course she was better than anybody else. It was unendurable that Alexander Dagg and his sluttish mother should take her name into their mouths. But—riding for a fall? Francis could not cast out the barbs planted by Alexander Dagg. All his life he would be naked to criticism, however foolish or unjust.

"D'you know what I'm going to tell yuh?

There's something funny about your house. People see lights where a light's got no right to be. My Maw says there's a looner in there somewheres. Somebody chained up. Does yer old aunt have to be chained up when her head gets too bad? People wonder a lot about your house. Do you know that?"

Yes, Francis knew that. Whoever lives in the finest house in a small Canadian town dwells in a House of Atreus, about which a part of the community harbours the darkest mythical suspicions. Sycophancy is present, but in small store; it is jealousy, envy, detraction, and derision that proliferate. In lesser houses there may be fighting, covert abortions, children "touched up" with a hot flat-iron to make them obedient, every imaginable aspect of parsimony, incest, and simple, persistent cruelty, but these are nothing to whatever seems amiss at the Big House. It is the great stage of its town, on which are played out the dramas that grip the imagination for years after the actors are dead, or have assumed new roles. With St. Kilda was linked its neighbour, Chegwidden Lodge, which provided in the Major and his beautiful wife a splendid addition to the cast of older actors. But only Francis had to listen, day after day, to what Blairlogie, as represented by Alexander Dagg's Maw, thought about it.

Most of all, Francis reflected about Dr. Upper. The local board of education, persuaded by who can tell what impulse toward modernity, had secured the services of Dr. G. Courtney Upper, who was making a tour of that part of Ontario, going to any school that asked for him, giving instruction in the mysteries of sex to boys and girls. The process took two days. For the first day Dr. Upper talked mysteriously and in general terms about the necessity to love and respect one's body, which was part of that British Empire that had shown its moral splendour in the war just ended. Any falling-off from the highest standards of clean speech, clean thought, deep breathing, daily washing of the armpits, was letting the Empire down. If you told dirty jokes you would quickly grow to look like a dirty joke. Girls were the future mothers of the Empire, and it behooved them to be models of daintiness and refinement in every possible way; boys would be the fathers of the Empire, and a slouching gait, sloppy grammar, smoking cigarettes, and spitting in the street would bring the Empire down as the Hun had never been able to do.

The Doctor himself was a pursy little man in a shabby black suit; his face was round and pudgy; his eyes ran and needed frequent mopping. But in the street he was a remarkable figure in an Inverness cape made for a bigger man, crowned by a bowler hat. His name was all over Blairlogie an hour after his arrival, for he had gone to Jim Murphy's barber-shop for a shave, and, hearing an oath from some patron who obviously sought to undermine the Empire, he had leapt from the chair, denounced the astonished blasphemer, and rushed into the street with half his face covered with lather. Before an audience of children his manner was hypnotic and powerfully emotional.

It was on the second day of his evangel that the Doctor really got down to serious business. The girls had been taken off to another room, where a lunar nurse initiated them in lunar mysteries of their own, and the boys were at the mercy of Dr. Upper.

He began with motherhood. His style was lyrical; he seemed almost to sing to the harp. No figure in a boy's life was so influential, so totally embracing, so holy and so good, as his mother. To her he owed the gift of life, for at the time of his birth she had gone down, down to the very gates of Hell itself, her body torn with pain, in order that her son might live. Just how this was done was not explained, which made the mystery doubly horrible. But that was what she had done, in the greatness of her love for the child she had not yet seen. Could any boy hope, however long he lived, to recompense her for that sacrifice, in which she had purchased his life at the danger of her own?

Plainly no boy could do so; but by complete obedience, and unfailing love, he might make a poor stab at it. Dr. Upper, assuming a whining voice and a cringing demeanour, spoke to a mother—whom he called Mommy—in a monologue in which worship and obedience were mingled. It would have brought blushes to the cheek of anyone not wholly under his spell, but the Doctor was a brilliant, if sickening, rhetorician.

141

He had worked up his great Apostrophe to Mommy over many years, and of its kind it was a masterpiece.

In the afternoon the pressure was doubled —trebled. Boys had it in their power to be the fathers of a great race, but they would never do so if they relaxed for an instant their determination to be pure in every respect. Purity of mind; he had spoken of that. Purity of speech; he had shown them how unmanly were swearing and dirty talk. But purity of body—on that all else depended, and without that the race would sink into the degeneracy so plainly to be seen among foreigners.

Purity of body meant a sentimental regard for one's testicles that was only slightly less whimpering than one's love for Mommy. Save for occasional washing they must never be touched, though they might be addressed, if they seemed to demand attention, in the Mommy-style of love but, in this case, also of rebuke. They must be told to be patient until the day when some lovely girl, who had kept herself pure, would become your wife on her way to the final apotheosis of motherhood. Were you going to throw away what was rightfully hers on base self-gratification—or worse? (What was worse was not defined.) Dr. Upper had known a boy so curious about his testicles that he had opened them up with his pocket-knife, to see what they were like, and had died of blood-poisoning in Dr. Upper's arms, imploring the Doctor with his last breath to warn other youths against his fatal lack of respect for his body.

If the testicles needed some stern talking-to from time to time, even more so did the penis. Yes, the Doctor urged boys always to use the medical terms, and not to sin by applying filthy names to these precious jewels. The penis might, from time to time, show a mind of its own, and when that happened, it had to be talked to kindly, but firmly (here the Doctor gave a little monologue that would bring any right-thinking penis to its senses), and wrapped in a cold wet towel until it was in a better frame of mind. On no account was it to be encouraged by thought or deed that would lead it to betray that noble mother or that almost equally wonderful girl who trusted you to bring her a love that was wholly pure and manly. Such thoughts, such deeds, were called masturbation, and it led rapidly to total degeneration of body and spirit. The Doctor had seen terrible ravages brought about by this sin of sins, and he could tell at a glance any boy who had succumbed to the loathsome practice.

Loathsome, yes, and dangerous, for the mighty gift of sex was not everlasting. Abuse it, and it would leave you, and then—what followed was too dreadful for the Doctor to say.

His peroration, the top of the show, came when the Doctor produced, after some rummaging, his own penis as an example of the adult member in its full splendour. He held it in his hand, as he thanked God for assisting him in bringing the

143

great message of purity of life to the boys of Blairlogie.

During the two days when he listened to Dr. Upper, Francis was sickening for whooping-cough, and shortly afterward he was in bed, warm under the blankets and loaded regularly with egg-nog by dutiful Aunt. The miseries of his illness were compounded by the urgings of his body, of those very organs upon which Dr. Upper had placed such spooky emphasis. They were unruly; they demanded attention and try as he might he could not banish their assertiveness by thoughts of his mother, or the Empire, or anything at all. He was sick not only in body but in mind.

The Doctor had told something, but not all, about the great mystery. That boys possessed some power that could make a girl a mother was clear enough, but how was it done? Not—oh, surely not by what he had seen, furtively and without comprehension, done by animals? What was the Limit, which was visited by such terrible consequences that a whole play was made about it, with Matinees for Ladies Only? There was nobody whom he could ask, of course. The atmosphere of St. Kilda was sternly Catholic, and Dr. Upper had not been asked to speak to Catholic children. Francis had made no mention of the Doctor at home, and he was sure that his knowledge was guilty knowledge, that might even reopen the wounds of Jesus. As for the Holy Mother, she must know of his plight, and would it not strain even her great pity? He was in misery, and his

144

misery made the whooping-cough worse. When at last it abated, after six long weeks, he was left with his old enemy, tonsillitis, and looked, Victoria Cameron assured him, like a ghost.

There were compensations, the best of which was that a return to school lay unimaginably far in the future. Even Miss McGladdery had given up her notion that pages of arithmetic problems would do anything for him. The next best thing was that during the daytime he was moved, partly dressed and bundled up in rugs and shawls, into Aunt's own sitting-room.

It was by far the most personal room in St. Kilda, for Marie-Louise's notions of decoration were strictly French-Canadian, and the downstairs rooms were stiff and grand with furniture almost too delicately upholstered in blue brocade to be sat upon by mortal man. But Aunt's room was a splendid muddle of all the things Aunt liked best, and there was a sofa for Francis in front of the fireplace, where Zadok Hoyle made him a fine fire every day. Zadok was a cheerful visitor, although his daily news for Francis consisted of a notice of what funerals he was driving for in the morning (Catholic) and afternoon (Protestant).

"I'm driving Madame V. de P. Delongpré at eleven," he would say. "A huge woman; not easy to embalm, let me tell you. Then back to the shop and get the Cross off the top of the hearse and put on the draped Urn to get old Aaron Wrong to the Presbyterian church by two sharp. He made it to ninety-four, you know. A tiny man at the last—

very easy to embalm because there was so little left of him. I'll just have time for a sandwich in between, but Miss Cameron has promised me a great feed tonight. I'll look in before me dinner and bring you some more wood. Keep your pecker up, dear man."

An unfortunate expression to use to Francis, for though Zadok meant it in its English sense of keeping cheerful, it had quite another message for Francis, who was aware that his pecker was too often indefensibly up and assertive during the day. Did Zadok know? Was Zadok mocking him? Adults were incomprehensible.

Zadok never broke his promise to return in the evening, with more wood and news of the day's diversions.

"Madame Delongpré would have been mortified," he would say. "Church not much more than a third full. But she was a bitter old gossip. Aaron Wrong, now, pulled a full church at St. Andrew's. I suppose it shows you what money and great old age can do. Long funeral. I was hard set to get back here to drive Madame Thibodeau home after the card-party. Between you and me, Francis, she's getting too old and too fat for the pony-trap. But she's still a great hand with the cards. She cleared over three dollars at the table this afternoon. D'you think she cheats?"

By such cheerful irreverences he relieved the warm, happy, but remorselessly devotional atmosphere created by Aunt, who would appear at eight o'clock to say the rosary, at its full length, with Francis, who now knew it by heart. It was not something to be mentioned to the Major, even if he should appear, which was unlikely. But now that Francis had been baptized by Father Devlin he was certainly a Catholic, and was not the poetry of the rosary his by right?

How much of Aunt's total dominance of their household was understood by the Senator and his wife? She was so humble, so deferential to Marie-Louise as the mistress, the wife, the mother; Aunt was so soft-voiced, so smiling, that her control of everything was hardly noticed. Marie-Louise often said that dear Mary-Ben was her Right Bower— an expression from Aunt's favourite game of euchre. She did not aspire to bridge, which was still new in Blairlogie, and fashionable, and beyond the understanding of a poor, addled old maid like herself; that was for such powerful intellects as Marie-Louise, and Madame Thibodeau, and the card-crazed group with whom they played five times a week, displaying astonishing avarice over the modest stakes. Of course, it could not be called gambling; the money was merely to give a little additional interest to the contest of wits, the severe post-mortems, and the occasional sharping which was not quite cheating. Ample meals and the green baize table were all Marie-Louise asked of life, now. As for the Senator, he had his business, his attendance in the Chamber in Ottawa, his politics, and his sun-pictures. Let his sister manage the household; he made her an ample allowance, most of which seemed to go to the Church.

Not all, however. Mary-Benedetta had her own craze. It was oil-paintings. She bought expensive reproductions from shops in Montreal, where she visited Reverend Mother Mary-Basil twice a year. Not all of these could be hung on the walls of her sitting-room, which were full from the ceiling to within three feet of the floor with Murillos, Ary Scheffers, Guido Renis, and all the masters of sweet piety that appealed to her; scores of others, unframed, were kept in portfolios, over which she brooded happily when the rosary had been said, and Francis was seated at her side, wrapped in shawls, in a reverential atmosphere. Masters of the Renaissance and masters of the nineteenth century were here, and not all the pictures were on sacred themes. Ladies languished on balconies, listening to cavaliers who played the guitar and sang in the garden below. Here was that lovely thing *Sir Galahad,* by G. F. Watts, O.M., R.A.— "the Order of Merit dear, and a Royal Academician, truly a great man"—in which the purity of the young man— "not a saint dear, but a great lover of our Lord"—and the purity of his horse were finely linked. And see, Francis, here is the Infant Samuel, wakened from his sleep by God's summons; can't you almost see the words on his lips, "Speak, for Thy servant heareth"? Remember that, Francis, if you should ever hear the Voice in the darkness. Oh, and look, dear, here is the Virgin of Consolation; see the poor soul who has lost her baby, comforted by the Holy Mother; painted by a Frenchman, dear, William Adolphe Bouguereau; oh, he must be a troubled soul, Francis, for he has painted some dreadful pagan pictures, but here he is, you see, painting this truly sacred picture that assures us of the Virgin's mercy. And here is *The Doctor* by Luke Fildes; doctors are very wonderful men, Francis, right next to priests in their pity and concern for human suffering; see him as he looks at the sick little boy, just as Uncle Doctor sat and looked at you when you were so bad with the whooping-cough. Well now, this one has got in here by mistake; it's called *Flaming June*, and you can see the girl is asleep, but why Lord Leighton wanted to shove her B.T.M. right into the front of the picture I'll never know; you may well ask why I bought it, but now I have it I can't quite bring myself to throw it away. Isn't the colour fine?

Francis could look at pictures for hours, absorbed in the world of fantasy they created, and their assurance of a life far beyond the reach of Carlyle Rural, and the moral squalor of Alexander Dagg's Maw. His convalescence began only a week or so before Christmas and when that day came Aunt had two gifts for him, in the choice of which she acknowledged him as a kindred spirit.

One was a head of Christ, for the picture of A Certain Person had been left in the nursery at Chegwidden Lodge. But that had been for a little child; this was unquestionably a work of the highest art. It was called *St. Veronica's Napkin*, be-

149

cause you know, dear, that when Our Lord stumbled and fell on the terrible walk to Calvary, St. Veronica wiped His dear Face with her napkin (no, not a dinner napkin, dear, more a hanky) and lo! His Image was imprinted on it forever. Just like the Shroud of Turin. As one looked at the calm face, its closed eyes seemed to open and gaze directly into your own. The work of a great Belgian master, dear; we'll hang it where you can see it from your bed, and you'll know He's looking at you all night long.

The other was secular, but though it was a "nude" it was not sensational; a boy, about Francis's own age, stood weeping at a door that the painter's art had made to look very firmly closed, but also as though it gave entry to something wholly delightful; it was called *Love Locked Out*. Painted by a lady, Francis—an American lady—but what a truly masculine grasp of art she must have to be able to think of and paint such a wonderful picture!

Love locked out. Francis knew all about that. Oh, Mother, darling Mother, why are you so far away? Why are you never here? Mother's visits were so few and so brief. Of course, it was her work in England, in the hospitals for Canadian soldiers, that kept her away, and Francis must be a brave soldier too, and not mind. Parcels at Christmas, and occasional brief letters that seemed to be written to a much younger boy, did not really make up for Mother's absence. Love Locked Out—even a brave little soldier could not keep back tears. The picture gave an outward, visible form to a longing that lived deep inside him, and surged to the surface whenever he was sad, or lonely, or when dusk was gathering outside the windows, and the fire made changing shadows on the wall.

That Christmas night, when Aunt thought he was fast asleep, Francis stood naked against the wall of his bedroom, and with a hand mirror he looked over his shoulder at his image in the big looking-glass on the other side of the room. Carefully composing his body, he assumed the attitude of the picture, and looked long and with sadness mixed with approval at what he saw. He could do it. He could enter and become the picture. He could do it well. He crept back into his pyjamas and returned to bed, his sadness mingled with a pleasure he did not understand but which was comforting. He would repeat that experience many times in the days to come.

You are letting your boy become rather odd, aren't you? said the Lesser Zadkiel.

—My dear colleague, you are allowing yourself to talk like Alexander Dagg, said the Daimon Maimas. I am pushing him gently in the direction dictated by his destiny, and I have not infinite means of doing that. I must work with whatever is at hand. He is to be a connoisseur, a patron of art, a man who understands art—though there will be dozens of Alexander Daggs of a more sophisticated sort to assert rancorously that he knew nothing whatever

151

about it. Don't expect me to make an omelette without breaking eggs.

—I was thinking about breaking hearts.

—Oh, hearts! Nobody gets through life without a broken heart. The important thing is to break the heart so that when it mends it will be stronger than before. If you will allow me to say so, my dear Zadkiel, you angels are very easily pulled toward sentimentality. If you had my work to do, you would know how ruinous that can be.

—I am disposed sometimes toward pity. If that is what you are talking about.

—If Francis was an ordinary boy he might have been lucky enough to have a guardian angel assigned to him, to keep him out of trouble and put pretty things in his way. But I am no guardian angel, as you well know: I am a daimon, and my work must sometimes seem rough. We haven't seen the last of Francis before the mirror, and next time he won't have his back to it.

—Ah, well. Let us go on with our story.

As Aunt managed everything in St. Kilda her taste was apparent not only in her own room, but everywhere, and especially in the pictures. In the dining-room, for instance, hung two large paintings by François Brunery, which had cost the Senator a pretty penny but which were, as Aunt explained to him, emblematic of his position in the world.

One was called, on the medallion at the bottom of the frame, *The Point of the Story.* At a dining-

152

table in what was plainly a palace in Rome sat five cardinals in scarlet, and a bishop in purple. Oh, how shrewd, how intelligent were the faces (three plump, two thin) that were inclined forward, intent upon the sixth, a cardinal whose upraised forefinger and twinkling eyes showed that the point of the good story was about to break upon his hearers. What could it be? Some tale of Vatican intrigue, some subtle reverse of fortune in the Curia, or, perhaps, some scandal about a lady? The look of discreet enjoyment on the face of the major-domo in the background suggested the last. And look at the table! What gold and silver objects, what crystal glasses, what ruby wine. (Oh, that's clever, contrasting the colour of the wine with the scarlet of the robes, without letting them swear at one another!) And what promise of further wine in the gorgeous silver wine cistern that stands in the foreground, on the finely painted hardwood floor. (Look, Hamish, there's wood for you!) A great picture, a real work of art, and just the thing for a dining-room.

On the opposite wall was an even jollier picture; jolly, but perhaps a little sly. It was called *The Tired Model*. A young monk, a Dominican by his robe, stands before the easel in his studio, upon which is a picture of a saintly old cardinal, his hands pressed against his breast. Just look at that delicate old flesh against the scarlet moiré, and his gaze raised to Heaven, from which is coming the light that enfolds him! But on the model-throne sits the old man, slumped in his chair, fast asleep;

the artist—a handsome young fellow with curly hair around his tonsure—is scratching his head in dismay.

Are not these pictures reverential, showing a devotion to the things of the Church and especially to its hierarchy, yet asserting that their owner shares a common humanity with the red-robed cardinals? These are such pictures as you might expect to find in the dining-room of a B.C.L. (as a Big Catholic Layman was jokingly called in Church circles), a man who knew his place, but who also knew his worth—a man who could re-gild a spire or contribute a splendid bell without having to think twice about the bill. Aunt had taken care that Hamish had what was right for him. When Father Devlin and Father Beaudry dined in that room they understood the subtle message; no domineering priests' ways in this house, if you please, gentlemen. Drink your wine and mind your manners.

Canada had officially embraced Prohibition in 1916, in order that when the brave boys returned after the War they would find a country purged of one of the major causes of evil-doing. In such houses as the Senator's the cellars contained stocks of wine bought long before, and there was no stint. But even substantial stocks dwindled, and this was reason for some unease. A good cellar needs regular replenishing. Marie-Louise's friends could nip their way through a surprising amount of white wine in an afternoon of bridge, before it was time for a substantial tea.

By the standards of Blairlogie, quite a lot of entertaining was done at St. Kilda, and in this, as in everything else, Aunt was the unobtrusive manager. Unobtrusive, that is, until it came to music, and then she shone. In every realm, without any hint of undesirable bohemianism or deviation from the strictest morality, Aunt was "artistic".

"Shall we have a little music?" she would say when, after dinner, the guests had had an hour in which to chat and digest. Nobody would think of replying that it might be more fun to go on talking; that would be an affront to the high aesthetic atmosphere of St. Kilda, which Aunt had created, to the greater glory of her brother and his wife.

When it had been enthusiastically agreed that nothing could be pleasanter than a little music, Aunt would go to the piano and, if there were someone present who had not been to dinner before, she would plunge immediately into a difficult and noisy piece, such as a Liszt Hungarian Rhapsody. The guest, if not of a positively turnip-like insensitivity, would be astonished at the noise, the pell-mell speed, the sheer cultivated racket that Aunt was producing. Even more astonished when, at the conclusion, when he was about to say, "Miss McRory, I never dreamed—" the other guests would break into mocking applause, and Aunt herself would turn on the piano stool, shaking with laughter.

For the piano was a Phonoliszt (World Renowned Pianists At Your Beck and Call . . . no pedals to push, no levers to learn . . .) and this was Aunt's little joke. The pianist had been the great Teresa Carreño, a famous matador of the instrument, imprisoned forever on a perforated roll of paper.

"But if you would like me to sing—" she would say, and all the guests agreed eagerly that they would like her to sing.

Aunt sang in English and French and it was generally agreed that her repertoire was very chaste. What was not chaste was the sound she made. She had a good voice, a true contralto, and produced a big, fruity tone surprising in such a small woman. She had always sung, and had been "finished" in Montreal in twelve lessons with Maestro Carboni. The maestro's method was simple, and effective: "All moving utterance is based upon the cry of the child," said he; "make a sound like a child crying—not in anger, but for love—and refine on it, Mademoiselle, and everything else will fall into place." Aunt had done so, and her singing was both good and astonishing, for it moved and troubled even musical ignoramuses.

The songs she sang were, in one way or another, cries for love. Songs in French, from the pen of Guy d'Hardelot, or in English, by Carrie Jacobs-Bond. Strongly emotional songs. Had Aunt known it, songs orgasmic in their slow, swelling climaxes.

But beyond any doubt Aunt's finest effort, her unfailing war-horse, was "Vale", by Kennedy Russell. Although Francis could see plainly on the

156

music that its name was "Vale", Aunt and all cultivated persons pronounced it "Wally", because it was Latin and meant "Farewell". In two brief verses by de Burgh d'Arcy (obviously an aristocrat of some kind) it caught the very soul of Aunt, and most of her hearers.

It was about a man who was dying. He begged somebody (wife? lover?—oh, surely not a lover, not when one was dying) to stay at his side during the creeping, silent hours.

Mourn not my loss, you lov'd me faithfully

(Obviously a wife, who had done her wifely duty.) The conclusion was dramatically splendid:

Then, when the cold grey dawn breaks silently,
Hold up THE CROSS . . . and pray for me!

For a dying person, Aunt made a remarkable amount of noise at *Hold up THE CROSS* and then faded almost into silence at *and pray for me!* as if the singer were actually pegging out. This was done by what Maestro Carboni called "spinning the tone", a very good Italian trick, and not easy to acquire.

Aunt sang this song often. It was always in demand when St. Bonaventura's had one of its concerts to raise money, and Father Devlin had said, in language that might have been more happily phrased, that when Miss McRory sang

"Wally" we all got as near to dying as we'd get before our time actually came.

Aunt's music had a lighter side, not for parties, but for those quiet evenings when it was just herself and the Senator and Marie-Louise, and Dr. J. A., who often dropped in after his evening rounds, tired out and wanting relaxation.

"Sing 'Damn Stupid', Mary-Ben," he would say, as he stretched his legs toward the fire.

"Oh, Joe, you do love to make fun of me," Aunt would say, and then sing the ballad from *Merrie England*:

> *Dan Cupid hath a garden*
> *Where women are the flowers—*

Which went on to declare that the sweetest flower loved by Cupid was the Lovely English Rose. She, the wholly Highland Scots old maid, and he, the wholly Irish old bachelor, found a distilment of their own stifled, unacknowledged romance in this very English song by Edward German Jones, born on the Welsh Border. Music, as Aunt often told Francis, knows no frontiers.

Francis heard it all. Sometimes he sat in the drawing-room, already in his pyjamas, but wrapped in rugs, because he had begged to hear Aunt sing, and what singer can refuse such a tribute, so obviously sincere? Sometimes, when there were guests and he was supposed to be in bed, he sat on the stairs, in his pyjamas and without any rugs. To the pictures he responded

158

with mind and heart, eager not only to understand what they had to say, but to know how they were made; to the music he listened with his heart alone.

He was finding out one or two things about pictures. He had the run of Aunt's collection of prints, and a number of books she possessed, with names like *Gems From the World's Great Galleries*. He was probably the only boy within a five-hundred-mile radius who knew what the Pitti was, or what *putti* were. But better than that, he was getting some notion of how pictures were put together.

His teacher was an unlikely one. Among Aunt's books was one which she had bought long ago, glanced at, and decided that it had nothing to say to her. It was called *How to Draw in Pen and Ink*, and the author was Harry Furniss. Indeed, he was still alive, and would be alive for a further five years after Francis first met with his book. Furniss was a remarkable caricaturist, but, as he explained in his genial prose, to draw caricatures it is first necessary to be able to draw people, and if you want to draw people you had better try your hand at drawing anything and everything. You cannot make Mr. Gladstone look like an old eagle if you cannot draw a serious Mr. Gladstone and a serious old eagle. You must develop an eye; you must see everything in terms of line and form. Andrea del Sarto was no Raphael, but he could correct Raphael's drawing; you could aim at drawing like del Sarto even if you hadn't a hope of being anything better than a Harry Furniss—which wasn't the easiest thing in the world to be, either.

Francis had access to unlimited paper and pencils; he had but to ask Aunt and plentiful supplies appeared. He did not tell Aunt about Harry Furniss, whom she had rejected as unworthy, and doubtless coarse in his methods. But a man who had been able, as a youth, to attend a London fire, make pages of rapid sketches, and then work them up into a full-page engraving for the *London Illustrated News* was just the man to catch Francis's imagination. A man who could make such vivid caricatures of people whom Francis had never heard of, but whose essence he felt in Furniss's drawings, was just the man to dispel the impression given by Aunt that it all had to be done by geniuses, usually foreigners, in studios, under the spooky guidance of the Holy Mother and perhaps even of A Certain Person. This was a gust of fresh air in art. This made art a possibility—remote, but still a possibility—for somebody like himself.

Always have paper in your pocket, said Harry Furniss. Never be without a notebook. Never miss a significant figure in the streets or at the theatre or in Parliament. Catch every turn of the head, every gleam in the eye. You can't draw pretty girls if you can't draw gutter crones. If you can't keep files of your notes, don't; but once having disciplined your hand and eye to capture every detail and nuance, perhaps you don't need files, for these things are filed in your brain and your hand.

Just the sort of sea-breeze to blow away the odour of sanctity. Francis was conscious of his notebook, which marked him as an artist. But where many a boy would have made a parade of what he was doing, and attracted attention from adults who wanted to see what he was up to, he mastered the trick of sitting quietly, making his rapid sketches without signalling.

A few weeks after Christmas he was able to go outside for limited airings, but he was not anxious to attract attention from Nosy Parkers who would want to know why he was in the streets when all decent boys were either in school, or at home with infantile paralysis, or simply with swollen glands. Not to be easily noticed is an acquirement, as is always being noticed; Francis studied the art of invisibility, and made sketches wherever he was.

He was perched on a bale of straw in the stable one February day, making sketches of the horses as they ate, when Zadok Hoyle said to him: "Frank, it's a fine day and I have to go over to The Portage this afternoon; why don't you ask your Aunt if you can come with me?" Aunt demurred a little, but finally said yes, he might go, but he must be well bundled up.

Bundled up he was, almost to the point of immobility, as he sat beside Zadok on the driver's seat. The wagon was not one of his grandfather's, but an odd cart with a low, boxed-in back; its purpose could not be immediately guessed. They drove perhaps four miles in the sharp air to a hamlet on a river-bank, which had a name of its own but from long custom was always called The Portage. Zadok pointed far beyond the river with his whip. "See that, Frankie? That's Quebec. And some funny things happen on this river."

They stopped on the river-bank at a shed, from which a fat, dark jowled man appeared, nodded to Zadok, returned to the shed, and shortly returned carrying a box; between them he and Zadok loaded six such boxes into the back of the cart. Not a word was said, and they drove off.

"That was the happy call," said Zadok. "Now we make the sad call." Happy? What was happy about it? Not a word said and the fat man had what Francis thought was a bad eye, and he wished he could have made a rapid sketch of it. And now—the sad call?

They drove somewhat less than a mile to a farmhouse, where Zadok spoke briefly with a woman in black; another, older woman, also in black, was to be seen in the background. A man appeared from the barn, and helped Zadok to carry a large package out of the house; a long package, wrapped in rough brown holland; it was clearly a man. They shoved it into the back of the cart, with the boxes, Zadok said something kindly, the man nodded and spat, and the horse was turned in the direction of Blairlogie.

"Is that a dead person, Zadok? Why are we carrying a dead person?"

"Why do you suppose, Frankie? It's Mr. Devinney's business; I pick 'em up, and I get 'em ready. I drive the hearse. Mr. Devinney does the business end. He sees to putting the death notice in *The Clarion*, and ordering and sending out the death-cards. He marches in the procession in his plug hat. He does all the condoling, which isn't easy work, but he has quite a poetic turn, sometimes. And of course he does all the billing, reckons up the number of plumes on the hearse, and all that. This one in the back is Old McAllister—a mean old sodbuster, but a customer now—and I'll have to get him ready for the funeral, lug him out to the farm again, and lug him back again on Friday, for the burial. Lot o' hauling in this business. We 're riding on the death-cart, Frankie. Didn't you know? Aw, but then a lot o' things are kept from a boy like you."

When they reached Blairlogie they drove up Dalhousie Street, which was the main and only business street, and stopped at a side door of Devinney's Furniture and Undertaking Parlours. Briskly, Zadok leaped down, opened the door of the shop, pulled out a light table on rubber wheels, shifted Old McAllister on to it, threw a sheet over him and had him into the shop in approximately fifteen seconds.

"Have to be quick. People don't like to see how things are done. A funeral's a work of art, y'see, dear boy, and all the rough part is no business of the public's."

This was as he was wheeling Old McAllister on his cart through the furniture part of the store, toward the back, which was closed off by a partition with a curtained double door. Beyond the

163

curtains, Zadok switched on the light—it was a dim light, afforded by two bulbs of modest power—and opened another double door, very heavy and with broad hinges. From inside came a cold breath, damp and stuffy, the smell of slowly melting ice. Quickly Old McAllister was wheeled inside, and doors were closed.

"Don't want too much melting," said Zadok. "Mr. Devinney is always complaining about the ice bill."

"But Zadok, what are you going to do with him?" said Francis. "Do you just leave him in there till the funeral?"

"I should say not," said Zadok. "I make him look better than he ever looked in his life. It's an art, Frankie, and though anybody can learn the elements of it, the real art's inborn.—You didn't know I was an artist, did you?"

It was then that Francis made his great confession. "Zadok, I think I'm an artist too." He rummaged in his outer clothes, and produced his sketch-book.

"By the Powers of Old Melchizedek," said Zadok (this was his mighty oath), "you are, dear boy, and no mistake. Here's Miss McRory to the life. Ah, Frankie, you've been a bit severe with the little cap, dear man. Ah, never be cruel, me dear. But b'God it's true enough, even if it is sharp. And here's Miss Cameron. You've made her look almost like one of your Aunt's spooky pictures. But it's true, too. And here's me! To think I was once accounted a handsome man! Ah, ye devil! That's the red nose to the life! Ah, Frankie, y' rascal! You make me laugh at myself. Oh, you're an artist. And what are you going to do about it?"

"Zadok—Zadok, promise me you won't tell. They'd be after me, and Aunt would want me to have lessons, and I don't want that yet. I have to find my own way first, you see. Harry Furniss says so; find your own way, and then let anybody teach you that can, but hang on to your own way."

"Here's Madame Thibodeau—ah, ye little scallawag—look at the way you've made her great bum hang off both sides of the chair. She'd have you killed if she ever saw that!"

"But that's it, Zadok! I've got to learn to see what's in front of my nose. That's what Harry Furniss says; most people don't see what's in front of their nose. They just see what they think they ought to see."

"True enough, Frankie, and don't I know that in my own art; you just have to encourage people to see what they think they ought to see. But come along, now. I've got to get you home, and the horse'll be gettin' cold."

On the way back to St. Kilda, Francis pleaded to know what Zadok was going to do with Old McAllister. If it was art of any kind, hadn't he the right of a fellow-artist to know? So at last it was clapped up between them that right after he had his supper Francis was to join Zadok again, because Aunt had to go out to a meeting at St.

Bonaventura's—something about the poor and needy—and he would see Zadok at his art, and Zadok would get him home in time to slip into his bed so that nobody, not even Miss Victoria Cameron, would suspect that he had been out.

In the barn Zadok's first care was to unload the six boxes which remained in the death-cart, and lock them in an unused stall in the stables.

"What is that, Zadok?"

"Oh, it's just some stuff your grandfather gets from a trusted man in Quebec. Mr. Devinney gets a little slice for the use of the cart. It's a sideline of his business that we never discuss. Everybody has his secret, Frankie. You have yours; Mr. Devinney has his." And as he heaved the last case into the stall, Francis thought he heard Zadok say, "And I have mine."

I question whether it was a good thing to steer a boy of thirteen into an undertaking parlour that is run by a bootlegger, said the Lesser Zadkiel.

—I don't, said the Daimon Maimas. He had been old-womaned far too much by Aunt. He needed a man in his life, and where was the Wooden Soldier? Saving the Empire across the ocean. And his mother was being wonderful to wounded soldiers, but had no time for her son. His grandfather was far too broken to be more than another gentle presence in the boy's life, though he was very kind, when he thought about it.

—Grandfather broken?

—The Senator never got over the destruction of

his idol. When Mary-Jacobine got into trouble and had to be married off to the likeliest comer— and a Protestant at that—he never quite believed in anything again. He was a strong man in business and in politics, but those are external things: only a fool gives his soul to them. The pith had been scooped out of him. Look at Marie-Louise: an aging, fat gambler. Look at Mary-Ben: she idolized her brother but she never understood more than half of him. Zadok was the strongest man around the place, as you well know.

—A rogue, my dear colleague. A rogue.

—Very well, but a kindly, decent rogue, in the thick of life and death. I had to work with what was at hand, you know.

—As you say. I have not had to do your work, so I certainly must not find fault with the way you did it.

—Quite so. And Zadok was something of an artist, as we'll see, if you will be so good as to go on with your narrative. By the way, do you know how it comes out?

—I cannot remember all these lives in detail. Like yourself, I am simply being reminded of the life of Francis Cornish.

The light in Mr. Devinney's workroom was like the light in Rembrandt, thought Francis; two mean bulbs, hanging above the narrow, slanted table on which Zadok had now placed the bundle which was all that was left of Old McAllister, a mean old sodbuster. Zadok was scrubbing his hands fiercely with yellow soap at a sink.

"Cleanliness is essential," he said. "Respect for the dead, and precaution for the living. You never really know what these people died of. So I'll just throw around some carbolic, and you keep well in your corner, me dear."

Well in his corner, perched on two coffin crates so that he had a good view of the scene, Francis had his notebook and pencil ready.

Respect for the dead; Zadok was gentle in unwrapping Old McAllister, who had apparently died in his long underwear, a baggy, liver-coloured extra skin. Quickly Zadok ripped the underwear with a curved knife which Francis recognized as a pruning-knife, and soon Old McAllister was naked, an unimpressive sight, but a Golconda for Francis.

This was something he had never reckoned on. He would be able to draw the nude figure, which even Harry Furniss insisted was the foremost necessity—after seeing what was in front of your eyes—in becoming an artist.

Old McAllister was balding and scrawny. His face and hands were tanned a deep brown by sixty-seven years of Ottawa Valley weather, but the rest of him was a bluey-white. His legs were like sticks, and his feet fell outward and sideways. Zadok had cut off his underwear because Old McAllister, according to local custom, had been sewed into it for the winter. Francis knew all about that; most of the children in Carlyle Rural were so encased and they stank amazingly.

"A bath, for a starter," said Zadok. "First, though, a thorough swilling-out." With a large squirt he neatly washed out the rectum of the corpse into a bucket. Then, with a dribble from a short hose, and frequent dabblings of carbolic, Zadok washed Old McAllister; the water fell to the cement floor and vanished down a drain. He washed Old McAllister's hands, with plentiful lathering of yellow soap, and cleaned the nails with his jack-knife.

"Always a problem, this," he said to the busily scribbling Francis. 'These fellas never clean their nails from Easter to Easter, but they have to have hands like a barber for the viewing. It's part of the art, you see. At the end they must look as they'd have looked on their wedding-day, or better. Probably better."

He shaved Old McAllister with ample lather and hot water. "Lucky I had some experience as a valet," he said, "but of course no valet could get away with this." He deftly poked a finger into the corpse's mouth to push out the hollow cheeks. The scrape of the razor told of the toughness of Old McAllister's beard. "Never been shaved more than once a week in his life, I don't suppose," said Zadok.

"Now didn't I have a roll of cotton-wool? For what we call the orifices."

The orifices were the ears, the nostrils, and, to Francis's surprise, the anus; into each a sufficient plug of wool was stuffed. Then a big chunk into the mouth, and before it was closed a large gob of beeswax was popped in and Zadok held the jaws until they were firmly clamped.

"This is easy enough in a winter funeral," he said, "but in summer it's another thing altogether. I've seen funerals where the wax went soft and the mouth opened unexpectedly and you wouldn't believe the screaming and fainting. But we'll have none of that with you, old boy, will we?" he said, and gave Old McAllister a friendly pat on the shoulder. "There, now we've done the clean-up jobs. Now comes the science. If you feel queer, dear soul, there's the bucket just by you."

Francis did not feel queer. He had got Old McAllister's right hand—what a hand for knots and lumps! He had got both feet, corns and bunions complete. He was now busy on a full-length, with difficult perspective. That picture that Aunt didn't like him to linger over in *Gems*—the *Anatomy Lesson*, was it called?—lived in his memory and came to his aid. This was great! This was life!

Zadok had drawn up a machine that sat on a wheeled cart, and looked like a tank with a hose coming out of it, beside his work-table. With a little fleam he lifted a vein in Old McAllister's arm, inserted a thickish needle that was attached to the hose, and began slowly and watchfully to work a pump-handle on his machine. As he pumped, he sang, in a fine bass, but *sotto voce*:

Yes! let me like a soldier fall
Upon some open plain,
This breast, expanding for the ball
To blot out every stain.

This went on for quite a long time—time enough for Francis to do another drawing, with Zadok's dark figure standing beside the body. He was proud of his professionalism in roughing in Old McAllister's privy parts; just six quick lines and a shadow, like Rembrandt. Nothing of the grossness of the boys who drew such things on fences. But of course they were not artists.

"Here we go for the big one," said Zadok. Quickly he nicked Old McAllister's navel, thrust in a larger needle—he called it a trocar—and pumped again. Then, something very delicate, involving the corner of the eye.

"There, old lad," he said. "That'll hold you for a week or two. Now for the real art, Frankie."

As he worked, Zadok, always a genial man, became positively merry. "No time to waste; don't want him to harden on me," he said, as he seemed to wrestle with Old McAllister, quickly getting him into socks, trousers, and a shirt that had come in a bundle from the farm. "On with your dancing-pumps, gaffer," he said, as he fitted the huge, misshapen feet into soft kid slippers. "Now, before the collar and tie, the real fancy-work."

"Where were you a valet, Zadok?" asked Francis.

"Oh, before the war—the Boer War, that's to

say—I was a lot o' things. Footman for a while; very good experience that, for any future job. Then a valet, because in the war I was batman to my young lord; I'd been a footman in his father's house, and we went into the Army together, you might say, but him as an officer and me as a private, of course. But we were never apart, not really. Keeping a young officer smart in the field, with them rotten Boers popping up everywhere you didn't expect them, was a job, I can tell you. Do you know them Boers didn't wear uniforms? Just fought in their farm clothes? You can't call that war. But I learned to dress a gentleman to look like a gentleman, dead or alive, so I don't have any trouble with a chap like this."

"But where did you learn all that—about the cotton-wool, and the needles and everything?"

"Always had a turn that way. I remember when I was just a little lad, at my grandfather's funeral. 'I want to see Granda, I want to see Granda' I kept on at my mother. She thought it was love, and very creditable to me, but it was just nosiness. He went by the palsy route, you see, and I was amazed that he'd stopped shaking. I thought it was the undertaker, old Smout, that had stopped him. Of course, Smout was just a Cornish village undertaker; coffin-maker, really; and he didn't have the scientific advantages of today. By my standards, Granda was just a mess, rigged up in a cheap shroud, his hair all combed the wrong way. But it was my start.

"Then in the war we had to bury the dead, and

in my lot that work was done under a farrier-sergeant who had no training and no ideas, but he wanted it done proper. That was where my talent came to light. There wasn't much we could do; no embalming, of course, but we could make 'em look like soldiers of the Queen, poor lads. With a face wound you could put on a decent piece of plaster. I would have got a medal for my work if it hadn't been for a misunderstanding, for which I bear no grudge, not now. Other outfits copied our methods, but they went too far. There was one bugger did a nasty business in hearts. He was an officer, so his mail wasn't censored—gentlemen don't read other gents' letters, you see—and he would write home, 'Dear Madam please accept my condolences on the death of your brave son, who fell like a man with the respect of all his regiment. His dying wish was that his heart should return to England and lay in the church where he learned to be a man when a boy. Can deliver said heart to you on my return to England, suitably preserved, at a very moderate fee. Yours, etc.' Rotten trick, but what mother could resist? God damn him, wherever he is now.

"Then I got a bit of real pro training in England, and that's where I picked up all this. Not that I learned the art of make-up in the embalmers' parlours. Not the real art. I had that off a pal of mine who played minor clowns in the panto at Christmas. Powder. That's the great secret."

Zadok raised a cloud of violet-scented *poudre de*

riz around the head. "That's the foundation," he said.

Old McAllister's face, which had turned a dark putty shade, was swiftly painted with a wash that left him a light salmon, and over the cheekbones Zadok brushed some dry rouge of a startling crimson. Next he worked on Old McAllister's mouth, gently massaging the grim, grey lips into an unaccustomed smile: this he touched up with a red salve that a harlot might have thought excessive. Then he rapidly massaged some vaseline into the thin hair, and combed it forward.

"How do you suppose he did his hair—when he did it? No indications, so we'll give him Old Faithful." He combed the hair with a left-hand parting, then quiffed the right-hand portion over his finger, giving Old McAllister a nifty, almost a dandified air. Quick work with the collar, the necktie; into the waistcoat, draping a huge silver watch-chain, from which the watch had been removed, over the sunken belly. On with the coat. A piece of card on the tip of which some white cambric was sewn was tucked into the breast pocket of the coat (Old McAllister had not used, or possessed, handkerchiefs of his own). The hands were folded on the breast, as if in Christian acceptance, and Old McAllister was a finished work of art.

Then, further astonishing Francis after an astonishing, rapturous evening, Zadok took Old McAllister's right hand in his own and shook it cordially. "Godspeed, old man," said he. Noticing

174

Francis's astonishment, he said, "I always do that. I'm the last, most personal attendant, you see; the priest is quite another matter. So I always shake the hand, and wish 'em well. You'd better shake, too, Frankie, as you've been here, and drawing pictures, and all."

Tentative, but game, Francis shook Old McAllister's chilly paw.

"There, old cully, back into the cooler with you, and I'll deliver you first thing in the morning, in plenty of time for the viewing. And as for you, Frankie my lad, I must get you home and to bed before anybody notices."

To Francis's surprise, Zadok not only took him back to St. Kilda, but came upstairs with him, and after the door had closed on his bedroom went—where? The sound was not of feet going downstairs, but of feet going upstairs, to the third floor, which was Victoria Cameron's private domain, and to which Francis was forbidden to mount under threat of the severest reprisals. Never, never up there, Francis. So why was Zadok going up there? Another astonishment at the end of an astonishing, enlarging, enlightening day. A memorable day on his journey toward being an artist, a man of the great world of events, like Harry Furniss.

In the weeks that passed, Francis spent many an enraptured hour in Mr. Devinney's back room, watching Zadok at work, and sketching for dear life. A variety of subjects came under his view and

175

his pencil. The old predominated, of course, but now and then there was somebody who had, in the prime of life, suffered an accident or an unaccountably severe illness. Once there was a girl of sixteen, whom Francis did not positively know, but whom he had seen in the streets and at the McRory Opera House.

With female subjects, Zadok's behaviour was exemplary. As he stripped them on the table, he draped a towel over the pubic region, so that Francis never saw a woman fully naked, much as he wished to do so.

"Professional discretion," said Zadok. "No Nosy-Parkering with the ladies. So we always lay a towel over The Particular, you see, dear soul, because no man, professional though he may be, has any call to behold The Particular of any female he deals with in a purely professional capacity."

But, oh, how Francis longed to see The Particular, about which he speculated so painfully. What could it be? The very few nudes in Aunt's collection seemed to have no Particular, or had averted it from the gaze, or put a hand over it. What was The Particular? He put the matter tactfully to Zadok; he was an artist, and ought to know everything about the human body.

"You must find out your own way, Francis," said Zadok solemnly; "the buzzem—well, it's very widely seen and indeed it's one of the first things any of us do see, but The Particular is quite another matter."

One night in March, as he took Francis to Devinney's, Zadok seemed depressed. "I don't care for this, dear lad; don't care for it at all."

What he did not care for, when it was taken out of the cooler, was the body of François Xavier Bouchard, a dwarf tailor, known to Blairlogie's English-speakers as Bushy.

His one-storey tailor-shop was a mean building at the top end of Dalhousie Street, and winter and summer Bushy could be seen leaning in the door, waiting for custom. It cannot have been much: sewing on a button or perhaps turning a suit for some thrifty soul, but he seemed to keep bread in his mouth, although, like many tailors, he was shabby in his own dress. He grinned without cease, a dog-like grin that seemed to implore tolerance, respect being beyond his hopes.

There he lay, on Mr. Devinney's table, his head huge and his trunk barrel-like, his arms and legs so short that there seemed to be little between shoulder and elbow, elbow and hand, his private parts huge above his tiny legs, although they would not have been excessive on a full-grown man. His head lay at an unusual angle.

"Hanged himself," said Zadok. "They found him this morning. Did it two or three days ago, I should guess. Poor, poor little soul. We've got to do our best for old F.X., Francis, not that anything can make up for a life like his."

The scene which preceded the final scene of Bushy's life, as Zadok recounted it, was something wholly outside any experience known to

Francis, except those terrible quarter-hours in the playground of Carlyle Rural, when boys blew up frogs and tortured cats. This would certainly have reopened the wounds of Jesus.

"The men in one of the lodges, Francis. I'm not going to tell you which one. Do you know what a lodge is? It's a lot of chaps who get together for a kind of religion that isn't quite the same as the real religion; they have altars and whim-whams, and they dress up in trick clothes and talk a lot of rubbish to one another. All very secret but somehow anybody who cares can find out.

"Every so often they let in some new members, and it's all very solemn; then they have to have some fun. You know how it is: after a solemn time you have to have a change. Like at funerals, where they joke and quarrel at the party after the burial. Well, these boys got the idea a while ago that it would be great fun to shanghai Bushy and take him up to the lodgerooms over De Marche's hardware, and give him a bath. They did it quite a few times. Everybody had a grab at him, or pushed the soap in his face, or tried to take the hide off him with the towel. Then they'd make him run up and down the room; they'd flick him with wet towels and sool him on so they could see his little legs go, and his big what's-its-name whack and thrash around. They had one of those affairs three days ago, and I guess the poor little mortal couldn't stand it any more, and went home and hanged himself. In a pair of braces, I understand.

Christ, Frankie, I hardly know whether to weep or puke. I've had a taste of humiliation myself, but poor old F.X.—" Zadok could not go on, but he bent to his work with special gentleness. Yes, let me like a soldier fall, upon some open plain.

Francis had seen pictures in Aunt's books called *The Entombment*. What dignity, what compassion was shown in the faces of those who handled the body of the dead Saviour. He had seen those pictures but he did not know them, encompass them, feel them, until he saw Zadok working over the body of the dead tailor. He sketched away like a man and an artist, but now and then he could not repress a sniff. That hour was to stay with him all his life.

When all was done, Zadok and Francis both shook hands with Bushy and wished him God-speed. And then, as always, for Zadok would not have it otherwise, he washed his hands carefully.

At night, when he was supposed to be in bed and asleep, Francis was sometimes very much awake, and engaged in—what were they? It would not be quite exact to call them games, and he himself could not have described them if he had been called on by some indignant or sorrowing adult to do so.

Thoughts and physical urges about sex rose to torment him several times a day, and even Dr. Upper's remedy of the cold towel was ineffective; Francis tried it once or twice, and then decided that it was silly; he did not really want to rebuke his penis for its insistence on being noticed. And noticed not only when his thoughts strayed to the mystery of The Particular, but often when he was thinking of something innocuous like food, or where he had put his tube of Chinese white. Was he wicked? But the wickedness was also thrilling. Was he in some special way afflicted or diseased, that he should be so teased by a part of his body he could not control? There was nobody to ask.

But the demand was frequent, and in an alarming way delicious. Sometimes he provoked it, knowing that he should not, by looking at his small store of movie magazines. These he had bought, from time to time, at a local store called The Beehive, which sold not only movie magazines but false-faces, rings made in the shape of serpents with glittering red-glass eyes, and books which told you how to be a magician or a ventriloquist. The movie magazines showed the screen favourites of the time—Mae Murray, Margarita Fisher, Gladys Walton—in bathing suits that exposed their legs to the knee, or in short skirts with rolled stockings; a picture of Gloria Swanson in some historical epic of a period when people were obviously dead to shame (or enjoyed it) showed one of her thighs almost to the hip. Long gazing at this picture was a hot excitement. So much more exciting than the few nudes to be found in Aunt's books, so often monumental people by Thorwaldsen, or some nineteenth-century artist with a strong hint of Dr. Upper in his attitude toward sex. They were no fun; the movie stars were alive, and exciting. But most exciting of all were the pictures of Julian Eltinge.

Francis had seen this popular female impersonator in *The Countess Charming* at Grand-père's theatre. Eltinge was a plump man of unremarkable appearance who could disguise himself as a woman of elegance and charm; the film showed the lacy undergarments, the corset, the wig that made the transformation. With some odds and ends of curtains and bits of silk he concealed in his chest of drawers Francis attempted to do what Eltinge did, and although the result would not have impressed anyone else it satisfied him deeply. He had to know about the human figure: he stuffed enough rags into his top to produce a buzzem something like that of Eltinge. The legs were a great feature of the pictures of movie stars: he disposed his legs in the manner of Gloria Swanson. He had no wig but he wrapped his head in a scarf. The effect in the mirror was gratifying to the point of urgency. What had Eltinge done about The Particular? Francis's own particular made it plain that disguise must have been extremely difficult.

Bedtime fantasies were partnered by night horrors. In dreams he was set upon by succubi who were nothing like Gloria Swanson or the tantalizing Clarine Seymour; no, in his dreams hags and women horribly like those he had seen in the embalming room tormented and whispered, until he awoke with the hot gush on his thighs that made him leap from his bed, dab at the sheets with a dampened cloth, and do what he could to wash the pants of his pyjamas. Suppose somebody found out? Suppose that Anna Lemenchick, who made the beds, told Victoria Cameron? What would happen? He could not guess, but it would be shame even beyond the rich vocabulary of Dr. Upper to describe. But he could not stop; posturing in the manner of Julian Eltinge was seductive beyond his power of resistance.

What do you make of that, my friend? said the Daimon Maimas.

—You had better tell me what you make of it, said the Lesser Zadkiel. I suppose you were at the root of it all?

—Indeed I was, said the Daimon Maimas, and I took care that nobody found Francis at his games, for he was right in supposing that there would have been a pious uproar. But surely you see what the boy was doing?

—Looking for something that his life denied him, obviously. Trying to cope with a problem for which his life in Blairlogie terms offered no solution and no solace. He seems not to have known any girls except in the most distant fashion, and the screen images were unlike anything he would have met with even if he had known some girls at school.

—Just as well, for it wasn't any palpable girl he was trying to evoke in front of his mirror, and it certainly wasn't Julian Eltinge. Of course, he didn't know it—they never do—but he was looking for The Girl, the girl deep in himself, the feminine

ideal that has some sort of existence in every man of any substance, and my Francis was a man of substance. It wasn't effeminacy which is what anybody who discovered him would have supposed. It certainly wasn't homosexuality, for Francis never had more than the usual dash of that. He was groping for the Mystical Marriage, the unity of the masculine and the feminine in himself without which he would have been useless in his future life as an artist and as a man who understood art. Useless as any sort of man—rich man, poor man, beggar man, thief; not to speak of tinker, tailor, soldier, sailor—who is destined to see more than a few inches beyond the end of his nose. This was the beginning of the search for the Mystical Marriage, which is one of the great quests, and as usual the quest was longer and more important than the eventual discovery.

—Aha! And I suppose the quest is what poor Simon Darcourt, labouring over his biography of Francis, apprehends dimly, but without really knowing what it is.

—We mustn't be extreme. And we certainly mustn't underestimate Darcourt. But he wouldn't think of describing Francis's quest as a search and a yearning to know the feminine side of his own nature, in order that he might be a complete and spiritually whole man. An idea like that, encountered head-on, is usually rather too much for human beings. They begin to see things they don't understand, and of course if they don't understand them, they are sure they must be monsters.

—*Like yourself, my dear Maimas?*

—*Yes, like me. Look at me, Zadkiel; what do you see?*

—*A handsome figure. Splendid breasts that any Venus might envy; a fine complexion and a glowing eye, and hyacinthine tresses of the deepest black. So far, a woman. But those elegantly narrow hips and sinewy legs; those handsome masculine organs of generation, which move and stir constantly with every change of your attitude and alteration of your thoughts. Hermes and Aphrodite wonderfully united in a single form. A simulacrum of a complete human creature, though of course you could not be what you are—a daimon—if you were not far above humanity as it now exists. Perhaps you are the creature of the future?*

—*Only as a symbol, brother. If humanity ever took on this form, they would have great trouble in reproducing themselves.*

—*Let us get on with the quest. As the Angel of Biography, that is what I have to record—indeed have recorded, for what we are watching is a record of the past. But as I have said, I can't remember everything about all these people. Did he follow the quest through to the discovery, I wonder? Not many of them do.*

—*No, but every quester has hints and intimations that are very precious and bring sudden light into his life. And of course you've noticed that forecast, that strong hint, that we see as we watch Francis, ludicrously garbed as a woman.*

—*I am being very dense, I fear, said the Angel.*

184

—Look behind the boy in his pathetic rags at the picture on the wall—the picture Aunt hung there in the goodness of her modestly wincing, power-greedy heart. Did she know it was a prophecy? Not consciously, but it was a prophecy and also the essence of life as everybody lived it at St. Kilda. The picture of Love Locked Out.

—Is Francis never to find love?

—You are unfolding the story, my dear friend. Please go on.

But it is impossible to go on without taking notice at this point of something with which Francis had nothing whatever to do, but which influenced his future decisively. This was the downfall—temporary only, as we shall see—of Gerald Vincent O'Gorman, who was, as the husband of Mary-Tess, his uncle.

G. V. O'Gorman was an unusually able man of business, and the Senator, with his fine eye for talent, had advanced him rapidly until Gerry, as everybody called him, was his second-in-command and managed everything in the ordinary way, giving advice when he was asked—and sometimes when he wasn't—but leaving the major decisions to the Senator himself.

He was a big, fleshy, fine-looking Canadian-Irishman, jolly and kind of heart, a loving husband to Mary-Tess and a careful father of their sons, Gerald Lawrence and Gerald Michael. He was a staunch Catholic, and after the Senator the

185

most prominent B.C.L. in Blairlogie and its district.

The O'Gormans came to dinner at St. Kilda every Sunday, and it did Aunt's heart good to see how loving they were. Their amorous speciality, in public, was a sort of graveyard chivalry, a declaration that each had a proven right to "go first" into the afterlife.

"Aw, Mary-Tess, if you go first, I'll never forgive you as long as I live, for my life would be a mockery without you, darlin'."

"Gerry, don't talk that way! You know it would kill me if you went before me; for the love of God, sweetness, let me go first! It will be the last of the thousand-and-one happinesses you've given me!"

"Aw, well; let's hope under God it'll be many a long day off, whichever it is. But I'll give no promise." Then a kiss—right at the table, after Gerry had gallantly wiped his lips with his napkin, as Aunt beamed, and Marie-Louise nodded approvingly, and the Senator looked down at his plate.

What could have been better? But then came the awful day when Mary-Tess, finding herself not far from the head office of the Senator's business affairs, dropped in after five o'clock, to walk home with her Gerald, and found him in his office, strenuously "at it" on his desk with his secretary, Blondie Utronki.

Oh, the tears! Oh, the protestations! Oh, the dreadful come-down! For Mary-Tess's howls attracted one of the cleaning women, who spread the tale through the whole of the Polish layer of the great fruit-cake, from which it mounted rapidly to the French layer, and in no time at all had reached the top, the Scots layer, where it was a cause of righteous jubilation.

Wouldn't you know it? Of course Blondie Utronki would be just the one for that sort of game! As if Gerry O'Gorman hadn't been shoving her forward whenever he could: getting her those chances to sing—at a hefty five dollars a warble—in the McRory Opera House, just before the feature film, when it was a specially good one! "I'm Forever Blowing Bubbles", and "Smile Awhile, I'll Kiss You Sad Adieu" and all that! Well, she'd blown her last bubble in Blairlogie, and she'll be kissing Gerry sad adieu now, you can bet!

And from Alexander Dagg's Maw: bad blood in that family! I've always said so. Piling on the agony, and now shamelessness on a glass-topped desk! We'll see the McRorys topple! Rot of the brain! Look at the old aunt!

Nor was this the worst. Aunt, that tireless backstairs arranger of destinies, had laboured for two years to bring about her latest coup in St. Bonaventura. Father Devlin was now Monsignor Devlin, and it was Aunt who had pushed and shoved at the Bishop to get him nominated for that honour. Indeed, it had been she who presented him with his first two pairs of violet socks, one of the distinguishing marks of his new splendour. But this was not Aunt's finest achievement.

St. Bonaventura had been very much to the fore in wartime charities, and Gerald Vincent O'Gorman, who was a little too old to be called up, and who felt that his brother-in-law, Major Francis Chegwidden Cornish, was brilliantly upholding the family honour in the Forces, had worked like a slave, and a dog, and a Trojan, for war charities. The whist-drives, the concerts, the fowl suppers! So successful was he that St. Bonaventura left all the Protestant churches nowhere in the extent of its contributions. Look at the Cigarette Fund—a triumph of organization and achievement! And everyone knew, because Aunt let it be heard, that Gerry did innumerable good works and paid for many a beautification of the church out of his own pocket, and never breathed a word about it. Surely something was owing for devotion like that?

Devotion was rewarded, for Aunt kept on at the Bishop, who kept on at the Cardinal of Apostolic Briefs, until Gerry was honoured by the Papacy itself, and Monsignor Devlin announced one Sunday morning at High Mass that henceforth Gerry was a Knight of St. Sylvester, as a recognition of his work for the Church, the Holy See and society at large.

Mary-Tess was the soul of modesty. Of course, it wasn't a Commander, or a Knight Grand Cross; just a simple Knight of St. Sylvester. No, no; nothing of the honour appertained to the spouse;

it was wholly a man's thing—but of course she was very proud. External badges of honour? Well, in future on great occasions, like a visit from the Bishop or at High Mass on St. Bonaventura's festal day, July 15, Gerry would be obliged to wear his coat with the gold buttons, and the gold embroidery on the velvet collar and cuffs, and the gold stripe down the side of the pants, and the bicorne hat with the Papal cockade. And the medal of the Order, with the Golden Spur hanging from it. And of course the sword. He'd have to put it on, whether he wanted to or not, and she'd have the job of making sure he got it all right, because you know what men are. Well, yes, Mary-Tess would admit under pressure, it was very nice.

Then—Blondie Utronki!

Monsignor Devlin, whose life was not a bed of roses, found that the hardest thing he had ever had to do was to inform Gerry that this sort of thing did not become a Papal Knight, and the Bishop had sent a peremptory inquiry. He would have to make a formal report to the Bishop, who would speed it to Rome, and the Knight would be un-knighted. Miserable in his violet socks, Monsignor Devlin made it as easy as he could. But Gerry was not inclined to take it easily.

"All I want to know—all I demand to know, Father Mick—is, who was the squealer?"

"Aw now, Gerry, no squealer was needed. The thing was all over town."

"A little bit of local gossip. Who squealed to the Bishop? That's what I want to know."

"Now Gerry, you know I have to write the report myself, even if my hand withers as I do it."

"All right; you have your duty. But who squealed to you?"

"The whole town, I tell you. The Presbyterians are laughing at us. When I met Mr. McComas in the Post Office he said to me: 'I'm very sorry to hear of your trouble,' he said. Me, to be pitied by a Presbyterian minister! They're jeering at us behind our backs."

"Yes, and to our faces, let me tell you! Yesterday in the office some joker stuck a memo up on the board saying, 'All swords that are to be returned to Rome must be left in the umbrella stand before Friday.'"

"Aw, that's very small! You must frown 'em down."

"D'you know who I bet it was? Now, don't take offence, but you know I've never liked him. Father Beaudry! I'll bet it was his letter put the Bishop on to you!"

"Now Gerry, I can't listen to that kind of thing."

"Oh, can't you? Well, priest though he is, he's a squealer and a whistle-tricker, and you can bet he'll never wear violet socks if I can stop it!"

"Now Gerry, you know the Order prescribes 'Unblemished character' and that's all there is to it. No more to be said.— Where's Blondie?"

"Gone to Montreal."

"Not the worst girl I've known. I hope you gave her something handsome? You've ruined her, you know."

"Aw Mick, don't talk so soft! She was wise enough when she came to me. I'm the one that's ruined."

Besides much of this, Monsignor Devlin had to listen to the wails and beseechings of his benefactress, Mary-Ben.

This was the Dark Night of the Soul for the McRorys, except perhaps for the Senator, who had government business that kept him in Ottawa for several weeks.

Francis knew nothing of the domestic and public miseries of the O'Gormans, as he was not going to school, and the morose atmosphere in St. Kilda did not greatly affect him. He had a scandal of his own.

He now knew for a certainty that several nights in every week Zadok Hoyle mounted the staircase that was forbidden to himself, because it led to Victoria Cameron's private domain. What went on up there? What was the relationship between these two important figures in his own life? If there was nothing fishy about it, why did Zadok take off his boots and go upstairs in his socks?

There were noises, too. Laughter, which he could distinguish as belonging to Zadok and Victoria. Singing, in what was plainly Zadok's voice. Sometimes thumps and bumps and scuffling. Seldom, but often enough to puzzle him, there was a sound that might have been a cat, but louder than a cat. He didn't like to ask Aunt; it might be squealing. Certainly he couldn't ask Zadok and Victoria, because if they were up to something they shouldn't be up to—something to do with the great mystery, perhaps, and related to the dark world half-unveiled by Dr. Upper— they would be angry with him, and his long, philosophical talks with Victoria, and his visits to Devinney's embalming parlour which were so necessary to his study of drawing, would be at an end. But he must know.

So, one night as Lent began, he crept slowly up the stairs in his pyjamas, feeling his way in the darkness until he became aware that the walls were covered with something soft, which felt like blanketing. On the landing he could see, by moonlight from a window high in the wall, that it was indeed blanketing, and that a heavy curtain of blankets hung directly in front of him. This was odd, for he knew that Victoria's room was in the other direction, and what lay toward the front of the house, beyond this curtain, was above his grandparents' large bedroom. An unlucky stumble, though a boy in his bare feet does not make much noise. But suddenly light, as a door opened, and there stood Zadok.

"You see, Miss Cameron, I told you he'd find his way up here one of these days. Come in, me little dear."

"Are you prepared to take responsibility for

this?" said Victoria's voice. "You know what my orders are."

"Circumstances alter cases: Shorter pants need longer braces," said Zadok. "He's here, and if you turn him away now, you'll regret it." And he beckoned Francis into the room, the door of which had been thickened and padded amateurishly but effectively.

The room was large and bare, and suggested a sick-room, for there was a table covered with white oilcloth, on which were a basin and pitcher. The floor was covered with what used to be called battleship linoleum. The light was harsh, from a single large bulb hanging from the ceiling, with a white glass shade that threw the light downward. But what Francis saw first, and what held his eyes for a long time, was the bed.

It was a hospital bed with sides that could be slid up and down, so that at need it became a sort of topless cage. In the cage was an odd being, smaller than Francis himself, dressed in crumpled flannelette pyjamas; its head was very small for its body, and the skull ran, not to a point, but to a knob, not very big, on which grew black hair. Because the top of the head was so small, the lower part seemed larger than it was, the nose longer, the jaw broader, and the very small eyes peeped out at the world without much comprehension. They were now fixed on Francis. The child, or the creature, or whatever it was, opened its lips and made the mewing sound that Francis had sometimes heard downstairs.

"Come along, Francis, and shake hands with your older brother," said Zadok. Then to the figure in the bed, "This is your brother, Franko, come to see you."

Francis had been taught to obey. He walked toward the cage, his hand out, and the figure sank back on its blankets, whimpering.

"This is Francis the First," said Zadok. "Be gentle with him; he's not very well."

Francis the Second had been ill for some months, and he was still weak. He fainted.

When he came to himself again, he was in his bed, and Victoria was sitting by him, dabbing at his brow with a cold towel.

"Now Frankie, you must promise me on your Bible oath that you will never tell where you've been or what you've seen. But I expect you want to know what's going on, and I'll answer a few questions. But not too many."

"Victoria, is that really my brother?"

"That is Francis Chegwidden Cornish the first."

"But he's in the graveyard. Aunt showed me the stone."

"Well, as you've seen, he's not in the grave-yard. That was just something I can't explain. Maybe you'll find out when you're older."

"But he's not like a human person."

"Don't say that, Frankie. He's not well and he'll never be any better, but he's human right enough."

"But why is he up there?"

"Because it would be very hard on everybody if

he was down here. There are problems. It wouldn't be nice for your grandparents. Or your parents. He may not live a long time, Frankie. Nobody expected he'd live as long as this."

"But you and Zadok spend a lot of time with him."

"Somebody must, and I was asked to do it by your grandfather, and I'm doing it. I'm not much good at cheering him up. Zadok does that. He's wonderful at it. Your grandfather trusts Zadok. Now you'd better go to sleep."

"Victoria—"

"Well?"

"Can I go to see him again?"

"I don't think it would be for the best."

"Victoria, I get so lonesome. I could be up there with you and Zadok sometimes. Maybe I could cheer him up."

"Well—I don't know."

"Oh, please!"

"Well, we'll see. Now you go to sleep."

Grown-ups always think children can go to sleep at will. An hour later, when Victoria looked in again, Francis was still awake, and she had to take the extraordinary step of giving him a glass of hot milk with some of his grandfather's rum in it to induce sleep.

During that hour his mind had raced over and over the same ground. He had a brother. His brother was very strange. This must be the Looner that Alexander Dagg's hateful Maw declared that

195

McRorys kept in their attic. A Looner! He could not encompass the idea.

But one thing was uppermost and demandingly powerful in his mind. He wanted to draw the Looner.

The very next night he was there, with his pad and pencil, and Victoria Cameron was angry: did he mean to mock the poor boy, and make a display of his trouble? No, certainly not; nothing more than he had been doing at Devinney's—just carrying out the advice of Harry Furniss to draw anything and everything. But in his heart Francis knew that his urge to draw the Looner was more than art-student zeal; drawing was his way of making something his own, and he could not hope to comprehend the Looner, to accept him as something related to himself, if he could not draw him, and draw him again, and capture his likeness in every possible aspect.

How much Victoria understood of that Francis could not tell, but the revelation about Devinney's made her open her eyes very wide, and breathe heavily through her nostrils, and look fiercely at Zadok. But Zadok showed no discomposure.

"We have to recognize, Miss C., that Francis isn't just your run-of-the-mill young scallawag, and circumstances alter cases, as I'm always saying. I wouldn't take just any boy to Devinney's, but for Francis, it's part of his education. It's not that he's nosy; he's a watcher, and a noter, and they're not the commonest people. Francis is deep, and with a deep 'un you have to give 'em something deeper than a teacup to swim in. This here's a deep situation. Francis the Second downstairs, sharp as a razor; Francis the First up here, and Dr. J.A. giving orders right and left about how to keep him as he ought to be. Aren't they ever to meet? Haven't they anything for one another? I put it to you fairly, Miss C., haven't they?"

Was Victoria convinced? Francis could not tell. But it was plain that she put great trust in the coachman-embalmer.

"I don't know, Zadok. I know what my orders are, and it wasn't easy for me to convince His Nibs that you should come up here sometimes— which you've extended to nearly every night."

"Ah, but the Senator trusts me. Would he let me make the journeys to The Portage if he didn't?"

"Well—I don't know. But you're a soldier, and you've travelled, and I just hope you know what you're doing."

"I do. Francis the First needs a new face to cheer him up. Shall we sing?"

Zadok struck up "Frère Jacques", which he sang in French, pretty well. But Victoria sang

Are you sleeping, are you sleeping
Brother John? Brother John?

because she spoke no French—could not "parley-voo the ding-dong" as the English speakers in Blairlogie put it—and would not try. But Francis piped up with the third voice, and they made a reasonable bilingual job of it.

The Looner was enchanted. It would be false to say that his face brightened, but he stood clinging to the raised side of his bed, and turned his little eyes from face to face of the singers.

Then Zadok sang "Yes, let me like a soldier fall", which was obviously a favourite. Most of it was in an extremely manly vein, but, as he explained to Francis, he always "came the pathetic" on

> *I only ask of that proud race*
> *Which ends its blaze in me,*
> *To die the last, and not disgrace*
> *Its ancient chivalry!*

"That's the way the Captain went in South Africa," he said solemnly, but who the Captain was he did not reveal.

This fine operatic piece was the gem of his repertoire, but as several evenings passed, Francis came to know it all. Zadok was a very personal performer. When he sang

> *There ain't a lady*
> *Livin' in the land*
> *As I'd swap for my dear old Dutch . . .*

he looked languishingly at Victoria, who pretended not to notice, but blushed becomingly. There were rowdy music-hall songs of the Boer War period, and "Good-bye, Dolly Gray". And there were songs that must have been the fag-ends of folksongs of great antiquity, but the words Zadok sang were those he had heard as a child, among the real folk, and not the cleansed and scholarly versions known to the English Folk Song Society.

> *The cock sat up in the yew-tree,*
> *King Herod come riding by,*
> *If you can't gimme a penny*
> *Please to gimme a mince-pie.*
> *God send you happy* (three times)
> *A Happy New Year.*

And there was a rough version of "The Raggle-Taggle Gypsies-O" that made the Looner hop up and down in his bed. When he did this he was likely to fart loudly, and Victoria would say, almost automatically, "Now then, none o' that, or I'll go downstairs." But Zadok said, "Aw now, Miss Cameron, the boy's a natural, and you know it." And, genially, to the Looner, "Better an empty house than a bad tenant, eh, Franko me dear?" Which seemed to comfort the dismayed Looner, who did not know what he had done that was wrong. Did he comprehend anything of the story of the gentle lady who left her noble husband and her goose-feather bed to go with the bright-eyed vagabonds? Nobody could tell how much the Looner understood of anything, but he responded to rhythm, and his favourite, which ended every concert, was a rollicking song to the beat of which Zadok, and Francis, clapped their hands:

Rule Britannia!
  God Save The Queen!
Hard times in England
  Are very seldom seen!
Hokey-pokey, penny a lump,
  A taste before you buy,
Singing O what a happy land is England!

After which Victoria demanded quieter entertainment, or Some Of Us would never get off to sleep.

Sometimes there were impromptu picnics, when Victoria brought up good things from the kitchen, and they all ate, the Looner noisily and merrily, but with an enjoyment that Francis saw as parody of the refined greed of Aunt and Grand'mère. In one caricature in his Harry Furniss manner he drew them all three at table. Yes, Grand'mère, and Aunt, and the Looner, all tucking into a huge pie. Zadok thought it wonderful, but Victoria seized and destroyed it, and gave Francis a scolding for his "badness".

As the Looner could not talk, Zadok and Victoria talked, with now and then a nod to include the quiet, attentive figure in the bed. Zadok would wave his pipe-stem at him, and interject "Isn't that right, old son?" as if the Looner were silent by choice, and reflecting deeply. Francis rarely spoke, but drew and drew and drew, until he had books full of pictures of the scene—the two adults, not fashionable or stylish figures but people who might have belonged

200

to any of five preceding centuries, Victoria knitting or mending, and Zadok leaning forward with his hands on his knees. Zadok sat in the old countryman's fashion: his back never touched the back of the chair. And, of course, there were countless quick studies of Francis the First, which were grotesque to begin, but with time became perceptive, and touched with an understanding and pity not to be expected in so young an artist.

"Is he really so bad, Victoria? Couldn't he come downstairs now and again?"

"No, Frank, he couldn't. Not ever. You haven't seen all of him. He's shameful."

"He's strange, right enough, but why shameful?"

Victoria shook her head. "You'd know if you had to watch over him every day. He has a festering mind."

A festering mind? Was it rotten brains, as charged by Alexander Dagg's Maw?

It was a few weeks before the explanation came. One night, at the beginning of Easter Week, the Looner was more than ordinarily stirred by Zadok's rendering of a seasonable hymn, "Who is this in gory garments?". The Looner began to puff and blow, and claw at the crotch of his pyjamas.

"Easy, Franko. Easy old man," said Zadok.

But Victoria was harsh. "Frank, you cut that right out, do you hear? Do you want me to get your belt? Eh? Do you?"

But the Looner paid no heed. He was now

masturbating, gobbling and snorting. A sight to strike shame into Francis the Second.

Quickly Zadok rose and restrained him. Victoria brought from the chest of drawers a strange affair of wire and tapes, and as Zadok pulled down the Looner's pyjama pants she fastened it around his waist, slipped a wire cage over his bobbing genitals, pulled a tape between his legs, and fastened the whole at the back with a little padlock.

The Looner fell to his mattress, whimpering in his catlike voice, and continued to whine.

"You shouldn't have seen that, me dear," said Zadok. "That's the trouble, you see. He can't leave himself alone, and in the daytime, when Miss Cameron is needed downstairs, we have to keep that on him, or nobody knows what might come of it. Sad, and that cage is a hateful thing, but Dr. J.A. says that's how it has to be. Now you and me had better go downstairs, and leave Miss Cameron to settle him for the night."

So that was it! This was plain evidence of the truth of what Dr. Upper had said. Self-abuse and the festering mind, and the shameful secret of the Looner, were all part of a notion of life which began to haunt Francis again, just as he had thought he was breaking free from that torment.

He dreamed terrible dreams, and thought fearful thoughts, as he lay looking without seeing it at the picture of *Love Locked Out*. Sometimes he wept, though tears were a shameful thing in a boy of his age. But what was he to make of this terrible house where the pious refinement of Aunt was under the same roof as the animal lust of the Looner, and the sweet music that Aunt played in the drawing-room was set against Zadok's singing in the attic, singing which was so vigorous, so full of gusto, that there seemed to be a hint of danger—something Dr. Upper would not have approved—about it. This house where there was so much deep concern for his welfare, but nothing of the love he needed except for the two servants, who did not precisely love him so much as accept him as a fellow-being. This house where he, the cherished Francis, was aware that in a sort of hospital-prison there was another Francis whom nobody ever mentioned, and, so far as he could find out, nobody ever visited, except the Presbyterian cook-nurse, whose opinions on the matter he sometimes heard, when she reluctantly spoke of the matter.

"We're not to judge, Frank, but something like what's upstairs doesn't happen just by chance. Nothing comes by chance. Everything's written down somewhere, you know, and we have to live the lives that are foreseen for us long before the world began. So you mustn't look on your brother as a judgement on anyone. But I won't say he isn't a warning—a rebuke to pride, maybe.

> *In Adam's Fall*
> *We sinned all.*

My grandmother worked that into a sampler

203

when she was a girl, and we've still got it on the wall."

"All sinners, Victoria?"

"All sinners, Frank, however your aunt throws scent over it with her religious pictures and fancy prayers. That's just the R.C. way of deceiving yourself, as if life was a fancy-dress party, with purple socks, and all. Life isn't just for fun, you know."

"But aren't we ever to be happy?"

"Show me the place in the Bible where it says we are to be happy in this world. Happiness for sinners means sin. You can't get away from it."

"Are you a sinner, Victoria?"

"Maybe the worst of sinners. How can I tell?"

"Then why are you so good to the fellow up-stairs?"

"We sinners have to stick together, Frank, and do the best we can in our fallen state. That's what religion is. I don't make the judgements. For all the silver and thick carpets and hand-painted pictures—your pictures too, clever though they are—this is a House of Sin."

"But Victoria, that's awful. And it isn't an answer. If you're a sinner, why don't you sin?"

"Too proud, Frank. God made me a sinner, and I can't change that. But I don't have to give in, even to Him, and I won't. I won't give it to Him to say. Though He slay me, yet will I worship Him. But I won't throw in the towel, even if He's damned me."

Thus, in addition to a little lukewarm Anglicanism, and much hot, sweet Catholicism, Frank imbibed a stern and unyielding Calvinism. It was no help with his personal difficulties. But he loved Victoria and he believed her, just as he believed Aunt. The only person who didn't seem to have a God who was out for his scalp was Zadok.

Zadok's religion, if it may be so called, was summed up briefly. "Life's a rum start, me little dear. I've good cause to know!"

The house of sin was, in its way, splendid, and Frank took satisfaction in its richness without having a clear idea of its ugliness. The drawing-room, so silvery blue, so crammed with uncomfortable "Louis" furniture, relieved only by the fierce mahogany gloss of the Phonoliszt, and the portly Victrola, repository of great music, including several records by the man-god Caruso. The dining-room, battleground of two great indigestions—Aunt's manifesting itself in sternly repressed gas, and Grand'mère's in a recurrent biliousness. Neither lady ever thought of moderating her diet. "I can take cream," Aunt would say, as if many other luxuries were denied her; she took cream at every meal. "Oh, I shouldn't, but I'll venture," was what Grand'mère would say, as she helped herself to another slice of Victoria's superb pastry, usually manifesting itself as the casing of a sweet fruit pie. The dining-room, with its red velvety paper and its pictures of cardinals, seemed an outward enlargement of two outraged, overloaded stomachs. And then, Grand-père's study, so complex and tormented in its panelling, where much the most interesting books were his many albums of sun-pictures. A House of Sin? Certainly a house of vexations and disappointments, quite apart from those that plagued Francis.

Late on the night of Good Friday, when in deference to Mary-Ben and Marie-Louise the Senator had taken no wine at the salmon dinner (a day of abstention and fasting, you see), the Senator sat in the hideous study, refreshing himself with a little of his excellent bootleg whisky. A tap at the door, which opened just wide enough for Dr. Joseph Ambrosius Jerome to slip in, smiling widely but not mirthfully, as was usual with him.

"Come in, Joe; I was hoping you'd look in. Will you take any spirits?"

"In spite of the day, Hamish, I will. And I'd like a word with you about the fellow upstairs."

"No change?"

"Just growing older, like the rest of us. You well know, Hamish, that I didn't give him long, years ago, when we moved him up there. He's proved me wrong."

"That was a bad decision, Joe."

"Don't I know it! But you remember we went into all that, and decided for Mary-Jim's sake, and the sake of the baby that was coming, it was the best we could do."

"Yes, but to pretend he had died! To pretend even to Mary-Jim! That awful pretended funeral—if Mick Devlin had known there was nothing in the coffin but some gravel he'd have had the hide off us both!"

"We had the support of Marie-Louise and Mary-Ben; they were sure we were doing the best thing. Do they ever speak of it now?"

"Not a word from either of them in years. Nobody goes up there but Victoria Cameron, and I believe Zadok, sometimes. I never go up. Can't stand the sight of him. My grandson! Now why, Joe, why?"

"Reasons better not gone into, Hamish."

"That's not an answer. Have you any notion, yourself? What's science got to say about it?"

"Did you read the book I lent you?"

"By that fellow Krafft-Ebing? I read some of it. When I read about the fellow who liked to eat his mistress's earwax, b'God I thought I'd spew. You can take it away with you when you go. What's all that got to do with Mary-Jacobine McRory, a beautiful, sweet-souled girl who got into a mess that might have happened to any girl, under the circumstances."

"Ah, but what were the circumstances? I told you at the time: go whoring after the English and a life of fashion, I said, and you'll be a sorry man. And what are you today, and what have you been ever since? A sorry man."

"Oh, of course, Joe, we know you're always right. And what has your rightness got you? You're a cranky, half-crazy old bachelor, and my sister is a cranky, religious-crazy old maid, and however much you boked at her torn-off scalp you'd have been better together than the way you are now—which is together but tortured apart. So don't preach to me."

"There, there, Hamish. Don't let's have any of your Hielan'man's hysterics. It hasn't been all bad. When last I saw Mary-Jim she looked happy enough."

"Happy enough isn't as happy as can be. Perhaps I was wrong. But I was trying to do the best for my child."

"God, Hamish, nobody can do the *best* for anyone. People can only rarely do the best for themselves. Mary-Jim's not over-bright, but God knows she's beautiful, and that entirely robbed you of good sense. Good intentions can make terrible mischief, but so long as love lasts, they'll last, and there you are. You didn't do too badly. You landed your Englishman."

"I wasn't fishing for any Englishman! But she had to marry, and where in this place, or in Ottawa even, would there have been anybody good enough for her?"

"The old problem of the rich Catholic girl: where is she to find a husband on her own level?"

"I met some very fine Catholics in England."

"Very fine? Well-born, I suppose you mean, and rich and educated? And I'm not saying that doesn't count for a lot. But you ended up with Cornish."

"And what's so bad about Cornish?"

"Oh, get away, Hamish! You know fine what's

wrong with Cornish. What about that paper he made you sign?"

"He overreached me; I don't say he didn't. But he's not turned out so badly. Listen, Joe, keep this under your hat, but there's to be some interesting news soon of Cornish."

"What's he up to now?"

"It's what he was up to all through the War. Working very much on the Q.T. and sometimes in serious danger, I understand. Well, when the next Honours List appears, he'll be a K.B.E.—Sir Francis—and my girl will be Lady Cornish. What d'you think of that?"

"I think I'm happy for you, Hamish, and for Mary-Jim. Maybe not so happy for Gerry O'Gorman and Mary-Tess. To lose one knighthood only to have another pop up in the same family won't sit well with them."

"Oh, that was only a Papal knighthood; this is a far more solid thing."

"Hamish, you astonish me! 'Only a Papal knighthood'! You're beginning to sound almost like a Prot."

"In this country if you're in the money business you have to learn to sit at the table with the Prots. They have most of it their own way. R.C.s and Jews needn't apply. And I'm thinking very hard about the money business."

"Surely you have all you need?"

"What a man needs and what he wants may be very different things. Don't forget, I came from very poor people, and the hatred of poverty is in my blood. Now listen: the lumbering business isn't what is was; it's changing, and I don't want to change with it; I want something new."

"At your age?"

"What about my age? I'm only sixty-seven. I've other people to think of. Now, you know that for years people—widows and old people and the like—have been coming to me and asking me to look after their money for them."

"And you've done it, and made money for them. For me, too."

"Yes, but I don't like it. You trust me, and I'm pleased you do, but this thing of private trust is no way to do business; in business nobody should have total responsibility for anybody else's money. So I'm thinking of unloading the lumber trade, and setting up one of these trust companies."

"In Blairlogie? Wouldn't it be very small potatoes?"

"No, not in Blairlogie. In Toronto."

"Toronto? Man, are you crazy? Why not Montreal, where the big money is?"

"Because there's other big money, and it's in the West, and Toronto will be the centre for that. Not yet, but you have to be ahead of the procession."

"You're away ahead of me."

"And properly so. Why wouldn't I be? You're a doctor and you look after my health; I'm a financier, and I look after your money."

"Well—when do you take the big step?"

"I've taken it. Not many people know, but

recent events are pushing me ahead fast. Gerry O'Gorman and Mary-Tess want to get out of Blairlogie; after that come-down over the Knight of St. Sylvester business they're very much out of love with this little place. They'll move to Toronto, and Gerry'll set the thing on its feet."

"God! Is Gerry up to a big thing like that?"

"Yes. Gerry has powers that have never been roused. And he's honest."

"Honest! What about Blondie Utronki?"

"Honest about money. Women are quite a different thing. And I've told Gerry there's to be no more of that monkey-business, and Mary-Tess has him under her thumb forever. He can do it. Gerry has great ability as an organizer, and people like him."

"He's no Prot."

"Not yet. But Gerry isn't nearly as good a Catholic as he was before that little sanctified rat Beaudry did the dirty on him. Give him time, and give him Toronto, and we shall see what we shall see. Anyhow, that needn't show too clearly. Didn't I tell you Cornish is to be a knight?"

"I don't follow you at all."

"Well—look here. The Cornish Trust—Gerry is Managing Director, I'm Chairman of the Board (and I'll keep the real power in my own hands, you may be sure), and Sir Francis Cornish is President, and the grand show-piece of the business. And Cornish is a bigoted Prot, as I have good cause to know."

"Will he do it?"

"Indeed he will. He's always been pestering me for a place in the business, and now there's a place just right for him."

"Can he manage it?"

"He's very far from being a fool. He's got a splendid war record, and that counts for a lot. And he doesn't want to come back to Blairlogie. As president he'll have no power I don't choose to give him, and Gerry'll watch him like a hawk. It's tailor-made, Joe."

"Hamish, I've always said you were a downy one, but this beats everything."

"It's not bad. Not bad at all. Everything has suddenly clicked into place."

"All things work together for good for those that love the Lord."

"Don't be cynical, Joe. But if you mean that, you're right. Even the third generation is taken care of. Gerry's boys are good lads, and they'll grow up to banking and trust business."

"And what about young Francis? Will Cornish let you cut his son out of this big game?"

"Francis is a fine boy. I like him best of the lot, and I won't see him pushed aside. But he's not just what I look for in a boy who's to grow up to be a banker. However, that's not too great a problem; Mary-Jim writes to her mother that there's another young Cornish on the way. If it's a boy—and as you always tell your patients, it's fifty-fifty that it will be—he can grow up to the family trade, which will be money, and a very good trade it is."

"I just hope he's all right."

"What do you mean, Joe?"

"Are you forgetting the lad upstairs?"

"He wasn't Cornish's son. Cornish is sound. The father of that poor creature must have been a degenerate."

"But he is Mary-Jim's son as well."

"I don't follow you."

"Now Hamish, you know I hate to say unpleasant things—"

"I know only too well that you love to say unpleasant things, Joe."

"That's a nasty dig at an old friend, Hamish. But you must remember I'm a man of science, and science has to come to terms with facts, however unpleasant they may be. It takes two to make a child, and if there's something wrong with the child, which of the two is responsible? You told me the father of that poor idjit upstairs was an unknown man, a soldier—"

"God knows what he may have been. Rotten with disease, probably."

"No, not probably at all, for Mary-Jim has never shown any hint of what you'd expect from any such association, so you can't blame it all on the man."

"Are you blaming it on my daughter?"

"Easy, now, Hamish! Easy, man. Just give me another dram of that fine whisky, and I'll explain. Because I've thought a lot about this matter, I can tell you, and I've read every book I can get hold of that might throw light on it. I lent you that book by Krafft-Ebing hoping you'd get a clue, but it seems you haven't."

"That book was full of dirty rubbish."

"Life's full of dirty rubbish. I'm a doctor and I know. If you'd read that book in a scientific spirit you'd have understood what it says. Krafft-Ebing's the great name in this field still, you know, though he died a while back. But I've been reading Kraepelin, his successor, who's the foremost man in this sort of medicine now, and there are certain points on which he and Krafft-Ebing are in full agreement. Now, if you'd read that book instead of skipping over to the earwax stories, you'd have taken in a very pertinent fact to what we're discussing: a healthy, well-brought-up young woman has no sexual desire whatever. Oh, some romantic notions out of books, maybe, but not the real thing. She's no notion of it, even if she has a rough idea how babies come. Now, look here: A very closely guarded, well-educated Catholic girl finds herself in a hotel room with a strange man. A servant, trained to keep his mind on his job, never to betray anything you might call humanity. Does he rape her? Not so far as we've been told. She said to you that one thing led to another. What thing was that one thing, Hamish?"

"That's enough, Joe. You'd better be on your way."

"No, it's not enough, Hamish. You've got your head in the sand, man. And don't order me to go, because I'm speaking to you as your family's medical adviser—have been since I don't know when—

and this is nasty medicine I'm giving you, to make you well. I'm not saying Mary-Jim is a light woman. May this whisky be my poison if I ever thought any such thing! But even the purest woman may be victim of a disease of the mind—"

"Joe—you don't mean Mary-Jim's touched?"

"It's not a permanent thing, Hamish, so far as I know. But it exists, and it attacks the young. In the profession we call it the *furor uterinus.*"

"You know I have no Latin. What's that mean?"

"Well—I'd translate it as the rage o' the womb. Uncontrollable desire. I've seen it in some cases of women—low women down at the end o' the town—and God forbid you should ever meet with such a thing. I mean, desire—well, sometimes a married woman, accustomed to that way of life— might feel something. On a hot night, for instance, in July. But many fine women never know any such trouble. So—what are we to make of it in poor Mary-Jim?"

"God! You tell me a terrible thing!"

"There are a lot of terrible things known to science, Hamish. And I don't say that some terrible people don't make capital of them. For instance this fellow Freud that we're beginning to hear about now that we're getting hold of medical books in German again. But nobody heeds him, and he'll soon peter out—or be run out of the profession. But well-authenticated medical science, based on great experience—you can't go against it."

"Joe, you hint at a world ridden and rotted with sex."

"I don't hint. I know. Why do you suppose I'm a single man? Even though I know that Mary-Ben would have taken me years ago, and perhaps even now. It's because I've seen too much, and I decided against it. Science has its celibates, as well as religion. And now the craze is for blathering about sex all over the place. Like that scoundrel Upper who was speaking in the public schools here, and telling innocent children God knows what! Did Francis say anything about him?"

"I never heard him mention the name."

"Perhaps he escaped, then. He's a frail lad. I don't imagine anything like that has come into his head yet. When the time comes, I'd better have a talk with him. Put him on his guard."

"Perhaps so. But—Joe, do you suggest that this—this trouble you say Mary-Jim had—might affect the child that's coming?"

"I can say truthfully that I don't know. But she has been leading the life of a married woman for many years now, and perhaps it's burned itself out. That's what we'll hope."

"Another like that one upstairs would kill Marie-Louise. It might finish me. Joe—can nothing be done?"

"Hamish, I told you once I wouldn't kill, and that's my answer now. Indeed, I'm sworn to keep that idjit alive; it's my sacred profession. That's why I had that wire affair made, to restrain his lust. Without it, he might rage and rip himself

216

into the grave, but that's not for me to encourage or condone. We must all of us just wait it out. But listen, Hamish: if family interests are moving to Toronto, why don't you send Francis to school there? Mary-Tess and Gerry would keep an eye on him. I hear the Christian Brothers have a fine school in Toronto. Get him out of here. Get him away from these women. Just suppose by bad luck he happens on that thing upstairs. What a brother for him!"

Dr. Jerome finished his third drink, shook hands warmly with his old friend, and left, with the warm consciousness that he was a man who had done a duty certainly painful, but in the best interests of everyone concerned.

Still no pity for Francis, brother? said the Lesser Zadkiel, pausing in the unfolding of his story.

—I have told you repeatedly, said the Daimon Maimas, that pity is not one of the instruments with which such agencies as I do our work. Pity at this stage of his life would not make Francis better; it would dull his perceptions and rob him of the advantages I have managed for him.

—Rough on the bystanders, would you not say?

—The bystanders are no concern of mine. I am Francis's daimon, not theirs. He has already met his Dark Brother. Everybody has one, but most people go through their lives without ever recognizing him or feeling any love or compassion for him. They see the Dark Brother in the distance, and they hate him. But Francis has his Dark Brother securely in his

drawing-books, and more than that. He has him in his hand, and his artist's sensibility.

—Nevertheless, my dear colleague, reluctant as I am to criticize or appear to teach you your business, is it good to conceal from everyone who the Dark Brother is, or how he came about?

—Well, in the obvious, physical sense, the Dark Brother in Francis's life is the outcome of Marie-Louise's well-intentioned meddling in London, when she made her daughter do everything she knew that might bring about a miscarriage. Those people thought a child had no real life until it was pushed into the outer world; they know nothing of the life in the womb, which is the sweetest and most secure time of all. If you jolt and shake and parboil the child, and batter it with cathartics and stun it with gin, you may kill it, or if it is very strong—and Francis the First was very strong or he wouldn't have survived the dance they led him—you may have an oddity to deal with. But Francis's Dark Brother is much more than an obvious, physical thing. He's a precious gift from me, and I think I did rather well to seize my opportunity of bringing him to Francis's notice so early.

—I suppose you know best, brother.

—I do. So let us go on and see how my gift to Francis shows itself. It's begun by getting him out of Blairlogie.

PART THREE

When the senator confided to Dr. J.A. that the Cornish Trust was in prospect, he was not entirely candid with his old friend; the Trust had been in his mind for at least five years, and had been in the process of assemblage for the last three. The business of the Papal knighthood had somewhat hurried matters, so far as the O'Gormans were concerned, and Gerry and Mary-Tess had already bought a house in Toronto on fashionable St. George Street. Major Cornish and Mary-Jim were talking with an architect about building a house in the rising suburb of Rosedale, appropriately near the residence of the Lieutenant-Governor. The Senator spoke to Dr. J.A. at Easter, and it was less than a month before the O'Gormans moved to Toronto, and at once made themselves known at St. James' Anglican Cathedral.

"It's no use trying to get a trust company on its feet unless you're seen and known where money is," said Gerald Vincent to his wife. She agreed, because he knew Toronto better than she; had he not been making visits to it for the last eighteen months? But she wondered aloud if in a city sometimes called "the Rome of Methodism" it might not be better to ally themselves with one of the Methodist churches where affluence and the godliness of John Wesley were mingled in a peculiarly Torontonian brew. When she discovered that the Methodist ladies appeared in the evening in a characteristic sort of gown in which the bosom was hidden as high as to the chin, and no jewellery was worn except a few discreet, chunky diamonds (good investments), she plumped for the more easy-going Anglicans. In their first three months of Toronto residence, before the Trust opened its doors to the public, the O'Gormans had caused themselves to be noticed in Toronto society. Noticed—and favourably noticed.

The question that was asked, of course, was whether they were Old Money, or New Money? The difference, though subtle to the vast population which was No Money, was important. Old Money usually reached back to colonial days, and some of it was Empire Loyalist; Old Money was Tory of an indigo that put to shame the weaknesses and follies of such wobblers as the first Duke of Wellington; Old Money sought to conserve and strengthen whatever was best in the body politic and knew precisely where this refined essence was to be found; it was in themselves and all that pertained to them. Even in the early twenties of this century, Old Money clung to its carriages, at least for ladies making calls, and had other tribal customs that spoke of assured distinc-

222

tion. The high priests of Old Money frequently wore top hats on weekdays, if they were going to do something priestly with money. They fought furiously against short coats for dinner dress, and white waistcoats with tailcoats. They kept mistresses, if at all, of such dowdiness they might almost have been mistaken for wives. For them the nineteenth century had not quite ended.

New Money, on the other hand, had taken its cue from Edward VII, who had a high regard for wealth however it was come by, and liked people with some "go" in them. New Money aspired to be Big Money, and did not greatly care if the drawing-rooms of Old Money were not easily opened. New Money wore dinner suits, which it called tuxedos, and smoked big cigars from which it removed the band before lighting up—an unthinkable solecism, for what if you should get a tobacco stain on your white glove? The O'Gormans knew they were New Money, but were aware that a trust company which was not on good terms with Old Money could run into quite unnecessary obstructions. The Senator, too, presented a problem. His gallant manners and handsome person recommended him anywhere, but it could not be concealed from the never-sleeping vigilance of Old Money that he was a Roman Catholic and a Liberal in politics. A difficult situation was avoided by the Cornish family, just as the Senator had foreseen.

Everything fell into place on June 3, when the Birthday Honours were announced, and Major

Francis Cornish, President of the soon-to-be-opened Cornish Trust, became Sir Francis Cornish, K.B.E. How did he get it? The whisper was that he had done extraordinary work in Intelligence during the War, and not simply Canadian Intelligence, which was rather small potatoes. Non-military people, and even a lot of military people, have a notion that Military Intelligence implies uncommon brilliance of intellect, extraordinary resource and daring, ability to solve codes over which the enemy has toiled for years, and iron control over beautiful and alluring female spies. Of course, this may be quite true, but nobody knows, and everybody speculates. The passing of time had given the Wooden Soldier an air of distinction, of the grizzle-headed, frozen-faced, uncommunicative variety. His monocle gleamed with suppressed secrets; his moustache spoke of Nature subdued, tamed, domineered over. Just the man to trust your money to: just the man to ask to dinner. And his wife! What a stunner! Could she have been a spy, do you think?

Thus the Cornish name shed lustre over the sturdy understructure of McRorys and O'Gormans. Long before the announcement of the honour, and before its doors were officially opened for business, the Cornish Trust was a financial certainty. No trust company opens for business until a great deal of solid and profitable business has already been done, and promises and assurances have been given. Sir Francis's knighthood gave strong assurance to what was already a reality.

This should by no means be taken as evidence that Toronto's social and business communities were snobbish. They would assure you, almost before you asked, that they were pioneers and democrats to a man, or a woman. But they were well-connected pioneers and democrats, and if they kept a sharp eye on Roman Catholics and Jews it was not to be interpreted as prejudice, but because Roman Catholics and Jews—fine people among them, mind you!—had not been particularly visible when the colony began its long pull toward nationhood. Their time would come, no doubt. But just for the present it was as well for Old Money, and such New Money as showed itself worthy, to keep things on an even keel. And what better guarantee of evenness of keel than a president of the trust company who had served his country well in war, whose intelligence was of a guaranteed respectable sort, and who *looked* so trustworthy?

What Sir Francis thought about it, nobody ever knew. Probably he believed some of what was said about him. Undoubtedly he understood the language of finance, and had the good sense to leave the deployment of finance to his father-in-law and his brother-in-law, and to take his generous reward while keeping his mouth shut.

In these circumstances, Dr. J.A.'s ludicrously provincial notion that the third generation of the family should attend the big school kept by the

Christian Brothers played no part. The young O'Gormans, Gerald Lawrence and Gerald Michael, were entered at Colborne College, a great stronghold of Old Money. At the same time the "Gerald" was discreetly dropped from their names; Mary-Tess sensed that the family habit of tacking the same dynastic label on several children might be very well for Blairlogie, but did not suit their changed situation.

Sir Francis also decided on Colborne for his son. The cousins did not see much of one another in their new school; the O'Gormans were in the Lower School because of their age, and were day-boys because their parents lived in Toronto. Sir Francis knew, and his wife (who had ceased to be Mary-Jim to anyone but her McRory family, and was known to everyone else as Jacko, which was what her husband called her) knew also, that they did not intend to be in Toronto for many months of the year. Sir Francis let it be known that his continuing relationship (never specified) with Very Important People in England would take him abroad often, and Jacko did not choose to be left behind. So Francis was to be a boarder at Colborne. Thus it was that Francis entered what looked like a new world, but which was not, in several respects that mattered to him, as new as it might appear.

Since Francis's days at Colborne, the reading world has been subjected to a flood of books written by men who hated their boarding-schools, and whose sensitive natures were thwarted and warped by early experience. It was not so with Francis. His life hitherto had made him philosophical and ingenious—not to say devious—in his dealings with his superiors and his contemporaries, and at Colborne he was philosophical and ingenious. He was not brilliant, in the prizewinning, examination-passing mode that makes for a splendid school career, but he was not stupid. He took life as it came, and some of what came was uncommonly like what had come at Carlyle Rural.

Much may be learned about any society by studying the behaviour and accepted ideas of its children, for children—and sometimes adults—are shadows of their parents, and what they believe and what they do are often what their parents believe in their hearts and would do if society would put up with it. The dominant group, though by no means the majority of the boys at Colborne College, were the sons of Old Money, and in their behaviour the spirit of Old Money was clear. They were the conservers of tradition, and they imposed tradition without discrimination and without mercy. The tradition best calculated to reduce a New Boy to his lowest common denominator was fagging.

On the first day of the autumn term, each senior boy was assigned, by decision of the prefects, a New Boy who was to be his fag for the year that followed, and it was clearly understood that the fag was the slave and creature of his fag-master, to do his bidding without question at any hour. There was an understanding that if a fag were seriously ill-used he could complain to the prefects, but to do so was squealing, and incurred contempt. Like all such systems it was conditioned by the people who practised it, and some fags had an easy time; it was even known for a fag-master to help a junior boy with his work. A few fag-masters were brutes, and a few fags lived in hell; the majority, like all slave classes, were genially derisive of their masters when they could get away with it, respectful when they had to be, and cleaned boots and put away laundry as badly as they could without incurring punishment. If the system taught them anything at all it was that all authority is capricious, but may be appeased by a show of zeal, unaccompanied by any real work.

Francis was assigned to a large boy named Eastwood, who came from Montreal, and who was on the whole good-natured and untroubled by intelligence. He was an officer in the Cadet Corps, and it was one of his fag's duties to polish the buttons on his uniform, and to bring his sword up to a high finish every Sunday night, ready for Monday's parade. Francis was never guilty of cheek; he allowed Eastwood to think that he admired him and took pride in his appearance on parade, and that did the trick. In his heart he thought Eastwood was a mutt.

Fagging had been good enough for your father, and it was therefore good enough for you. A certain amount of servitude and humiliation made a man of you. There may even have been some truth in this belief. Everybody ought to have some experience of being a servant; it is useful to know what virtually unlimited authority is like for those on the receiving end.

Francis was good enough at his work to escape any particular notice; he was always in the upper half of his form, undistinguished but respectable. He was able to hold his place, while having plenty of time to study the masters, whose personal character was often more educational than anything they taught.

It was on Prize Day that they presented the most interesting spectacle, when they appeared on the platform of the Prayer Hall in their gowns, beneath which they wore, in some cases, old-fashioned morning coats, preserved from far-off weddings. About half of them were Englishmen, and rather more than half were veterans of the recent war. They wore their medals of honour, some of substantial distinction. One or two limped; Mr. Ramsay had a wooden leg and walked with a clumping gait; Mr. Riviere had an artificial hand under a black glove; Mr. Carver had a silver plate in his head, and was known to have had spells when he climbed the water-pipes in his classroom and taught from that elevation. Their hoods were old and crumpled, but some of them were from ancient universities and spoke of a brilliance that had not brought any reward except a position as a schoolmaster. In the eyes of the boys as a whole, they were glorious; but to Francis there was an air of melancholy about them, for he was perhaps the only person in the Hall who saw what was in front of his nose, who really observed how they stood, and what their faces were really saying. Of course, he never spoke to anyone about what he saw.

His life held many secrets—things he could not talk about to anyone, although he had friends, and was passably well-liked. The religion of the School, for instance; it was a kind of middle-brow Anglicanism, not too heavily stressed because the School contained boys of all denominations, including several Jews, and some richly coloured boys from South America who were probably Papists. The hymns were loud, chiefly unexceptionable admonitions to live decently and honourably, and the music to which they were sung was superior stuff from the Public School Hymnal—Holst, Vaughan Williams, and unsentimental tunes that would not have been strange to Luther. The Headmaster preached a short extempore sermon every Sunday night, and because he was a man whose enthusiasms sometimes outran his judgement, he was likely to say things which a more discreet man would have left unsaid. Musing on the theme of sin and perhaps forgetting where he was, he once quoted Nietzsche, declaring: "Sins are necessary to every society organized on an ecclesiastical basis; they are the only reliable weapons of power; the priest lives upon sins; it is necessary to him that there be sinning." Fortunately few boys were listening, and of those who were, few understood what he was saying. Francis may have been the only one of those who hugged this wisdom to his heart. But upon the whole the School's religion puzzled him. It seemed to lack heart. There was nothing in it of the mystery, the embracing warmth, the rich gravy of the religion of Mary-Ben. It was a religion well suited to Old Money and to the toadies of Old Money. It was a religion that Never Went Too Far.

Never too far. That was the constant admonition of Old Money and the toadies of Old Money. Those who had any pretension to classical education likened it to the Greek doctrine: Nothing in excess. Some, who had dabbled a little in Shakespeare, might say "Look that you o'erstep not the modesty of Nature". Of the blatant immodesty of Nature they had no conception. But Francis had; he had sensed it in the abyss that lay at his feet in Carlyle Rural, and in what he had seen of the exactions and vengeance of life among the corpses in Devinney's embalming room. Francis knew in his heart that life was broader, deeper, higher, more terrifying, and more wonderful than anything dreamed of by Old Money. A schoolboy is not supposed to know such things, and he scarcely admitted them even to himself. But they emerged, sometimes, in his drawings.

In the circumstances of life in a large boarding-school it is impossible to draw without being observed. As a fag he was required to do an extensive business in decorating raincoats; these were slickers made of yellow oilskin, on the back of which, between the shoulders, it was demanded that he draw a funny face, which was then shellacked, so that it was permanent. These raincoats were greatly prized. Two or three came dangerously near to being identifiable caricatures of masters; one in particular, a severe Scottish face with beetling brows and an extraordinary amount of hair growing from its nose, was certainly Mr. Dunstan Ramsay, the history master. Mr. Ramsay called Francis into his study one night after prayers.

"Caricature is a rare and fine gift, Cornish, but you ought to consider it carefully before it gets you completely in its grip. It's the exaggeration of what is most characteristic, isn't it? But if you see nothing as characteristic except what is ugly, you'll become a man who values nothing but ugliness, because it's his trade. And that will make you a sniggering, jeering little creature, which is what most caricaturists have been—even the best. There are some quite good art books in the library. Look at them, and learn something larger than caricature. Don't forget it, but don't make it the whole of what you can do."

Francis was glad not to be caned for *lèse-majesté* and supercheek, and promised that he would look at the art books in the library. And there, in a not very extensive or distinguished collection, he found what he missed in the religion of the school.

As is likely to happen (to people who have a daimon) the discovery coincided with something else, not obviously related to it. The fags often sang, when they were mustered to haul the big roller over the cricket pitch, or sweep snow from the open-air hockey rink, and what they sang was what they liked, not what the music master made them sing in class; his taste was for "Searching for Lambs" and other folksongs he valued because they were in five-quarter time and demanded some musical skill. But the fags sang a sentimental song in waltz time that a few of them knew and the others quickly learned:

> *To the knights in the days of old,*
> *Keeping watch on the mountain height,*
> *Came a vision of Holy Grail*
> *And a voice in the silent night,*
> > *Saying—*
> *Follow, follow the gleam,*
> *Banners unfurled, o'er all the world;*
> *Follow, follow the gleam*
> *Of the chalice that is the Grail.*

How many knew what the Grail was, or why it should gleam, does not matter. Francis knew, for he had read it in a book that came, of course, from Aunt Mary-Ben. The Grail was the Cup from which Christ had drunk at the Last Supper, and anybody lucky enough to catch sight of it was ensured a very special life forever after.

Among the art books recommended by Buggerlugs—which was what the boys called Mr. Ramsay—was one that dealt with the work of the Pre-Raphaelite Brotherhood, and in the illustrations—Francis did not bother much with the text—was something of the Grail in the light that shone from the eyes of the men, and the rich, swooning beauty of the women. It was a light that fed the hunger he felt because of the starved, wholly external religion of the school, and a lush depiction of Nature that balanced the world of wretched desks, spattered ink, chalk dust, constipating food, and the unceasing, unimaginative, perfunctory obscenity of schoolboys' talk. It was an enlargement that made even compulsory games and the Rifle Corps open up to a light that came from somewhere outside the school. And then the Headmaster, who kept his ears open, seized upon the slave-song of the fags and preached one of his Sunday-night sermons about the Grail, as a vision, an unresting aspiration, and with his usual fine disregard of probability urged the boys to read Malory at once, and to make the Grail quest a part of their own lives.

Francis hunted down *Le Morte d'Arthur* in the school library, and was soon compelled to recognize that it was a dense, intractable, difficult book and he could not get through enough of it to find the Grail or anything else he wanted. Nor was the encyclopaedia more helpful, with its tedious explanation of where parts of the legend came from, and its dowdy, scholarly rejection of all the good stuff about Joseph of Arimathea and King Arthur—the stuff that fed his imagination and made the Grail a glowing reality. So he hugged the book about the Pre-Raphaelites, and kept it out of the library far longer than was permitted, even though nobody else wanted it. He considered stealing it, but a strong feeling from the Blairlogie past told him that A Certain Person would not like it—His wounds might even be reopened—and that a life of noble feeling could not be founded on a crime, especially a crime that would be so easily detected.

All boys were expected to be "keen". The most admired form of keenness was not obvious success, but pitting yourself against some form of school contest where you were not likely to succeed, but where your quality as "a good loser" might be seen and admired. Francis found it in the Oratory Contest.

Of course, nobody expected anything that could be seriously called oratory. To excel at verbal expression was a suspect gift. But a sufficient number of boys came forward every year who could force themselves to stand before an audience of the staff and their peers, and control their terror as they talked for ten minutes on a topic that was handed to them on a folded slip of paper by the Headmaster, who arranged that each contestant should have ten minutes in a secluded room—most certainly not the library—to collect whatever thoughts he might have. The slip handed to Francis read "The Gift of Sight".

That was why Francis mounted the platform and embarked with considerable confidence on a criticism of the portraits that hung on all four sides of the Prayer Hall. These were, he said, pictures that everybody in the school saw every day, but that nobody really was aware of except as interruptions of the walls. The pictures were not good as works of art, and if they were not good works of art, had they a place in an institution of education? Were they worthy of the finest school in Canada? (He thought this a fine touch, certain to please his audience.) He pointed out the low level of artistic competence they represented, and asked rhetorically if any of them were by painters who could be named by anybody in the audience? Two or three of them, he mentioned, were already flaking badly, although they could not be more than fifty years old, and it was clear that they had been done in inferior pigments. He was lightly jocose about the fact that the ample beard of one Headmaster of the nineteenth century was rapidly going green. He said that the painters had obviously been hacks or amateurs. He spent his last three minutes explaining how a painter of acknowledged genius, such as Michelangelo or Bouguereau, would have presented these grave figures, making them not only records of Heads past, but vivid evocations of strong intelligence and character, and a daily refreshment to the eyes of the school. He sat down amid a heavy silence.

The Headmaster, in his judgement of the speeches, praised Cornish's obvious sincerity. But it was a boy who laboured mightily with "Sabbath Observance: For or Against", and who came down heavily for the closed Toronto Sunday, who was awarded the cup.

Afterward the Head said: "That was good, Cornish. Unexpected and I suppose true. But tactless,

Cornish, tactless. There were two or three of our Governors in the audience, and they didn't like it. You must be careful with words like 'hack': the world's full of hacks, unfortunately. You must learn to keep your claws in. But there was one Governor who thought you ought to have some recognition. So go to the school bookseller with a note I'll give you, and get yourself a book about art. But don't tell anybody how you came by it. That's an order."

That was the beginning of the substantial library about art in its various forms that was one of the valuable things Francis left behind him when he died. The bookseller, a kindly man, found him Burckhardt's *History of the Renaissance* for four dollars—it was illustrated, and thus expensive—and threw in a second-hand set of Vasari's *Lives of the Painters*, which was marked at a dollar-fifty, but which he reduced for a promising boy.

Francis obediently kept quiet about his special prize, but he could not avoid the reputation he now had for knowing about pictures, and being what some of the hostile masters hissingly condemned as an "ESS-thete". Francis had not heard the word before, though he knew what "aesthetic" meant; but it was plain from the way it was said that an "ESSthete" was a pretty feeble chap, wasting his time on art when he ought to be building up his character and facing the realities of life—as the hostile masters, failures to a man, understood life. But not all the masters shared this view, and in particular Mr. Mills, the senior classics master, began to look on Francis with favour.

It was the same among the boys. Most of them thought that being interested in pictures was girls' stuff, and not even for the kind of girls they knew—girls who were simply themselves in a different biological package. Old Money girls, in fact. But there were others, including most of the Jews, who wanted to talk about art to Francis. Art as they understood it, that is to say.

For some years a few Canadian painters, who came to be called the Group of Seven, had been trying to reveal the Canadian landscape in a new way, seeing it freshly, and not as it would have appeared to an eye darkened by a nineteenth-century English landscape painter's notion of what Nature ought to be. Their work was of course much derided and they were thought to be outrageously modern, although they would not have seemed so to a European or an American critic. What the parents said was parroted by the children, and Francis was beset with "Whaddya think of the Group of Seven? My mother says it looks like what our Swedish cook used to paint on her day off. My father says he could do as well, if he had the time. I mean—look at it! Can you see Georgian Bay in it? My father says he's hunted through all that country every autumn since he was a boy, and he says he knows it better than any of those birds, and he never sees anything like that. Blue snow! I ask you!"

Francis gave non-committal answers, not because he had any interest in new painting, but because the world he wanted to paint was not the world of Nature but the world of his imagination, dominated by the Grail Legend. This was now the food upon which he fed his spirit, and so far as he retained any of the Catholicism Aunt Mary-Ben had bootlegged into his supposedly Anglican world, it was attached to what he knew about the Grail. That was almost entirely what he derived from Tennyson; if by chance he hit on anything that associated the great legend with the pre-Christian world he left it unread; what he wanted was the world of Rossetti, of Burne-Jones, of William Morris. It was not easy to be a Pre-Raphaelite in Canada in the third decade of the twentieth century, in a school that was cheerfully Philistine about art (though certainly not about scholarship), but in so far as it could be done, Francis did it.

This involved a certain amount of mental contortion, and even something approaching a double consciousness. To his school companions he was just Cornish, not a bad fellow, but with a bee in his bonnet about pictures. To his schoolmasters he was Cornish, a boy somewhat above the middle except in Classics, where he showed ability. To both companions and masters Francis paid his dues; he was mediocre at games, but he played, and he took part in enough other school activities to avoid being despised as a slacker; he worked conscientiously at his studies, was always top of his class in French (but this was discounted by the School, because he had been raised to speak French, which the School regarded less as a key to another culture than as an obstacle course and a brain-teaser), and was good in Latin and Greek, which were also brain-teasers. Nobody knew how his mind was seized by the heroes of Virgil and Homer, and how easy Classics became if you cared about what they said. It was a period when educators believed that the brain could be strengthened, like a muscle, by attacking and conquering anything it might at first find difficult. Algebra, geometry, and calculus were the best developers of mental muscle; to master them was really pumping iron; but Classics wasn't bad—indeed sufficiently repellent to the average boy's mind to rank as a first-rate subject of study. But the inner chamber of Francis's mind was dominated by the Grail, as it appeared to him to be—something fine, something better than his life at present could provide, something to be sought elsewhere, something that made sudden, fleeting appearances at home.

Whether Francis's parents had neglected him is a matter about which there could be many opinions. They had left him for long periods in the care of his grandparents and Aunt Mary-Ben, but surely that was not neglect? They had not noticed that his schooling in Blairlogie had been at odds with his life at St. Kilda. They had sent him to Colborne College because it was the kind of school Sir Francis understood, without any consideration of what kind of school Francis might need. They had done everything for him that money could provide, and that they could imagine, but they had not seen much of him or given much thought to him. Their reason was, of course, the War, and the part Sir Francis had played in it as what would be called in a later, different war "a backroom boy", and the necessity for Mary-Jacobine to do what complemented her husband's career and augmented his position. Long after the War was officially over, these necessities seemed to prevail over any serious attention to Francis.

Did this make him feel neglected, rejected, bitter? Far from it. It made it possible for him to idealize his parents and love them as distant, glorious figures, quite apart from the everyday world. At school, and at the expensive camps where he spent his summers, he had always with him a folder in which were pictures of his father, looking distinguished, and his mother, looking beautiful, and these were holy ikons that comforted and reassured him when he doubted himself. And as the Grail took command of his inner life, they were associated with it, not directly and foolishly, but as the kind of people who made such splendour possible and perpetuated it in the modern world.

When the business of the Cornish Trust required Sir Francis to be in Canada for much of each year, his son saw him at weekends, talked with him, was sometimes taken for splendid meals at his club, and was often shown his medals. But, as the Major explained, medals were not the measure of a man's service; it was what the chaps at the War Office and the Foreign Office thought of you that established your true measure. It was the degree of access you had to the People Who Really Knew. These people were not named, but that was not because they had no reality, for there was nothing of the phoney about the Major when it came to his profession; these significant people were not named because they were not in the limelight, although in a very real sense they controlled the limelight and chose the people on whom it should shine. These people were by no means all soldiers; some of them were scientists, some were officially explorers, some were dons. It was never said, but it was clear enough that the Major was associated in some way with what was still called the Secret Service. Secrecy was bred in Francis's bones.

As for his mother, she was a beauty, in a time before beauties had become entirely professional beauties. It would have been vulgar and un-Grail-like to say it, but she was a Society Beauty.

Being a beauty always means constellating some ideal related to the historical period where it appears, and Mary-Jacobine, now known as Jacko Cornish, was a Beauty of the Twenties. She did not languish; she danced vigorously and joyously. She was not swathed in embroideries; she wore tight sheaths that came barely to her beautiful knees. Her figure was boyish but not flat or muscular. She smoked a great deal, and had a variety of long holders for her Turkish cigarettes. She drank cocktails to the extent that made her laugh delightfully, but never until she hiccuped. Her hair was cut short in styles that had various names from year to year, but were basically the Eton Crop. She used make-up, but her own high complexion made make-up an ornament rather than a disguise. Her underclothes were few, and although they were splendidly embroidered they were never so much so as to spoil the set of her wonderful frocks. Her scent was bought in Paris, and only somebody like the President of the Cornish Trust could have afforded it. She flirted with everybody, even her elder son.

For there was now a second son, old enough to be sent to the Lower School at Colborne, and he was Francis's brother Arthur. There was more than ten years between them, and Arthur did not figure largely in Francis's life, but he was a nice kid, and Francis was civil to him. Arthur was everything Francis was not, a noisy, exuberant, strong little boy, and a great success at school. If Francis had not sat on Arthur from time to time, for his soul's good, Arthur would have patronized Francis, whom he recognized with the instinct of his kind as the sort of fellow who would never be Captain of Games in the Upper School, which was the goal Arthur had set for himself, and which after the required number of years he attained. Francis never knew it—it was not proper that he should know it—but the Major thought more highly of Francis than he did of Arthur. The younger boy was the type who would some day be a good soldier, if he were so unlucky as to be involved in a war, but he was not a Secret Service type, and the Major rather suspected that Francis was precisely that.

It was in May 1929, when Francis was nineteen, going on twenty, that several matters which had been hanging fire resolved themselves.

The first came when he was training for Track, on the oval path that surrounded the school's main cricket pitch. Francis was a fair runner, but not a star. On this day he ran a few yards, felt short of breath, pressed on in the best School tradition, lost consciousness, and fell to the ground. Sensation! Boys collected; the drill-sergeant rushed up shouting, "Back, back all of you; give him air!", and when Francis came round, which he did in a few seconds, detailed four boys to take him up to the Infirmary, where Miss Grieve, the school nurse, packed him into bed at once. It was a Thursday, which was one of the days when the doctor visited the School; he listened to Francis's heart, looked grave to hide his want of opinion, and said that he would arrange a visit to a specialist, immediately.

The following morning Francis felt perfectly well, went to Prayers as usual, and was astonished when the Headmaster announced a list of awards, in which his name appeared as winner of the School Prize in Classics. He was also named as one of those who should report to the Head's secretary immediately Prayers were over.

"Oh, Cornish," said Miss Semple; "you're to be excused classes this morning. You're to go to the General Hospital to see Dr. McOdrum at ten. So you'd better hurry."

Dr. McOdrum was very important, but he worked in a mercilessly overheated, windowless little kennel in the basement of the big hospital, and was himself so pale and stooped and over-burdened in appearance that he was a poor adver-tisement for his profession. He made Francis strip, hop up and down, pretend to run, step on the seat of a chair and then step down again, and finally lie on a cold, medical-smelling trolley while he went over him very carefully with a stetho-scope.

"Aha," said Dr. McOdrum, and having deliv-ered himself of this opinion, allowed Francis to go back to school, greatly puzzled.

As it was a Friday, and Francis was a prize-winner, he was given special leave to go home for the weekend. Ordinarily he would have had to wait until Saturday morning. So it was about five o'clock when he went into the new house in Rosedale, and made for the drawing-room, hoping there might still be some tea left. There he found his mother, kissing Fred Markham.

They did not start like guilty creatures. The smiling Markham offered Francis a cigarette, which he took, and his mother said, "Hello dar-ling, what brings you home tonight?"

"Special leave. I won the Classics Prize."

"Oh, you clever creature! Kiss me, darling! This calls for a celebration!"

245

"Sure does," said Fred Markham. "White Lady, Francis?"

"Oh, Fred, are you sure? He doesn't have cocktails."

"Then it's time he started. Here you are, old man."

The White Lady was delicious, specially the white of egg part. Francis drank, chatted, and felt worldly. Then he went up to his room, dropped on his bed, and burst into tears. Mum! Imagine it, Mum! With Fred Markham, who had a gold inlay in one of his front teeth, and must be forty if he was a day! Mum—she wasn't a bit better than Queen Guenevere. But that would set Fred Markham up as Sir Launcelot, which was ridiculous. If Fred was anything, he was a base cullion, or perhaps a stinkard churl. Anyway, he was an insurance broker, and who did he think he was, getting fresh with Lady Cornish? But it had looked as if Mum were in on the kiss; she wasn't resisting, and maybe it wasn't the first. Mum! God, she must be almost as old as Markham! He had never before thought of his mother as anything but young. Older than he, but not in any exact chronological way.

The door opened and his mother came in. She saw his tears.

"Poor Francis," she said, "were you very surprised, darling? No need to be. Doesn't mean a thing, you know. It's just the way people go on nowadays. You wouldn't believe how things have changed, since I was your age. For the better, really. All that tiresome formality, and having to be old so soon. Nobody has to be old now, unless they want to. I met a man last year when we were in London who had had the Voronoff operation—monkey glands, you know—and he was simply amazing."

"Was he like a monkey?"

"Of course not, silly! Now give me a kiss, darling, and don't worry about anything. You're almost done with school, and it's time you grew up in some very important ways. Did you like the White Lady?"

"I guess so."

"Well, they're always rather strange at first. You'll get to like them soon enough. Just don't like them too much. Now you'd better wash your face and come down and talk to Daddy."

But Francis did not hurry to talk to Daddy. Poor Father, deceived like King Arthur! What did Shakespeare call it? A cuckold. A wittoly cuckold. Francis was not pleased with the part he had played in the talk with his mother; he should have carried on like Hamlet in his mother's bed-room. What had Hamlet accused Gertrude of doing? "Mewling and puking over the nasty sty" was it? No, that was somewhere else. She had let her lover pinch wanton on her cheek, and had given him a pair of reechy kisses, and let him paddle in her neck with his damned fingers. God, Shakespeare had a nasty mind! He must look *Hamlet* up again. It was a year since Mr. Blunt had coursed his special Lit. class through it, and

Mr. Blunt had gloated a good deal over Gertrude's sin. For sin it was. Had she not made marriage vows as false as dicers' oaths? Well—must wash up and talk to Father.

Sir Francis was greatly pleased about the Classics Prize, and opened a bottle of champagne. Poor innocent, he did not know that his house was falling about his ears, and that the lovely woman who sat at the table with him was an adulteress. Francis had two glasses of champagne, and the White Lady was not altogether dead in his untried stomach. So it was that when Bubbler Graham phoned after dinner he was more ready to fall in with her suggestion that they should go to the movies than he would otherwise have been.

He still had to say where he was going at night, and what he was going to do.

"Bubbler Graham wants to go to the movies," he mumbled.

"And you don't want to? Oh, Francis, come off it! You don't have to pretend to Daddy and me. She's charming."

"Mum—is it all right for Bubbler to call me? I thought the boy was supposed to do the calling."

"Darling, where do you get these archaic ideas? Bubbler is probably lonely. Frank, give the prize-winner five dollars. He's going to have a night out."

"Ah? What? Oh, of course. Do you want the car?"

"She said she'd bring her car."

"There, you see? A thoroughly nice girl. She

doesn't want you to carry all the expense. Have a marvellous time, darling."

Bubbler wanted to see a film with Clara Bow in it, called *Dangerous Curves,* and that was where they went. Bubbler had taken Clara Bow as her ideal, and in restless energy and lively curls she was a good deal like her idol. During the show she let her hand stray near enough to Francis's for him to take it. Not that he greatly wanted to, but he was rather in the position of the man upon whom a conjuror forces a card. Afterward they went to an ice-cream parlour, and sat on stools at the counter and consumed very rich, unwholesome messes of ice cream, syrup, and whipped cream, topped with fudge and nuts. Then, as they drove home through one of Toronto's beautiful ravines—which was certainly not on their direct route—Bubbler stopped the car.

"Anything wrong?" said Francis.

"Out of gas."

"Oh, come on! The tank registers more than half full."

Bubbler bubbled merrily. "Don't you know what that means?"

"Out of gas? Of course I do. No gas."

"Oh, you mutt!" said Bubbler, and rapidly and expertly threw her arms around Francis's neck and kissed him, giving a very respectable version of the way Clara Bow did it. But Francis was startled and did not know how to respond.

"Let me show you," said the practical Bubbler. "Now ease up, Frank; it isn't going to hurt. Easy, now." And under her instruction Francis showed himself a quick study.

Half an hour later he was decidedly wiser than he had been. At one point Bubbler unbuttoned his shirt and put her hand over his heart. Tit for tat. Francis opened her blouse, and after some troublesome rucking up of her brassiere, and accidentally breaking a strap on her slip, he put his hand on her heart, and his scrotum (if schoolboy biology were true) sent a message to his brain that was the most thrilling thing that he had ever known, because her heart lay beneath her breast, and although she was a girl of the twenties, Bubbler had a substantial breast, crushed and bamboozled though it was by a tight binder. His kisses were now, he felt, as good as anything in the movies.

"Don't snort so much," said the practical Bubbler.

When she dropped him at his house Francis said slowly and intently, "I suppose this means we're in love?"

Bubbler bubbled more than she had done at any time during a bubbling evening. "Of course not, you poor boob," she said. "It's just nice. Isn't it? Wasn't it nice, Frank?"—and she gave him another of her Clara Bow kisses.

Just nice? Frank prepared for bed, very much aware that he was "all stewed up" as Victoria Cameron would have put it. Bubbler had stewed him up, and to Bubbler it was just nice. Did girls really do all that—fumbling under the blouse and hot kissing—just because it was nice?

He was, after all, a Classics prize-winner. A line of Virgil rose in his mind—a line that Mr. Mills read with sad insistence:

> *Varium et mutabile semper*
> *Femina*

Even in his mind he was careful to get the arrangement of lines correct. *Fickle and changeable always is woman.*

Stewing, regretting, yearning for more but angry to have been used for somebody else's pleasure, Francis went to bed, but for a long time he could not sleep.

"Frank, I'd like you to have lunch with me at my club," said Sir Francis, when he met his son at breakfast.

His club was large, gloomy, untouched by any sort of modern taste, and extraordinarily comfortable. Ladies were not allowed, except on special occasions and under heavy restraints. His father ordered two glasses of sherry—not too dry—and Francis reflected that in his experience this was a weekend of heavy boozing.

"Now, about luncheon—what do you say to a bowl of oxtail, with grilled chops to follow and—Oh, I say, they've got tapioca pudding down for today. I always say, it's the best tapioca pudding I get anywhere. So we'll have that, and—waiter—a couple of glasses of club claret.

"This is a celebration, Frank. A celebration of your Classics prize."

"Oh—thanks, Father."

"A good sort of prize to get—what?"

"Well, lots of the fellows don't think much of Classics. Even some of the masters wonder what use it is."

"Pay no attention. Classics is good stuff. Anything that gives you a foot in the past is good stuff. Can't understand the present if you don't know the past, what? I suppose you'll do Classics at Spook? Or will you leave that till Oxford?"

"Oxford?"

"Well, I've always assumed you'd go to Oxford after you'd been to Varsity here. Of course, you must go here, and I suppose Spook's the best college for you. I mean, as I'm head of a big Canadian business, it wouldn't do to send you out of the country for your 'varsity work altogether. Spook, then Oxford. Give you lots of time."

"Yes, but oughtn't I to be getting on?"

"With what?"

"I don't know, yet. But everybody at school thinks he ought to get on with whatever he's going to do as fast as possible."

"I don't think what you're going to do needs to be hurried."

"Oh? What am I going to do?"

"What do you want to do?"

"I'd really like to be a painter."

"Excellent. Nothing wrong with that. That fellow who painted your mother—de Laszlo, was it?—he seems to do extremely well at it. Mind you, he has talent. Have you got talent?"

"I don't really know. I'd have to find out."

"Excellent."

"I thought perhaps you might want me to go into the business."

"Your grandfather doesn't think you're cut out for it. Neither do I, really. Perhaps Arthur will lean that way. He's more the type than you are. I'd thought that you might skip the business and have a look at the profession."

"I don't follow—"

"My profession. Let's not be coy about this. You know, or you probably guess, that I've been pretty close to Intelligence for the past while. Fascinating world. You don't know what I've done, and you shan't. I don't have to tell you that it's a matter of honour never to hint that I've even been near such work. The real work, I mean. People get wrong ideas. But I think you might have what's wanted, and this Classics prize is nearer to what's wanted than it would be in the financial game. But some of the best Intelligence men must be seen by the world to be doing something else—something that looks as if it took all their time. Being a painter would be very good cover. Able to mix widely, and people wouldn't be surprised if you travelled and were a bit odd."

"I've never thought about it."

"Just as well. People who dream about it and

253

hanker for it are just bloody hell at it. Too much zeal. At best they're just gumshoe men—and women. You know you've got a heart?"

A heart? Did Father mean Bubbler Graham?

"I see McOdrum didn't tell you. Yes, you've got a dicky heart, it appears. Not bad, but you mustn't push yourself too hard. Now, that's just the thing for the profession. Anybody wants to know why you're loafing around, you must tell 'em you've got a heart, and most of 'em will assume you're a bit of an invalid. Loaf and paint. Couldn't be better. They thought I was just a soldier. Still do. Nobody expects a soldier to have any brains. Rather like being an artist."

"You mean—I'd be a spy?"

"Oh, for God's sake, Frank, don't use that word! That's Phillips Oppenheim stuff. No, no; just a noticing sort of chap who goes anywhere and does what he pleases, and meets all sorts of people. Not false whiskers and covering your face with walnut juice and letting on to be Abdul the Water-Carrier. Just be yourself, and keep your eye peeled. Meanwhile, go to Spook and then Oxford and pack your head with everything that looks interesting, and don't listen to fools who want you to do something that looks important to them. You've got a heart, you see."

"But what would I have to do?"

"I can't say. Perhaps just write letters. You know—friendly letters to chaps you know, about this and that. Mind you, I'm talking rather freely. There'd be nothing doing for a while. But you

254

ought to meet some people, as soon as possible. I can arrange for you to meet them when you're in England this summer."

"Am I going to England?"

"Don't you want to?"

"Oh yes; it's just that I hadn't thought about it."

"It's time you met some of my people. I haven't said anything about it, Frank, because after all they're your mother's people, but there's more to you than just that lot at St. Kilda. I mean old Mary-Ben with her priests and her fusspot ways, and your grandmother—nice woman, of course, but she's going to end up like old Madame Thibodeau. There are other people in your life. You ought to meet my lot. We're half of you, you know. Maybe the half that will appeal to you more than the Blairlogie crowd."

"Did you hate Blairlogie, Father?"

"Not hate, exactly; I don't let myself hate any place where I have to be. But a little of Blairlogie was enough. Why do you ask?"

"I remember at the farewell party you gave at the hotel at Blairlogie, and you and Grandfather were the only men who wore evening dress, and Alphonse Legaré came up to you half-slewed and laughed in your face and struck a match on the front of your dress shirt."

"I remember."

"You didn't move an inch or bat an eye. But it was worse than if you had hit him, because you didn't think he was in the same world as you

255

were. He couldn't touch you. I admired that. That was real class."

"Awful word."

"It's the word we use for the real goods. You had the real goods."

"Well—thanks, my boy. That's the profession, you understand. No losing your temper. No doing stupid things."

"Not even if your honour is affected? Not if somebody you trusted with everything turned out to be not worthy of it?"

"You don't trust people till you've learned a lot about them. Obviously you are thinking of someone. Who is it?"

"Father, what do you really think of Fred Markham?"

The Wooden Soldier rarely laughed, but he laughed now.

"He's good enough for what he is, but that isn't much. I think I know what's on your mind, Frank; don't let Fred Markham worry you. He's a trivial person, a kind of recreation for a lot of women. But he hasn't got what you call the real. goods."

"But Father, I saw him—"

"I know you did. Your mother told me. She thought you were taking it quite the wrong way. People must have recreations, you know. Change. But a day on the golf-course isn't running off across the world. So don't worry. Your mother can take care of herself. And take care of me, too."

"But I thought—vows—"

"Loyalties, you mean? You find out that loyalties vary and change outwardly, but that doesn't mean they are growing weaker inwardly. Don't worry about your mother and me."

"Does that mean that Mother is just another form of what you call cover?"

"True, and not true. Frank—I don't suppose you know much about women?"

Who likes to admit he doesn't know much about women? Every man likes to think he knows more about women than his father. Frank would have bet that he had seen more naked women than his father had ever dreamed of, though he was not boastful about the quality of what he had seen. Those pallid figures at Devinney's. No beauty chorus. But Francis had long outgrown the ignorance of Blairlogie days; he knew what people *did*. Like animals, but love made it splendid. He thought patronizingly of poor Woodford at school, who had revealed during a bull-session that he thought children were begotten through the woman's navel! At seventeen! How they had kidded Woodford and pictured what it would be like on his wedding night! Francis knew all about the Particular that the encyclopaedia and a lot of Colborne school-biology could tell him. And he knew anatomy, and could draw a woman without her skin on—out of a book. Father obviously meant intimacy with women, and Francis was aware that though he could draw quite a decent flayed woman he had never touched a warm one

257

until Bubbler Graham had made it easy for him. The Wooden Soldier was going on.

"I've had quite a bit to do with women. Professionally, as well as personally. They can be useful in Intelligence work. D'you know, I even met the famous Mata Hari a few times. A stunner. Fine eyes, but chunkier built than they like 'em today. When they shot her at last she was forty-one—just about the age your mother is now and every bit as beautiful as your mother. In the profession, you know, their usefulness is limited, because it's all business with them, and they're always looking for a better deal. Now the men—lots of them are mercenary, of course, but some of the best will work for a cause, or love of country. I sometimes think a woman has no country; only a family. And of course there are the men who can't resist adventure. Not women, though they're often called adventuresses. They work with their bodies, you see, and of course their outlook is different. Mind you, I've met some astonishing women in the profession. Marvellous at code and cypher, but they're an entirely different sort—the puzzle-solving mentality. Those are the bluestockings; not usually very interesting as women. The adventuresses are bitches. Always on the take.

"Still—I didn't ask you here to talk about that. Just about women in general. My advice is: never have anything to do with a woman, high or low, who expects to be paid. They're all crooks, and unless you pay very high you're likely to end up with something you never wanted to buy. No pay:

that's a good rule. I'd say—stick to widows. There are lots of them, especially since the War, and you don't have to go outside your own class, which is important if you have any real respect for women. Be generous, of course, and play decent and straight, and you'll be all right. That's that, I think. Now, what do you intend to do?"

"I don't think I know any widows."

"Oh, you will. But that's not what I meant. Will you go to England this summer? Spook in the autumn?"

"Yes, Father. It sounds great."

"Good. And when you're in England you'd better meet one or two of the chaps. I'll arrange it."

Frank missed his chance to ask his father about the Looner, said the Lesser Zadkiel.

—Did you think he had a chance? The Major was a very accomplished talker—which took the form of not seeming to be accomplished at all, but never losing his grip on the way things were going. He overwhelmed Francis with new ideas—the profession, going to England to meet the Cornishes, how to cope with women. With a glass of sherry and a glass of club wine in his unhabituated gizzard, Francis never had a chance to initiate any new subject, or challenge a long-held secret. You know about secrets: they grow more and more mysterious, then suddenly they crumple away and everybody wonders why they were ever secret. The secret of the Looner was some years behind him in Blairlogie,

and Francis couldn't keep up with the extraordinary things his father was telling him—that he didn't much mind his mother kissing Fred Markham, that he had really been in the Secret Service, that widows were the thing. The Major was an old hand at important conversations.

Francis sat in the ruins of the Castle of Tintagel, trying to think about King Arthur. This was holy ground, the very place in which Arthur was begotten by Uther Pendragon upon the beautiful Igraine, wife of the Duke of Cornwall. The enchanter Merlin had made that possible. But try as he would to think about the great story, all Francis could do was to look north-west over the heaving, gleaming sea from which came, so it seemed, all the light of Cornwall. This sea-light, reflected back toward the sky as if the sea itself had some source of light beneath it, had puzzled and dominated him during the whole month he had spent with the Cornishes of Chegwidden. The light gave new meaning to the legends he had brought, as appropriate luggage for a Cornish holiday. This was not the light of the pre-Raphaelite pictures, the moony glow that bathed those impossibly noble men and perversely beautiful women; this was a world-light, a seemingly illimitable light that the sea, like a dull mirror, yielded in a form so diffused that the whole peninsula of Cornwall was pervaded by it, and although manifestly there were shadows to be seen, nevertheless the light seemed to defy shadows, and cast itself on every side of every object.

In this extraordinary, unfamiliar light—unfamiliar to Francis, who had never lived near the sea— it was surely possible to plunge oneself into the world of legend? Looking from this storied head-land might one not imagine one saw the painted sails of the ship that bore Tristan and Iseult to-ward their meeting with King Mark? But try as he would to bully his thoughts into this legendary and poetic mode, all Francis could think of was the Cornishes of Chegwidden, and how odd they were.

Odd because they lived in this enchanted land, and appeared to be utterly impervious to enchant-ment. Odd because they lived where the saints of the ancient Celtic Church had proclaimed Christ's gospel in a truly Celtic voice, long before the dark-skinned missionaries of Augustine had come from Rome with their Mediterranean Catholicism, to preach and impose belief with all the fanaticism of their kind. Apparently the Cornishes of Cheg-widden had never heard of Celtic Christianity, or, if they had, could not understand that it might be something more interesting than the Low Church faith of St. Ysfael, in whose parish they lived and were the great folk. Surely the name of St. Ysfael was Celtic enough and old enough to nudge the most sluggish historical sense? The church had been there, in one form or another, since the sixth century; they knew that. But what really inter-ested them was that in the nineteenth century a devout Cornish had contributed the thumping sum of five hundred pounds to have St. Ysfael done up in the height of Victorian Gothic style, and they were determined that not a brass ornament or an encaustic tile should be changed. There was a family story that this pious Cornish had caused a lot of old panelling—fifteenth-century or something of the sort—to be ripped out and burned, as rubbish, when the great work of restoration was done.

Odd because they seemed unaware that King Arthur might have ridden over what were now their own parklands, and that some of their oldest trees might have grown from grandacorns of trees under which the great King—the *dux bellorum* of the earliest records—had reined in his horse to rest and look about him in the mysterious light of the peninsula that was Cornwall. When Francis had mentioned this as a possibility, his uncle—who was named Arthur Cornish, of all things—had looked at him queerly and said that unquestionably there was a tree in the park that had been planted to celebrate the coronation of Queen Victoria, and it was coming into promising maturity, for an oak, at this very moment, having survived two serious periods of blight.

What really interested Uncle Arthur was something called the Local Bench, upon which he sat as a magistrate as every Cornish had done for as long as there had been a Bench, and which he was now disagreeably expected to share with tradesmen and even a local socialist, who could not understand that the essence of local justice lay in knowing the local people—which ones were decent folk and which were known poachers and riff-raff—and treating them accordingly. Uncle Arthur owned a good deal of property in lands and cottages, and it was on the rents of these that Chegwidden and all its ancient glory depended. If Uncle Arthur had ever heard of Oscar Wilde as anything but a damned bad type who would have received no mercy from the Local Bench, he had certainly never heard Wilde's comment that land gives one position and prevents one from keeping it up. He would have agreed that there, at least, the bugger knew what he was talking about. The merciless exactions of modern government on landowners was his favourite topic, and if any of his kin had ever heard the word paranoia, they might have recognized that on this theme Uncle Arthur was distinctly paranoid. Modern government, he was sure, was a gigantic plot to ruin him, and in him all that was best in rural England.

His wife, Aunt May, would have described herself with appropriate modesty as a religious woman, for the doings of the parish and the services at St. Ysfael's were her chief concern. Helping the poor, so far as the waning fortunes of the Cornishes would allow, and a repressive hand on any clergyman who showed a tendency to be High, were her great cares. What she believed, nobody knew, for she was firm in her reticence on all matters relating to the inner life. In church she was seen to pray, but to What, and what she said to It, and how It worked in her daily life, nobody knew. The chances were strong that she prayed for her son Reginald, who was with his regiment in India, and her son Hubert, who was in the Navy and hoped for a command soon, and her daughter Prudence, who had married Roderick Glasson, another oppressed neighbouring squire. Unquestionably she prayed for her tribe of grandchildren, but how efficacious such prayers were was a matter of speculation, for they were a wild lot and gave Francis a good deal of trouble.

He never, during his month at Chegwidden, got them properly sorted into families, for they came and went inexplicably, roaring in and out of the house with cricket bats and bicycles, and small guns, if they were boys. As for the girls, they were doing their uttermost, it seemed to the quiet Canadian, to get themselves killed, riding ponies in a horrible parody of polo, which they played in a meadow full of rabbit holes, so that the ponies were always stumbling, and the girls were always pitching over their heads into the path of other charging ponies. They all regarded him as a huge joke, even when he tried to impress them with his skill (learned at an expensive boys' camp) in making a fire without matches. Because of this they called him the Last of the Mohicans, and treated his enthusiasm for King Arthur as a form of American madness. He never could be sure whose were Reginald's, and whose Hubert's, though he knew that two of the girls must be

Prudence's, because they assured him daily that if their older sister, Ismay Glasson, could only meet him, she would soon put him to rights. They were very proud of Ismay because she was a Terror, even among the Chegwidden lunatics. But Ismay was abroad, staying with a French family to improve her accent, and doubtless terrorizing the French.

At the family table, over bad food in restricted quantities, Francis had tried to introduce some topic that would reveal whether or not the Chegwidden Cornishes knew what a great man his father was, and how intimate he was with the Chaps Who Knew, up in London. But he discovered that Sir Francis was merely a younger brother, so far as Uncle Arthur was concerned, and that in Aunt May's mind it was a pity that if there had to be a Lady Cornish at all, that Lady Cornish should be an American—for the Cornishes were pig-headedly determined that the pretence of Canadians not to be Americans was sheer affectation, to be rebuked whenever possible. As for the fortune that the Wooden Soldier had acquired by his marriage and his value as a trust company figurehead, it was plainly a sore touch at Chegwidden; to be a younger son, and to have money, when the elder son was struggling to keep his head above water, was intolerable cheek. So Francis was made to feel that he was not only the Last of the Mohicans, but a Rich American. He was sure the Chegwidden Cornishes did not mean it unkindly; it was simply that their excellent manners were not strong enough to keep their jealousy in complete abeyance.

From the family table Francis sometimes lifted his eyes above his plate of congealing mutton stew to look at the family portraits that hung above the wainscot. They were, he had to admit, ghastly. They were worse, because older and more blackened and scabby, than the portraits in the Prayer Hall at school. But out of them all, though the form varied, stared the family face, a long, horsy face with gooseberry eyes in which, in some portraits, a distinction, an air of intelligence and command, showed itself. As he looked around the table, at Uncle Arthur and at the grandchildren (for of course Aunt May did not count, being a mere breeding machine in the great complex of Cornishes), that face, disappointed and severe in Uncle Arthur, and peering through puppy-fat, or schoolboy awkwardness, or under ill-braided pigtails, was repeated in a variety of styles, but always, in form and mannerism, the same. And, when he went to bed in his chilly room, he could see, in the whorled mirror, that even under the black hair he had from the McRorys, it was his own face, and that his black hair and his gooseberry eyes gave him a look which would some day be startling.

Chegwidden: a disappointment, really. After all he had suffered because of that difficult name, which was not only queer in itself but a nuisance in pronunciation, he had at least expected an impressive dwelling and, as the name suggested, a white building. But no: Chegwidden was a large, low, grubby-looking mansion of brownish-grey stone, with a lowering, unfriendly front door, pinched little windows, and a slate roof on which moss grew in patches. Old it unquestionably was; such inconvenience could not have been achieved in anything less than four centuries. Smelly it was, too, for a much-tinkered Victorian system of plumbing had never really come to terms with what was demanded of it. As it seemed to be a family habit never to throw anything away, it was cluttered with furniture and ornaments, pride of place being given to things that various Cornishes had brought home from military or naval service abroad. But the total effect was faded, down-at-heel, uncomfortable, and valetudinarian. School had habituated Francis to shabbiness and discomfort and stinks, but his notion of a family dwelling was the rich, velvety ugliness of St. Kilda, or his mother's uncompromisingly fashionable house in Toronto. How did the Cornishes put up with a house where every chair, in the midst of summer, embraced the sitter like a cold sitz-bath, and every bed was dank from the sea mists?

Yet Father had assured him that at least half his root was here.

Try as he might, he could not evoke King Arthur, even in the ruins of Tintagel. He bicycled back through Camelford to Chegwidden, glad that tomorrow he would return to London, and after a few days take ship for Canada.

"Did you enjoy your visit to Cornwall?"

"Thank you, sir. It was very interesting."

"But not enjoyable?"

"Oh, very enjoyable. But I thought people living there would have been more aware of the history of the place."

"The Cornishes *are* the history of the place. I suppose they think of history as something that happens elsewhere. A bit provincial, was it?"

"I wouldn't like to say that."

"You're a cautious fellow, aren't you, Francis?"

"I don't like to make hasty judgements. This is my first time in England, you see."

"But it certainly won't be your last, your father tells me. Going up to Oxford eventually?"

"That's the plan."

"By that time you might be quite a useful chap. Your father tells me you might end up in the profession."

So that was what it was! That was why Colonel Copplestone had asked him to lunch in the Athenaeum, an impressive club in the West End, though certainly not much ahead of Chegwidden in the matter of food. Francis had been expecting something like this, Colonel Copplestone must be one of the Chaps Who Knew.

"Father spoke about it."

"And you liked the idea?"

"I was flattered."

"Well—no promises, of course. Just follow your nose. But we're always on the lookout for promising young men, and if they're promising enough, we might make a few promises later on."

"Thank you, sir."

"Are you a letter-writer?"

"Sir?"

"Write interesting letters, do you? If you're really interested, I want you to write letters to me."

"What about?"

"About what you're doing—and seeing—and thinking. I'd like a letter from you not less than once a fortnight. Write to me at this address; it's my country place. And in the letters you address me as Uncle Jack, because I'm an old friend of your father's, and that's appropriate. I'm your godfather."

"Are you, sir? I hadn't known."

"Neither had I, till I met you today. But that's what I am now. So you write to me as a godfather, which is a very good relationship, because it can mean nothing very much, or quite a lot. Just one thing, though; don't mention that your father, or your godfather, has anything whatever to do with the profession."

"I'm not really very sure what the profession is."

"No, of course not. For the present, it's just the profession of men who follow their noses and see whatever's to be seen. I don't think we want any blancmange, do you? Let's take our mud coffee upstairs."

Dear Uncle Jack:

Cornwall was really great, but I liked
London better. I have never seen such pictures
before. Our gallery in Toronto is small, and not
very good, because we have no money to buy
the really first-rate pictures. Not yet. Maybe it
will come. I am trying now to find out about
the new pictures, by the new men, and I went
to as many private galleries in London as I
could, and saw a lot of stuff that puzzled me. I
might as well tell you, though, that the people
who ran the galleries, or perhaps I should say
the young men who showed off the pictures to
possible buyers, were as interesting as the
pictures themselves. They are so *silky*, and they
talk so easily about tactile values and *nouveau
vague,* and a lot of things that were away over
my head. I hadn't really understood what an
ignoramus I am.

I've read a bit about the new stuff. Quite a
lot, really. And I understand (or think I do)
that a picture shouldn't really be *about*
anything. Not like those awful pictures that tell
a story, or show upper-class kids feeding robins
in the snow, or show you Hope, or the Soul's
Awakening or something that is intended to
make you feel religious, or wistful. No, a
picture is just patterns of line and colour
arranged on a flat surface, because it's no good
kidding yourself that it isn't flat, is it? I mean,
perspective is all very fine if it's mathematics,
but if it tries to kid you that you are looking

into depth it's a cheat. Pictures are pure form and colour. Anyway, that's what the new books say, and certainly that is what the silky chaps in the galleries say. Nix on emotion. Perhaps even nix on meaning anything except what is in front of one's nose.

The trouble is that in some of the best of the new stuff emotion and meaning keep breaking in. Like this chap Picasso. I saw some of his stuff at one of the galleries, and if it's just form and colour on a flat surface, I'm dreaming. It's a statement of some sort. Not that I could tell you what the statement is, but I'm sure it's there, and I'm sure that if I can stick with it long enough, I'll find the meaning.

And Old Masters! Of course I've done my best with the new painting, but I admit I liked the Old Masters best. I think I know why. As you know, I was raised a Catholic—or perhaps not exactly *raised* one but a lot of Catholicism was bootlegged into my early days by a great-aunt, and unless I can drain every drop of it out of me—and I don't seem to have much luck doing that—those Nativities and Adorations and Crucifixions and Trans-figurations can never be simply clever arrangements of line, volume, and colour for me. They are statements, some strong, some not so strong, some fancy, some terribly plain. Were the old boys wrong? I try to think so, but it won't work.

You are partly to blame, godfather. You say

follow your nose, and if I do it takes me in some very unmodern and unfashionable directions. If I'm to see pictures the modern way, and no other way, I guess I'll have to cut off my nose. And that would spite my face, wouldn't it?

I don't intend to spite my face, ever, or turn my back on old friends. Do you know of a caricaturist and illustrator called Harry Furniss? I owe a lot to him, or I should say to a book of his that was my Bible for a while. The other day, in a shop that sells drawings and pictures, I found an original sketch of an actor called Lewis Waller (never heard of him) by H.F. and I bought it, just for old sake's sake, for ten pounds. Which is pretty steep for my pocket. But I couldn't resist it. Just to have something H.F. had touched. How the silky boys would despise it, but it's a wonder of artistic economy.

I have sore feet from trudging through the National Gallery, the Tate, the Wallace, the Victoria and Albert. All full of marvels. And what do you think? I have a favourite picture! I know I shouldn't, and crushes on works of art are the worst kind of amateurism, but it absolutely stuns me. In the Nat. Gal. a big picture called *An Allegory of Time* by Bronzino; 1502-72 it says and otherwise I know nothing about him. But what a statement! And what is the statement and what is the allegory? I stare and stare and can't figure it out.

Do you know it? What hits you first is the nude figure of a beautiful woman, superbly fleshly and naked as a jaybird except for a coronet of jewels. I mean she isn't just nude, which can be like a corpse on the embalmer's table, but astonishingly naked. A youth who looks about fourteen stoops toward her from the left, kissing her, and it's plain that her tongue is pushing between his lips—French kissing they call that, godfather—and if they are really mother and son it's a pretty queer situation; furthermore his right hand is on her left breast, the nipple peeping between his index and second fingers, which it wouldn't do unless the kiss meant more than just good-morning or something like that. His left hand is drawing her head toward him. On the right a stout baby, with a knowing smile, is winding up to throw some roses over them. So far, so good. But a vigorous, muscular old man, looking as though he wasn't very pleased by the goings-on, is either drawing a blue curtain over this scene, or else he is revealing it. Can't be sure. A woman is helping him, only her head visible, but beneath her and just behind Cupid's out-thrust rump is another woman whose face is torn with pain—is it? or could it be jealousy? Behind the fat baby is a creature with a childlike but not an innocent face, and the body attaching to it ends in a serpent's tail and the terrible feet of a lion.

Two masks, one young and one old, lie on the ground.

What do you make of that fine thing? God only knows, at present, but I mean to make it my business to know, because it's saying something, just as my great-aunt's awful, skilful pictures of Cardinals joking and boozing say something. Those are saying that the Church is powerful and classy, but Bronzino says—something about a very different world, and a world I want to learn about. Nobody is going to tell me it's just an arrangement of form and colour. It's what my great-aunt calls A Good Lesson.

I am learning fast. I have already caught on that Bouguereau wasn't really a great painter, though he was an astonishing technician. Bought another drawing yesterday, just some scratches of the Virgin and Child, with a scribble that might be one of the Magi. Cost me twenty-five pounds and I shall not be eating at the Café Royal tonight I assure you. But I'm sure it's a Tiepolo. Maybe School Of.

Off on the boat-train in the morning. It was wonderful to see you. Shall write again soon.

Yr. affct. godson
Frank

Not bad for a lad of nineteen, thought Colonel John Copplestone, as he tucked the letter into a newly opened file.

By the time Francis had completed four years at the College of Saint John and the Holy Ghost (irreverently called Spook by all students and by faculty members when they were not obliged to be on their best behaviour) in the University of Toronto, the file in Colonel John Copplestone's study was a fat one, and there was an additional file, not so fat, in which the Colonel's old friend and an honoured member of the profession who simply signed himself J.B. reported now and then on things which Francis might not have told his godfather. J.B. was officially the Warden of the Students' Union at the University of Toronto, but he was a great letter-writer, and although most of his letters were simply dutiful communications with his aged mother in Canterbury, quite a few of them went to Colonel Copplestone, and some of these went farther still, to the Chaps Who Knew. Even in a trusted, if not beloved, Dominion, things may happen about which inside information is welcome to the Secret Service of the mother country, and J.B. supplied a good deal of it.

His comments on Francis, boiled down, would not have seemed particularly significant unless one happened to be recruiting for the profession. Francis was fairly well liked, but was not one of the most popular undergraduates; nothing of the Big Man on Campus about him. He seemed not to have much to do with girls, although he was not indifferent to them. On the other hand, his friendships with young men were not intense.

Francis had made one or two attempts to appear in productions at the University Theatre, and was a wooden, disastrous actor, his black hair and green eyes making him look odd under theatre circumstances. Outside his studies he did not cut much of a figure, but he was a surprisingly useful member of the Union Pictures Committee; he could spot a good thing, and urge that it be bought, when the other undergraduates who worked with J.B. simply didn't know their Picassos from a hole in the ground. Francis was already buying Canadian pictures for himself in the twenty-five- to hundred-dollar range. Though he came of a rich family he didn't have a lot of money to throw around, and once J.B. had asked him why he was wearing no overcoat on a sub-zero day, to be told that Francis had hocked his coat to buy a Lawren Harris that he couldn't resist. He hoarded what money he had in order to buy pictures. Spent none of it on himself, and had the reputation of being "close" with money, which probably accounted for his lack of contact with girls, who are great eaters and drinkers. He drew a good deal, and had decided talent as a caricaturist, but for some reason didn't choose to exploit it; nevertheless the caricaturist's gleam was often seen in his green eye, when he thought nobody was looking. Did pretty well in his studies, and astonished everybody when at the end of his fourth year he took the Chancellor's Prize in Classics, even though Classics wasn't in vogue. This would give him a good push forward at Oxford, and

J.B., who had drag at Oxford, would see that it did not go unheeded.

A candidate for the profession? Possibly. The Oxford days would tell, thought Colonel Copplestone. After all, the boy was still only twenty-three.

During the summer before his departure for Oxford, Francis paid a visit to Blairlogie. He might not have thought of doing so if his mother had not urged him to make the effort. The people there are getting old, she said; you see Grand-père now and then, but Grand'mère and Aunt have not seen you for—oh, more than ten years. It's the least you can do, darling. So, in hot August weather, off he went.

The journey, once he had left the main line and taken the train which struck northward toward Blairlogie, seemed to be almost violent in its reversal of time. From the excellent modern train in which, because his parents had paid for his ticket, he travelled in the chair-car, which had radio earphones at every seat, he changed to a primitive affair in which an ancient, puffing engine pulled a baggage coach and one passenger coach at a stately twenty miles an hour through the hinterland. The passenger coach was old without being venerable; it had a great deal of fretwork ornamentation in wood that had once been glossy, but the green plush seats were mangy and slick, the floor was poorly swept, and it stank of coal-dust and long use. Because of the heat the windows that would still open were opened, and grit and smoke from the engine occasionally swept through the car. There were stops at tiny stations in the middle of nowhere, usually in order that some small piece of freight might be unloaded. There were other stops in order that the journal-boxes might cool; the train was prone to that plague of old running-stock, the hot-box.

At noon the train halted in the midst of rocky scrubland where there was not a roof in sight. "If any of yez haven't brought yer lunch, yez can get dinner up on the hill at th' old lady's. Costs a quarter," said the conductor, and himself led a small procession up the hill where, in the old lady's kitchen, chunks of fat bacon and fried potatoes were ready on the back of the wood-stove; on top of each plate of meat was laid a slab of rhubarb pie. The etiquette, Francis saw, was to remove the pie delicately (so as not to break it) and lay it on the pine table beside the plate, until the latter had been cleared and wiped with a chunk of bread; then the pie was lifted back to the plate to be devoured with the well-sucked fork, and washed down with the old lady's coffee, which was boiling hot, but not strong. Fifteen minutes were allowed for this repast, and when the conductor rose everybody rose, and put a quarter into the hand of the unsmiling, unspeaking old lady. The conductor, it seemed, did not pay; he led his pilgrims in single file down the hill to the waiting train. The engine-driver and the fireman (who doubled as brakeman) had eaten thriftily from lunchboxes by the side of the line. They clambered back into the cab, belching enjoyably, and the train resumed its sleepy, stately course.

Late in the afternoon the conductor tramped importantly through the car, shouting, "Blairlogie! End of the line! Blairlogie!", as if some passengers could possibly have been in doubt about the matter. Then the conductor hastened to be first off the train and was well away up the street toward his home before Francis could get his suitcase down from the overhead rack, and set foot once again in the place of his birth.

Blairlogie had changed, if the old train had not. Few horses were to be seen on the streets, and some of the streets themselves had been paved. Shops bore different names, and the Ladies' Emporium, where Grand'mère had always bought her hats (because the Misses Sim, though Protestants, had undoubtedly the best taste, and the deftest hands with artificial cherries and roses, in town), had vanished altogether, and weeds grew where it had stood. There was a movie-house, too, which seemed to mean that a gaudy front had been stuck on a failed grocery-store. The McRory Opera House, farther up the street, was closed, and had an offended, snubbed look. Trees were taller but buildings were smaller. Donoghue's blacksmith-shop was not to be seen and, most significant change of all, a motor truck laden with cut timber was making its way up the street, and the name on its side was not his grandfather's name.

But when he got away from the business street

and up the hill, St. Kilda looked as it always had looked, and when he rang the bell it was undoubtedly Anna Lemenchick, though broader and seemingly shorter, who answered. She said nothing—she never did say anything when she answered the door—but there was a scampering upstairs, and Aunt Mary-Ben came rattling down, rather dangerously on the polished hardwood, and threw herself at him. She was so tiny; had he really grown so much?

"Francis! Dear, *dear* boy! How big you are! Oh, and so handsome! Oh, Mother of God, isn't this a happy day! Did you take the taxi? We'd have sent, only there's nobody to send just now—Zadok in hospital and all. Oh, what will Grand'mère say when she sees you! Come, come right away and see her, Frankie, my own dear. It'll do her more good than anything!"

Grand'mère was in bed, a mountain of flesh, but yellow and sour-smelling. Conversation with her was in French, because she found English an effort now. She was considerably younger than the Senator—who was, as usual, away in Ottawa, or in Montreal, or in Toronto, on some business or other—but chronology had nothing to do with what ailed her, and she might have been ten years older than her real age, which was sixty-eight.

"Dr. J.A. is reserved about dear Marie-Louise," said Aunt Mary-Ben, as she and Francis ate the bad dinner that evening. "We fear what's wrong, of course, but he won't be plain about it. You remember how he always was. You can't undo

280

nearly seventy years of overeating, he says. But could hearty eating really bring on *that?* I pray for her, of course, but Dr. J.A. says the age of miracles is past. Oh, Frankie, Frankie, it's a dreadful thing, but we must all go in the end, mustn't we, and your dear Grand'mère has led such a *good* life—not a thing to reproach herself with—so though it's hard for us, we must bow to His will."

The ruling passion, it appeared, was still strong. That night Francis played for three hours with Aunt and Grand'mère, who could summon up spirit for the game. It was euchre. The deck of thirty-two cards was ready when they went upstairs, and on and on, remorselessly and almost without speaking, they played hand after hand. Francis, as the least experienced, was euchred again and again, and he could not but notice that frequently his grandmother's hand would disappear beneath the covers, presumably to press some aching part or to ease her bedgown, and when it reappeared—could that have been the flash of a card that had not been there before? An unworthy thought, and he pushed it down, but not quite out of sight. Mary-Ben was willing enough to lose, but Francis had not come to the time of life when he understood that winning is not always a matter of taking the trick.

As they parted at bedtime, he whispered to Aunt, "What's the news of Madame Thibodeau?"

"She doesn't get out much now, Francis; she's become so stout you see. But she's wonderful.

Stone deaf, but she plays cards three times a week. And wins! Oh dear me, yes; she wins! Eighty-seven, now."

Where was Victoria Cameron? Who was caring for the Looner?

It appeared that Aunt had been forced to get rid of Victoria Cameron. She had kicked over the traces just once too often, and Aunt had turned her out lock, stock, and barrel. She had not been replaced as cook, but Anna Lemenchick did her best, helped out by old Mrs. August's youngest girl, who was willing, though not very bright. Anna's best was not good, but with poor Marie-Louise reduced to a diet of liquids, Aunt had no heart to look for another first-rate cook, in spite of her brother's urging. It seemed heartless, didn't it, to hire somebody to cook dishes poor Grand'mère could not hope to taste?

Francis was still incapable of telling Aunt that he knew about the Looner, but on his first night at St. Kilda he crept upstairs while he knew Aunt would be busy on her prie-dieu. All the curtains that had deadened sound were gone. Nobody slept up there because Anna Lemenchick came by the day. He tried the door of the room which had once been hospital and madhouse and prison, but it was locked.

In his childhood room, which seemed to have lost substance, like everything else at St. Kilda, Francis caught sight of himself as he undressed, in the long mirror before which he had once

282

postured in a mockery of women's attire. A young
man, with hair on his chest and legs, black curls
clustering about his privates; moved by an impulse he could have denied, but to which he
yielded, he once again drew the bed cover about
him and looked at what he saw—looked hungrily
for the girl who should have been behind the
mirror, but was not. Where was she? He had not
found her in any of the girls with whom, at
Spook, he had sought her. She must be somewhere, that girl from the world of myth, from the
real Cornwall of his imagination. He would not
believe it could be otherwise. But the consequence
of his gazing brought on such arousal that he had
to "choke the ghost", which was school slang for
masturbation. As always, the act brought relief
and disgust, and he fell asleep in a bad temper.
He didn't want crushes and affairs and the student amusements he heard so much about at
Spook. He wanted love. He was twenty-three,
which he thought very old to be without love, and
he wondered what could possibly be the matter
with him, or with his fate, or whatever decreed
such things. Hell!

He had no trouble, the next morning, in finding Victoria Cameron. She was smack in the middle of the main street, in a small shop which said,
over the door, CAMERON FANCY BAKED GOODS, and
inside she stood behind the counter amid a profu-
sion of her best work.

"Well, you never thought leaving your grandfather's house would be the ruin of me, did you,

Frankie? It's been the making of me. Dad and the boys baking the bread as always, and me making the fancy stuff here, we're doing a land-office business, let me tell you. No, I'm not married, nor will I ever be, though it's not for want of offers, let me tell you. I've better things to do than slaving for some man, and you can bet on that."

"Zadok? That's a sad story. He wanted to marry me, but can you imagine that? I told him straight: Not as long as you do what you do at Devinney's, I told him, and don't give it up, because I wouldn't marry you even if you gave it up. I'm too fond of my own way, I said. But it hurt him. You could see that. I don't pretend that was all of it, but it may have been part of it.

"I think it was that poor boy's death that hit him hardest. You hadn't heard about that? No, I don't suppose there'd be anybody tell you. Zadok felt he'd done it, in a way."

A pause, during which a group of customers, who looked curiously at Francis, were accommodated with a half-dozen of lemon-curd tarts, another half-dozen of the raspberry tarts, two lemon pies promised for a wedding anniversary, and a big bag of cream puffs. Not to speak of two crusty white and two brown and two raisin loaves. When this press of business was completed, Victoria continued. "Zadok was always one for his beer, you remember. And after I told him flat there was nothing doing so far as I was concerned he took to bringing it up to that room on the top floor, to drink while he sang to Frankie—the other Frankie. You know, Francis, he loved that boy. You might almost have thought he was his own. Zadok had a heart in him, you've got to give him that. I didn't like him bringing in the beer, but I couldn't have stopped it without more trouble than it seemed to me to be worth. And I think there was some spite in it. Men are funny, you know, Francis. I think Zadok wanted to show me that if I wouldn't have him, he'd go to the Devil, hoping maybe I'd change my mind to save him. But I wasn't raised to think you can save people. If they can't save themselves—that's to say, as far as anybody *can*—nobody else can do it for them. We all have our fate to live out, and I knew it wasn't my fate to save Zadok. So he'd drink a lot, and get silly, and drink healths to Frankie, and Frankie knew something cheerful and jolly was meant, and he'd laugh in that sort of lingo that was all he could manage. But I was firm on the one thing: I wouldn't let Zadok give Frankie any of the beer.

"Probably that's what did it. Instead of beer, Frankie drank a lot of water. Harmless, wouldn't you say? He'd just piss it into his diaper, and no harm done. But one night Zadok and I had a real knock-down row, because he was drinking more than usual and making too much noise, and at last I walked out on the two of them and told Zadok he could get Frankie ready for sleep by himself.

"Of course I knew he couldn't. The boy relied on me to get him ready for the night, and I wouldn't fail him. So after an hour or so, when I knew Zadok had gone, I went in to settle Frankie down, and I did, but I thought he looked a little queer, and he was heavy to lift. In the morning he was dead.

"Do you know what it was? *Drownded!* I had to get the old Aunt, and she sent for Dr. J.A., and after he looked at Frankie he said that was what it was. Drownded! You see, that poor boy wasn't like other people. There was some gland right in the top of his head that wasn't right, and when he went on that water toot with Zadok he must have drunk about—I don't know—gallons maybe, and it was more than he could stand. The doctor said some of it must have got into his blood, and then into his lungs, and he drownded. The doctor called it pulmonary oedema. I've remembered it, because—well, you wouldn't expect me to forget it, would you? So there had to be another funeral at night, though there was no priest this time, and now there really is a Frankie under that stone that was a fake for so long.

"No, they didn't tell your parents. In fact, your mother never knew what was up there in the attic all those years. But your grandfather knew, of course, and he and Dr. J.A.—well, it'd be hard to say exactly what happened. They were both relieved, but it wouldn't have done to let that show. I knew some money changed hands, to make sure Zadok kept his mouth shut. And in an awful way I suppose it was gratitude.

"The money was the end of him. Drank worse

and worse, and his work at Devinney's suffered; he did some jobs that scared the bereaved when they looked into the coffins—all swollen around the face, and a kind of boiled colour. So Devinney had to get rid of him. And the upshot of that was that he fell down drunk one winter night in the lane behind Devinney's—because he had a sort of unnatural pull toward the place—and nearly froze, and they had to take both his legs off, and even at that they don't seem to have been able to stop the gangrene. He's up in the hospital now. It would be kind of you to go and see him. Yes, I go, once a week, and take a few tarts and things. That hospital food is worse than Anna Lemenchick's.

"After poor Frankie was buried for the second time I didn't last a week at St. Kilda. One morning the old Aunt and I went right to the mat, there in the kitchen, and she told me to go. Go, I said! It's you that'll go if I leave this kitchen! You and the Missus cramming yourselves at every meal worse than Zadok and his beer! Don't think you're firing me! I'm the one that's doing the firing! Just see how you get along without me! *You pair of old stuff puddings!* That was common of me, Francis, but I was worked up. Not even your grandfather could persuade me to stay after that. How could I stay in a place where I'd showed myself common?"

Francis knew that something had to be said, and though it is not easy for young people to say such things, he said it.

"Victoria, I don't suppose anybody will ever

know what you did for that fellow—Francis the First, I call him—but you were wonderful, and I thank you for him, and for everybody. You were an angel."

"Well, I don't see any need to get soft about it, Francis. I did what had to be done. As for thanks, your grandfather was very generous when the parting came. Your grandfather sees farther than most people. Who do you suppose is paying for Zadok in the hospital? And the money that allowed me to set up this place was a gift from him."

"I'm glad. And you can play the tough Presbyterian all you please, Victoria, but I'll go right on thinking of you as an angel." And Francis kissed her soundly.

"Frank—for Heaven's sake! Not in the shop! Suppose somebody saw!"

"They'd think there were more tarts in here than the ones in the showcase," said Francis, and dodged through the door as the outraged Victoria called after him.

"That's quite enough of that sort of talk. You're worse than Zadok."

Was it possible to be worse than Zadok? When Francis visited him in the hospital later that day it seemed that Zadok's decline could not be equalled. The ward was hot and stuffy; there were no patients in the other two beds, so Francis could talk freely to the wasted trunk that lay in the bed nearest the window, with a kind of cage under the sheet to lift it from where the legs had once been.

The stench of disinfectant was oppressive, and from Zadok's bed there came, from time to time, a whiff of something disgusting, a scent of evil omen.

"It's this gang-green, they call it, Frankie. I can feel it all through me. B'God I can taste it. Can't seem to stop it, though they've taken my legs. It's an eating sore, y'know. Dr. J.A. says he's never seen it so bad, though he's seen some bad cases in the lumber camps. Says he doesn't know why I'm not dead, because I'm a mass of corruption. He can talk like that to me because I'm an old soldier, me dear, and I can bear the worst. He's not unkind; it's just that he sees the world as a huge disease, and we're all part of it."

"It's very, very bad luck, Zadok."

"I've known very bad luck in my time, me dear. I've looked it right in its ugly mug, and it's a terror. Yes, it's a rum start what can happen to a man. I've never told you about South Africa, have I?"

"I knew you'd fought there."

"I fought well there. I did some good work. I was up for promotion and a decoration. Then it all fell to pieces because of love. You wouldn't think of that, would you? But love it was, and I'm not ashamed of it now.

"I was in a regiment raised in Cornwall, you see, and I went under the lead of a young man who was the son of the great family in my part. His father was an Earl, so he was a Lord. The Captain, he was. God, he was a handsome man,

Frankie! We'd grown up together, almost, because I'd followed him all my life, hunting, fishing, roving, everything boys do. So of course I joined the regiment under him, and I was his batman—his personal servant, like. Before I joined I'd been two or three years in his father's house as an under-servant, a footman that was, so it seemed a very natural thing that I should go on looking after his clothes, and even trimming his hair, like. We were friends, great friends, the way a master and a servant can be. And I swear to God he never laid a finger on me nor I on him in a way that would bring shame on either of us. It wasn't like that; I've seen some o' that, in the Army and out of it, and I swear it wasn't like that. But I loved the Captain, the way you'd love a hero. And he was a hero. A very brave, fine man.

"Like many a hero, he was killed. Stopped a Boer sniper's bullet. So we buried him, and I did my best for him right to the end. Dressed him, and saw his hair was washed, and he looked very fine in the cheap coffin that was all there was, of course. 'Yes, let me like a soldier fall.' Remember that song?

"I thought I'd die, too. At night I used to sneak out after Lights Out, and sit by his grave. One night a picket noticed me, lying on the grave and crying my heart out, and he reported me, and there was an awful fuss. I was charged, and the Colonel had a lot to say about how such behaviour was unworthy of a soldier and could be harmful to morale, and how such immoral relationships must be sharply discouraged, and I was discharged without honour and sent back home, and bang went my medal, and a big part of my life. The Colonel wasn't one of our lot. Not a Cornishman, and he didn't understand me. I wonder if he ever loved anything or anybody in his life. So that was very bad luck."

"Terrible bad luck, Zadok. But I understand. It was like the love that held the Grail knights together, and the people who served them in innocent love."

"Ah, well, I don't know anything about that. But of course you're part Cornish, aren't you, Frankie? Not that I'd say they were a very loving lot, on the whole. But they're a loyal lot."

"What did you do in England?"

"Whatever I could. Servant, mostly, and some jobs for undertakers. But there was one thing that seemed almost as if it was meant to make up for the other, and it was love too, in a funny way.

"It was like a dream, really. That's the way it seems to me now.

"There was one regimental sergeant-major—good bloke—that I'd known, and he was kind to me now and then. He had a funny sideline. Used to supply men—soldiers mostly—to places that wanted servants for big dos, just to dress the place up, you know; not really do much except wear the livery and look tall and trustworthy. Well, I'd been a footman, hadn't I? Get a few bob for an easy night's work.

"One night was a big night in one of the big

hotels, and I was on the job, all gussied up in breeches and a velvet clawhammer and white wig. No moustache then, of course. A servant must shave clean. We'd done our job and I was just about to take off the fancy clobber when some fellow—one of the upper waiters—rushed up to me and said, 'Here, we're short-handed; just take this up to number two-four-two will you, and give it in before you leave.' And he handed me a tray with a bottle of champagne and some glasses on it, and dashed away. So up I went, knocked on the door, very soft as I'd been taught in the castle, and went in.

"Girl in there. Alone, so far as I could see. Beautiful girl, I remember, though I couldn't say now what her face was like, because she was so beautifully dressed, and a servant isn't supposed to stare, or even look anybody in the eye, unless asked. 'Open it, please,' she said. Soft voice; might have been French, I thought. So I opened and poured, and said, 'Will that be all, madam?' Because orders were that any lady had to be 'madam', not 'miss'. 'Wait a minute,' said she. 'I want to have a good look at you.' And I still didn't raise my eyes, you see, Frankie. I don't know how long she looked. Might have been a minute. Might have been two. Then she says, very soft, 'Do you ever go to the theatre?' 'Not much in my line, madam,' said I. 'Oh, you should,' says she. 'I've been and it's perfectly wonderful. You haven't seen *Monsieur Beaucaire?*' 'Don't know the gentleman, madam,' I said. 'Of course you don't,' she said; 'he's imaginary. He's in a play. He's a valet who's really a prince. And the actor who plays Monsieur Beaucaire is the most beautiful man in the world. His name is Mr. Lewis Waller,' she said.

"Well, then I knew a little more. I'd heard of Lewis Waller. Matinee idol, they used to call him. A real swell. Then what she said really surprised me, and I had to look in her face.

" 'You're the very image of him in *Monsieur Beaucaire*,' she said. 'The costume, the white wig. It's astonishing! You must have a glass of champagne.'

" 'Strictly against orders, miss,' I said, forgetting myself when I called her that.

" 'But strictly according to my orders,' said she, very much the little princess. 'I'm lonely, and I don't like to drink alone. So you must have a glass with me.'

"I knew that was just swank. She wasn't used to drinking much any time, not to speak of alone. But I did what she said. And I made my glass last, but she had three. We talked. She did, that's to say. I kept mum.

"There was something amiss with her. Don't know what it was. All excited, and yet not happy, as if she'd lost a shilling and found a sixpence, if you follow me.

"Well, I soon saw what it was. I had seen something of life, and I'd seen a good deal of women, of all kinds. She wanted it. You know what I mean? Not like some old woman who's crazy with vanity and foolishness and fear of her own age. She wanted it, and I swear, Frankie, I didn't take advantage of her. I just lived in the present, so to speak, and after some more talk I did what she wanted—not that she asked bolt outright or even seemed to know much about how it was managed. And I swear to you I was perfectly respectful, because she was a sweet kiddie and I wouldn't have harmed her for the world. It was lovely. Lovely! And when it was over she wasn't crying or anything, but looked as if she was ready for bed, so I carried her into the bedroom and laid her down, and gave her one good kiss, and left.

"Frank, it was the sweetest thing that ever happened in my whole life! A dream! It'd be hard to tell it to most people. They'd grin and know best, and think badly of her, and that would be dead wrong, for it wasn't that way at all.

"When I was out in the corridor I passed a big mirror, and saw myself, in the livery and the white wig. I looked hard. Maybe I was Monsieur Beaucaire, whoever he was. Anyhow, it did something wonderful for me. I was able to put the Army disgrace and the dishonourable discharge behind me, and try to get on in the world.

"Not that I did, not in any big way. But after a while I decided to try my luck in Canada, and fetched up here. And now I've ended like this.

"No, I never saw her again. Never knew her name. A rum start, me dear. That's all you can say about it. A rum start."

Zadok was weary, and Francis rose to go. "Is there anything I can do for you, Zadok?"

"Nobody can do anything for me, me dear. Nothing at all."

"That's not like you. You'll get well. You'll see."

"Kindly meant, Frankie, but I know better. Suppose I did get well? No legs—what'd that add up to? Old soldier with no legs, playing the mouth-organ in the street? Not me! Not for Joe! So it's good-bye, me dear."

Zadok smiled a gap-toothed, red-nosed smile, but his moustache, once proudly dyed and now a yellowish grey, had still a dandified twist.

Francis, moved by an impulse he had no time to consider, leaned over the bed and kissed the ruined man on the cheek. Then he hurried from the room, for fear Zadok should see that he was weeping.

The little hospital was at some distance from the town. As Francis emerged, one of Blairlogie's two taxis had just set down a passenger and was about to drive away. But the driver pulled up suddenly, and shouted: "Hey, Chicken! D'yuh want a taxi?" It was Alexander Dagg.

"No, thanks. I'll walk."

"Where yuh been?"

"I haven't lived here for a good many years."

"I know that. I ast yuh where yuh been."

Francis did not answer.

"Visiting somebody in the hospital? That old bum Hoyle, I'll bet. He's dying, isn't he?"

"Maybe."

"No maybe about it. Say—d'yuh know what I'm going to tell yuh? Nobody was surprised what happened. My Maw says what happened to him is a warning to all boozers."

During his time at Colborne College and Spook, Francis had learned a few things in the gymnasium he had not known when he was at Carlyle Rural. He was now more than six feet tall, and strong. He walked to the taxi, reached through the window by the driver's seat, seized Alexander Dagg by the front of his shirt, and yanked him sharply toward the door.

"Hey! Go easy, Chicken. That hurts!"

"It'll hurt worse if you don't shut your big, loud mouth, Dagg. Now you listen to me: I don't give a good god-damn what you think or what your evil-minded old bitch of a Maw thinks. Now you be on your way, or I'll beat the shit out of you!" Francis thrust Alexander very hard against the steering-wheel, then wiped his hands on his handkerchief.

"Oh, so that's how it is! Oh, I'm very sorry, Mr. Cornish, very sorry indeed, your royal highness. Say—d'yuh know what I'm going to tell yuh? My Maw says the McRorys are all a bunch of bloodsuckers, just using this town for whatever they can get out of it. Bloodsuckers, the lot of yez!"

This was hurled bitterly from the window as Alexander Dagg drove away, his head dangerously twisted so that he could not see where he was going; he narrowly missed hitting a tree. Francis should have kept his dignity and his undoubted victory, but he was not quite old enough for that. He picked up a stone and hurled it at the flying car, and had the satisfaction of hearing it strike with a force that undoubtedly damaged the taxi's paint.

"Oh dear, I had promised a duck for your last dinner, Francis, but this doesn't seem to be a duck, does it? So what I said must have been *un canard*."

"Certainly *un canard*, and this is *un malard imaginaire*, Mary-Ben. Look at this! The blood follows the knife as you cut it."

"I'm afraid you're right, J.A. Don't eat it, Francis. You don't have to be polite here."

"I was brought up to be polite at this table by you, Aunt. I can't stop now."

"Yes, but not to the point of eating raw—what do you suppose it is, J.A.?"

"At a rough guess I should say that whatever is on our plates approached the oven believing itself to be a capon," said the Doctor. "Mary-Ben, you can't go on like this; Anna Lemenchick can't cook and that's all there is to it."

"But J.A., she believes herself to be the cook."

"Then you must shatter her illusion, before she kills you and Marie-Louise. I insist, on behalf of my patients. Ah, it was a sorry day when you let Victoria Cameron leave this house."

"J.A., there was no help for it. She had become

297

a tyrant—an utter tyrant. Kicked right over the traces if I made the slightest criticism—"

"Mary-Ben, learn to know yourself before it's too late to learn anything! You nagged her without mercy because she was a Black Protestant, and you hadn't the bigness of spirit to see that her quality as an artist raised her above mere matters of sect—"

"Joe, you are unkind! As if I could nag."

"You're a sweet nagger, Mary-Ben—the very worst kind. But we mustn't wrangle on Francis's last evening here. Now, what's to follow this horrible duck or whatever it is? A pie, is it? God send the pastry isn't raw."

But the pastry was raw. Anna Lemenchick, stolid and indifferent to the amount of uneaten food she removed on the plates, now brought in a tray on which was a bowl of hot bread-and-milk for the patient upstairs. Aunt excused herself, and hurried off with the tray to feed Marie-Louise, who liked company with her meals of slops. Dr. J.A. rose and fetched a bottle of the Senator's port from the sideboard, and sat down with Francis.

"Thank God, Anna can't get her murderer's hands on this," he said, pouring out two large glasses. "This house is sinking into the earth, Francis, as you well can see."

"I'm worried, Uncle Doctor. Nothing seems to be right here. Not just the food, but the whole feel of the place."

"Francis, it's stinginess. Senile parsimony is what ails Mary-Ben. She's rolling in money, but she thinks she's poor and won't hire a decent cook. Your grandmother can't eat the stuff, and Mary-Ben just eats this garbage to prove she's right."

"Uncle Doctor, tell me honestly—is Grand'mère going to die?"

"Oh yes, eventually. We all are. But when I couldn't say. She hasn't got cancer, if that's what you're worried about. Just a totally ruined digestion and gallstones like baseballs. But she and Mary-Ben carry on as if the retribution of a lifetime of overeating the richest possible foods was something unique in the annals of medicine. B'God they make it almost religious. 'Behold and see, if there be any acidity like unto my acidity.' The oddity is that Mary-Ben's eaten the same stuff, chew for chew, as her sister-in-law, and she's still at it—a mighty little knife-and-fork is Mary-Ben. D'you know she visits old Madame Thibodeau every day for tea? Christian charity? Get away! It's because Madame Thibodeau gets all her cakes and tartlets from the infidel Victoria Cameron, that's why! That's female logic for you, Francis."

"Then Grand'mère is not as bad as she looks?"

"No, she's just as bad as she looks, but if she keeps on bread-and-milk and my peppermint mixture she could last a good long time. But Mary-Ben's the one to last. The McRory strain is a very strong strain, Francis. So look after it in yourself. It's a golden inheritance."

"Is it all good?"

"How do you mean?"

"No madness? No oddity? I know about the fellow that was upstairs; what explains him?"

"That's not for me to tell you, Francis. That may have been a matter of chance—what they call a sport. Or it may be something that is bred in the bone."

"Well—it's very important to me. If I married, and had children, how great is the danger—?"

"On chance, perhaps not very great. Look at you, and look at your brother Arthur; both perfectly sound. Or it could happen again. But let me give you some advice—"

"Yes?"

"Go ahead. Keep on with your life. If you want to have children, take the risk. Don't stay single or childless on some sort of principle. Obey instinct; it's always right. Look at me and Mary-Ben. There's a lesson for you! Yes, Francis, I've come to the time of life when I'm less of a teacher or adviser than I'm an object lesson:

> *The sin I impute to each frustrate ghost*
> *Is—the unlit lamp and the ungirt loin—*

D'you know any Browning?"

"Not really."

"Mary-Ben and I used to read him together, long ago. Very clever fellow. Away ahead of all these so-called psychologists you hear about nowadays."

When the long, tedious bout of euchre was com-

300

pleted in Grand'mère's room, Aunt Mary-Ben insisted that Francis should come into her sitting-room for a last chat. He was leaving early in the morning. The room was almost unchanged, only somewhat shabby from use and the passing of time.

"Aunt, why is Grand-père so seldom here now?"

"Who's to say, Francis? He has so much business to attend to. And I dare say he finds it dull here."

"It wouldn't have anything to do with the food, would it?"

"Oh, Francis! What a thing to say!"

"Well, you heard what Uncle Doctor said. It'll kill you."

"No, no it won't; Dr. J.A. must have his joke. But the truth is, Frank, I can't hurt Anna Lemenchick. She's the last of the old servants, and the only one who has never cost me a moment's uneasiness. Old Billy, you remember, drank so terribly, and Bella-Mae has given herself up totally to that Salvation Army, and do you know sometimes they have the neck to play right outside the church, just before High Mass! And Zadok—well you know I never really trusted him; there was a look in his eye, as if he were thinking impermissible thoughts when he was driving the carriage. D'you know I once caught him imitating Father Devlin? Yes, right in the kitchen! He had a tablecloth over his shoulders, and was bowing up and down with his hands clasped, and moaning, 'We can beat the Jews at do-minoes!', pretending he was singing Mass, you see. And Victoria Cameron was laughing, with her hand over her mouth! I don't care what your grandfather and Uncle Doctor say, Francis, that woman was evil at heart!"

On the subject of Victoria Cameron, Aunt was implacable, and declared furthermore that with the wages servants wanted nowadays—forty dollars a month had been heard of!—you had to look out that you weren't simply made use of. So Francis led the conversation to his future, in which Aunt was passionately—the word is not too strong—passionately interested.

"To be a painter! Oh, Frankie, my dear boy, if ever there was a dream come true, that's it, for me! When you were so ill as a child, and used to sit in this room and look at the pictures, and draw pictures of your own, I used to pray that it might flower into something wonderful like this!"

"Don't say wonderful, Aunt. I don't know even if I have any talent, yet. Facility—probably. But talent's something very much beyond that."

"Don't doubt yourself, dear. Pray that God will help you, and He will. What God has begun, He will not desert. Painting is the most wonderful thing—of course, after a life in the Church—that any man can aspire to."

"You've always said that, Aunt. But I've wondered why you say it. I mean—why painting, rather than music, for instance, or writing books?"

"Oh, music's all very well. You know I love it. And anybody can write; it just takes industry. But

302

painting—it makes people *see*. It makes them see God's work truly.

> *. . . we're made so that we love*
> *First, when we see them painted, things we have*
>   *passed*
> *Perhaps a hundred times, nor cared to see:*
> *And so they are better, painted.*

That's Browning—*Fra Lippo Lippi*. I used to read a lot of Browning once, with a great friend, and that always made me cry. Yes, yes, it's true! The painter is a great moral force, Frankie. It's truly a gift of God."

"Well—I hope so."

"Don't hope. Trust. And pray. You still pray, don't you, Francis?"

"Sometimes. When things are bad."

"Oh my dear, pray when they are good, too. And don't just ask. Give! Give God thanks and praise! So many people treat Him like a banker, you know. It's give, give, give, and they can't see that it's really lend, lend, lend. Frankie—you've never forgotten what happened when you were so sick that time?"

"Well—wasn't that just a bit of panic?"

"Oh, Frank! Shame on you! That was when Father Devlin baptized you. You're a Catholic forever, my dear. It's not something you can shrug off at a fashionable school, or among unthinking people, like your father, though I'm sure he's a

303

good man so far as he understands goodness. Frank—you still have your rosary?"

"It's somewhere, I suppose."

"Dear boy, don't talk like that! Now look, Frankie; you always liked my rosary, and it's a fine one. I want you to have it—no, no, I have others—and I want you to take it with you everywhere, and use it. Promise, Frank!"

"Aunt, how can I promise?"

"By doing so now. A solemn promise, made in love. A promise made to me. Because you know, I'm sure, that at least in part you are my child, and the only one I'll ever have."

So, after some further weak demurrers, Frank took the rosary, and gave the promise, and the next morning he left Blairlogie, as he then thought, forever.

So that poor wretch the Looner was the outcome of a chance meeting between the romantic Mary-Jacobine and the destroyed soldier Zadok? said the Lesser Zadkiel.

—If you wish to talk of Chance, said the Daimon Maimas. But you and I know how deceptive the concept of Chance—the wholly random, inexplicable happening—is as a final explanation of anything.

—Of course. But I am keeping in mind how dear the notion of Chance is to the people on Earth. Theirs is the short view. Rob them of Chance and you strike at their cherished idea of Free Will. They are not granted the time to see that Chance may have its limitations, just as Free Will has its limitations. Odd,

isn't it, that they are glad enough to have their scientists show them evidence of pattern in the rest of Nature, but they don't want to recognize themselves as part of Nature. They seem persuaded that they, alone of all Creation, so far as they know it, are uninfluenced by the Anima Mundi.

—Well, we see that they have some choice within the pattern, but the pattern is strong, and now and then it shows itself nakedly. Then something like this happens: Mary-Jacobine chooses Zadok—against probability, but because she has a crush on an actor; Zadok begets a child in a single coupling with a virgin—again against probability, but because he is a compassionate, unhappy man. Do we call that chance? But then, she does not recognize her chance lover when he appears and he does not recognize her because they are in a world they think of as the New World. Then—Marie-Louise destroys a child in the womb, which is very probable considering who and what she was. Zadok does not know his own son— how would he? Just Chance and Likelihood in their old familiar muddle, said the Daimon.

—I suppose they would call it coincidence.

—A useful, dismissive word for people who cannot bear the idea of pattern shaping their own lives.

—Coincidence is what they call pattern in which they cannot discern something they are prepared to accept as meaning, said the Lesser Zadkiel.

—But we see the meaning, do we not, brother? Of course we do. The Looner brought love back into the life of Zadok, for only love can explain his behaviour toward him. The Looner brought motherhood into *the life of Victoria Cameron, who did not choose—probably feared—to seek it in the usual way.*

—And for your man Francis, my dear colleague?

—Ah—for Francis the Looner was a lifelong reminder of the inadmissible primitive in the most cultivated life, a lifelong adjuration to pity, a sign that disorder and abjection stand less than a hair's breadth away from every human creature. A continual counsel to make the best of whatever fortune had given him.

—But surely, also, a constant pointer to humility? said the Angel.

—Very much so. And I think that although I had nothing to do with the begetting of the Looner, I made good use of him in the shaping of Francis. So the Looner did not live in vain.

—Yes, you did well there, brother. And where is the helm set for now?

—For Oxford.

—Oxford certainly won't strengthen the Blairlogie strain, said the Angel.

—Oxford will strengthen whatever is bred in the bone. And I have already made sure that the Looner, in every aspect, is bred in the bone of Francis. Francis will need all his wits and all his pity at Oxford, said the Daimon.

PART FOUR

PART FOUR

What would not
Out of the Flesh?

"Everybody agrees that your first year at Oxford was a triumph," said Basil Buys-Bozzaris.

"That's very kind of everybody," said Francis. He was being patronized by the fat slob Buys-Bozzaris and he was beginning to wonder how much longer he would put up with it.

"Now, now; let's have no false modesty. You have made a nice little name as a speaker in the Union; you have gained a place on the committee of the O.U.D.S.; your sketches of Oxford Notables in the *Isis* are admitted to be the best things of their kind since Max Beerbohm. You are known as one of the aesthetes, but you are not a posturing fool. You must admit that's very good."

"Those are pastimes; I came to Oxford to work."

"Why?"

"Well, there's a widely accepted notion that one comes here to learn."

"To learn what?"

"The foundation for whatever one means to do with one's life."

309

"Which is—?"

"I haven't really decided."

"Oh, God be praised! For a few moments I feared you might be one of those earnest Americans with a career before you. *Too* middle-class! But Roskalns says you told him you meant to be a painter."

Roskalns? Who was he? Oh yes; that grubby chap who hung about the edges of the O.U.D.S. and was a private coach in modern languages. Had Francis confided in him? Possibly he had said something to somebody else when Roskalns was listening—as Roskalns always seemed to be doing. Francis decided he had had quite enough of Buys-Bozzaris.

"I think I'd better be going," he said. "Thanks for the tea."

"Don't hurry. I'd like to talk a little more. I know some people you might like to meet. You're fond of cards, I hear."

"I play a little."

"For pretty high stakes?"

"Enough to make it interesting."

"And you win pretty consistently?"

"About enough to come out even."

"Oh, better than that. Your modesty is charming."

"I really must go."

"Of course. But just one moment; I know some people who play regularly—really good players—and I thought you might care to join us. We don't play for pennies."

"Are you asking me to join some sort of club?"

"Nothing so formal. And we don't just play; we talk, as well. I hear you like to talk."

"What do you talk about?"

"Oh, politics. World affairs. These are lively times."

"Several people have gone to Spain, to see what they can do there. Even more say they would be in Spain in a moment, if they could see their way clear. Is that the sort of talk?"

"No, that is youthful romanticism. We are much more serious."

"Perhaps I could look in once or twice?"

"Of course."

"Tonight?"

"Admirable. Any time after nine."

A few days later Francis wrote one of his letters to Colonel Copplestone:

Dear Uncle Jack:

Second year at Oxford is a great improvement. One knows where the things are that one is likely to want and where the people are one is certain not to want. The nice thing about being at Corpus is that it is so small. But that means that only first-year men and a few specials can live in college, so I am in digs, and have secured a very nice set of rooms virtually on the college doorstep. Canterbury House the place is called, because it's by the Canterbury Gate of Christ Church. I have the top floor; big living room and small bedroom; superb view down Merton Street, which must be the prettiest street in Oxford, and the only drawback is that when Great Tom gets off his 101 peal at midnight it is almost as if he were in my bedroom. I am thinking of writing to the Dean and suggesting that this ancient custom be discontinued. Do you suppose he would listen?

Have met a few new people. The ground-floor set of rooms here—most expensive, worst view—is occupied by a man called Basil Buys-Bozzaris, which is a name to conjure with, don't you think? He conjures a bit; a few days ago as I was running up the stairs beside his door he popped his head out and said, "A Virgo; I know him by his tread!" which was arresting enough to make me stop and chat, and he waffled a bit about astrology; rather interestingly, as a matter of fact. I don't go for astrology by any means, but I have found that sometimes it provides useful broad clues about people. Anyhow, he wanted me to come to tea with him, and yesterday I did.

In the interim I made a few inquiries about BBB. Our landlord was very forthcoming: rich, he said, and a count, and a Bulgarian. He entertains a lot, and whenever he is having people to lunch, he has the same lunch served to himself the day before, wines and all, and then edits it for errors of cooking or choice!

This impresses the landlord no end, as well it might.

Somebody else who knew a bit about him said he was an oddity. Probably thirty-five, and is here ostensibly studying international law; I am sure you know what a vague area that can be, if somebody wants to hang around a university. BBB seems to be interested in Conflict of Laws, which is of course an even more tangled briar-patch. My informant says he is one of those hangers-on all universities attract. As for being a count, I don't know whether Bulgaria has them or has ever had them, but it is a vague title roughly indicative of some distance from the peasant class. So I knew a bit about him before going to tea.

Usual polite questions, to establish the ground. What was I studying? Flattery about some sketches I did last spring for the *Isis* of Oxford people who are in the eye of the University. Velvety request for my birth date and hour, as he would be delighted to cast my horoscope. I yielded; no reason not to, and I cannot resist horoscopes. And what are you interested in, I said. I am a connoisseur, said he, and this surprised me, because the room was not that of a connoisseur; just the landlord's perfectly good, dull furniture, and a few photographs framed in silver of Middle-European-looking people—choker collars and fancy whiskers on the men, and the women with an awful lot of hair and that kind

313

of fat that is kindly referred to as "opulence".
Not a good object anywhere, and across one
corner an ikon of the Virgin in the most
offensively sweet nineteenth-century taste, with
a *riza* in decidedly *not* sterling silver covering
all but the face and hands. BBB smiled, for he
must have seen my surprise. Not a connoisseur
of art, he said, but of ideas, of attitudes, of
politics in the broad sense. Then he talked a bit
about the present European situation, about
this man Hitler in Germany, about the misery
in Spain, all in a distant, removed fashion, as if
only ideas and not people were involved. Asked
me to come back, to play cards, and I said I
would, not because I like him but because I
didn't.

The card-playing, when I went back, was
interesting enough to repay me for an evening I
would not ordinarily have chosen to spend in
such uncomfortable circumstances. Lots to
drink and expensive cigars for the grabbing,
but the concentration was on two tables of
bridge—all the room would comfortably hold.
The atmosphere was very serious for a friendly
game. BBB was the leader at one and a rather
scruffy fellow called Roskalns, who coaches
first-year men in Latin and does a variety of
languages for others who want them (not
employed by the University, an independent
coach), took care of the other. The rest of us
changed tables from time to time but these two
remained where they were. Brisk play, and the

stakes were substantially above what is usual here, where anybody who loses a pound in an evening feels he has been living dangerously. I was particularly interested in another man—in his second year at Christ Church—named Fremantle, because he is a Canadian though he has lived a good deal in England.

Fremantle had the real wild gambler's eye. Life with my mother and grandmother and great-grandmother has taught me quite a bit about cards, and the first rule is—keep calm, don't *want* to win, because the cards, or the gods, or whatever rules the table will laugh at you and take your last penny. Only what my mother calls "intelligent, watchful indifference" will carry you through. If you see that look in somebody's eye—that hot, craving gleam—you see somebody who has lost himself first, and will probably lose his money so long as he sits at the table. When the time came to settle up at the end of the evening Fremantle was in hock to BBB about twelve quid, and he didn't look happy about it. I came out exactly seven shillings to the good, which was part luck and part my fourth-generation skill with the pasteboards. Anybody who has played skat with my gran and great-gran knows at least how to shuffle without dropping the cards.

Knows a few other things, too, and I kept my eye open for those. Nothing to be seen except that Roskalns has just the teeniest inclination to deal from the bottom of the deck now and then, though not very injuriously, so far as I could tell. I enjoy a mild flutter, and shall go to BBB's evening game from time to time, though I can play cards more comfortably in several other places.

Why go, then? You know how inquisitive I am, godfather. Why has BBB one Dutch name as well as his genuine Bulgarian one? Does he float his heavy hospitality on what he makes at the table? Is Charles Fremantle really as hell-bent on ruin as he seems to be? And why, as I was leaving, did BBB give me an envelope that contained a pretty good horoscope which said, among other things, "You are very shrewd at piercing through what is hidden from others"? Sounds like a come-on. I have never found anything in my horoscope that suggested unusual perception—beyond what a caricaturist might have, of course.

Obedient to your advice, I am not writing this on College stationery, as you see. I swiped this paper the other day when I visited the Old Palace to pay my yearly respects to the R.C. chaplain, Monsignor Knollys, as my Aunt Mary-Benedetta strictly charged me to do. The chaplain is a queer bird and rather dismissive to Canadians, whom he merrily terms "colonials". I'll colonial him if I get the chance.

Yr. affct. godson,
Frank

Two days after his evening with Buys-Bozzaris,

Frank was working in his sitting-room when the door burst open after a short, loud knock, and a girl burst in.

"You're Francis Cornish, aren't you?" said she, and dumped an armful of books on his sofa. "I thought I'd better have a look at you. I'm Ismay Glasson, and we're sort of cousins."

Since his visit to Cornwall and Chegwidden House five years ago, Frank had forgotten that he had a cousin named Ismay, but he recalled her now as the terrible older sister of the obnoxious Glasson children, who had assured him that if Ismay had been at home, she would have given him a rough time. He had been rather afraid of girls then, but in the interval had gained greatly in self-possession. He would give her a rough time first.

"Marry come up, m'dirty cousin," said he; "don't you usually wait to be asked before you barge into a room?"

"Not usually. 'Marry come up, m'dirty cousin'—that's a quotation, isn't it? You're not reading Eng.Lit., I hope?"

"Why do you hope that?"

"Because the men who do are usually such dreadful fruits, and I'd hoped you'd be nice."

"I am nice, but apt to be formal with strangers, as you observe."

"Oh balls! How about giving me a glass of sherry."

During his first year, Francis had become thoroughly habituated to the Oxford habit of swim-

317

ming in sherry. He had also discovered that sherry is not the inoffensive drink innocent people suppose.

"What'll you have? The pale, or the old walnut brown?"

"Old walnut. If not Eng.Lit., what are you reading?"

"Modern Greats."

"That's not so bad. The kids said something about Classics."

"I considered Classics, but I wanted to expand a bit."

"Probably you needed it. The kids said you mooned about and talked about King Arthur and said Cornwall was enchanted ground, like a complete ass."

"If you judge me by the standards of your loathsome and barbarous young relatives, I suppose I was a complete ass."

"Golly! We're not precisely hitting it off, are we?"

"If you burst into my room when I am working and insult me, and tuck up your muddy feet on my sofa, what do you expect? You've been given a glass of sherry; isn't that courtesy above and beyond anything you've deserved?"

"Come off it! I'm your cousin, aren't I?"

"I don't know. Have you any papers of identification? Not that they would say any more than your face. You have the Cornish face."

"So have you. I'd have known you anywhere. Face like a horse, you mean."

"I have not said you have a face like a horse. I am too well-bred, and also too mature, for this kind of verbal rough stuff. And if that means to you that I am a complete ass, or even a fruit, so be it. Go and play with your own coarse kind."

Francis was enjoying himself. At Spook he had learned the technique of bullying girls: bully them first and they may not get to the point of bullying you, which, given a chance, they will certainly do. This girl talked tough, but was not truly self-assured. She was untidily and unbecomingly dressed. Her hair needed more combing than she had given it recently and the soft woman's academic cap she wore was dusty and messy, as was her gown. Good legs, though the stockings had been worn for too many days without washing. But in her the Cornish face was distinguished and spirited. Like several other girls he had seen in Oxford, she might have been a beauty if she had possessed any firm conception of beauty, and related it to herself, but in her the English notion of neglected womanhood was firmly in command.

"Let's not fight. This is good sherry. May I have another shot? Tell me about yourself."

"No, ladies first. You tell me about yourself."

"I'm in my first year at Lady Margaret Hall. Scholarship in modern languages, so that's what I'm doing here. You know Charlie Fremantle, don't you?"

"I think I've met him."

"He says you met at a card game. He lost a lot. You won a lot."

319

"I won seven shillings. Does Charlie fancy himself as a card-player?"

"He adores the risk. Says it makes his blood run around. He adores danger."

"That's expensive danger. I hope he has a long purse."

"Longish. Longer than mine, anyhow. I'm poor but deserving. My scholarship is seventy pounds a year. My people, with many a deep-fetched groan, bring it up to two hundred."

"Not bad. Rhodes Scholars only get three hundred, at present."

"Oh, but they get lots of additional money for travel and this and that. What have you got?"

"I look after my own money, to some extent."

"I see. Not going to tell. That's your Scotch side. I know about you from Charlie, so you can't hide anything. He says your family is stinking rich, though a bit common. The kids said you were bone mean. Wouldn't even stand them an ice cream."

"If they wanted ice cream, they shouldn't have put an adder in my bed."

"It was a dead adder."

"I didn't know that when I put my foot on it. Why are you at Oxford? Are you a bluestocking?"

"Maybe I am. I'm very bright in the head. I want to get into broadcasting. Or film. If not Oxford, what? The days are gone when girls just came out and went to dances and waited for Prince Charming."

"So I hear. Well—is there anything I can do for you?"

"Doesn't look like it, does it?"

"If you have no suggestions, I suppose I could take you to lunch."

"Oh splendid! I'm hungry."

"Not today. Tomorrow. That will give you time to smarten up a little. I'll take you to the O.U.D.S. Ever been there?"

"No. I'd love that. I've never been. But why do you say O.U.D.S? Why don't you call it OUDS? Everybody does, you know."

"Yes; I know, but I wasn't sure you would know. Well—my club, and ladies are admitted at lunch."

"Isn't it full of dreadful fruits? People with sickening upper-class names like Reptilian Cork-Nethersole? Isn't it crammed with fruits?"

"No. About one in four, at the outside. But dreadful fruits, as you so unpleasantly call them, have good food and drink and usually have lovely manners, so no throwing buns or any of that rough stuff you go in for at women's colleges. Meet me here—downstairs, outside the door marked Buys-Bozzaris—at half past twelve. I like to be punctual. Don't trouble to wear a hat."

Francis thought that he had sat on his young cousin enough for the moment.

The advice about the hat was not simply gratuitous insult. When Ismay found herself lunching in the O.U.D.S. dining-room the following day

321

there were two elegant ladies wearing hats at the President's table. They were actresses, they were beauties, and the hats they wore were in the Welsh Witch fashion of the moment—great towering, steeple-crowned things with scarves of veiling hanging from the brim to the shoulders. The hats, as much as their professional ease and assurance, separated them irrevocably from the five hatless Oxford girls, of whom Ismay was one, who were dining with male friends. The O.U.D.S. did not admit women as members.

Ismay was not the aggressive brat of the day before. She was reasonably compliant, but Francis saw in her eye the rolling wickedness of a pony, which is pretending to be good when it means to throw you into a ditch.

"The ladies in the hats are Miss Johnson and Miss Gunn. They're playing in *The Wind and the Rain* at the New Theatre over the way; next week they go to London. Smart, aren't they?"

"I suppose so. It's their job, after all."

But this indifference was assumed. Ismay was positively schoolgirlish when, after lunch, a handsome young man stopped by their table and said: "Francis, I'd like to introduce you and your sister to our guests."

When the introductions and polite compliments to the actresses were over, Francis said, "I should explain that Ismay is not my sister. A cousin."

"My goodness, you two certainly have the family face," said Miss Johnson, who seemed to mean it as a compliment.

"Is that chap really the president of the club?" said Ismay, when the grandees had gone.

"Yes, and consequently a tremendous Oxford swell. Jervase Featherstone; everybody agrees he's headed for a great career. Did you see him last winter in the club production of *Peer Gynt?* No, of course you didn't; you weren't here. The London critics praised him to the skies."

"He's wonderfully good-looking."

"I suppose so. It'll be part of his job, after all."

"Sour grapes!"

Francis had achieved in a high degree the Oxford pretence of doing nothing while in fact getting through a great deal of work. He had learned how to study at Colborne, where success was expected, and he had improved on his technique at Spook. At Oxford he more than satisfied his tutor, hung about the O.U.D.S. meddling a little with the decorative side of its productions, contributed occasional caricatures to the *Isis,* and still had time to spend many hours at the Ashmolean, acquainting himself with its splendid collection of drawings by Old Masters, almost Old Masters, and eighteenth- and nineteenth-century artists whom nobody thought of as masters, but whose work was, to his eye, masterly.

The Ashmolean was not at that time a particularly attractive or well-organized museum. In the university tradition, it existed to serve serious students, and wanted no truck with whorish American ideas of drawing in and interesting the general public. Was it not, after all, one of the oldest museums in the Old World? It took Francis some time during his first year to persuade the museum authorities that he was a serious student of art; having done so, he was able to investigate the museum's substantial riches without much interference. He wanted to be able to draw well. He was not so vain as to think that he might draw like a master, but it was the masters he wished to follow. So he spent countless hours copying master drawings, analysing master techniques, and to his astonishment surprising within himself ideas and insights and even flashes of emotion that belonged more to the drawings than to himself. He did not trust these whispers from the past until he met Tancred Saraceni.

That came about because Francis was a member, though not a very active one, of the Oxford Union. He would not have joined if he had not been assured in his first year that it was the thing to do. He sometimes attended debates, and on two or three occasions he had even spoken briefly on motions related to art or aesthetics about which he had something to say. Because he knew what he was talking about, when most of the other debaters did not, and because he spoke what he believed to be the truth in plain and uncompromising language, he gained a modest reputation as a wit, which amazed him greatly. He was not interested in politics, which was the great preoccupation of the Union, and his interest in the place was chiefly in its dining-room.

In his second year, however, a House Committee that was looking for something significant to do decided that the lamentable state of the frescoes around the walls of the Union's library must be remedied. What was to be done? The budding politicians of the membership knew nothing much about painting, though they were sufficiently aware of the necessity to have some sort of taste to decorate their rooms with reproductions of Van Gogh's *Sunflowers* or—greatly daring—the red horses of Franz Marc. The library frescoes were, they knew, of significance; had they not been done by leaders of the Pre-Raphaelite Brotherhood? This was just the kind of thing the Union liked and understood, for they could make a debate of it: should relics of a dead past be brought back to life, or should the Union advance fearlessly into the future, getting the frescoes replaced by artists of undoubted reputation, but equally undoubted fearless modernity?

The first thing, of course, was to find out if the frescoes could be restored at all, and to this end, guided by a couple of dons who knew something about art, the Union House Committee invited the celebrated Tancred Saraceni to examine them.

The great man appeared, and demanded a ladder, from which he examined the frescoes with a flashlight and picked at them with a penknife; descending, he declared himself ready for lunch.

Francis was not a member of the House Committee but he was invited to lunch because he was supposed, from his three or four brief speeches, to know something about art. Did he not do those drawings, almost but not quite caricatures, for *Isis?* Was he not known to have drawings—"originals", not reproductions—in his rooms? Just the man to talk to Saraceni. And, when asked, he was eager to meet the man who had the reputation of being the greatest restorer of pictures in the world. Even French museums, so reluctant to look outside their own country for art experts, had called upon Saraceni more than once.

Saraceni was small, very dark, and very neat. He did not look particularly like an artist; the only unusual aspect of his appearance was a pair of discreet side-whiskers that crept down beside his ears and stopped modestly just at the point where they could be described as side-whiskers at all. His customary expression was a smile, which was not mirthful, but ironic. Behind spectacles his brown eyes wandered, not perfectly synchronized, so that he sometimes seemed to be looking in two directions at once. He spoke softly and his English was perfect. Too perfect, for it betrayed him as a foreigner.

"The points to be considered are, first, whether the frescoes can be restored at all, and second, are they worth the cost of restoration?" said the President of the Union, who saw himself as a cabinet minister in embryo, and liked clarifying the obvious. "What is your frank opinion, sir?"

"As works of art, their value is very much a matter of debate," said Saraceni, the ironical smile working at full force. "If I restore them, or supervise their restoration, they will appear as they were originally seen when the artists took down their scaffolds seventy-five years ago, and in their restored form they will last for two or three hundred years, if they are properly cared for. But of course then they will be paintings by me, or my pupils, painted precisely as Rossetti and Burne-Jones and Morris originally meant them to be, but in greatly superior paint, on properly prepared surfaces, and sealed with substances that will preserve them from damp, and smoke, and the influences that have turned them into almost incomprehensible smudges. In short, I shall do professionally what the original painters did as virtual amateurs. They knew nothing about painting on walls. They were enthusiasts." He spoke the last word over a tiny giggle.

"But isn't that what restoration always is?" asked another committee member.

"Oh no; a picture that has suffered damage through war, or accident, may be repaired, re-backed, re-painted where nothing of the original remains, but it is still the work of the master, sympathetically and knowledgeably revived. These pictures are ruins, because they were painted in the wrong way with the wrong kind of paint. Faint ghosts of the original paintings remain, but to bring them to life again would mean re-painting, not restoration."

"But you could do that?"

"Certainly. You must understand: I make little claim to being an artist in the romantic sense of

327

that mauled and blurred word. I am a fine crafts-man—the best at my trade, it is said, in the world. I should rely on what craft could do; I should not call upon the Muse, but on a great deal of chemistry and skill. Not that the Muse might not assert herself, now and then. One never knows."

"I don't follow you, sir."

"Well—it is an aspect of my work I do not talk about very much. But if you work on a painting with all your skill, and sympathy, and love, even if you have to re-invent much of it—as would be the case here—something of what directed the first painter may come to your aid."

It was at this point that Francis, who had been listening attentively, felt as though he had been given a sharp, quickening tap on the brow with a tiny hammer.

"Do I understand, Signor Saraceni, that the spirit of the Pre-Raphaelites might infuse you, from time to time, as you worked?"

"Ah—ah—ah! This is why I do not usually speak of such things. People like you, Mr. Cor-nish, may interpret them poetically—may speak of something almost like possession. I have had too much experience to speak so boldly. But consider: these men who painted the pictures we are talking about were poets; better poets than painters, ex-cept for Burne-Jones, and as you probably know he wrote very well. What was their theme? The pictures illustrate The Quest for the Grail, and that is much more a theme for a poet than a painter. Surely one can evoke the Grail spirit better in words than in images? Am I a heretic to say that each art has its sphere of supremacy, and invades another's at its deep peril? Painting that is illustrative of a legend is only that legend at second-best. Pictures that tell a story are useless because they are immobile—they have no movement, no nuance or possibility of change, which is the soul of narrative. I suppose it is not unduly fanciful to think that the poets who made asses of themselves with these old, dirty, obliterated pictures might have something to say to somebody who was a masterly painter, even though he might be no poet?"

"You have known that to happen?"

"Oh yes, Mr. Cornish, and there is nothing spooky about it when it happens, I assure you."

"So we might get these pictures back on our walls as Morris and Rossetti and Burne-Jones would have painted them if they had understood fresco-work?"

"Nobody can say that. Certainly they would be much better pieces of craftsmanship. And such inspiration as the original painters possessed would still be there."

"Surely that answers all our questions," said Francis.

"Oh no. Pardon me, there is one question of the uttermost importance that we have not touched on," said the cabinet-minister-in-embryo. "What would you judge the cost to be?"

"I couldn't tell you, for I have not thoroughly

329

examined the walls under the pictures, or even measured the extent of wall that is covered," said Saraceni. "But I am sure you know the story about the American millionaire who asked another American millionaire what it cost him to maintain his yacht? The second American millionaire said, If you have to ask that question, you can't afford it."

"You mean it might run up to—say, a thousand?"

"Many thousands. There would be no point in doing it any way but the best way, and the best way always runs into money. When I had done my work you would have some enthusiastic illustrations of the Grail Legend, if that is what you want."

That effectively concluded the conversation, though there were further courtesies and assurances of mutual esteem. The House Committee was by no means displeased. It had done something, something no previous committee had done in many years. It could make a report on what it had done. So far as the pictures were concerned it really did not care if they were restored or not. The Union was, after all, a great school for budding politicians and civil servants, and this was how politicians and civil servants worked: they consulted experts and ate lunches and worked up a happy sense of behaving with great practicality. But practicality was against spending much money on art.

Francis, however, was in a high state of excitement, and with the full concurrence of the President—who was glad to have Saraceni taken off his hands, once the issue of the pictures had been settled—he invited the little man to dine with him that evening at the Randolph Hotel.

"Quite clearly, Mr. Cornish, you were the only member of the committee who knew anything about pictures. You also showed keen interest when I spoke of the influence of the original painter on the restorer. Now I must tell you once again that I meant nothing at all mystical by that. I am no spiritualist; the dead do not guide my brush. But consider: in the world of music many composers, when they have completed an opera, rough out the plan of the overture and give it to some trusted, gifted assistant, who writes it so much in the style of the master that experts cannot tell one from t'other. How many passages in Wagner's later work were written by Peter Cornelius? We know, pretty well, but not because the music reveals it.

"It is the same in painting. Just as so many of the great masters entrusted large portions of their pictures to assistants, or apprentices, who painted draperies, or backgrounds, or even hands so well that we cannot tell where their work begins and leaves off, it is possible today for me—I don't say for every restorer—to play the assistant to the dead master and paint convincingly in his style. Some of those assistants, you know, painted copies of masterworks for people who wanted them, but the master did not emphasize that when he presented his bill. And today it is very hard to tell some of those copies from originals. Who painted them? The master or an assistant? The experts quarrel about it all the time.

"I am the heir, not to the masters—I am properly modest, you observe—but to those gifted assistants, some of whom went on to become masters themselves. You see, in the great days of what are now so reverently called the Old Masters, art was a trade as well. The great men kept ateliers which were in effect shops, where you could go and buy anything that pleased you. It was the Romanticism of the nineteenth century that raised the painter quite above trade and made him scorn the shop—he became a child of the Muses. A neglected child, very often, for the Muses are not maternal in the commonplace sense. And as the painter was raised above trade, he often felt himself raised above craftsmanship, like those poor wretches who painted the frescoes we were looking at earlier today. They were full up and slopping over with Art, but they hadn't troubled to master Craft. Result: they couldn't carry out their ideas to their own satisfaction, and their work has dwindled into some dirty walls. Sad, in a way."

"You don't think much of the Pre-Raphaelites."

"The ones with the best ideas, like Rossetti, could hardly draw, let alone paint. Like D. H. Lawrence, in our own time. He had more ideas than any half-dozen admired modern painters, but he couldn't draw and he couldn't paint. Of course, there are fools who say it didn't matter; the conception was everything. Rubbish! A painting isn't a botched conception."

"Is that what's wrong with modern art, then?"

"What's wrong with modern art? The best of it is very fine."

"But so much of it is so puzzling. And some of it's plain messy."

"It is the logical outcome of the art of the Renaissance. During those three centuries, to measure roughly, that we call the Renaissance, the mind of civilized man underwent a radical change. A psychologist would say that it changed from extraversion to introversion. The exploration of the outer world was partnered by a new exploration of the inner world, the subjective world. And it was an exploration that could not depend on the old map of religion. It was the exploration that brought forth *Hamlet*, instead of *Gorboduc*. Man began to look inside himself for all that was great and also—if he was honest, which most people aren't—for all that was ignoble, base, evil. If the artist was a man of scope and genius, he found God and all His works within himself, and painted them for the world to recognize and admire."

"But the moderns don't paint God and all His works. Sometimes I can't make out what they are painting."

"They are painting the inner vision, and working very hard at it when they are honest, which by no means all of them are. But they depend only on themselves, unaided by religion or myth, and of course what most of them find within themselves is revelation only to themselves. And these lonely searches can quickly slide into fakery. Nothing is so easy to fake as the inner vision, Mr. Cornish. Look at those ruined frescoes we were examining this morning; the people who painted those—Rossetti, Morris, Burne-Jones—all had the inner vision linked with legend, and they chose to wrap it up in Grail pictures and sloe-eyed, sexy beauties who were half the Mother of God and half Rossetti's overblown mistresses. But the moderns, having been hit on the head by a horrible world war, and having understood whatever they can of Sigmund Freud, are hell-bent for honesty. They are sick of what they suppose to be God, and they find something in the inner vision that is so personal that to most people it looks like chaos. But it isn't simply chaos. It's raw gobbets of the psyche displayed on canvas. Not very pretty and not very communicative, but they have to find their way through that to something that is communicative—though I wonder if it will be pretty."

"It's hell for anybody who thinks of being an artist."

"As you do? Well—you must find your inner vision."

"That's what I'm trying to do. But it doesn't come out in the modern manner."

"Yes, I understand that. I don't get on very well with the modern manner, either. But I must warn you: don't try to fake the modern manner if it isn't right for you. Find your legend. Find your personal myth. What sort of thing do you do?"

"Might I show you some of my stuff?"

"Certainly, but not now. I must leave first thing in the morning. But I shall be back in Oxford before long. Exeter College wants to consult me about its chapel. I'll let you know in plenty of time, and I shall keep some time for you. Where shall I send a note?"

"My college is Corpus Christi. I pick up letters there. But before you go, won't you have another cognac?"

"Certainly not, Mr. Cornish. Some of the masters drank a great deal, but we assistants and apprentices, even three centuries afterward, must keep our hands steady. I won't have another cognac, and unless you are certain that you are a master, you won't have one either. We must be the austere ones, we second-class men."

It was said with the ironic grin, but for Francis, suckled at least in part on the harsh creed of Victoria Cameron, it was like an order.

Late in the autumn, and not long after his meeting with Saraceni, Francis was surprised and not immediately pleased to receive the following letter:

My dear grandson Francis:

    I have never written to you at Oxford before this, because I did not feel that I had anything to say to a young man who was deep in advanced studies. As you know, my own education was scant, for I had to make my way in the world very young. Education makes a greater gulf in families even than making a lot of money. What has the uneducated grandfather to say to the educated grandson? But there are one or two languages I hope we still speak in common.

One is the language, which I cannot put a name to, that you and I shared when you were a lad, and used to come on afternoon jaunts with me, making the sun-pictures with my camera. It was a language of the eye, and also I think chiefly a language of light, and it gives me the greatest satisfaction to think that perhaps your turn for painting and your interest in pictures had a beginning, or at least some encouragement, there. You now speak that language as I never did. I am proud of your inclination toward art, and hope it will carry you through a happy life.

Another language is something I won't call religion, because all through my life I have been a firm Catholic, without truly accepting everything a Catholic ought to believe. So I cannot urge you sincerely to cling to the Faith. But don't forget it, either. Don't forget that language, and don't be one of those handless fellows who believes nothing. There is a fine world unknown to us, and religion is an attempt to explain it. But, unhappily, to reach everybody religion has to be an organization, and a trade for a lot of its priests, and worst of all it has to be reduced to what the largest mass of people will accept and can be expected to understand. That's heresy, of course. I remember how angry I was when your father demanded that you be raised a Protestant. But that was a while since, and in the meantime I have wondered if the Prots are really any bigger turnip-heads than the R.C.s. As you grow old, religion becomes a lonely business.

The third language we speak in common is money, and it is because of that I am writing to you now. Money is a language I speak better than you do, but you must learn something of the grammar of money, or you cannot manage what your luck has brought you as my grandson. This is much on my mind now, because the doctors tell me that I have not a great way farther to go. Something to do with the heart.

When my will is executed, you will find that I have left you a substantial sum, for your exclusive use, apart from what you will share with my other descendants. The reason I give in my will is that you do not seem to me to be suited by nature to the family business, which is the banking and trust business, and that therefore you must not look for employment or advancement there. This looks almost like cutting you out, but that is not so at all. And this is between us: the money will set you free, I hope, from many anxieties and from a kind of employment that I do not think you would like, but only if you master the grammar of money. Money illiteracy is as restrictive as any other illiteracy. Your brother Arthur promises well as a banker, and in that work he will have opportunities to make money that will not come your way. But you will have another kind of chance. I hope this will suit your purpose.

Do not reply to this letter, for I may not be able to deal with my own letters for very long, and I do not want anyone else to read what you might say. Though if you chose to write a farewell, I should be glad of that.

With affct. good wishes . . .
James Ignatius McRory

Francis wrote a farewell at once, and did his utmost with it, though he was no more a master of the pen than his grandfather; lacked, indeed, the old man's self-taught simplicity. But a telegram told him that it came too late.

Was there anything to be done? He wrote to Grand'mère and Aunt Mary-Ben, and he wrote to his mother. He considered going to Father Knollys at the Old Palace and asking for—and paying for—a requiem mass for his grandfather, but in the light of what the letter had said he thought that would be hypocritical and would make the old colonial laugh, if he knew.

Was his feeling of grief hypocritical? It struggled in his heart with a sense of release, and new freedom, a feeling of joy that he could now do with his life what he liked. His grief for the old Scots woodsman quickly turned to elation and gratitude. Hamish was the only one of his family who had ever really looked at him, and considered what he was. The only one of the whole lot, perhaps, who had ever loved the artist in him.

Christmas was drawing near, and Francis decided that duty called him back to Canada. After one of those penitential mid-winter sea voyages across the Atlantic he was once again in the up-to-the-minute decor of his mother's house, and little by little became aware of what his grandfather had meant to the Cornishes and the McRorys, and the O'Gormans. To the bankers a real regard for the old man was greatly tempered by the delightful business of administering his affairs. He seemed more splendid in death than he had ever been in life. Gerald Vincent O'Gorman in particular was loud in his praise for the way the old man had disposed of his estate. There was something for everybody. This was a Christmas indeed!

Gerry O'Gorman was understandably better pleased than was Sir Francis Cornish, for Gerry now succeeded his father-in-law as Chairman of the Board, while Sir Francis remained in his honourable but less powerful place as President. But then Lady Cornish inherited substantially, which was very agreeable to Sir Francis, and took much of the salt out of the tears of his wife. Even Francis's younger brother, Arthur, who was just twelve, seemed enlarged by Grand-père's death, for his future in the Cornish Trust, always sure, was now clearer than it had been before, and Arthur, at school, was taking on the air of a young financier, stylish, handsome, well-dressed, and adroit in his dealing with contemporaries and elders.

The stricken ones, of course, were Grand'mère and Mary-Ben, but even they had their benefit from the Senator's death; had not Reverend Mother Mary-Basil from Montreal, and His Grace the Rev. Michael McRory from his archdiocese in the West, come to Blairlogie for the funeral, and stayed on to visit the two old women, dispensing comfort and good counsel that was none the less sweet for the handsome remembrances the Senator had made of his brother and sister in the great will.

The will! It seemed that they talked of nothing but the will, and the part that Francis played in it, singularized as he was by the largest of all the personal bequests (his mother and Mary-Tess were beneficiaries of a special trust), surprised and puzzled his family. It was Gerry O'Gorman who summed it up briefly and bluntly: you would think Frank could study art on less than the income from a cool million.

Not that he was just to have the income; the old man had left it to him outright. Now, what would Frank know about handling money in that quantity? But Francis remembered what his grandfather had said about learning the grammar of money, and before he took the dismal voyage back to Oxford he had given directions as to what was to be done with his money when it became available, and even Gerry had to admit that he had handled it well.

So Francis returned to Corpus Christi and Canterbury House, and the inner rooms of the Ashmolean, a rich man, in terms of what he was and what responsibilities he had. Rich, and with the prospect of being richer, for his grandfather had made him a participant in that family trust which at the moment carried Grand'mère, and Aunt, and his mother and Mary-Tess, and as these died off his portion would increase. You're sitting pretty, boy, said Gerry, and Sir Francis, putting it with the dignity of a President, said that his future was assured.

How quick people are to say that someone's future is assured when they mean only that he has enough money to live on! What young man of twenty-four thinks of his future as assured? In one respect, Francis knew that his future was painfully uncertain.

He had known something of girls at Spook—a little hugging and tugging at parties, though the girls of that time were cautious about what he still thought of as The Limit. He had experienced The Limit in a Toronto brothel with a thick-legged woman who came from a country district—a township—not inappropriately named Dummer, and for a month afterward he had fretted and fussed and examined himself for the marks of syphilis, until a doctor assured him that he was as clean as

341

a whistle. On these slender experiences he was sure he knew a good deal about sex, but of love he had no conception. Now he was in love with his cousin Ismay Glasson, and she was plainly not in love with him.

Perhaps she was in love with Charlie Fremantle. He met them together often, and when he was with her she talked a good deal about Charlie. Charlie found Oxford painfully confining; he wanted to get out into the world and change it for the better, whether the world wanted it or not. He had advanced political ideas. He had read Marx—though not a great deal of him, for Charlie found thick, dense books a clog upon his soaring spirit. He had made a few Marxist speeches at the Union, and was admired by other untrammelled spirits like himself. His Marxism could be summed up as a conviction that whatever was, was wrong, and that the destruction of the existing order was the inevitable preamble to any beginning of the just society; the hope of the future lay with the workers, and all the workers needed was sympathetic leadership by people like himself, who had seen through the hypocrisy, stupidity, and bloody-mindedness of the upper class into which they themselves had been born. In all of this Ismay was his submissive disciple. If anything, she was even more vehement than he against the old (people over thirty) who had made such a mess of affairs. Of course, they dressed their ideas up in language more politically resonant than this, and they had plenty of books—or Ismay had—that supported their emotions, which they called their principles.

Charlie was just twenty-one and Ismay was nineteen. Francis, who was twenty-four, felt middle-aged and dull when he listened to them. His was not a political mind, nor was he quick in argument, but he was convinced that something was wrong with Charlie's philosophy. Charlie had not spent three years at Carlyle Rural, or he might have thought differently about the aspirations and potentialities of the workers. Charlie's grandfather had not hacked his way out of the forest and into the seat of a Chairman of the Board with a woodsman's broadaxe. Educate the workers, said Charlie, and you will see the world changed within three generations. Thinking of Miss McGladdery, Francis was not so sure the workers took readily to education or to any change that went beyond their immediate and obvious betterment. Charlie was a Canadian like himself, but Charlie's family were Old Money. Francis had seen enough of Old Money at Colborne College to know that hypocrisy, stupidity, and bloody-mindedness were just as natural to that class as Charlie said they were. Francis was cursed with an ability, not great but real, to see both sides of the question. It never occurred to him that three years in age might make a difference in Charlie's outlook, and certainly it never entered his head that he himself had the temperament of the artist, detesting both high and low, and anxious only to be let alone to get on with his own work. Charlie was the upper

343

class flinging itself into the struggle for justice on behalf of the oppressed; Charlie was Byron, determined to free the Greeks without having any clear notion of what or who the Greeks were; Charlie was a Grail knight of social justice.

Francis cared little what might happen to Charlie, but he grieved and brooded over Ismay. He had a strong intuition that Charlie was a bad influence, and the more he saw of Charlie at Buys-Bozzaris's gambling sessions the stronger that intuition became. There were now too many regulars at the evening sessions for bridge, and the game had become poker; for poker Charlie had no aptitude at all. Not only was he a rash gambler; he delighted in the role of the rash gambler. He seemed almost to claw his chips toward him; he flung down his cards with an air of defiance; he took stupid risks—and lost. He did not pay, he gave IOUs which Buys-Bozzaris tucked in his waistcoat pocket almost as if he did not notice them. Francis knew quite enough of the grammar of money to know that an IOU is a very dangerous scrap of paper. Worst of all, on the rare occasions when Charlie won, he exulted in an unseemly way, as if by pillaging the Oxonians around him he was vindicating the have-not class. Francis fretted about Charlie, without quite seeing that Charlie was a fool and a gull. For Charlie had something that looked like romantic sweep and dash, and these were qualities that Francis knew he lacked utterly.

He saw a lot of Ismay, for Ismay was drawn by

344

the easy glasses of excellent sherry, the meals at the George, the visits to the cinema and the theatre that Francis could provide, and was eager to provide. Ismay was even willing to let Francis kiss her and paw her (paw was her expression when she was impatient and wanted him to stop) as a reasonable return for the luxuries he commanded. This gave Francis even deeper anxiety; if she allowed him such liberties, what did she permit to Charlie?

He was miserable, as only a worried lover can be, but his love had another and happier aspect. Ismay was willing to pose for drawings, and he did many sketches of her.

When he had completed a particularly good one she said: "Oh, may I have that?"

"It's not much more than a study. Let me try for a really good one."

"No, this is terrific. Charlie would love it."

Charlie did not love it. He was furious and tore it up, and made Ismay cry—she did not often cry—because he said he would not have that oaf Cornish looking at her in the way the sketch made it very clear that he did look at her—as a lover, an adorer.

Ismay, however, rather enjoyed Charlie's pique, so much more fiery than Francis's sluggish jealousy, disguised as concern, so stuffy and possessive. So things went further, and when one day Francis worked himself up to the pitch of asking Ismay if he might draw her in the nude, she consented. He was overjoyed, until she said, "But none of the old Artists-and-Models-in-Paris stuff, you understand?" which he thought reflected on his phlegmatic, objective artist's attitude toward the unclothed figure. He admitted to himself that Ismay had a coarse streak—but that was part of her irresistible allurement. Coarse, like some splendid woman of the Renaissance aristocracy.

So he sketched Ismay in the nude, as she lay on the sofa in his sitting-room on the top floor of Canterbury House, where the light was so good and the coal fire kept the room so warm, and on many subsequent occasions he sketched her in the nude, and though his excellent experience in Mr. Devinney's embalming parlour enabled him to do it very well, the thought of all those work-worn corpses never entered his head.

One day, when he had finished a good effort, he threw down his pad and pencil and knelt beside her on the sofa, kissing her hands and trying to keep back the tears that rushed to his eyes.

"What is it?"

"You are so beautiful, and I love you so much."

"Oh Christ," said Ismay. "I thought it might come to this."

"To what?"

"To talk about love, you prize ass."

"But I do love you. Have you no feeling for me at all?"

Ismay leaned toward him, and his face was buried between her breasts. "Yes," she said. "I love you, Frank—but I'm not in love with you, if you understand."

This is a nice distinction, dear to some female hearts, which people like Francis can never encompass. But he was happy, for had she not said she loved him? Being in love might follow. So, when he had agreed to her condition that he must not talk about love, it was decided by Ismay that the afternoons of posing in the nude might continue from time to time. She liked it. It gave her a sense of living fully and richly, and Francis's adoring eyes warmed her in places where the glow of his generous coal fire could not reach—places that Charlie did not seem to know existed.

Who taught you to draw? In one of the guest-rooms at Exeter, where he was staying for a few days in the Spring Term, Saraceni was looking over the sketches and finished pictures that Francis had brought him.

"Harry Furniss, I suppose."

"Extraordinary! Just possible, but—he died—let me see—surely more than ten years ago!"

"But only from a book. *How to Draw in Pen and Ink*—it was my Bible when I was a boy."

"Well, you have his vigour, but not his coarse style—his jokey, jolly-good-fellow superficial style."

"Of course, I've done a great deal of copying since those days, as you can see. I copy Old Master drawings, at the Ashmolean every week. I try to capture their manner as well as their matter. As you said you did when you restored pictures."

"Yes, and you didn't learn anatomy from Harry Furniss, or from copying."

"I picked it up in an embalming parlour, as a matter of fact."

"Mother of God! There is a good deal more in you than meets the eye, Mr. Cornish."

"I hope so. What meets the eye doesn't make much impression, I'm afraid."

"There speaks a man in love. Unhappily in love. In love with this model for these nude studies that you have been trying to palm off on me as some of your Old Master copies."

Saraceni laid his hand on a group of drawings of Ismay that had cost Francis great pains. He had coated an expensive handmade paper with Chinese white mixed with enough brown bole to give it an ivory tint, and on the sheets thus prepared he had worked up some of his sketches of the nude Ismay, drawing with a silver-point that had cost him a substantial sum, touching up the drawing at last with red chalk.

"I didn't mean to deceive you."

"Oh, you didn't deceive me, Mr. Cornish, though you might deceive a good many people."

"I mean I wasn't trying to deceive anybody. Only to work in the genuine Renaissance style."

"And you have done so. You have imitated the manner admirably. But you haven't been so careful about the matter. This girl, now: she is a girl of today. Everything about her figure declares it.

Slim, tall for a woman, long legs—this is not a woman of the Renaissance. Her feet alone give the show away; neither the big feet of the peasant model nor the deformed feet of a woman of fortune. The Old Masters, you know, when they weren't copying from the antique, were drawing women of a kind we do not see today. This girl, now—look at her breasts. She will probably never suckle a child, or not for long. But the women of the Renaissance did so, and their painters fancied the great motherly udders; as soon as those women had given up their virginity they seemed to be always giving suck, and by thirty-five they had flat, exhausted bladders hanging to their waists. Their private parts were torn with child-bearing, and I suppose a lot of them had piles for the same reason. Age came early in those days. The flesh that showed such rosy opulence at eighteen had lost its glow, and fat hung on bones far too small to support it well. This girl of yours will be a beauty all her life. This is the beauty you have captured with a tenderness that suggests a lover.

"I am not pretending to be clairvoyant. Looking deep into pictures is my profession. It is simple enough to see that this model is a woman of today, and the attitude of the artist to his sitter is always apparent in the picture. Every picture is several things: what the artist sees, but also what he thinks about what he sees, and because of that, in a certain sense it is a portrait of himself. All those elements are here.

"None of this is to say that this is not good

work. But why go to such pains to work in the Renaissance style?"

"It seems to me to be capable of saying so much that can't be said—or I should say that can't be said by me—in a contemporary manner."

"Yes, yes, and to compliment the sitter—I hope she is grateful—and to show that you see her as beyond time and place. You draw pretty well. Drawing is not so lovingly fostered now as it used to be. A modern artist may be a fine draughtsman without depending much on his skill. You love drawing simply for itself."

"Yes. It sounds extreme, but it's an obsession with me."

"More than colour?"

"I don't know, I haven't really done much about colour."

"I could introduce you to that, you know. But I wonder how good a draughtsman you really are. Would you submit to a test?"

"I'd be flattered that you thought it worth your trouble."

"Taking trouble is much of my profession, also. You have your pad? Draw a straight line from the top of the page to the bottom, will you? And I mean a *straight* line, done freehand."

Francis obeyed.

"Now: draw the same line from the bottom to the top, so exactly that the two lines are one."

This was not so easily done. At one point Francis's line varied a fraction from the first one.

"Ah, that was not simple, was it? Now draw a

line across the page to bisect that line—or I should say those two indistinguishable lines. Yes. Now draw a line through the centre point where those two lines bisect; draw it so that I cannot see a hint of a triangle at the middle point. Yes, that is not bad."

The next part of the test was the drawing of circles, freehand, clockwise and anti-clockwise, concentric and in various ways eccentric. Francis managed all of this with credit, but without perfection.

"You should work on this sort of thing," said Saraceni. "You have ability, but you have not refined it to the full extent of your capabilities. This is the foundation of drawing, you must understand. Now, will you try a final test? This is rather more than command of the pencil; it is to test your understanding of mass and space. I shall sit here in this chair, as I have been doing, and you shall draw me as well as you can in five minutes. But you shall draw me as I would look if you were sitting behind me. Ready?"

Francis was wholly unprepared for this, and felt that he made a mess of it. But when Saraceni looked at the result, he laughed.

"If you think you might be interested in my profession, Mr. Cornish—and I assure you it is full of interest—write to me, or come and see me. Here is my card; my permanent address, as you see, is in Rome, though I am not often there; but it would reach me. Come and see me anyhow. I have some things that would interest you."

351

"You mean I might become a restorer of old paintings?" said Francis.

"You certainly could do so, after you had worked with me. But I see you do not take that as a compliment; it suggests that your talent is not first-rate. Well, you asked me for an opinion, and you shall have it. Your talent is substantial, but not first-rate."

"What's wrong?"

"A lack of a certain important kind of energy. Not enough is coming up from below. There are dozens of respected artists in this country and elsewhere who cannot begin to draw as well as you, and who have certainly not as fine an eye as you, but they have something individual about their work, even when it looks crude and stupid to the uninstructed eye. What they have is what comes from below. Are you a Catholic?"

"Well—partly, I suppose."

"I might have known. You must either be a Catholic, or not be one. The half-Catholics are not meant to be artists, any more than the half-anything-elses. Good night, Mr. Cornish. Let us meet again."

"What would you like for your birthday?"

"Money, please."

"But Ismay, money isn't a present. I want to give you something real."

"What's unreal about money?"

"Will you promise to buy something you really want?"

"Frank, what do you expect me to do with it?"

So Francis gave her a cheque for ten pounds. When Charlie came to Buys-Bozzaris's poker-night two days later with ten pounds to risk, Francis was immediately suspicious.

"Did you give Charlie that ten quid?"

"Yes. He was in a hole."

"But I meant it for you!"

"Charlie and I believe in property in common."

"Oh? And what does Charlie share with you?"

"What right have you to ask that?"

"Damn it, Ismay, I love you. I've told you so more times than I can count."

"I think the porter at the Examination Schools loves me; he always looks sheepish when I speak to him. But that doesn't give him the right to ask me about my private life."

"Don't talk like a fool."

"All right, I won't. You think I'm sleeping with Charlie, don't you? If I were—and I don't say I am—what would it be to you? Aren't you pushing the cousin thing a bit far?"

"It isn't the cousin thing."

"Do you remember what you said, the first time you spoke to me? 'Marry come up, m'dirty cousin.' I said I'd trace that, and I have. A chap in Eng.Lit. ran it down for me. It's from an old play: 'Marry come up, m'dirty Cousin; he may have such as you by the Dozen.' Is that what you mean, Frank? Do you think I'm a whore?"

"I never heard that; I just thought it was something you said to pushy people. And you were very pushy and you still are. But not a whore. Certainly not a whore."

"No; not a whore. But Charlie and I have ideas far beyond yours. You've some frightfully back-woods notions, Frank. You must understand: I won't be questioned and I won't be uncled by you. If that's the way you want it, we're through."

Apologies. Protestations of lover-like concern for her welfare—which made her laugh. An expensive lunch at the George. An afternoon during which she posed for him again; before they settled to work, Ismay struck a number of whorish poses which tormented him, and made her laugh at his torment. And before she went, he gave her another cheque for ten pounds, because she must have a present for herself, and no, no, no, don't stake Charlie at poker if you really care for him at all, because it will be his ruin.

What Ismay bought with the cheque Francis never knew, for he dared not ask her, and he knew from his bank statement that the cheque was not cashed. Doubtless she was keeping it until something appeared that she really wanted.

What Basil Buys-Bozzaris wanted was becoming clear. After the poker sessions he always asked Francis to stay and talk for a while, and as they lived in the same house there was no need for Francis to leave before midnight; they were free of the rule governing all junior members of the University, who must be in their lodgings or their colleges by midnight, or risk expulsion. Roskalns

354

stayed, as well, because he was not a member of the University, and could come and go as he pleased. And what was the drift of the talk?

Francis understood it long before Buys-Bozzaris knew that he did. The count (if he were a count) from Bulgaria (if that were his place of origin) had what he called advanced political ideas, and although these were not so naive as Charlie's, they tended in Charlie's direction. It was not difficult to broach such subjects at Oxford at that time, where it was common talk among shoals of undergraduates that the political world was, in the popular expression, "polarized". Democracy had failed, and its forms of government might be expected to collapse at any time. Everybody with a head on his shoulders was aware, whether he formulated the thought clearly or not, that he was either a fascist or a communist, and if his head was a good head, there was only one choice. Not to take a side was to be an "indifferentist", and when the show-down came the indifferentists would surely suffer for their foolishness. Buys-Bozzaris knew which way the cat would jump.

Certainly this political cat would not jump toward fascism, which was essentially a bourgeois concept, under the guidance of people like Hitler and Mussolini who wanted to found strong nations—even empires—on the impossible foundations of some version of capitalism. Only a Marxist world, which was to say a world in which the primary doctrines of Marx had been refined and hammered out through trial and error, had any

355

chance of survival. Was it not time for anybody who had his eye on that jumping cat to throw in his lot with the side that would dominate the civilized world, probably in less than ten years? Wasn't it every intelligent man's duty to push things along?

Francis could be of help, perhaps of very great help, but until he had made a firm decision, it was not possible for Buys-Bozzaris to say precisely how it was to be done. Francis was, as Buys-Bozzaris knew—oh, yes, he was not so much the simple student of international law as a casual observer might think—a young man with a certain background. He had money; that was easily to be seen, if you knew what money was, and Buys-Bozzaris knew. He had an invaluable possession in his Canadian citizenship and his Canadian passport, because with those credentials he could go almost anywhere without arousing suspicion. Surely Francis knew that Canadian passports were greatly valued in the world of international espionage? The genuine article, capable of surviving any amount of probing, was a gift of the gods. If Francis chose, he could be immensely useful, and in the course of time his usefulness would not go unrewarded. Had Francis any idea what he was talking about?

Francis admitted that he could dimly guess what lay behind such conversation. But it was such a novel idea. He needed time to think. Gee, it had never been put to him quite that way before. (Francis thought "Gee" a good stroke; it

356

was just what somebody like Buys-Bozzaris would expect a Canadian to say, when the heavens of political opportunity were opened to him.) Could they talk further? He had to get it sorted out, and in such matters as this, he was a slow thinker.

Take plenty of time, said Buys-Bozzaris.

Francis did take plenty of time. He did not want to attract the attention of the Bulgarian count, who seemed to watch all his comings and goings, by doing anything uncommon. So he waited until the Easter vacation to meet Colonel Copplestone and tell him all he knew. Once again they lunched at the Athenaeum. Francis understood that the Colonel thought a crowded room, with lots of noise, the best place for confidences. Two people leaning across a table, talking as quietly as possible, attracted no attention. The Colonel listened to all he had to say.

"Your man is quite well known to the profession," he said, when Francis had finished. "Not a very serious person. Rather an ass, in fact. Quite a common type; he has no important contact with the people he talks about, and no real influence. But he likes to suggest that he has a lot of power. Of course, he scorns the out-in-the-open student Communist group: he likes subtlety and secrecy and all the allurement of the classy spy. He isn't one, believe me. Your fellow-Canadian is much more interesting, really. Hot-heads like that can reveal quite a lot by what they do, or try to do, rather than what they know. Keep me posted."

"I'm sorry not to have been more useful," said Francis. This was his first attempt to show that he was worthy of the profession, and it was disappointing to find that he had not really uncovered anything.

"Oh, but you have been useful," said the Colonel. "You've corroborated some information, and that's useful. My job needs an enormous amount of work that isn't at all dramatic, you know. Don't be influenced by novels that suggest that extraordinary things are done by some wonderful chap working entirely on his own."

"Aren't there any wonderful chaps?"

"There may be. But there are far more who just get on quietly, noticing something here, something there, corroborating something for the fifteenth time."

"Wasn't Father wonderful?"

"You should ask him. I can guess what he'd tell you. His best work was understanding and collating things he heard from dozens of chaps who were doing what you're doing. He was awfully good at putting two and two together."

"And I'm likely to go on doing this for quite a while?"

"Quite a while, I should say. Yes."

"I'm not likely to be a permanency, then?"

"Paid, you mean. Oh, my dear fellow, don't be silly. Chaps with incomes like yours don't get paid for the kind of thing you're doing."

"I see. That seems to be the English way. A while ago I was talking to the chief of the curators of the Ashmolean, asking if there were any chance of my getting an appointment there when I've taken my degree. 'What private income have you?' he asked, very first thing. Listen, Uncle Jack, suppose BBB were to offer me a job—a job with money—wouldn't it be a temptation?"

"Not if you've got any brains at all. He won't, you know, but if he did, you should tell me at once. Because you'd never get away with it. You aren't as much alone, or as unknown, as you might suppose. But why are you fussing about money? You've got plenty, haven't you?"

"Yes, but everybody seems to think I'm to be had cheap. Everybody thinks I'm a money-bags. Haven't I any value, apart from my money?"

"Of course you have. Would I be talking to you now if you hadn't? But nobody gets rich in the profession. And nobody who is once in it—even as far in as you are, which isn't far—ever quite gets out of it. Do you think for a moment that your man has lashings of money from his side, to pass out to people like you? He's probably being squeezed, and that can be very uncomfortable. Now, you just get on with what you're doing, and if the time ever comes when we should talk about money, I'll bring the subject up myself."

"Very sorry, Uncle Jack."

"Don't mention it, Francis. And I mean that in every sense of the words."

There had been a look in Colonel Copplestone's eye that surprised and humbled Francis. The benevolent uncle had suddenly turned tough.

It was the fourth week of the Oxford summer term; Trinity Term, as the ancient custom of the University called it.

It was Eights Week, when the colleges raced their boats to determine which college should be Head of the River. Francis was taking a leaf out of Colonel Copplestone's book, and he was having a very important conversation with Ismay in the open air, sitting comfortably on the upper deck of the Corpus barge, amid a din of cheering, as they ate strawberries and cream and watched the sweating oarsmen.

"I had a queer message from my bank a couple of days ago."

"I never get anything but queer messages from my bank."

"I'm not surprised if you go on the way you're going."

"Meaning what?"

"I think you know very well what. A cheque made out to you and signed by me, for a hundred and fifty pounds."

Ismay seemed to be chewing a difficult strawberry. "What did they say?"

"Called me in to have a look at it and inquire a little."

"What did you say?"

"Oh, we just chatted. Banker and client, you know."

"Frank, you've got to understand about this.

My bank cashed the cheque and I haven't got the money."

"I didn't suppose you had. Charlie's got it, hasn't he?"

"Do we have to talk here?"

"Why not? Just keep your voice down, and if you have anything particularly important to say, whisper it when I'm shouting 'Well rowed, Corpus!' I'll hear you. I have excellent hearing."

"Oh for God's sake don't be so facetious! Do you suppose I'm a forger?"

"Yes. And if you want to know, I've suspected it for some time. Do you think I was taken in when you admired my elegant Italic hand suddenly, and wanted me to show you how it was done? You're one of Nature's scrawlers, Ismay; if you wanted to learn Italic, it was so you could write like me. Enough to change a cheque, for instance. And why would you want to do that, you little twister?"

"Why did the bank ask you, anyway?"

"The banks all have an agreement with the Proctors that if a junior member of the University cashes a particularly big cheque they will tip the Proctors off. It's a way of keeping an eye on gambling. I suppose the money went to pay off Charlie's debts to Buys-Bozzaris?"

"It will. But you've got to understand; Charlie was being threatened."

"By the fat count? Don't be funny."

"No, by some other chaps—real thugs. Frank, Buys-Bozzaris is a crook."

"You amaze me! Crooks on all sides! You make me tremble!"

"Oh, for God's sake be serious!"

"I am serious. These races stir the blood. Listen to those people shouting, 'Well rowed, Balliol!' Doesn't that excite you?"

"Some terrible toughs came to see Charlie and threatened him. They had all his IOUs that he gave to Buys-Bozzaris. That fat bugger had sold them!"

"Mind your language. This is the barge of the College of Corpus Christi, and we must not disgrace our sacred name. Are you surprised that BBB sold the IOUs? I suppose he needed ready cash and sold them at a discount."

"I've never heard of anything like it!"

"Oh, but you will, Ismay, you will. When you've gone a little farther in the forging game, you'll hear some things that will astonish you. The conversation in prison is most illuminating, I'm told."

"Be serious, Frank. Please!"

"I can be awfully serious about a hundred and fifty nicker. That's an underworld expression, by the way; you'll pick up the lingo soon."

"What did you tell the bank about the cheque?"

"As they'd cashed it, I didn't think I needed to say much. They were looking very coy, you know the way bankers do when they think you're a perfect devil of a fellow."

"You mean you didn't tell?"

"And shame my bank? When you had done

such a lovely job, neatly transforming that birthday cheque for ten quid? How could they have faced me, if I'd told them it was a forgery?"

"Oh, Frank, you are a darling!"

"A darling or a complete mug, do you mean?"

"Well—it was one of those tight squeezes. I'll make it up to you, honestly I will."

"Honestly you will? What could you do honestly, Ismay? Sleep with me, do you suppose?"

"If that's what you want."

"You know it's what I want. But not with a price on it, the price being Charlie's skin. I don't think that would have quite the right romantic savour, do you? Though, let's see: woman sacrifices herself to the lust of her wealthy pursuer, to save the honour of her lover. Rather good, isn't it? Only I don't like the casting; either I'm the lover and Charlie is the villain, or it's no deal. May I get you some more strawberries?"

Francis was looking forward to his visit to Buys-Bozzaris. His confusion and ineptitude which had made it impossible to cope with a blow in the face or a kick in the rump at Carlyle Rural was long behind him; he was prepared to be moderately rough with the fat count if that should be necessary. His banker's blood, which he had not known he possessed, was running hot, and he wanted his money. After dinner at Corpus he made his way the short distance back to Canterbury House, and knocked on the familiar door.

"Cornish? Happy to see you. Let me give you a

drink. Am I to suppose that you have made up your mind about joining us in our political work? You can talk freely. Roskalns here is one of us, and this isn't a poker-night, so nobody else is likely to drop in."

"I've come about those IOUs that Charlie Fremantle gave you."

"Oh—no need to worry. That's all over. Charlie has paid, like an honest chap."

"Come on, Basil. You flogged those notes."

"Well—same thing, isn't it? Charlie is clear."

"No, Charlie bloody well isn't clear. The money to pay came from a cheque that was forged in my name. I want a hundred and fifty pounds from you."

"A hundred and fifty—Oh, come, Cornish, Charlie owed me exactly ninety-seven pounds, fourteen and elevenpence, and I haven't had it yet. I am expecting a visit from the collectors, this evening, as a matter of fact. Did that naughty boy sophisticate a cheque for a hundred and fifty? That wasn't very honest of him, was it?"

"No, and it wasn't very honest of you to give those notes to collectors, as you call them, who are shaking Charlie down for a hundred and fifty, out of which you will presumably get your ninety-seven, fourteen and eleven. I want the names of those fellows. I'm going to turn them over to the Proctors."

"Now, now, Cornish, you're heated. You wouldn't do that. There are rules, unwritten rules, among gentlemen about debts of this sort. Not bringing in the Proggins is almost Rule Number One. Of course Rule Number One is, always pay up."

"But not with my money."

"What about *my* money? Why are you talking to me? Talk to Charlie. He's the naughty boy."

"I'll certainly talk to Charlie. But I'm out a hundred and fifty, and I thought you might have been paid already."

"Not a bean. I'm waiting, as I told you. And I shall have something to say to those collectors. A hundred and fifty pounds for a debt of ninety-seven, fourteen and eleven. It's outrageous!"

"Yes, and so is selling IOUs. Why didn't you collect yourself?"

"Oh, Cornish, you're impossible. One has a certain position. One doesn't go about with a little greasy book, rapping on doors. Or do they, where you come from?"

"Never mind where I come from."

This might have become rancorous, if there had not been a tap on the door. If Francis had not been so busy with Buys-Bozzaris, he could have heard shuffling and whispering out-side. Roskalns answered, tried to shut the door after he had peeped through a crack, and was flung backward, as two determined men thrust their way in. In Oxford there are several gradations of society: members of the University, in all their diversity, attendants and servants of members of the University, in all *their* diver-sity, and people who are not associated with the University, who are also various, but look entirely different from the other two classes. These men were very plainly of class number three.

"Look here, Mr. Booze-Bozzaris, this will never do. Young Fremantle has scarpered."

"You mean he has gone?"

"What I said. Scarpered."

"I don't understand."

"Well then, let me put you straight. We visited him, as per arrangement, and he said, gimme a little time to get the money together, and we said rightyho, but no funny stuff, see? Let's have it, and in cash. Because we are well aware that there can be dishonesty in these matters of collection, and we didn't want none of that. So we kept an eye on the place, and he came and went, and came and went, quite normal. It's one of the colleges he's in; New College. Whenever we inquires, the porter says he's in. But those fellows would say anything. When we didn't see him yesterday we went quiet up to his rooms, and the long and short of it is, he scarpered."

"You're telling me you can't pay me?"

"What do you mean, pay you, Mr. Booze-Bozzaris? We paid you fifty quid on account for those notes, agreeing to make up the rest of the ninety-seven, fourteen and eleven after we'd collected from Fremantle—"

"After you collected a hundred and fifty quid from him, you mean," said Buys-Bozzaris.

"That's by the way. We have to have something for our trouble and risk, haven't we? But now we shall have to ask for that fifty quid back, because we been diddled."

"But not by me."

"Never mind who by. Let's have it."

"Don't be absurd."

"Now look, Mr. Booze-Bozzaris, we don't want trouble in any shape nor form, but it's pay up now or my colleague here may have to do a little persuading."

The colleague, who said nothing, cleared his throat softly, and flexed his hands, rather like a pianist. For the first time the collector who did the talking spoke to Francis. "You'll want to leave, sir," he said; "this is just some private business."

"Not private from me," said Francis. "I have some money to recover from Charlie myself."

"This is getting too complicated altogether," said the collector. "We got no time to waste. Now just stand perfectly still, Mr. Booze-Bozzaris, and you two other gents keep out of the way, while my colleague makes a search that will be perfectly polite and easy, so long as there is no resistance."

The colleague moved toward Basil gently but firmly, his hands extended as if he might be going to tickle him. Buys-Bozzaris backed toward a corner, and as he did so his hand went to the pocket of his jacket.

"Oh no you don't!" said the talking collector. The colleague seized the arm that Buys-Bozzaris jerked upward. The pistol caught in the top of his pocket, went off with a roar that was like a cannon in the room, and Buys-Bozzaris fell to the floor with a scream that was louder still.

"Christ! Shot himself!" said the collector.

"Shot off his goolies!" said the colleague, speaking for the first time. The two rushed to the door, through the small hall and into the street, and were gone.

Gunfire in Oxford is uncommon. The University Statutes strictly forbid it. In a few seconds Mr. Tasnim Khan from the first floor, Mr. Westerby from the second, Mr. Colney-Overend from across the hall, and the landlord were all in the room, shouting contradictory advice. It was Francis who lugged Buys-Bozzaris into a chair, and it became apparent that he had shot himself, not very seriously, in the foot.

Half an hour later the injured man, moaning like a cow in labour, had been taken by Roskalns to the Radcliffe Infirmary in a taxi. Francis had been with the landlord to hunt up the Proctors, and give an account of the affair which said only that two men had visited the Bulgarian, demanded money related apparently to a debt, that nobody had fired a gun at anyone, and the wound was pure accident. The Junior Proctor, who heard it all, raised his eyebrows at the word "pure", took names, warned Francis not to leave Oxford until the matter had been fully investigated, and called the hospital to say that Buys-Bozzaris was not to be released until he had been questioned.

Francis went to Lady Margaret Hall, where, as

368

it still lacked a quarter of an hour before the closing of the gate, he was able to have a short talk with Ismay.

"Oh yes, Charlie's scarpered. I knew he would."

"Where's he gone?"

"I don't suppose it matters if you know, because he won't be back and he won't be found. He's gone to Spain to join the Cause."

"Which of the many possible Causes would that be?"

"The Loyalists, obviously. Thinking as he does."

"Well—at least your name hasn't been mentioned. And won't be, if you have enough sense to keep your mouth shut."

"Thanks, Frank. You're sweet."

"That's what I'm beginning to be afraid of."

Being sweet might mean being a gull, but there were compensations. Francis was invited by his Aunt Prudence Glasson to spend a fortnight at St. Columb Hall, the Glasson family seat, when the Oxford term ended. He seemed, said Aunt Prudence, to have become a great chum of Ismay's, and they would be delighted to welcome him, as it was such a long time since he had stayed at nearby Chegwidden. At that time, Francis remembered, the Glassons had not troubled to ask him to visit them, though Aunt Prudence was his father's sister, and her pestilent younger children had seen a great deal of him and found him mockable. But he had no mind for resentment;

369

the thought of having Ismay under his eye for two weeks, without Charlie and the pleasures of Oxford to distract her, was irresistible.

The horrible children had become more tolerable since last he saw them. The two girls, Isabel and Amabel, were lumpy, fattish schoolgirls, who blushed painfully if he spoke to them and giggled and squirmed when he reminded them of the dead adder in his bed. Their older brother, Roderick, who was seventeen, was at this stage very much a product of Winchester, and seemed to have become a Civil Servant without ever having been a youth; but he was not seen much, as he spent a lot of time winding himself up for a scholarship examination that lay some time in the future. Ismay alone retained any of the wildness he had associated with his Glasson cousins.

She was offhand and dismissive with her mother, and contradicted her father on principle. The older Roderick Glasson, it is true, provoked contradiction; he was of the same political stripe as Uncle Arthur Cornish—that is to say, his Toryism was a cautious echo of an earlier day— and though he never quite sank to saying that he didn't know what things were coming to, he used the word "nowadays" frequently in a way that showed he expected nothing from a world gone mad, a world that had forgotten the great days before 1914. This extended even to female beauty.

"You should have seen your mother when your father married her," he said to Francis. "An absolute stunner. There aren't any women like that now. They've broken the mould."

"If he had seen his mother when his father married her," said Ismay, "it would have been rather a scandal, wouldn't it?"

"Ismay, darling, don't catch Daddy up on everything he says," said Aunt Prudence, and a familiar wrangle was renewed.

"Well, why can't people say what they mean, and not simply waffle?"

"You know perfectly well what I meant, but you can't resist any opportunity to show how clever you've become at Oxford."

"If you didn't want me to become clever at Oxford, you shouldn't have nagged me to go for that miserable, inadequate scholarship. I could have stayed at home and studied stupidity. That would have had the advantage of being cheap."

"As I suppose you are too old to be sent from the table, Ismay, I have no recourse but to leave it myself. Francis, would you like a cigar?"

"We've finished anyway, and I wish you wouldn't take refuge in Christian-martyring, Daddy. It isn't argument."

"I do so well remember your mother's wedding," said Aunt Prudence, the peacemaker. "But Francis, didn't you have an older brother? I seem to remember a letter from Switzerland, from your father."

"There was an older brother, also Francis, but he died."

It was the memory of that older Francis that

softened the opinions of the living Francis about Ismay and her parents. In a world that contained such secrets as the Looner, these disputes seemed trivial. What did Wordsworth call it? The still, sad music of humanity—to chasten and subdue? Something like that. The underlying, deep grief of things. One must try to understand, to overlook sharp edges. Of course he was on Ismay's side, but certainly not as a combatant. Her parents were dull and tedious, and she was too young, too radiant and full of life, to have learned to be patient. Probably she had never had to be patient about anything. Without knowing it, Francis's view of family life was much like that of Shakespeare; parents, unless they happened to be stars like King Lear, were minor roles, obstructive, comic, and not to be too much heeded. Only Coriolanus paid attention to his mother, and look what happened to him!

If Shakespeare was not present in his mind, the Grail legend had returned to it in full force. Once again he was on the holy ground of Cornwall, and the pedal-point of his passion for Ismay was the story of Tristan and Iseult, and another more primitive and magical tale.

A passion it certainly was. He was twenty-four years old, so he did not moon and brood like a boy, but he ached for Ismay, and longed to see her happy and pleased with life. He had the lover's unjustified belief that love begets love. It was impossible that he should love Ismay so much without her loving him by infection. He did not

372

think ill of himself; he did not consider himself deficient, compared with other young men. But faced with the splendour of Ismay he could only hope that she might let him serve her, devote his life to her and whatever she wanted.

Ismay knew all of this, and therefore it was perhaps surprising that she let him persuade her to spend a day with him at Tintagel. She tormented him, of course. Shouldn't they take Isabel and Amabel, who did not get many outings; they mustn't be selfish, must they? But it was Francis's intention, on this occasion, to be wholly selfish.

They had a fine day for their picnic, though as it was Cornwall it was certainly not a dry day. Ismay had never been to Tintagel, and Francis held forth about its history: the castle of the Black Prince, and before that the monastic community that had gathered around the hermitage of St. Juliot, and, far back in the mists, Arthur, that mysterious fifth-century figure who might have been the last preserver of Roman order and Roman culture in a Britain overrun by savage northerners, or—even better—have been the mighty figure of Welsh legend.

"Did he live here?" said Ismay, who seemed to be yielding a little to the nature of the story and the spirit of the place.

"Born here, and strangely begotten here."

"Why strangely?"

"His mother was a wonderfully beautiful princess, who was wife to the Duke of Cornwall. Her name was Ygraine. A very great Celtic chieftain,

Uther Pendragon, saw her and desired her and could not rest until he had possessed her. So he took counsel of the magician, Merlin, and Merlin surrounded this castle with a magical spell, so that when her husband was absent Uther Pendragon was able to come to her in her husband's guise, and it was here that he begot the marvellous child who grew to be Arthur."

"Didn't the Duke ever find out?"

"The Duke had no luck; he was killed and cuckolded the same night, though not by the same man. Arthur was brought up by another knight, Sir Ector, and educated by Merlin."

"Lucky lad."

"Yes. Didn't you ever learn any of this at school? You, a Cornish girl—a Cornish princess."

"My school thought mythology meant Greeks."

"Not a patch on the great Northern and Celtic stuff."

Thus Francis began the casting of a spell that had been long working in his mind, and with such success that Ismay yielded to it, becoming tenderer and more compliant than he had ever known her, until at last on a motor rug in the embrace of what might have been part of the Black Prince's castle, or one of the hermitages of the companions of St. Juliot, or just possibly a remnant of that castle of Duke Gorlois (who figures ignominiously in legend as cuckolds must) in which Arthur was begotten, he possessed Ismay, and it seemed to him that the world could never have been so splendid, or blessing so perfect, since the days of the great legend.

Ismay was subdued as they made their way back to the Glasson family car (itself almost a vehicle of legend) and walked somewhat uneasily.

"Anything wrong?"

"Not seriously. But there were a few stones under that rug. Frank, do you know the one—

There was a young fellow named Dockery
Who was screwing his girl in a rockery;
Oh what did she wail
As they thumped on the shale?
"This isn't a fuck—it's a mockery!"

Francis was so lost in the splendour of the afternoon that he was ready to accept this as the plain-spoken jesting of the age of legend, befitting a Celtic princess.

Francis had taken seriously Saraceni's advice that he should stop flirting with colour and find out what it truly was. That meant working in oils, and except for some tentative messing he had never done much with oils, and knew he must make a serious beginning. When he left Cornwall, reluctantly but aware that his fortnight could not be extended, he went to Paris, and during the summer months worked almost every day at La Grande Chaumière, an art school directed at the time by Othon Friesz. He bought the tickets that were sold by the concierge, arrived early and left late, spoiled a substantial amount of canvas, and achieved some dreadful messes of dirty colour until, in time, he was able to put into practice the few precepts Friesz threw to him, almost inaudibly and apparently with contempt.

Always paint fat on lean. Always lay in your warms over your colds. The groundwork should be done in paint well thinned with turpentine: afterward your fat colour, mixed with mastic or Venice turps. Don't mess your paint about on the palette: fresh paint gives the best quality. Never put more of a colour over the same colour. Always paint warm on cold and after your body coat every successive coat must be thinner until you get to the top. Always fat on lean.

Simplicity itself, like the few notes Mozart wrote on the back of a letter and gave to his pupil Sussmayer to explain how to compose music. But not easy to do. It was Francis's skill in drawing that saved him from abject failure. There were plenty of students in the atelier who knew nothing of drawing, and from their easels Friesz sometimes turned with a murmured "Quelle horreur!" But Friesz did not turn up often. Having given advice, he allowed the student to struggle until he had mastered it or abandoned the contest. Friesz provided a place to work, an ambience, a name, and infrequent, good advice; it was enough.

After ten weeks of hard work Francis thought he had earned a holiday, and would go to Rome. He would see the sights of Rome, and he would find out if Tancred Saraceni had meant anything more than pleasantry when he said to hunt him up.

Saraceni meant much more than that. He insisted that Francis stay with him, and allow him to display the wonders of the great city. There was more than enough room in his apartment.

The apartment was a marvel of splendid clutter. For thirty years Tancred Saraceni had never been able to deny himself a bargain, or a good piece of painting or furniture, or tapestry, or embroidery, or sculpture, whenever one turned up that he could afford, and in his life such things turned up all the time. It was not a pack-rat's nest and there was not a thing in it that was not fine of its own kind; everything was disposed with taste and effect, so far as space allowed. But even in the generous space of that apartment there were limitations, and though Saraceni would not have admitted it, the limitations had long ago been exceeded. The effect was overwhelming.

Why overwhelming? Because it was vastly more than the sum of its parts. It was a collection various in kind, but coherent in representing the taste of one avid, brilliant, greatly gifted connoisseur. It was Saraceni swollen to immense proportions. It was a man's mind, the size of a house.

The apartment itself was part of an old palace that faced what had once been a charming little square with a fountain playing gently in its middle. But that had been in the days before the motor car degraded and despoiled Rome as it has degraded and despoiled so many cities. Now the little square was every day parked full of cars that came and went, leaving their stink on the heavy September air. The little fountain still played, but its basin was full of food wrappers and trash, rarely cleared out. Because the air outside was fouled by cars, Saraceni logically refused to open his windows, and this did nothing to lighten the oppressive feeling of his dwelling. Literally it had an air of an earlier day.

He was alone. A woman came every morning and did such cleaning as he would permit; he dusted all the objects of art, and himself polished whatever needed to be polished. He had been married, yes, to a wonderful English lady who had at last decided that she could no longer bear to live under such circumstances, and they had parted amicably. Tancredo, she had said, you must make a decision—shall it be the collection or me? He had not needed long to decide. My dearest one, he had said, the collection is timeless and you, alas that it should be so, are trapped in time. She had laughed so marvellously that he had almost been tempted to change his mind, but had not done so, in the end. A wonderful woman! They met and had delightful encounters every time he visited England. He had a daughter, also, but she was happily married and lived in Florence, where he saw her from time to time. She could not be tempted back to the apartment, even for a brief visit.

Saraceni was philosophical about the lonely state. He had made his choice. If it was art or human relationships, art unquestionably had the prior call.

He was an admirable host. He took Francis everywhere, and showed him things that even a privileged tourist could not have seen. It may not be said that at the Vatican doors flew open, because they moved gently on oiled hinges, but there were few doors that did not move for Saraceni; there were cardinalical palaces to which the public was not admitted, but where the chamberlain knew Saraceni as a privileged friend of the household. And in many great churches, chapels, and palaces he let it be known, with modesty, that such-and-such a splendid piece had regained its beauty because he had worked on it.

"You keep the Renaissance in repair," said Francis, meaning it as a joke.

But Saraceni did not take it as a joke. "I do," said he; "it is a trust that must be taken very seriously. But it is not repair. Call it re-creation. That demands special knowledge and special techniques. But if you want to know what these are, you must come and work with me." And he looked intently at Francis.

"I must get my degree first. No sense spending two years on it and then chucking it away. I have a third year to go. Then, if you will have me."

"By then I shall be busy on a long and tricky problem. A private collection that has been allowed to decline fearfully. But I think much of it may be reclaimed. I shall want an assistant. I promise that you could learn a great deal."

"I have everything to learn. Working in Paris I have found out what a totally incompetent painter I am."

"No, no, no; you have learned some basic things, and it takes time to make them work for you. All that you tell me about laying fat over lean, and so forth, is excellent, and you were doing it with modern paint. If you come to me you will have to learn to do it with old paint, which is harder in some ways, easier in others."

"Old paint? Where does it come from?"

"I make it. Make it as the masters made it. They did not buy their paint in tubes, you know. They mixed their own, and much of the work is to discover what they used, and how they mixed it. Did you know that Nicholas Hillyard used ear-wax in those splendid Elizabethan miniatures? What is ear-wax, when you have painstakingly gathered the yield of many ears? I know. Chemistry is the secret. You cannot satisfactorily repair an old picture with a paint that is too much unlike what the painter used. And when you have done that—Ah, well, you shall see what follows, what *must* follow if restoration is to be that, and not simply cobbler's work."

At night they sat in the awesome apartment sipping Scotch whisky, which was Saraceni's preferred tipple, and as they mellowed, Francis talked about his own taste in art. He was inclined to deplore the fact that, strive as he would, he liked the painting of an earlier day better than that of contemporary artists. What was he to make of

380

himself? How could he hope to be an artist, even of the humblest rank, if he did not live and feel in tune with his own time? When the paintings that haunted him were not modern either in technique or in taste? The Bronzino, for instance . . .

"Ah, the Bronzino, The so-called *Allegory of Love*. Who gave it that inexpressive name, I wonder? It is not about love at its highest, but about Luxury—the indulgence of the senses. For all its erotic splendour and evocation of sensual pleasure it is a profoundly moral picture. Those old painters were great moralists, you know, even such a man as Angelo Bronzino, who so many imperceptive critics have called a cold and heartless artist. Surely you have seen the morality behind it?"

"I've looked at it literally for hours, and the more I look the less I know what is behind it."

"Then you must look again. You, who once won a prize for Classics!"

"It isn't really a classical theme. Venus and Cupid are the principal figures, but not doing anything I can associate with any classical reference I know."

"You must understand the classics as the Renaissance understood them, which is not the way a boys' school understands them. You must penetrate the classical world, which is by no means dead, I assure you; classical morality, classical feeling. Venus is tempting her son Cupid to a display of love that is certainly not simply filial. Is not that what many mothers do? Since Freud there has been a great deal of cocktail-hour chatter about the Oedipus complex and the love of a son for his mother, but who ventures on the dangerous theme of the mother's part in that affair? Come now, Francis, has your mother, whose beauty I have heard you praise, never flirted with you? Never caressed you in a way that was not strictly maternal?"

"She never put her tongue in my mouth or coaxed me to play with her breast, if that is what you are talking about."

"Well—but the possibility—was there never the possibility? If you had been of the pagan world and hot for pleasure, and not frightened out of your wits by Christianity, might you have recognized the possibility?"

"Maestro, I don't really follow you."

"I puzzle over it sometimes. So much talk since Dr. Freud about fathers who rouse erotic feeling in their daughters: never any talk about mothers who do the same with their sons. Does such one-sidedness seem really likely?"

"Where I grew up we had lots of incest. I knew one fellow, the son of a logger who was killed in the forest, and from twelve years of age onward he had to stand and deliver for his mother at least five times a week. When last I heard of him he had two brothers who were probably his sons. He never married; no necessity, I suppose. But that was in what the Renaissance would call very primitive conditions."

"Don't be too sure what the Renaissance would call it. But I speak of possibilities, not of completed acts. Possibilities—things that merely float in the air and are never brought to earth—can be extremely influential. It is the artist's privilege to seize such possibilities and to make pictures of them, and such pictures are among the most powerful we have. What is a picture of the Madonna—and we have seen many of them this week—but a picture of a Mother and her Son."

"A Holy Mother and the Son of God."

"In the worlds of myth and art all mothers are holy because that is what we feel in the depths of our hearts. No, not the heart: that is where modern people think they feel. During the Renaissance they would have said, the liver. In the gut, in fact. Worship of the Mother, real or mythical, comes from the gut. Have you never wondered why in so many of those pictures Joseph, the earthly father, looks such a nincompoop? In the very best of them Joseph is not even permitted to enter. That is one of the unspoken foundation stones of our mighty Faith, Francis; the love affair between Mother and Son, and according to the Scriptures no other woman ever challenged her place of supremacy. But in these Madonnas there is nothing overtly erotic. There is in Bronzino; in that picture he cast off the Christian chains and showed truth as he saw it, of love despised and rejected.

"Have you really looked at the picture? You have looked at the artist's achievement, but have you understood what he is saying? Venus holds an apple in one hand, and an arrow in the other.

383

What does that say: I tempt you, and I have a wound for you. And look at all the secondary figures—the raving figure of jealousy behind Cupid, speaking so clearly of despair, of love despised and rejected; the little figure of Pleasure who is about to pelt the toying lovers with rose leaves—see at his feet the thorns and those masks of the concealments and cheats of the world, marked with the bitterness of age; and who is that creature behind the laughing Pleasure—a wistful, appealing face, a rich gown that might almost blind us to her lion's feet, her serpent's sting, and her hands that offer both a honeycomb and something beastly—that must be the Cheat—Fraude, in Latin—who can so prettily turn love to madness. Who are the old man and the young woman at the top of the picture? They are plainly Time and Truth, who are drawing aside the mantle that shows the world what is involved in such love as this. Time—and his daughter Truth. A very moral picture, is it not?"

"Certainly as you interpret it, and as I have never heard anyone else explain it I cannot quarrel with you. But I'm horrified that Bronzino thought of love in that way."

"So you might well be. But he didn't, you know. The picture that has enthralled you in the National Gallery in London was half of a design that was meant to be two tapestries. One tapestry is completed and you can see it in Florence, in the Arazzi Gallery. It is called *L'innocentia del Bronzino* and it shows Innocence threatened by a dog (for

Envy), a lion (for Fury), a wolf (for Greed), and a snake (for Treachery); Innocence is being powerfully protected by Justice, a female figure with a mighty sword, and there again you will see Time with his hourglass and his wings (because he flies, as every parrot knows) and he is taking the cloak from a naked girl, who of course is Truth, his daughter. So really the pictures ought to be called the Allegories of Truth and Luxury, and they are splendid Renaissance sermons. Together they tell us much about life and about love, as it appeared to a Christian mind refreshed by the newly found classicism."

"Maestro, you remind me very much of my dear old Aunt Mary-Ben. She insisted that pictures were moral lessons, and told stories. But you should have seen the pictures she showed me to prove it."

"I am quite sure I have seen many of them. Their morality is of their own time, and the stories they tell are sweet and pretty, suited to people who wanted a sweetly pretty, stunted art. But they are in a long tradition quite different from those innumerable landscapes and figure pictures, and abstracts painted by men who did not want to tell anybody anything except what their personal vision discovered in easily accessible things. The tradition that your aunt and I admire, in our different ways, is not to be brushed aside, nor should its works be discussed as though they belonged to the other, purely objective tradition. There is nothing in the least wrong with having something to say, and saying it as best you can, even if you are a painter. The best moderns often do it, you know. One thinks of Picasso. Think about him."

It was impossible to think of Picasso, or of anything but immediate concerns, after Frank had read the letter which was sent on from Corpus and reached him two days before he was to return to England.

Dear Frank:
    The news is that I am well and truly up the spout. Two months gone. I had meant to keep this jolly secret from the parents until you were back in England, but that hasn't been possible. Not that I am all bagged out, and stumbling about in my bare feet like Tess of the D'Urbervilles, but some determined chucking up in the a.m. gave the show away. So there have been great family conferences, and after Daddy had had his prolonged and mournful say, and Mum had wept, the question was: what to do? My suggestion that I go to London and have the little intruder given what-for by a really competent doctor was shouted down. Daddy is a churchwarden and takes it greatly to heart. What they want is a wedding. Keep your hair on. They do not in the least regard you as an old black ram who has tupped their white ewe. (Shakes.) Indeed there were one or two nasty hints that they thought their white ewe might

have been a not-unwilling collaborator. No, they think you a highly desirable *parti*, as they used to say in Mum's day. When I said that I didn't know if you would want to marry me they said that blood was thicker than water (messier, too) and we were cousins (which in other circs they might well have thought an objection), and there was a lot more to be said for it than just saving face. The Glassons, as you will have divined, have an awful lot of face and precious little else. So—what about it? Don't waste time. Think hard and let me know. If my plan is to be taken, it must be done pretty soon.

Love, and all that that implies,

Ismay

After a morning's reflection Francis sent a telegram:

PROCEED WEDDING PLANS INSTANTER STOP WITH YOU IN A WEEK LOVE TO ALL

FRANK

The eagerness in the telegram was not from the heart. Francis did not want to marry Ismay, or anybody; he discovered that what he really wanted was to be in love, but not tied down to marriage, of which his experience had not been particularly appetizing. Against abortion he had an insuperable Catholic objection, partnered by an equally insuperable Calvinist objection that sprang from his association with Victoria Cameron. How had it happened? Why had he not taken precautions? The answer to that was that he thought precautions unromantic, and with Ismay at Tintagel, everything must be romantic. A standing prick has no conscience; that was a piece of bleak wisdom he had acquired at Colborne College, and that would certainly be the way the Glassons would look at it. The fact that he had not meant it in that spirit at all simply could not be explained and was irrelevant to the situation. What was to be done? He couldn't for a moment think of leaving Ismay in the lurch, quite apart from the fact that the Glassons and his own parents would probably hunt him down and kill him if he did such a dirty trick. His career, about which he had no firm plans but vast, unmoulded expectations, would be a ruin, for Ismay only fitted into that scene as The Ideal Beloved, not by any means as a wife and mother. He was to be the Grail Knight who ventured forth, returning to his lady only between adventures. But after all thoughts of this sort had been rehearsed again and again, the nagging feeling crept into his consciousness that he was really a very dim young man, considering that he was twenty-six and thought to be clever.

Greeting the Glassons in his new character caused him greater dread than reunion with a pregnant Ismay. He had not then got, nor would he ever get, Dr. Upper fully out of his system, and deep within himself he thought that he had done a dirty thing, and would doubtless be appropriately punished. But when he arrived at the nearest railway station to St. Columb's Hall the Glasson parents greeted him with more warmth than they had ever shown before, and his most difficult task was to kiss Ismay on the station platform with the proper sort of affection—as accepted wooer rather than as too successful seducer. Nobody said anything about what was in all their minds until after tea, when Roderick Glasson suggested with terrible casualness that he and Francis might take a walk.

All that was said on that walk was said a score of times afterward, the intention becoming clearer every time. It was too bad that things had been a little premature, but Francis must realize that we were living in 1935, and not in the dark ages of Queen Victoria, and with clever management all would be well. The marriage would take place in a little over a fortnight's time; the banns had already been called once in the parish church. It would be a quiet affair—not more than sixty or seventy people. Then Ismay and Francis would go somewhere on an extended wedding trip, and when they returned in a year or so with a child, who was to be the wiser? Whose business was it, after all, but the family's?

Francis was aware that this was a path that had already been travelled in the family history, but Roderick Glasson could not have known why it struck so coldly into his heart. It was from Victoria Cameron that he had heard of his parents' return from such a wedding trip with the Looner. God!

Would this child be another such goblin as that? Did he carry that dark inheritance? Reason was against it, but a strain of the mythical in Francis's thinking put reason firmly in its place. Was the Looner a punishment for something? He dared not contemplate what it might be, for he was sure his parents had never put themselves in such a pickle as he and Ismay had done. Everything about them made it unthinkable. In any case he was unquestionably his father's truly begotten son; the family face was the clearest evidence. The Looner must have been bad luck of some sort. But what sort?

It was incoherent; it was superstitious; it was irrational, this mass of torturing speculation, but it was unquestionably real. And what did the telegram mean that reached him from Canada?

NEWS TODAY FROM RODERICK WE SEND LOVE AND CONGRATULATIONS CANNOT ATTEND WEDDING WORD TO WISE BE VERY CAREFUL ABOUT ALL MONEY ARRANGEMENTS

FATHER

Money arrangements? He had already had some hint of that. The Glassons, Roderick explained during another walk, were feeling the pinch, as did all landowners. Rents had not kept up with expenditures; taxes were punitive; without heavy investment in equipment agriculture could not survive. New money spent on the estate was imperative if large sales of portions of land that had been part of the Glasson patrimony for generations were to be avoided. Not that sales would bridge the gap for long. Roderick had looked into the future fearlessly, and he saw only one hope for St. Columb Hall and its estates, and that hope was—new money. It was a case of substantial refinancing now or—well, eventual ruin.

Had Francis ever given any thought to agriculture? No, Francis had not. He didn't think he wanted to be a landowner and farmer.

Roderick laughed, almost musically. No question of that. The estate must go to Roderick, his only son. Not that it was tied down by law, but that was how it had always been. However, young Roderick had set his heart on a career in Whitehall, and certainly he seemed to have a talent that way. Now if—just suppose—Francis and Ismay lived at a very decent dower house on the property, and Roderick and Prudence lived at the Hall until at last they were forced by the inevitable to leave it (manly acceptance of age and death here, almost like the "business" of a none too accomplished actor), it would be possible to totally re-finance the estate, and a family property—Francis was already a cousin and would soon be doubly family—would be revitalized in the best possible way. Francis wouldn't have to worry about the farm; Roderick knew farming like the palm of his hand, and they had an excellent agent who, with real money strength behind him, would put things in apple-pie order before you knew it. In time, young Roderick would return, and anyway he would always have St. Columb's behind him. Francis could do whatever he pleased. Paint, if he liked. Mess about with Cornish history and legend, if it suited him. He would be, Roderick thought the phrase was, a sleeping partner. It was not said how the sleeping partner was to benefit, except in terms of moral satisfaction.

Slowly, it sank in. This was why the Glassons were so philosophical about Ismay's false step, over which they might otherwise be raising the roof. The price of Ismay was—one million Canadian dollars, with accrued interest, because Francis had not been drawing heavily on his income. Of course, they knew all about it; the Cornishes of Chegwidden would have gossiped and probably exaggerated. One million Canadian dollars was rather more than two hundred thousand pounds, which to people like the Glassons was wealth illimitable.

That was where the price began. The larger part would be his thraldom to life in a dower house, under the shadow of St. Columb's and the shadow of Chegwidden, free to paint and dream about myth if he were fool enough to want to do that. He was to be the money-bags, that was plain. More kids, undoubtedly. But such a fate could be avoided; the Glassons could not trap him there. No; after thinking about it painfully and honestly, Francis recognized that it was the money that really meant most, and he was brought to the shameful conclusion that he wanted Ismay, but he didn't like her price.

Still, as Grandfather McRory always said, nobody has your money so long as it's still in your own pocket. Roderick Glasson seemed to think that money would be made over to him in lumps. Francis made it clear that the uttermost he could manage, so far ahead as he could see, was four thousand pounds paid quarterly for the first year. This was not true, for not only had he his grandfather's handsome bequest, but he also received enough from the trust that included his aunts and his mother to make up a good income in itself. But as Francis sat in his bedroom and did reckonings, he was astonished to find how fond of money he was, and how reluctant to let any of it out of his grasp. When he stated his terms to his uncle, Roderick's face fell, but as he had no way of knowing what Francis really possessed, he had to make the best of it. After all, Francis pointed out, he would have to support Ismay and probably Aunt Prudence somewhere on the Continent for the greater part of a year, and that would be another call on his income. Capital, he explained, was not a thing one ever diminished. Roderick nodded sagely at this, knowing very well that he had himself diminished his capital almost to invisibility, and that this was what had brought him to his present position. But he was optimistic; after the first year things might look very different.

Ismay and Aunt Prudence on the Continent, said Roderick, as it sank in. But where would

Francis be? At Oxford, said Francis. He was determined not to sacrifice his degree and he had another year to go. But what did he need with a degree? It would be useless if he were living the life of a country gentleman. Roderick had no degree; he had come out of the Navy to assume the splendours and miseries of St. Columb's when he inherited it, and had never felt the want of a university training. It was at this point that Ismay joined in the genteel wrangling; she too wanted to complete her studies and receive some sort of university stamp. Francis had thought about that, too. She certainly could not return to Oxford; the colleges did not encourage married undergraduates—indeed objected to them, and understandably so. But she could go to the continent, and pursue her modern-language studies very effectively at Lausanne, and live near by at Montreux; continental universities did not give as much individual concern to their students as did Oxford. Such a stay abroad would dissemble the early arrival of the child, which was also a consideration. He would pay—within reason.

"You've got it all planned, haven't you?" said Ismay to him when her parents were not near. "You've got them completely outgeneralled." She spoke with admiration.

"It's a short plan," said he; "but it gives us a year to think about what we intend to do. I don't want to settle here and become 'Francis Cornish, whose sensitive landscapes follow in the path of B. W. Leader'." He was really thinking about the profession, of which he had said nothing to Ismay, and which he was determined not to mention unless it became inescapable. Ismay as the Desired One was being replaced in his heart and mind by Ismay the Promised One, not to say the Inescapable One, and there were some things she must not know. She was worse than a blabber; she was a hinter. It gave her pleasure to rouse curiosity and speculation about dangerous things.

These family deliberations took place in the evenings, after Aunt Prudence and in a lesser degree Uncle Roderick had spent a toilsome day planning the wedding. So much to do! And all to be done on a shoestring—for the Glassons insisted that it would be indefensible, and even perhaps unchancy, to let Francis pay for any part of that. They greatly enjoyed the excitement, protesting that they did not know how they could get through another day like the one just completed.

Two nights before the wedding day Francis and Ismay escaped from the general hubbub, and were walking in a lane at dusk. Overhead the sky was deepening from a colour which reminded Francis of the cloak that Time and Truth deploy so effectively in the Bronzino *Allegory*.

"You feel trapped, don't you?" said Ismay.

"Do you?"

"Yes, but my trap is a physical one. The kid. That has to be dealt with before I can do anything else. But you're not trapped in that way."

"No, but I have an obligation. Surely you see

that? Apart from loving you, and wanting to marry you, of course."

"Oh Frank, don't be so stuffy! I hate to think what your upbringing must have been. You've still got a chance."

"How?"

"Scarper, of course."

"Desert you? Now?"

"It's been done."

"Not by me. I'd feel the most terrible shit."

"I wouldn't think so."

"Maybe not. But I'd think so."

"All right, my dear-O-dear. It's your neck."

"I'm really surprised you think I might."

"Don't ever say I didn't give you a chance."

"You're a tough little nut, Ismay."

"Not the Celtic princess of your dreams? Maybe I'm more like a Celtic princess of reality than you suppose. From all I've heard they could be very tough nuts, too."

When the wedding day came neighbours arrived from far and wide: county families, the professional bourgeoisie, tenants of St. Columb's (who had been badgered by the agent into presenting the couple with a mantel clock, engraved in suitably modified feudal terms), such old women as attended all weddings and funerals without distinction of class, and the Bishop of Truro, who did not read the Marriage Service, but gave the blessing afterward. Ismay, tidy for once, and robed in virgin white, looked so lovely that Francis's heart ached toward her. The Service was read by the local parson, who was from the very lowest shelf of the Low Church cupboard. He stressed the admonition that marriage was not to be taken in hand wantonly, to satisfy men's carnal lusts and appetites, like brute beasts that have no understanding, but for the propagation of children. All of this he spat out with such distaste that he alarmed Ismay's two sisters, Isabel and Amabel, present in white dresses to signify virginity in its rawest and meatiest guise, and caused the Glassons and Francis to wonder if the good man smelt a rat. But it was soon over; "The Voice That Breathed o'er Eden" was sung, the Bishop said his say, and Francis and Ismay had been licensed to go to bed in future without shame.

The wedding had not bothered Francis unduly, but the wedding breakfast was a different matter. At this affair, which was held on the lawn at St. Columb's because it was a fineish day, Roderick Glasson the Younger took charge, and conducted the affair in the manner of a Best Man who was aimed at Whitehall, and wanted everything to be done with precision, and with only such enthusiasm as was compatible with his ideal of elegance—which kept enthusiasm well in check.

Roderick gave a good impression of what he would be like at forty-five. He read, like one communicating a knotty minute to a Civil Service superior, some telegrams of congratulation, most of which were from Canada and one or two from Oxford friends which had to be read with restraint. The Bride was toasted by Uncle Arthur

Cornish, who described her in terms that made Ismay giggle unsuitably and chilled Francis, who detected in it allusions to his money, and satisfaction that it was not going out of the family. Francis replied, briefly, and made insincere protestations of humility and gratitude toward the Bride's parents, who liked that part of his speech very much, but thought it could have been even more forcibly put. As he spoke, Francis had to overcome whispering among the guests who had not met him, and hissed, "An American? Nobody told me he was an American." "Not American—Canadian." "Well, what's the difference?" "They're touchier, that's what." "They say he's very wealthy." "Oh, so that's it." Then the Best Man toasted the bridesmaids, and was arch about the fact that, as they were his little sisters, he could not say too much in their favour, but he had hopes that they would improve. The bridesmaids took this with scarlet faces and occasional murmurs of Oh, I say, Roddy, pack it in, can't you? Roderick told about the time he and his sisters had put a dead adder in the groom's bed, and an indecency had to be frowned down when Old George Trethewey, a cousin but not a favourite, shouted drunkenly that they'd put something a damned sight better in his bed now. And finally the tenant who farmed the biggest of St. Columb's farms toasted The Happy Couple, and was somewhat indiscreet in hinting that the coming of new blood (he did not say new money) into the family promised well for the future of agriculture at St. Columb's. But at last it was over, the wedding cake had been deflowered and distributed, every hand had been shaken; the Bride had flung her bouquet from the front door with such force that it took her sister Amabel full in the face, and the couple sped away in a hired car toward Truro, where they were to catch a train.

In Lausanne there was no difficulty about having Ismay entered as a student, with credit for the year she had already completed at Oxford. In Montreux it was not hard to find a pension with a living room and a bedroom, the latter containing a couch on which she or Aunt Prudence could sleep when they occupied the place together. But it all meant laying out money in sums small and large, and Francis, who had never had experience of this sort of slow bleeding, undertaken in a cause which was not nearest his heart, suffered an early bout of the outraged parsimony which was to visit him so often in later life. Stinginess does nothing to improve the looks, and Ismay commented that he was becoming hatchet-faced.

His life with Ismay was agreeable, but it had none of the old lustre. She was more beautiful than ever, and the carelessness with which she had always dressed now seemed a fine disdain for trivialities. Only a very sharp eye would have discerned that she was pregnant, but when she was naked she had a new opulence, and Francis drew her as often as was possible. A really beautiful woman should have a figure like a 'cello, he said, running his hand appreciatively over her swelling belly. But though he loved her, he had ceased to worship her, and sometimes they snapped at one another, because Ismay's broad speech, which he had once thought so delightful, grated on his nerves now.

"Well, if you didn't like the way I talk, you shouldn't have knocked me up."

"I wish you wouldn't use vulgar expressions like that, as if we were that sort of person. If you want to talk dirty, talk dirty, but for God's sake don't talk common."

Irritatingly, Ismay would respond to this sort of thing by singing Ophelia's song, quietly and reflectively, in a Cockney accent:

> *B'Jeez and by Saint Charity,*
> *Alack and fie for shame!*
> *Young men will do't, if they come to't;*
> *By cock, they are to blame.*
> *Quoth she, before you tumbled me,*
> *You promised me to wed,*
> *So would I ha' done, by yonder sun,*
> *An thou hadst not come to my bed.*

"That should be all right," she murmured, apparently to the walls. "Shakespeare. Good old Shakers, the darling of the OUDS. Nothing common about him. You can't get classier than Shakers."

Francis could not linger in Montreux. He had to return to Oxford, and he did so with no time to spare before the beginning of the Michaelmas

Term. He had made a mess of things with Ismay, he told himself. Not that he was sorry to have married her, but that should have come later. Now he had to leave her when surely she needed him with her—though she had been calm enough when he went. After all, Aunt Prudence was going to her in a few weeks. He knew nothing about the matter, but he had a vague impression that a pregnant woman needed her husband close by, to run out and get her pickles and ice cream if she should have a sick fancy for them in the middle of the night, and to gloat romantically over the new life that was gathering within her. The doctor in Montreux had taken it philosophically when he explained that he must return to England, and assured him that everything would be quite all right. Well—it had to be all right. He was determined to get his degree, and get the best class he could manage. This sudden bump in the road should not rob him of that. So he settled to work, and worked very hard, almost entirely giving up drawing and painting, and refusing a tempting offer to assist a distinguished designer in preparing a garden performance of *The Tempest* for the OUDS.

He was able to spend Christmas with Ismay, and found her, now obviously pregnant, and even more obviously a European student, accustomed to speak French more often than English, and deep in Spanish studies. She had enjoyed herself, once she had persuaded her mother to return to England and stop fussing over her. This sort of student life suited her as the formality of Oxford had never done. They spent, on the whole, a very amicable Christmas holiday, much of it in Ismay's living-room, smoking countless stinking French cigarettes and pursuing their university work. They conversed entirely in French and Ismay liked his lingering French-Canadian accent. It was "of the people" she said and she approved of anything that was of the people.

He was with her in February, when the child was born. Pensions are not accommodated to childbirth, and Ismay was in a small private hospital, which cost a lot of money. Aunt Prudence was there, too, and she and Francis had an uneasy time of it in the pension rooms. Francis hauled the couch out of the bedroom into the sitting-room for himself, and Aunt Prudence, though well aware that the bed was due to her sex and seniority, nevertheless accused herself daily of being a nuisance.

The child was born without incident, but surrounded by the usual grandmotherly and fatherly anxiety. Indeed, Francis was nervously wretched until he had seen the little girl and been assured by the doctor that she was perfect in every way. Had he expected anything else? Francis did not say what he had feared.

"She's the absolute image of her father," said Aunt Prudence, smiling at Francis.

"Yes, she's the image of her father," Ismay agreed, smiling at no one.

To Francis the child looked like every baby he had ever seen, but he did not say so.

The question of a name for the child arose almost at once. Francis had no ideas, but Ismay was perhaps more maternal than she liked to admit. The child was sucking at her breast when she made a suggestion.

"Let's call her Charlotte."

"All right. But why?"

"After her father."

Francis looked blank.

"Frank, I've been trying to get around to this for quite a while, but the time never seemed just right. But this is it. You know, of course, that this is Charlie's child?"

Francis still looked blank.

"Well, it is. I know for a certainty. We were very close before he scarpered."

"And you sucked me in to give cover for Charlie's child?"

"I suppose I did. But don't think I liked doing it. You're a dear, and you've behaved beautifully. But there's a basic difference between you and Charlie: he's the kind that makes things happen, and you're the kind things happen to, and for me there's no question of choice. Don't forget that before the wedding I gave you a chance to get away, and you decided not to take it. This is Charlie's child."

"Does Charlie know?"

"I don't suppose he knows or cares. I've had some indirect news of him, and you know how things are hotting up in Spain, so I suppose that if he did know he couldn't do anything about it. He's got bigger fish to fry."

"Ismay, this puts the lid on it."

"I didn't expect you to be pleased, and I honestly meant to say something earlier, but you see how it is. I wanted to be square with you, and now I have."

"Oh, so that's what you've been, is it? Square? Ismay, I'd hate to be near when you were being crooked."

Back to Oxford, miserable and beaten so far as his marriage was concerned, but with a compensating fierce ambition to distinguish himself in his Final Schools, which he faced in June. It is impossible to prepare for Final Schools by extreme exertions during the last ten weeks; preparation should have been well begun two years before. That was when Francis had started to work, and thus his last ten weeks was free for finishing touches, rather than the acquirement of basic knowledge. His tutor was pleased with him—or as pleased as a tutor ever admits to being—and polished him up to a fine gloss. The consequence was that when he had written his papers and waited out the obligatory period during which they were read and marked, he had the satisfaction of seeing his name posted in the First Class. He telegraphed to Canada, and the next day received an answer: "Congratulations. Love to Ismay and Charlotte." Did his parents, then, see them as a happy trio, a Holy

Family, with Baby Bunting prettily innocent of Daddy's distinction?

Ismay and the child were at St. Columb's; Aunt Prudence had insisted that a summer in the country, with country food and air, was just what Ismay and Baby needed. It was to St. Columb's, therefore, that Francis sent his second telegram about his academic success. He was surprised to receive a telephone call on the following day. The telephone was not a favourite agent of the Glassons, nor was Oxford, with its great population of students and its paucity of telephones, an easy place with which to communicate. But Uncle Roderick called, and Francis was found by the Porter of Corpus, and there, in the Porter's lodge, while one undergraduate bought a stamp and another inquired about the whereabouts of his bicycle, he heard his uncle, distant and mouse-like of voice, saying that Ismay was not at St. Columb's but had said she was going up to Oxford for a couple of days to see Francis. That had been a week ago. Was she not with him?

It was on the following day that he received a letter from Lausanne:

Dear Frank:

It's no good pretending something will work when it obviously won't. By the time this reaches you I shall be in Spain. I know where Charlie is, and I'm joining him. Don't try to find me, because you won't. But don't worry. I shall be all right, or if I'm not I shall be all wrong in a cause I think is more important than any personal considerations. You are the best of chaps, I know, and won't let Little Charlie down, and of course when I get back (and if I do) I'll take on again. Sorry about the money. But really you love that stuff too much for your own good. Love,

Ismay

The money, he discovered, was what he had deposited in an account for her use. She had cleared it out.

Scarpered!

"I want to beat up a woman with my fists. Are you interested, and if so what would your price be?"

Francis had put his question to at least eight prostitutes on Piccadilly, and had had eight refusals, ranging from amusement to affront. Obviously he was in the wrong district. These girls, most of them fragile and pretty, were high-priced tarts, not hungry enough to consider his proposal. He found his way into Soho, and on the fourth try had better luck.

She was fortyish, with badly dyed hair and a gown trimmed with imitation fur. On the stout side, and underneath a heavy paint job her face was stupid but kindly.

"Well—I don't know what to say. I've had gentlemen who had special tastes, of course. But usually it's them that wants to be beaten up. A few slaps, you know, and some rough talk. But I don't know. With your fists, was it you said?"

"Yes. Fists."

"I'd have to think it over. Talk it over with my friend, really. Have you got a moment?"

From the depths of her bosom she pulled out a crucifix which, when she put it in her lips, proved to be a little whistle, on a chain. She gave a discreet double tweet. Very soon a small, dark man, quietly dressed and wearing a statesman's black Homburg, appeared, and the woman whispered to him.

"How rough would this be?" asked the man.

"Hard to say, till I got into it."

"Well—it could come very dear. Broken teeth, now. Bruising. That could put her out of business for a fortnight. No; I don't think we could look at it, not at any price that would make sense."

"Would one good punch be any help?" said the woman, who seemed to have a pitying heart. "One good punch at, say, ten quid?"

"Twenty," said the man, hastily.

They went to the woman's flat, which was near by.

"You understand I've got to stick around," said the man. "This isn't your ordinary call. You might get carried away, and not in control of yourself. I've got to stick around, for both your sakes."

The woman was undressing, with rapid professional skill.

"No need for that," said Francis.

"Oh, I think she'd better," said the man. "In

fact, I'd say she'd rather, seeing as you're paying. Professional, you understand. Her birthday suit is her working clothes, isn't it?"

"Okay. Ready when you are," said the woman, now naked and bracing herself on stout legs. She had, Francis saw with an embalmer's eye, an appendicitis scar of the old-fashioned kind that looks rather like a beetle with outspread legs.

Francis raised his fist, and to summon anger he thought hard of Ismay at her most defiant, her most derisive, her most sluttish. But it would not come. It was the Looner who dominated his feeling, not as an image, but as an influence, and he could not strike. He sat down suddenly on the bed, and to his deep shame burst into sobs.

"Oh, the poor love," said the woman. "Can't you, darling?" She pushed a box of tissue handkerchiefs toward him. "Don't feel it so. There's lots that can't, the other way, you know. They've very good reasons, too."

"He needs a drink," said the man.

"No, I think he needs a cup of tea," said the woman. "Just put on the electric, will you, Jimsie? There, there, now. You tell me about it." She sat beside Francis and drew his head down on her large scented breast. "What did she do to you, eh? She must have done something. What was it? Come on, tell me."

So Francis found himself sitting on the bed with the woman, who had pulled a silk peignoir trimmed with rather worn marabou about her, and her ponce, or her bully, or whatever the term might be for Jimsie, sipping hot, strong tea, giving a shortened, edited version of what Ismay had done. The woman made comforting noises, but it was Jimsie who spoke.

"Don't take me up wrong," he said, "but it certainly looks as if she done the dirty on you. But why? That's the way we have to look at it. There's always a reason, and it may not be one you'd ever think of. Why, would you say?"

"Because she loves another man," said Francis.

"O Gawd; sod love!" said Jimsie. "You never know where you are with it. A great cause of trouble." And as he went on to anatomize love, as it appeared to him both as a man and as a professional dealer in sexual satisfaction, it seemed to Francis that he heard the voice of Tancred Saraceni, explaining the Bronzino *Allegory*. The face that was clearest in the picture, as he thought of it, was the woman-headed beast with a lion's claws and a dragon's tail, who proffered the sweet and the bitter in her outstretched hands. The figure called the Cheat, or in Saraceni's Latin explication, Fraude. He must have whispered the name.

"Fraudy? I should think it was fraudy, and rotten, too, walking out on you and the baby," said the woman.

When at last Francis was fit to go, he offered the woman two ten-pound notes.

"Oh, no dear," said she; "I couldn't think of it. You never had your punch, you see. Not that I'd have blamed you if you'd really socked me."

409

"No, that wasn't the agreement," said the man, taking the notes himself, swiftly but delicately. "You've got to consider time spent, and an agreement entered into even if not carried out. But I'll say this, sir. This night does you credit. You've behaved like a gentleman."

"Oh, sod being a gentleman," said Francis, then regretted it, and shook hands with them both before running down the stairs into the Soho street.

The premises of Sir Geoffrey Duveen and Company were elegant and awesome; Francis would never have presumed to enter on his own volition, but it was here that Colonel Copplestone had said he was to meet him, and the wording of the message had suggested without actually saying so that it was a matter of importance. Something of importance was just what Francis needed. He had never felt so insignificant, so diminished, so exploited in his life since the days at Carlyle Rural. He was smartly dressed and punctual as he presented himself in the great London centre of art dealing and art exportation. The Colonel was in a small panelled room in which hung three pictures that made Francis's eyes pop. This was the sort of thing that very rich collectors could afford, and that they looked to the Duveen Company to supply.

"But you have your degree. First Class honours; I saw it in *The Times*. Just remind me of what that degree implies."

The Colonel seemed inclined to brush aside Francis's story of his marriage and its outcome as something of secondary importance. How callous these old fellows were!

"Well, it's called Modern Greats, but the formal name is Philosophy, Politics, and Economics. I concentrated on philosophy, and having a Classics degree already I had a certain advantage over the men who worked with translations; you begin at Descartes, but it's very useful to know what came before. And modern languages: mine were French and German. The politics is pretty much British constitutional stuff. I did as little economics as I could. Not my thing: I prefer my astrology without water."

"Aha. Well, you didn't waste your time at Oxford," said the Colonel. "Don't let the other thing bother you too much. Painful, of course, but I can offer you something that will make you forget it—or almost forget it."

"In the profession?"

"Yes. Not bang in the middle of the profession, of course. That's for quite a different sort of chap. But something you can do very well, I should think. Better than anyone else available at the moment, certainly. I want you to work with Tancred Saraceni."

"Is he—?"

"Most certainly not. And you must never let him think you are, or you'll be in the soup. No; Saraceni is in a queer game of his own, which interests us at the moment, and could be important. By the way, quite a few people who believe in that sort of thing say he has the Evil Eye. I don't completely dismiss that, so watch your step. You told me he had suggested that you might like to work with him? Learn his special trade, or craft, or whatever he calls it?"

"Yes, but I'm not really sure that's what I want. I want to be a painter, not a craftsman who tarts up paintings that have been allowed to decay."

"Yes, but what the profession wants is that somebody should be with Saraceni on the job he's undertaking now. Do you know anything about the Düsterstein collection?"

"Never heard of it."

"It's not well known, though these people here at Duveen's know about it, of course. It's their business to know such things. It's a lot of Renaissance and post-Renaissance and Counter-Reformation pictures—not all of them the best, I believe, but still remarkable—that are housed in Schloss Düsterstein in Lower Bavaria, about seventy miles from Munich. The owner is the Gräfin von Ingelheim, and she is interested in having her pictures put in A-1 condition, with a view to sale. Not a vulgar sell-out, you understand; not an 'Everything Must Be Sold To The Walls By The End Of The Month' thing. No, a gradual, very high-class unloading that should bring in a great deal of money. We want to know where the pictures are going. She's persuaded Saraceni to do the work of getting the stuff ready, rather on the quiet, without actually being secret. Saraceni needs an assistant, and we would like the assistant to be a member of the profession. And that's you, my boy."

"I'm to report to you? But what? And how?"

"No written reports to me, unless something totally unlikely happens. But you'll come back to England now and then, won't you? Don't you want to see little Charlotte and find out how she is getting on? What kind of a father would you be if you didn't? But there will also be another form of written report, and this afternoon you had better go to Harley Street, where Sir Owen Williams-Owen will see you, and take a look at your heart, and tell you how to report back to him on how it's getting on."

It was plain to Francis that Uncle Jack was enjoying being mysterious, and that his best course was to play straight man, and let his instructions come in due course.

"Williams-Owen knows all about hearts. He will give you a regimen of health that you must follow, which will include regular reports to him on how your heart is functioning. How many heartbeats after strenuous exercise—that sort of thing. But in actual fact it will be a key to observations we want you to make about trains.

"Schloss Düsterstein sits in a considerable estate, with some parkland and a lot of farms. Less than a mile from the house, or the castle or whatever it is, there is a branch of a railway, and that branch leads to a large compound—a concentration camp, as Lord Kitchener called them, to which freight and cattle cars are taken from time to time, not on any regular schedule but always late at night. You can tell how many cars there are because the train travels quite slowly—what they call a Bummelzug—and at one place it crosses an intersection point, and makes a characteristic sound with its wheels. If you keep your ears open, and count the times you hear that sound, and then divide by two, you can reckon the number of freight or goods vans that have passed over the point, and are thus bound for the camp. And that's what you report to Williams-Owen, every fortnight, according to a scheme he will give you, in a letter in which you can whimper and play the hypochondriac as much as you please. He'll see that the information gets to the right place."

"It's better than staying here and feeling sorry for myself, I suppose."

"Much better. It's your first professional job, and if you haven't thought so already, you're damned lucky to get it."

"Well, but what about—oh, sod being a gentleman! Sorry to be sordid, Uncle Jack, but—am I paid anything?"

"As I told you, this is something of a sideline, and we haven't any appropriation for it. But I think you may count on something eventually. Anyhow, you needn't pretend to me that you need money. I've heard about your grandfather's will. Your father mentioned it in a letter."

"I see. I'm in training, as it were?"

"No; it's a real job. But take my advice, Frank, don't fuss about money. The profession is run on a shoestring, and there are lots of people fighting for a quarter-inch of the string already. When there's anything for you, you can rely on me to let you know. But if there's no money, I can at least offer you some information. We know where Charlie Fremantle is."

"Is she with him?"

"I suppose so. He's in a very hot place to be at the moment. If those two are counting on a peaceful old age, they're out of their minds. Oh, and your friend Buys-Bozzaris is dead."

"What? How?"

"Carelessness. Actually he was a futile agent, and his recruiting was a joke; Charlie Fremantle was the only fish he caught, and even Charlie— who is an idiot—managed to cheat him about some gambling money. So Basil found himself in what we might call an untenable position, and it looks as if he shot himself."

"I don't believe it. I doubt if he could hit himself—on purpose, anyhow."

"Perhaps not. Perhaps he had expert assistance—Well, anything more?"

"Just a matter of curiosity, Uncle Jack. These goods vans—these freight cars—what's in them?"

"People."

Your man was lucky to be quit of Ismay, said the Lesser Zadkiel.

—My man was lucky to have known her, said the

415

Daimon Maimas. She doesn't show up well in Francis's story: an unscrupulous little sexual teaser and a crook about money; if she had stayed with him, what sort of cat-and-dog life would they have had? They would have torn one another apart and quite soon she would have betrayed him with somebody. But she thought herself a free agent, and that always leads to trouble.

—Oh quite. She was really an adjunct of Charlie Fremantle; one aspect of his fate. Odd, isn't it, that these adventurous, feather-brained fools like Charlie always have some woman who is ready to put up with anything to serve him and his folly? My records show it again and again.

—What lies before her in Spain? Scampering around from one squalid, endangered hovel to another, always under threat, often under gunfire, imagining she is serving the people's cause—which neither she nor Charlie could have defined—but really just Charlie's woman and slave. If pity lay in my sphere, said the Daimon, I think I should pity her.

—But pity is not in your sphere, brother. You don't even pity poor Francis, who broke his heart over her.

—Certainly not. A heart is never really stout until it has broken and mended at least once. Francis might be grateful to me for finding him such an interesting heart-breaker. Lots of men break their hearts over women who are no more interesting than turnips.

—Yet he knew she was no good. Not to him, anyway. What was she to him?

—Surely you remember how, in his bedroom at Blairlogie, he used to posture in front of his mirror,

rigged up as a sort of woman? *Searching for the Mystical Marriage, though he didn't know it; looking for the woman in himself for the completion of himself and he thought he had found it in Ismay. And he most certainly did find part of it in Ismay, for she was what he was not, she had qualities he would never possess, and she had the beauty and the sluttish irresistible charm to make him love her whatever she did, and whatever he knew about her. I think I did rather well in enlarging his life with Ismay.*

—As when she told him he was the kind of man things happened to, and not the kind that made them happen?

—Oh, come, brother, you were not taken in by that old chestnut, were you? You know as well as I that people often make the most astonishing reversals of what seems to be their basic nature, when they are compelled to do it. Really, my dear colleague, you astonish me! I don't wish to be offensive, but here we are, a couple of Minor Immortals, watching Francis's life unfold before us, as you have it filed away in your archive, and yet sometimes you talk as if we were no wiser than a pair of human beings watching television, where the unexpected, the unpredictable is rigorously forbidden to happen. The laws of such melodrama are not binding on us, brother. You have typed Francis, and you talk of Ismay as if she were vanished forever. As for me, you seem to degrade me to the level of that detestable theological fraud, a Guardian Angel! Come, come!

—Don't scold, brother. I am sorry if I have appeared to underestimate your daimonic role in this

417

affair. But I have so much to do with mortals that sometimes I think a little of their sentimentality is rubbing off on me.

—Don't be distracted by trivialities, said the Daimon Maimas. What do the theologians say? Circumcise yourself as to the heart and not as to the foreskin. And never neglect what is bred in the bone. Do you think it was bred in Francis to be a victim all his life? How would that reflect on me? As a rather superior mortal once said to a sentimental friend, Clear your mind of cant! Shall we continue?

PART FIVE

PART FIVE

Click-clack . . . click-clack . . . twenty-four repetitions of the sound, and a melancholy toot as if from an entirely innocent Bummelzug passing over a switch-point. But why would an innocent Bummelzug be rumbling through the Bavarian countryside at half past eleven at night, when all decent freight-trains were at rest on their sidings? Twenty-four click-clacks meant twelve vans. Twelve vans, loaded, perhaps, with people, were being hauled to the internment camp that lay obscurely in a nearby valley.

Francis made a note in the book he carried always in his breast pocket. Tomorrow he would write to Sir Owen Williams-Owen in Harley Street, to report on the condition of his heartbeat under particular conditions of stress.

This was the first such observation he had made during his first week at Schloss Düsterstein. It was providential that his bedroom lay on the side of the great house that was nearest to the railway line.

The great house had been a surprise—was still

a surprise, after a week's exploration. To begin, in spite of its name it was not particularly suggestive of melancholy. Old it unquestionably was, and large even as country houses go, but its chief quality was that of the centre of a large farming district, and on its own lands and tenant-farms adjacent the Gräfin von Ingelheim conducted a big agricultural industry with exemplary efficiency. Motor trucks took vegetables, fowls, and veal or pork every week to the railway that carried them on to Munich, where wholesale dealers awaited them, and distributed them to a number of hotels, restaurants, and butchers. In a wing of the castle was an office from which the farms were managed and the dispatching of the foodstuffs was arranged, probably in some of the goods vans that now and then visited the camp in the hills. Schloss Düsterstein was, as agricultural matters go, big business.

Castle it was called, but there was nothing of the medieval fortress about it. There were reminders of the seventeenth century and a large square tower that was considerably earlier, but its appearance and plan were of the latter part of the eighteenth century; if shabby in some of its details and furnishings—the sort of shabbiness that suggests an aristocratic indifference to newfangledness rather than poverty—it was comfortable and as pleasant as a decidedly grand house could be. It was not domestic in the English sense, but it was not a comfortless imitation of a French château, either. Francis's bedroom, for instance: a heavily furnished room so large that the big bed seemed accidental rather than central, with armchairs and a desk and plenty of room for all his artist's equipment, and in one corner a large and fine porcelain stove. True, he washed in a little closet concealed in one of the walls, to which hot water was brought through an inner passage, so that he never saw the servant who carried it; but the ewer and basin, the two large chamber-pots, and the slop-pail were of an expensive eighteenth-century china, marked with the crest of Ingelheim. Slops were spirited away every day by means of the same inner passage. Baths were to be taken in a large chamber set out with Empire furniture and a marble tub of almost Roman aspect, into which rather rusty water gushed through huge brass taps; it was a long walk from the bedroom, but as an Oxford man Francis was accustomed to distant baths.

Francis's room was in the rear of the castle; the family were in another wing into which he never penetrated, but he met them in the living quarters, a series of large drawing-rooms and a dining-room behind the rooms of state, which were now never used except for the display of the collection of pictures that had made Düsterstein and the Ingelheim family famous among connoisseurs for two centuries. Not that the pictures in these private rooms were inconsiderable; they were family portraits by a variety of masters, not always of the foremost rank, but by no means unknown or lightly esteemed.

Ever since his arrival Francis had looked with astonishment from the pictures on the walls to the two representatives of the family who sat below them, the Countess Ottilie and her granddaughter, Amalie, whose features the portraits reflected in a bewildering but always recognizable variety. Here was the Family Face indeed, the Countess's square and determined as became a great landowner and a farmer of formidable talents, and that of Amalie, which was oval, still unmarked by experience but filled with beautiful expectancy. The Countess was not yet sixty; Amalie was probably fourteen. He conversed with them in English, as the Countess was anxious that Amalie should be perfect in that language.

These evenings were not long. Dinner was at eight, and was never over before nine, for though not a heavy meal it was served with what seemed to Francis extraordinary deliberation. Saraceni talked with the Countess. Francis was expected to talk to Miss Ruth Nibsmith, the governess. Amalie spoke only when spoken to by her grandmother. After dinner they sat for an hour, during which the Countess made one cup of coffee and one glass of cognac last the full time; sharp at ten Amalie kissed her grandmother, curtsied to Saraceni and Francis, and retired under the care of Miss Nibsmith. Then the Countess went to her private room, where, Saraceni told him, she worked over the farm accounts until eleven, at which hour she went to bed, in order to rise at six and spend two hours out of doors, directing her workers, before breakfast at eight.

"A very regular existence," said Saraceni.

"Does nothing else ever happen?" said Francis.

"Never. Except that on Sundays the priest comes for Mass at seven; you aren't expected to attend, but it will give satisfaction if you do, and you shouldn't miss the chapel; it is a Baroque marvel that you won't see otherwise. But what do you mean—'Does nothing else ever happen?' What do you suppose is happening? Money is being made, to begin with. This family was almost beggared during the War and the Countess's father and now Countess Ottilie have made them almost as rich as they ever were—out of veal, which, as you know, is the staple diet of people in this part of the world. Amalie is being prepared for a brilliant marriage to somebody who hasn't been chosen yet, but who will have to measure up to exacting standards. Great fortunes don't go to fools—not at Düsterstein, anyhow. And there is the collection to be put into first-class order, and you and I will work on that like galley-slaves, for the Countess expects it. Isn't that enough activity to satisfy your North American soul?"

"Sorry to bring it up, but—do I get paid?"

"Most certainly you do. First of all, you are privileged to work with me, and there are hundreds of young artists who would give anything for that high distinction. Next, you have an opportunity to study one of the very few notable collections still to remain in private hands. That means that you will be able to make an intimate day-by-day and mood-by-mood study of pictures that even the directors of world-famous galleries see only by carefully controlled appointment. The greatest are on loan to the Munich gallery, but there are splendid things here—things any of those galleries would be glad to possess. You are privileged to live on familiar terms with aristocrats—the Ingelheims of blood, myself of talent—in beautiful country surroundings. Every day you are given real cream and the best of veal. You have the cultivated conversation of La Nibsmith, and the transporting silences of Amalie. You can keep your little car in the stables. But as for money—no, no money; that would be adding sugar to honey. The Countess receives you here as my assistant. I am paid, of course, but not you. What do you want money for? You're rich."

"I'm beginning to be afraid that stands between me and being an artist."

"There are worse disabilities. Want of talent, for instance. You have talent, and I shall show you how to use it."

To begin with, learning to use his talent seemed to mean a lot of dirty work, about the performance of which Saraceni was tyrannical and sarcastic. The silky expert Francis had met at Oxford and the patrician connoisseur he visited in Rome was an unappeasable slave-driver in the studio. During his first few days Francis did no work at all, but wandered freely through the castle to get the feel of things, as Saraceni put it.

But on the first Sunday there was a violent change. Francis was up in time for chapel, and, as Saraceni had said, it was a Baroque marvel. At first sight it seemed to have a splendid dome in which the Last Judgement was set forth in swirling movement, but on examination this proved to be a *trompe-l'oeil* work of extraordinary skill, painted on a flat ceiling, and effective only if the observer did not go too far forward toward the altar; viewed from that point the supposed dome was distorted, and the *sotto in su* figures of the Trinity looked toad-like. The worshipper who went forward to receive the Host was not wise if he looked upward when he returned to his seat, for he would see a fiercely distorted God the Father and God the Son spying on him from the contrived dome. The chapel itself was small, but seemed big; the fat priest had to squeeze himself into the tiny elevated pulpit as if he were putting on tight trousers. The whole room was a wonder of gilding and plaster painted in those pinks and blues that look like confectioner's work to the critic who refuses to surrender himself to their seductions. Francis was surprised to find himself alone in the chapel with Saraceni; the Countess and her granddaughter sat at the back, in an elevated box, as if at the opera, invisible to the less distinguished worshippers below. Theirs was the best view of the magical ceiling.

After chapel, breakfast, at which Saraceni and Francis were served by themselves.

427

"Now, to work," said Saraceni. "Have you brought any overalls?"

Francis had no overalls, but Saraceni fitted him out with a garment that might once have been a laboratory technician's white coat, filthy with paint and oil.

"Now to the studio," said Saraceni, "and when we are in the studio, you had better call me Meister. Maestro is not quite right for these surroundings. And I shall call you Cornish, not Francis, when we are at work. Corniche. Yes, you shall be Corniche."

What was happening to the Meister? In the studio he was shorter, more darting and nervous in movement, and his nose seemed hookier than elsewhere. At work, Saraceni was not the urbane creature of his social life. Francis recalled what Uncle Jack had said about the Evil Eye, though of course he did not believe in any such thing.

The studio was like a studio only in its fine north light, which came from a wall of windows that opened on the park. It had been, explained Saraceni as Francis gaped in wonderment, one of those amusements that pleased the aristocracy of the eighteenth century. It was a very long room the walls of which were encrusted with shells in many varieties, so set in the plaster that the inner sides of some and the convexities of others were outward toward the light, and they had been used to form an intricate decoration of panels, pillars, and baroque festoons. Not only shells, but minerals of several varieties had been used to decorate the walls, forming pilasters of white and pink and golden marble and—could it be?—lapis lazuli, between which depended clustered ropes of shells, each of which culminated at its fattest richness in a huge piece of brain coral. When it was new, and when it was loved and admired, it must have been a splendid folly, a rococo pavilion to lift the heart and sharpen the senses. But now the shells were dusty and dingy, the dry fountain in the wall showed rust and dirt in its basin, and the occasional mirrors were like eyes over which cataracts had grown. The shell benches had been shoved into a jumble at one end, and the room was dominated by several easels, a laboratory bench whose water supply came from visible, ugly piping that made a toe-catcher in the floor, and a large metal affair, suggesting a furnace, that had been hitched up to the castle's meagre dynamo with equal disregard for the propriety of the room.

"What love and skill must have gone into the making of this," said Francis.

"No doubt, but the less must give way to the greater, and now it is my workroom," said Saraceni. "This was a costly, ingenious toy, and those who played in it are dust. Ours is the greater task."

What was the task? Francis was never told directly; he made his discoveries by deduction, with growing incredulity. From after breakfast until four o'clock in the afternoon, when the light changed too much for Saraceni's needs, with a short interval for sandwiches and a glass of good

Munich beer, he toiled at a variety of jobs from early September until mid-December. He learned to grind minerals to powder in a mortar, and mix them with various oils; the mixing was a tedious process. He learned to use and prepare mineral colours and gums—cinnabar, manganese dioxide, calcined umber, and sticky, messy gamboge. He learned to chip bits from the least visible parts of the splendid lapis pilasters, and grind his chippings fine with mortar and pestle before uniting the powder with lilac oil, to make a splendid ultramarine. It gave him particular pleasure to make the acquaintance of woad, the *iastis tinctoria*, from the juice of which a dark blue could be extracted. At the laboratory bench he learned to make up a compound of carbolic acid and formaldehyde (the whiff of which reminded him poignantly of nights with Zadok in Devinney's embalming parlour) and bottle it firmly against evaporation.

"I don't suppose you ever thought painting involved so much chemistry and cooking," said Saraceni. "You are making the true colours used by the Old Masters, Corniche. These are the splendid shades that do not fade with age. Nowadays you can buy colours somewhat like them in shops, but they are not the same at all. They are labour-saving and they save time. But you and I have precisely the same amount of time as the Old Masters—twenty-four hours in every day. There is no more, and never any less. For the true work of restoration on an old panel or canvas you must use the colours the original master employed. The

honesty of your craft demands it. It is also undetectable.

"Oh, I suppose some very clever investigator
with rays and chemicals might be able to say what
parts of a picture had been restored—though I
prefer to say revived—but our task is to do a job
of revival that will not provoke foolishly inquisitive persons to resort to rays and chemicals. It is
not the purpose of a picture to arouse unworthy
suspicions, but to give pleasure—delight, or awe,
or religious intimations, or simply a fine sense of
the past, and of the boundless depth and variety
of life."

This had a fine ring of morality and aesthetic
probity about it. Saraceni making the past live
again. But there were elements in what was really
happening that Francis did not understand.

If the past was to be recovered, why not the
best of the past? There were pictures hanging in
Schloss Düsterstein that plainly needed the attention of a restorer, pictures by distinguished masters—a Mengs, a van Bylert, even a Van Dyck
that wanted cleaning—but these did not come to
the shell-pavilion. Instead there were several pictures, usually painted on panels, some of which
were in bad repair and all of which were dirty.
One of Francis's jobs was to wipe these as clean as
possible with soft, damp cloths and then—but
why?—wash these cloths in as little water as possible and dry out the pan until the dust from the
picture was dust again, and could be sucked up

with a syringe and put in a numbered small bottle.

Most of the little pictures were portraits of Nobody in Particular, in all his and her dull variety; just noblemen and merchants, burgomasters and scholars, and their pie-faced wives. But Saraceni would place one of these competent, uninteresting daubs on his easel, and study it with care for hours before removing certain portions with a solvent so that the painting beneath was blurred, or else the undercoating of the panel was revealed. Then he would repaint the face, so that it was the same as before but with a greater distinction—a keenness of aristocratic eye, a new look of *bürgerlich* astuteness, a fuller beard; women, if they had hands, were given rings, modest but costly, and better complexions. Sometimes he placed, in the upper left-hand corner of the panel, some little heraldic device, which might indicate the status of the sitter, and on one picture, rather larger than the rest, he introduced an ornamental chain, the collar and emblem of the Saint-Esprit. He is tarting up these four-hundred-year-old dullards, thought Francis, but why, and for whom?

Saraceni's method of painting was wholly new to Francis. On his palette he laid out his colours—the colours that Francis had so laboriously prepared—in small, almost parsimonious dibbets; but elsewhere on the palette was some of the phenol and formaldehyde mixture mingled with a little oil, and before he took paint on his brush he dipped it first in this resinous gum, which served him as a medium. A strange way to paint, surely? Late in November Francis decided that the time had come to ask a question.

"You shall see why I do that," said the Meister. "Indeed, you cannot help but see. Overpainting on a restored—or revived—picture is easily detected with the naked eye. As a picture ages, and the paint dries out—it takes about fifty years—it cracks in a certain pattern. What we call the *craquelure*. The cracks are mere hair-lines; only a poor picture develops a hide like a crocodile. But those hair-lines penetrate right through all the coatings of paint, as deep as to the ground you have used to prepare your canvas—or panel—like these I have been working on. So—how do I produce a *craquelure* in the new work I have done that blends undetectably with the old work? Well, as you see I am using a fast-drying paint—or rather, that phenol mixture that I use as my medium. Tomorrow I shall show you how I produce the *craquelure*."

So this was what the electric furnace was for! Francis had assumed it might be to heat the cold, damp grotto-room, but such heat as there was came from a brazier—not much more than a pan of burning charcoal set on a tripod, which gave out about as much heat as a dying baby's last breath, in Francis's opinion. On the day following their talk about *craquelure* Saraceni turned on the electricity in the furnace, and in time, with much rumbling and moaning, it achieved a heat by no means great, but which taxed the primitive electrical system of the castle, where electric light was scant and dim, and did not proceed above the ground floor.

When Saraceni declared the heat to be sufficient he and Francis carefully inserted the painted panels and after about fifty minutes of slow baking they emerged with, sure enough, tiny hairlines that satisfied the Meister. While they were still warm he surprised Francis yet again.

"Before these cool, you must take a sable brush and put back as much as you can of the dust that was originally on these pictures, taking special pains to get it into the tiny cracks over the new work. Don't be too eager; but be sure to cover the whole picture and especially whatever is new. Of course, you will use the dust from the bottle that bears the number of the picture. We must not insult Bürgermeister A with dirt that the hand of time has sown on the portrait of the wife of Bürgermeister B. And hurry up. The dust must adhere. Now—on with your work, you understudy of Father Time."

The next day Saraceni was in high excitement. "Everything now will have to wait until I return from Rome. I must visit my apartment before Christmas; I cannot be separated forever from my darlings, my pictures, my furniture—not even from my bed-curtains, which once belonged to the Empress Josephine. Antaeus had to touch his foot to the earth to gain strength, and I must touch and see my beauties if I am to have the resolution

434

I need for this work.—You are looking at me oddly, Corniche? Does my passion for my collection really surprise you so much?"

"No, Meister, not that. But—precisely what is it you are doing here?"

"What do you suppose?"

"I don't want to be presumptuous, but this restoration, or revitalizing, or whatever you call it, seems to go a bit farther than is necessary."

"Oh, Corniche, speak what is in your mind. The word you want to use is faking, isn't it?"

"I wouldn't use that word to you, Meister."

"Certainly not."

"But it does look rather fishy."

"Fishy is just the right word! Now, Corniche, you shall know everything that is proper for you to know in good time. Indeed, you shall know a great deal when Prince Max visits us. He is coming for Christmas, and I shall be back in plenty of time to show him all these greatly improved panels. Prince Max talks a great deal more freely than I do. Of course, it is his right.

"Meanwhile, during the fortnight that I am absent, you shall have a little treat. A treat and a rest. You have seen how I work, and I promised to teach you as much of what I know as you can take in. While I am away, I want you to paint a picture for me. See, here is this little panel. Almost a ruin as a picture, but the panel is sound enough, and so is the leather that covers it. Paint me a picture that is all your own, but would not look out of place among the other panels. Do the best you can."

"What is the subject to be? One of these *bürgerlich* turnip-heads?"

"What you think best. Use your invention, my dear fellow. But make it congruous with the others. I want to see what you can do. And when I return we shall have a splendid Christmas, showing these pretty baked cakes to Prince Max."

Use his invention? Well, if that was what Saraceni wanted, that is what Francis would do, and he would surprise the Meister, who seemed to think his invention would be limited. Saraceni set off for Rome the day after he told Francis how to use his time, and Francis sat down to his table in the chilly shell-grotto to plan his surprise.

Saraceni was not the only one to leave the castle. The Countess and Amalie left on the same day, to go to Munich to enjoy some of its pleasures before Christmas, and Francis and Miss Ruth Nibsmith were left in possession.

Miss Nibsmith was by no means bad company; in the absence of the Countess she expanded considerably, and although Francis never saw her during the day, they met at dinner, which was served at the same stately pace as always. To fill up the time between courses they drank a good deal of the Countess's excellent wine, and resorted after dinner to the brandy bottle.

"I can never really settle myself in these German rooms," said Miss Nibsmith, kicking off her substantial shoes and putting her feet on the side of the splendid porcelain stove in the family drawing-room. "They have no focus. You know what I mean? *Focus,* in the true Latin meaning of the word. No hearth. I long for an open fire. It is as good as a dog in a room to give it life. These German stoves are beautiful, and they are certainly practical. This room is warmer than it would be if it had a fireplace, but where does one look for the centre of the room? Where does one stand when making a pronouncement? Where does one warm one's bottom?"

"I suppose the focus is wherever the most important person is," said Francis. "When the Countess is here, she is obviously the focus. Now—you ought to know these things, as an intimate of Düsterstein: I understand that for Christmas we are to entertain a Prince Max—will he be the focus? Or does the Countess always top the heap in her own castle?"

"Prince Max will be the focus," said Miss Nibsmith, "but not just because of his rank. He is quite the bounciest man I have ever met, and his laugh and his chatter make him the centre wherever he is. The Countess adores him."

"A relative?" said Francis.

"A cousin—not the nearest sort. A Hohenzollern, but poor. Poor, that is, for a prince. But Maxi is not one to repine and blame Fortune. No, no; he stirs his stumps and deals extensively in wine, and he gets rid of a lot of it in England and especially in the States. Maxi is what our Victorian ancestors would have called a smooth file. He will be the focus, you will see. The hot air from Prince Max will keep us all warm, and perhaps uncomfortably hot."

What did Miss Nibsmith do with herself all day? Francis made a polite inquiry.

"I write letters for the Countess in French, English, and German. At the moment I keep an eye on the business. I type quite well. I give lessons to Amalie, chiefly in history; she reads a lot and we talk. History is my thing. My Cambridge degree is in history. I'm a Girton girl. If I have any spare time I work on my own notes, which might be a book some day."

"A book? About what?"

"You'll laugh. Or no, I think you have too much intelligence to laugh. Anybody who works with Tancred Saraceni must be used to odd ventures. I'm making a study of astrology in Bavaria, particularly during the sixteenth and seventeenth centuries. What do you make of that?"

"I don't make anything of it. Tell me about it."

"Astrology is part of the science of the past, and of course the science of the present has no place for it, because it is rooted in a discredited notion of the universe, and puts forward a lot of Neo-Platonic ideas that don't make much sense—until you live with them for a while."

"Does that remark mean that you believe in astrology yourself?"

"Not as hard-boiled science, certainly. But as psychology—that's quite another thing. Astrology is based on a notion nobody wants to accept in our wonderfully reasonable Western World, which is that the position of the stars at the moment of your birth governs your life. 'As above, so below' is the principle in a nutshell. Utterly dotty, obviously. Lots of people must be born under the same arrangement of stars, and they don't have similar fates. Of course, it's necessary to take careful heed of precisely *where* you were born, and that varies greatly, so far as the stars are concerned. But anyhow, if the astrologer has your date, and time, and place of birth he can cast a horoscope, which can sometimes be quite useful— sometimes no good at all."

"You sound as if you half believe it, Ruth."

"Half yes: half not. But it's rather like the *I Ching*. Your intuition has to work as well as your reason, and in astrology it's the intuition of the astrologer that does the trick."

"Are you strongly intuitive?"

"Well, Girton girl though I am, I have to say yes, against what my reason tells me. Anyhow, what I'm studying is how widespread and how influential astrology was in this part of the world at the time of the Reformation and Counter-Reformation, when most people here were fierce Catholics and were supposed to leave all spiritual things—and that meant all psychological things as well—to the Church, which of course knew best, and would see you through if you were a good child. But lots of people didn't want to be good children. They couldn't fight down the pull of whatever was in the depths of their being; couldn't fight it down and couldn't channel it into being a contemplative, or whatever the Church approved. So they sought out astrologers, and the astrologers were usually in hot water with the Church. Very much like our modern world, where we are supposed to leave everything to science, even when science is something as spook-ridden as psychoanalysis. But people don't. Astrology is very big business in the extraverted, science-ridden U.S.A., for instance. The Yanks are always whooping it up for Free Will, and every man's fate being his own creation, and all that, but they're just as superstitious as the Romans ever were."

"Well! You're a funny historian, Ruth."

"Yes I am, aren't I?"

"But as a wise man I know—or knew, for the poor fellow is dead now—used to say, Life's a rum start."

"The very rummest. Like this room, in a way. Here we are, cosy as can be, even if we have no focus. What makes us so snug?"

"The stove, obviously."

"Yes, but have you never thought what makes the stove so warm?"

"I've wondered—yes. How is it fed?"

"That's one of the interesting things about these old castles. Dividing all the main rooms are terribly narrow passages—not more than eighteen inches wide, some of them, and as dark as night— and through those corridors creep servants in soft slippers who poke firewood into these stoves from the back. Unseen by us, and usually unheard. We don't give them a thought, but they are there, and they keep life in winter from being intolerable. Do they listen to us? I'll bet they do. They keep us warm, they are necessary to us, and they probably know a lot more about us than we would consider comfortable. They are the hidden life of the house."

"A spooky idea."

"The whole Universe is a spooky idea. And in every life there are these unseen people and—not people exactly—who keep us warm.—Have you ever had your horoscope cast?"

"Oh, as a boy I sent away money for a horoscope from some company in the States that advertised them in a boys' magazine. Awful rubbish, illiterate and printed on the worst kind of paper. And at Oxford a Bulgarian chap I met insisted on casting a horoscope for me, and it was blatantly obvious that what he found in the stars was pretty much what he wanted me to do, which was join some half-assed Communist spy outfit he thought he commanded. Not a very deep look into astrology, I am sure you would say."

"No, though the Bulgarian one has a familiar ring. Lots of horoscopes used to be cast that way, and still are, obviously. But I'll do one for you, if you like. The genuine article, no punches pulled. Interested?"

"Of course. Who can resist anything so flattering to the ego?"

"Dead right. That's another element. A horoscope means somebody is really paying attention to you, and that is rarer than you might think. Where, and when, were you born?"

"September 12, apparently at seven o'clock in the morning, in 1909."

"And where?"

"A place called Blairlogie, in Canada."

"Sounds like the Jumping-Off Place. I shall have to consult the gazetteer to get the exact position. Because the stars over Blairlogie weren't precisely like the stars over anywhere else."

"Yes, but suppose somebody else had been born at just that moment, in Blairlogie, wouldn't he be my twin, in all matters of Fate?"

"No. And now I shall let the cat out of the bag. This is what separates me from your boys'-paper fraud, and your Bulgarian Commie fraud. This is my great historical discovery that the real astrologers guarded with their lives, and if you breathe it to anybody before my book comes out, I shall hunt you down and kill you very imaginatively. When were you conceived?"

"God, how would I know? In Blairlogie; I'm sure of that."

"The usual answer. Parents are terribly niminy-piminy about telling their children these things. Ah, well; I shall just have to count backward and make an approximation. But anyhow—when were you baptized and christened?"

"Oh, I can tell you that, right enough. It was about three weeks later; September 30, actually, at roughly four o'clock in the afternoon. Church of England rite. Oh, and now I come to think of it, I was baptized again, years later, Catholic, that time. I'm sure I can remember the date if I try. But how does that come in?"

"When you were begotten is obviously important. As you seem to be a healthy chap I presume you were a full-term baby, so I can get the date fairly near. Date of entry upon the stage in the Great Theatre of the World is important, and that is the only one the commoner sort of astrologers bother with. But the date when you were formally received into what your community looked upon as the world of the spirit, and were given your own name, is important because it supplies a few shades to your central chart. And to be baptized twice!—spiritual dandyism, I'd call it. You let me have all that on a piece of paper at breakfast, and I'll get to work. Meanwhile, just one more teensy cognac before we retire to our blameless couches."

Days alone in the shell-grotto and nights with Ruth Nibsmith were doing much to restore Francis's battered self-esteem. Getting away from England had been a bruising experience. There was all the trouble of explaining to Ismay's parents what had happened, and putting up with their obvious, though unexpressed, opinion that it must have been his fault. Then there was the trouble of making arrangements about the child Charlotte—Little Charlie as everybody but Francis insisted on calling her, slurring the "Ch" so it sounded like "Sharlie"—because the Glassons wanted to have control over her, but did not particularly want to be bothered with her. Their days of bringing up children were, they said reasonably, in the past. Were they now to take on a baby, who needed care every hour of the day? They worried, understandably, about Ismay, who was God knows where with God knows who in a country on the brink of civil war. The girl, they admitted, was a fool, but that did not seem to lessen their conviction that Francis was to blame for everything that had happened. When he was pushed at last to the point of telling them that Little Charlie was not his child, Aunt Prudence wept and Uncle Roderick swore, but they were no more sympathetic toward Francis. Cuckolds are fated to play ignominious and usually comic roles.

Never had Francis felt so low as when at last he came to an arrangement with the Glassons; in addition to the money already promised to keep the estate afloat, he agreed to pay all the costs of maintaining Little Charlie, which were substantial, because the child must have a first-rate nanny, and money for whatever a child needs—and the Glassons were not prepared to stint their granddaughter—and also a sum indefinitely allocated but definitely estimated for unforeseen costs. It was all reasonable enough, but Francis had the feeling that he was being exploited, and when his honour and his affections were under ruinous attack, he was astonished to find how greatly the assault on his bank-account affected him also. It was ignoble, under the circumstances, to think so much about money, but think about it he did. What did he care about Little Charlie, at present a dribbling, squalling, slumbrous lump?

In the circumstances, it was not surprising that he had jumped at Uncle Jack's offer of something to do, some place to go, a necessary task to undertake. But that had resolved itself into three months of grubby devilling for Tancred Saraceni, who had kept him grinding away with mortar and pestle, boiling up the smelly muck that went into the "black oil" the painter needed for his work, and generally acting as chore-boy and sorcerer's apprentice.

What was the sorcerer up to? Faking pictures, or at least improving existing worthless pictures. Could the great Saraceni really be sunk in this worst sort of artistic sin? Certainly that was what it looked like.

Well, if this was the game, if this was what he had been dragged into, he might as well play it to the hilt. He would show Saraceni that he could daub in the sixteenth-century German manner as well as anyone. He was to paint a picture that would agree in quality and style with the panels that had been completed and that now sat all around the shell-grotto, staring at him with the speculative eyes of the unknown dead. As Francis sat down to plan his picture he laughed for the first time in several months.

He did many preliminary drawings, and just to show what a conscientious faker he was, he did them on some of the expensive old paper culled from old books and artists' leavings he had from his Oxford days, coating it with an umber base, and making his careful preliminaries (for they were not sketches in the modern sense) with a silver-point. Yes, it was coming quite well. Yes, that was what he wanted and what would surprise the Meister. Rapidly and surely, he began to paint on his miserable old panel, in the Meister's own careful mode, with unexceptionable, authentic colours, and every stroke mixed with the magical formula of phenol and formaldehyde.

He realized with surprise that he was happy. And in his happiness, he sang.

Many painters have sung at their work, as a form of incantation, an evocative spell. What they sing may not impress an outsider as having much to do with their painting. What Francis sang was an Oxford student song to the tune of the Austrian national anthem of an earlier and happier time, *"Gott erhalte Franz den Kaiser"*:

> *Life presents a dismal picture,*
> *Home is gloomy as the tomb:*
> *Poor old Dad has got a stricture,*
> *Mother has a fallen womb;*
> *Brother Bill has been deported*
> *For a homosexual crime,*
> *And the housemaid's been aborted*
> *For the forty-second time.*

On and on he moaned, happy at his work. The

Happy Faker, he thought. As I do this, no one can touch me.

"Are you happy? I am." Ruth Nibsmith turned her head on the pillow to look at Francis. She was not a beautiful woman, or a pretty woman, but she was well-formed and she was incontestably a jolly woman. Jolly was the only possible word. A fresh, high-spirited, merry, and, it proved, an amorous woman, who had in no way set out to lure Francis into her bed, but had cheerfully agreed to his suggestion that they advance their friendship in this direction.

"Yes, I am happy. And it's nice of you to say that you are. I haven't had much luck making anyone happy in this way."

"Oh, but it's good sport, isn't it? How would you rank our performance, in university terms?"

"I'd give us a B +."

"An excellent second class. Well, I dunno—I'd call it an A-. That's modest, and keeps us well below the Romeo and Juliet level. Anyhow, I've enjoyed it immensely these last few days."

"You speak as if it were over."

"It is over. The Countess brings Amalie back from Munich tomorrow, and I must take to my role as the model of behaviour and discretion. Which I do without regret, or not too much regret. One has to play fair with one's employers, you know; the Countess trusts me, and so I can't be having it off with another of the upper servants in the Castle when I am watching over Amalie.

447

Oh, if Amalie could see us now she'd be green with envy!"

"What? That kid?"

"Kid my foot! Amalie's fourteen, and warm as one of those porcelain stoves. She adores you, you know."

"I've hardly spoken to her."

"Of course. You are distant, unattainable, darkly melancholy. Do you know what she calls you? Le Beau Ténébreux. She's eating her heart out for you. It would plunge her into despair to think you were content with her governess."

"Oh, shut up about the governess! And about upper servants; I'm nobody's servant."

"Balls, my boy! One's lucky if that's all one is. The Countess isn't a servant; she's a slave to this place, and to her determination to restore the family fortunes. You and I are just paid hands, able to leave whenever we please. I like being an upper servant. Lots of my betters have been upper servants. If it wasn't too much for Haydn to wear the livery of the Esterhazys, who am I to complain? There's a lot to be said for knowing one's place."

"That's what Victoria Cameron used to say."

"One of the women in your gaudy past?"

"No. Something like my nurse, I suppose. I have no gaudy past, as I'm sure you've read in the stars. My wife was always rubbing it in."

"A wife? So that's the woman in the horoscope?"

"You've found her, then?"

"A woman who gave you the most frightful dunt."

"That's Ismay, right enough. She always said I was too innocent for my own good."

"You're not innocent, Frank. Not in any stupid way. Your horoscope makes that extremely clear."

"When are you going to unveil the great horoscope? It'd better be soon, if the Countess comes back tomorrow."

"Tonight's the night. And we must get out of this nest of guilty passion right away, because I've got to dress and so have you, and we both want a wash."

"I'd been thinking about a bath. We both reek, in an entirely creditable way."

"No, no bath. The servants would be on to us at once if we bathed during the late afternoon. In the Bavarian lexicon of baths, an afternoon bath means sex. No, you must be content with a searching wash, in your pre-dinner allowance of hot water."

"Okay. 'Ae fond kiss, and then we sever'."

" 'Ae farewell, alas, forever'."

"Oh Ruth, don't say forever."

"Of course not. But until dinner, anyhow. And now—up and out!"

"I hope there's something good for dinner."

"What would you guess?"

"Something utterly unheard of in Düsterstein. What would you say to veal?"

"Bang on! I saw the menu this morning. *Poitrine de veau farci*."

"Ah, well; in the land of veal, all is veal.

> *I'm wearin' awa', Jean*
> *Like snow-wreaths in thaw, Jean*
> *I'm wearin' awa'*
> *In the land o' the veal."*

"Lucky to get it. I could eat a horse."

"Hunger is the best sauce."

"Frank, that's magnificent. What an encapsulation of universal experience! Is it your own?"

Francis gave her a playful punch, and went back to his own room, for a searching wash before dinner.

After dinner, the horoscope. Ruth had an impressive clutch of papers, some of which were zodiacal charts, upon which she had added copious notations in a handsome Italic hand.

"The writing oughtn't to swear at the material, you see, so I learned to write like this."

"Yes. Very nice. The only trouble is that it's so easily forged."

"Think so? I'm sure you could spot a forgery of your own fist."

"Yes, I've done so."

"There you go, being Le Beau Ténébreux. Could it have been the Dream Girl who appears so strongly in your chart?"

"It was. Clever of you to guess."

"A lot of this work is clever guessing. Making

hints from the chart fit in with hints from the subject. That girl is an important figure for you."

"Thank God she's gone."

"Not gone. She'll be back."

"What then?"

"Depends if she's still the Dream Girl. You ought to get wise to yourself, Francis. If she treated you badly, some of it was your own fault. When men go about making Dream Girls out of flesh-and-blood girls, it has the most awful effect on the girl. Some fall for it, and try to embody the dream, and that is horribly phoney and invites trouble; others become perfect bitches because they can't stand it. Is your wife a bitch?"

"Of the most absolute and triple-distilled canine order."

"Probably only a fool. Fools make more trouble than all the bitches ever whelped. But let's look at your full chart. Let's get down on the floor, where I can spread it out. Put some books on the corners to hold it down. That's it. Now—"

It was a handsome chart, handsome as the zodiac can be, and as neatly annotated as a governess could make it.

"I won't overwhelm you with astrological jargon, but take a look at these principal facts. The important thing is that your Sun is in midheaven, and that's terrific. And your eastern horizon—the point of ascent—is in conjunction with Saturn, who is a greatly misunderstood influence, because people immediately think, Oh yes, Saturn, he must be saturnine, or sour-bellied, but that's not what it really means at all. Your Moon is in the north, or subterranean midheaven. And—now this is very significant—your Sun is in conjunction with Mercury. Because of your very powerful Sun, you have lots of vitality, and believe me you need it, because life has given you some dunts, and has some others in waiting. But that powerful Sun also assures you of being right in the mainstream of psychic energy. You've got spiritual guts, and lots of intuition. Then that wonderful, resilient, swift Mercury. Psychologically, Francis, you are very fast on your feet.

"Now—here's that very powerful and influential Saturn. That's destiny. You remember about Saturn? He had it tough, because he was castrated, but he did some castrating himself. What's bred in the bone, you know. Patterns necessarily repeat themselves. All kinds of obstacles, burdens to be borne, anxieties, depressions and exhaustion—there's your Beau Ténébreux personality for you—but also some compensations because you have the strong sense of responsibility that carries you through, and at last, after a struggle, a sense of reality—which is a fine thing to have, though not always very comfortable. Your Mars supports your Sun, you see, and that gives you enormous endurance. And—this is important—your Saturn has the same relationship to your Moon that Mars has to your Sun, but it's a giver of spiritual power, and takes you deep into the underworld, the dream world, what Goethe called the realm of the Mothers. There's a fad now for calling them the Archetypes, because it sounds so learned and scientific. But the Mothers is truer to what they really are. The Mothers are the creators, the matrixes of all human experience."

"That's the world of art, surely?"

"More than that. Art may be a symptom, a perceptible form, of what the Mothers are. It's quite possible to be a pretty good artist, mind you, without having a clue about the Mothers.

"Saturn on the ascendant and the Sun in midheaven is very rare and suggests a most uncommon life. Perhaps even some special celestial guardianship. Have you ever been aware of anything like that?"

"No."

"You really are a somebody, Francis."

"You're very flattering."

"Like hell I am! I don't fool around with this stuff. I don't make a chancy living by casting horoscopes for paying customers. I'm trying to find out what it's all about, and I've been very lucky in discovering that old astrologer's secret I told you about. I'm not kidding you, Francis."

"I must say my remarkableness has taken its time about showing itself."

"It should start soon, if it hasn't started already. Not worldly fame, but perhaps posthumous fame. There are things in your chart that I would tell you if I were in the fortune-telling and predicting business. Being at Düsterstein is very important; your chart shows that. And working with Saraceni is important, though he simply shows up as a Mercurial influence. And there are all kinds of things in your background that aren't showing up at present. What's happened to all that music?"

"Music? I haven't been much involved with music. No talent."

"Somebody else's music. In your childhood."

"I had an aunt who sang and played a lot. Awful stuff, I suppose it was."

"Is she the false mother who turns up? There are two. Was one the nurse?"

"My grandfather's cook, really."

"A very tough influence. Like granite. But the other one seems to be a bit witchy. Was she queer to look at? Was she the one who sang? It doesn't matter that what she sang wasn't in the most fashionable taste. People are so stupid, you know, in the way they discount the influence of music that isn't right out of the top drawer; if it isn't Salzburg or Bayreuth quality it can't be influential. But a sentimental song can sometimes open doors where Hugo Wolf knocks in vain. I suppose it's the same with pictures. Good taste and strong effect aren't always closely linked. If your singing aunt put all she had into what she sang, it could have marked you for life."

"Perhaps. I often think of her. She's failing, I hear."

"And who's this—this messy bit here? Somebody that doesn't seem fully human. Could it have been a much-loved pet?"

"I had a brother who was badly afflicted."

"Odd. Doesn't look quite like a brother. But influential, whatever it was. It's given you a great compassion for the miserable and dispossessed, Francis, and that's very fine, so long as you don't let it swamp your common sense. I don't think it can; not with that powerful Mercury. But immoderate compassion will ruin you quicker than brandy. And the kingdom of the dead—what were you doing there?"

"I really believe I was learning about the fragility and pitiful quality of life. I had a remarkable teacher."

"Yes, he shows up; a sort of Charon, ferrying the dead to their other world. What I would call, if I were writing an academic paper, which God be thanked I'm not, a Psychopomp."

"Handsome word. He'd have loved to be called a Psychopomp."

"Was he your father, by any chance?"

"Oh, no; a servant."

"Funny, he looks like a father, or a relative of some kind. Anyhow—what about your father? There's a Polyphemus figure in here, but I can't make out if he's your father."

Francis laughed. "Oh yes, a Polyphemus figure sure enough. Always wears a monocle. Nice man."

"Just shows how careful you have to be about interpreting. Polyphemus wasn't at all a nice man. But he was certainly one-eyed. But was he your real father? What about the old man?"

"Old man? My grandfather?"

"Yes, probably. The man who truly loved your mother."

"Ruth, what are you talking about?"

"Don't get up on your ear. Incest. Not the squalid physical thing, but the spiritual, psychological thing. It has a sort of nobility. It would dignify the physical thing, if that had occurred. But I'm not suggesting that you are your grandfather's child in the flesh, rather his child in the spirit, the child he loved because you were born of his adored daughter. What about your mother? She doesn't show up very clearly. Do you love her very much?"

"Yes, I think so. I've always told myself so. But she has never been as real as the aunt and the cook. I've never really felt that I knew her."

"It's a wise child that knows his father, but it's one child in a million who knows his mother. They're a mysterious mob, mothers."

"Yes. So I've been told. They go down, down, down into the very depths of hell, in order that we men may live."

"That's very Saturnine, Francis. You sound as if you hated her for it."

"Who wouldn't? Who needs such a crushing weight of gratitude toward another human being? I don't suppose she thought about the depths of hell when I was begotten."

"No. That seems to have been quite a jolly occasion, if your first chart isn't lying. Have you told her about your wife? Running off with the adventurous one?"

"No I haven't. Not yet."

"Or about the child?"

"Oh yes, she knows about the child. 'Darling, you horrible boy, you've made me a grandmother!' was what she wrote."

"Have you relieved her mind by telling her that she isn't really a grandmother?"

"Damn it, Ruth, this is too bloody inquisitorial! Did you really see that in this rigmarole?"

"I see the cuckold's horns, painfully clear. But don't fuss. It's happened to better men. Look at King Arthur."

"Bugger King Arthur—and Tristan and Iseult and the Holy sodding Grail and all that Celtic pack. I made a proper jackass of myself about that stuff!"

"Well, you could make a jackass of yourself about much more unworthy things."

"Ruth, I don't want to be nasty, but really this stuff of yours is far too vague, too mythological. You don't honestly take it seriously, do you?"

"I've told you already; it's a way of channelling intuitions and things that can't be reached by the broad, floodlit paths of science. You can't nail it down, but I don't think that's a good enough reason for brushing it aside. You can't talk to the Mothers by getting them on the phone, you know. They have an unlisted number. Yes, I take it seriously."

"But this stuff you've been telling me is all favourable, all things I might like to hear. Would you tell me if you saw in this chart that I would die tonight?"

"Probably not."

"Well, when will I die? Come on, let's have some hard information, hot from the planets."

"No astrologer in his right mind ever tells somebody when they are going to die. Though there was once a wise astrologer who told a rather short-tempered king that he would die the day after the astrologer died himself. It assured him of a fine old age. But I will tell you this: you'll have a good innings. The war won't get you."

"The war?"

"Yes, the coming war. Really Francis, you don't have to be an astrologer to know that there's a war coming, and you and I had better get out of this charming, picturesque castle before it does, or we may find ourselves making the journey on the Bummelzug that passes behind here every few days."

"You know about that?"

"It's not much of a secret. I'd give a lot to have a peep at that place, but the first rule for aliens is not to be too snoopy. I hope you don't go too near there when you are out for spins in your little car. Francis, surely you know that we are living in the grasp of the greatest tyranny in at least a thousand years, and certainly the most efficient tyranny in history. And where there's tyranny, there's sure to be treachery, and some of it is of a rarefied sort. You don't know what Saraceni's doing?"

458

"I'm beginning to wonder."

"You'll have to know soon. Really, Francis, for a man with your strong Mercury influence you are very slow to catch on. I said you weren't stupid, but you *are* thick. You'd better find out what you've got yourself into, my boy. Maybe Max will tell you. Listen—Mercury is the spirit of intelligence, isn't he? And also of craft, and guile, and trickery, and all that sort of thing. Something of the greatest importance is very near you. A decision. Francis, I beg you, be a crook if you must, but for the love of God, don't be a dumb crook. You, with Saturn and Mercury so strong in your chart! You want me to tell you the dark things in your chart—there they are! And one thing more: money. You're much too fond of money."

"Because everybody is trying to gouge it out of me. I seem to be everybody's banker and unpaid bottle-washer and snoop and lackey—"

"Snoop? So that's why you're here! Well, it relieves me that you're not just a lost American wandering around in a fog—"

"I'm not an American, damn it! I'm a Canadian. You English never know the difference!"

"Sorry, sorry, sorry! Of course you're a Canadian. Do you know what that is? A psychological mess. For a lot of good reasons, including some strong planetary influences, Canada is an introverted country straining like hell to behave like an extravert. Wake up! Be yourself, not a bad copy of something else!"

"Ruth, you can talk more unmitigated rubbish than anybody I have ever known!"

"Okay, my pig-headed friend. Wait and see. The astrological consultation is now over and it's midnight and we must be fresh and pretty tomorrow to greet our betters when they come from Munich, and Rome, and wherever the ineffable Prince Maximilian is arriving from. So, give me one more cognac, and then it's goodnight!"

"Heil Hitler!" Prince Maximilian's greeting rang like a pistol shot.

Saraceni started, and his right arm half rose in response to the Nazi salute. But the Countess, who had sunk half-way down in a curtsy, ascended slowly, like a figure on the pantomime stage, rising through a trapdoor.

"Max, do you have to say that?"

"My dear cousin, forgive my little joke. May I?" And he kissed her affectionately on the cheek. "Saraceni, dear old chap! Dear little cousin, you're prettier than ever. Miss Nibsmith, how d'you do? And we haven't met, but you must be Cornish, Tancred's right hand. How d'you do?"

It was not easy to get a word in with Prince Max. Francis shook his outstretched hand. Max did not stop talking.

"So kind of you to ask me to spend Christmas with you, cousin. It's not celebrated as cheerfully in Bavaria as we remember, though I saw a few signs of jollification on the road. I came by way of Oberammergau, because I thought that there, if anywhere, the birth of Our Lord would be gratefully acknowledged. After all, they must sell and export several hundred thousand board-feet of crêches and crucifixes and holy images every year, and even they can't utterly forget why. In Switzerland, now, Christmas is in full, raving eruption. Paris is *en fête,* almost as if Christ had been a Frenchman. And in London people otherwise quite sane are wallowing in the Dickensian slush, and looting Fortnum's of pies and puddings and crackers and all the other artifacts of their national saturnalia. And here—I see you've put up some evergreens—"

"Of course. And tomorrow there will be Mass, as usual."

"And I shall be there! I shall be there, not having eaten a crumb or drunk a swallow since midnight. I shall not even clean my teeth, lest a Lutheran drop might escape down my gullet. What a lark, eh? Or should I say, 'Wot larks', Cornish? Should I say 'Wot larks'?"

"I beg your pardon, sir?"

"Oh, not sir, please! Call me Max. 'Wot larks' because of Dickens. You must be a real Dickensian Protestant, no?"

"I was brought up a Catholic, Max."

"You don't look in the least like one."

"And exactly how does a Catholic look?" said the Countess, not pleased.

"Oh, it's a most becoming look, cousin, an other-wordly light in the eyes, never seen among Lutherans. Isn't that so, Miss Nibsmith?"

461

"Oh, but our eyes shine with the light of truth, sir."

"Good, very good! No trapping the governess, is there? Are you taking on any of that light, Amalie?"

Amalie blushed, as she always did when she was singled out for special notice, but had nothing to say. There was no need. The Prince rattled on.

"Ah, a real Bavarian Christmas, just like childhood! How long will it last, eh? I suppose so long as none of us are Jews we shall be allowed to celebrate Christmas in our traditional way, at least in privacy. You're not a Jew, by any chance, Tancred? I've always wondered."

"God forbid," said Saraceni, crossing himself. "I have worries enough as it is."

Amalie found her tongue. "I didn't know Jews celebrated Christmas," she said.

"Poor devils! I don't think they get much chance to celebrate anything. We'll drink to better times at dinner, won't we?"

The Prince had arrived in a small, sporting, snorting, coughing, roaring, farting car, loaded with packages and big leather cases, and when the company assembled for dinner, these proved to contain presents for everybody, all speaking loudly of Bond Street. For the Countess a case of claret and a case of champagne. For Amalie, a photograph of Prince Max in dress uniform, in a costly frame from Asprey's. For Miss Nibsmith a beautiful if somewhat impractical diary bound in blue leather, with a gold lock and key—for astrological notations, said Prince Max, slyly. For Saraceni and Francis leather pocket diaries for the year to come, obviously from Smythson's. And for the servants, all sorts of edible luxuries in a hamper from Fortnum's.

Of course there were other gifts. The Countess gave Francis a book that had been written about the Düsterstein pictures by some toilsome scholar many years before. Amalie, with much blushing, gave him six handkerchiefs which she had embroidered with his initials. Saraceni gave everybody books of poetry, bound in Florence. Francis won high distinction by giving the Countess and Amalie sketches of themselves, done in his Old Master style, in which he had taken special care to emphasize the family resemblance. He had nothing for the men, or for Miss Nibsmith, but it did not seem to matter. And when the gift-giving was finished, they sat down to a dinner of greater length than usual, with venison, and roast goose, and a stuffed carp, which was nicer to look at than to eat. And when cheese had been consumed the Countess announced that in special compliment to Francis they would conclude with a traditional English dish, which the chef identified, he being an Italian-Swiss, as *Suppe Inglese*. It was a dashing attempt at a sherry trifle, rather too wet but kindly meant.

The meal was accompanied by what was less a conversation than a solo performance by Prince Max, filled with casual references—fairly casual but by no means inevitable—to "my cousin Carol, the King of Rumania" and one or two stories about "my ancestor, Friedrich der Grosse (though of course we are of the Swabian branch of the family)" and quite a long account of how he had studied canon law as a boy "so that the priests couldn't cheat us—we had more than fifty parishes, you know." And at last when toasts were to be proposed and the Countess, and Amalie, and Miss Nibsmith, and the splendours of Italian art "as represented by our dear Maestro, Tancred Saraceni", and the King of England, had all been drunk, the Prince insisted with much merriment that they drink also to "the Pretender to the British Throne, my cousin Prince Rupert of Bavaria, whose claim is through his Stuart ancestry, as of course you know." After this toast Francis insisted on smashing his glass (having made sure it was not too precious) in order that no lesser toast should ever be drunk from it.

Francis emerged somewhat too abruptly from his character as Le Beau Ténébreux, for he was feeling the wines stirring within him. When Amalie, daring greatly, asked him if it were true that there were many bears in Canada, he replied that when he was a boy a child had been eaten by a bear within three miles of Blairlogie. That was true, but not content, he went on to say that the bear had later been seen, walking on its hind legs, wearing the child's tuque and carrying its satchel of books, making its way toward Carlyle Rural. Even Amalie refused to believe him.

"My dear Amalie, the English wit tends always

toward some *fantaisie*," said the Countess with grandmotherly solemnity. And then Prince Max took over again, to tell about a boar-hunt he had once enjoyed in the company of several highly placed relatives.

"What does Prince Max do now?" Francis asked Ruth Nibsmith, after dinner.

"Travels for a wine company that has headquarters in London," she whispered. "Lives on what he makes, which is pretty good, but not of course a fortune. He's a real aristocrat, a shameless, joyful survivor. Hitler will never down Max. Did you notice the little Wittelsbach thingummy on the door of his car? Max is the real goods, but not tongue-tied, like our English hogen-mogens."

Christmas morning. Mass had been heard, breakfast had been eaten, and without any words having been spoken about it—though Prince Max talked without a stop about other things—Saraceni led the way to the shell-grotto workroom, and the Countess, the Prince, and Francis followed. The panels on which Saraceni had been working all through the autumn were propped up on tables and walls and against the pillars of lapis lazuli.

Slowly the Prince made a tour of inspection.

"Marvellous," he said; "really, Tancred, you are greater than your reputation. How you have transformed these dismal daubs! I would never have believed it if I did not have the evidence before me. And you say it is truly undetectable?"

"A determined critic, armed with various testing acids, and special rays to pick up inevitable discrepancies in the brushwork, could probably see what was done—but I doubt if even then he would be sure. But as I have been telling our friend Corniche every day, our task is to do our work so well that suspicion will not be aroused, and prying investigators will not come with their rays and begin to arouse suspicions. As you see, the pictures are rather dirty. And the dirt on them is their very own. No Augsburg dirt where one might expect Nürnberg dirt. Doubtless they will be given a good cleaning before they are hung in the great gallery."

"Perhaps you will be called in to supervise the cleaning. That would be rather good, wouldn't it?"

"I should certainly enjoy it."

"You know, some of these are so good I almost covet them for myself. You have really made it seem as if some uncommonly clever, and quite unknown and unrecognized, portraitists of authentic German style had been at work among the rich merchants of the fifteenth and sixteenth centuries in these parts. The one thing you have not been able to disguise is your talent, Meister."

"You are very kind."

"Look at this one. The Fuggers' jester. Unquestionably this is one of the Fools whom we know the Fuggers always kept in their entourage after they became Counts, but which one? Do you think it could be Drollig Hansel, the favourite of Count Hans? Look at him. What a face!"

"Poor wretch," said the Countess; "to be born a dwarf and kept as a Fool. Still, I suppose it was better than being a dwarf whom nobody kept."

"This one will certainly delight our friends when they see it," said Prince Max.

"I am sorry, but that one is not included with the others," said Saraceni.

"Not included! But it's the pick of the lot! Why is it not included!"

"Because it is not a touched-up genuine picture. It is wholly and simply a fabrication, made by our young friend Corniche. I have been teaching him the technique of this sort of painting, and as an exercise I left him to produce something solely on his own responsibility, to show how well he had mastered the art."

"But it is superb!"

"Yes. A superb fake."

"Well—but could anybody spot it?"

"Not without a scientific examination. The panel is old and quite genuine, and it is covered in leather as old as itself. The colours are correct, made in the true manner. The technique is impeccable, except that it is rather too good for a wholly unknown painter. And this ingenious scoundrel Corniche has even seen that the *craquelure* incorporates some authentic dust. I don't suppose one observer in a thousand would have any doubt about it."

"Oh, but Meister—that observer would surely spot the old Fugger *Firmenzeichen*, the pitchfork and circle, that can just barely be perceived in the

467

upper left-hand corner. He would pride himself on having spotted it and guessed what it is, although it is almost obscured."

"Yes. But it is a fake, my dear Max."

"Perhaps in the substance. Certainly not in the spirit. Consider, Meister: this is not imitating any known painter's work—that would be a fake, of course. No, this is simply a little picture in a sixteenth-century manner. Now what makes it different from these others?"

"Only the fact that it has been done in the past month."

"Oh, that is almost Lutheran pernickety morality! That is an unworthy servitude to chronology. Cousin, what do you say? Isn't it a little gem?"

"I say it speaks of the dull, inescapable misery of being a dwarf, of having to make oneself ridiculous in order to be tolerated, of feeling that God has not used you well. If it makes me feel these things so strongly, it is certainly a picture of unusual quality. I should like to see it make the journey with the others."

"Of course, cousin. Just the sort of good sense I should expect from you. Come on, Tancred, relent."

"If you say so. The greatest risk is yours."

"Let me worry about the risk. Is everything ready for the journey, cousin?"

"The six big hogsheads are in the old granary."

"Then let us get to work at once."

Francis, Max, the Countess, and Saraceni spent the next three hours wrapping the panels—eighteen of them, including the picture of the jester—in oiled paper, after which they were sewn into packages of oiled silk and the seams caulked with tar Saraceni heated on the brazier. To the silken packages a number of small lead weights were attached. Then they carried them to the old granary, where there were no workmen because of the holiday, and there they removed the tops from the six hogsheads, and carefully sank the packages in the white wine they contained—fifty-two gallons to a barrel. When Prince Max tapped the last top back into place, eighteen pictures had been drowned, snug and dry in their casings, and were ready to travel to England, to the warehouses of a highly respected London wine-merchant. It was a good morning's work, and even the Countess relaxed some of her usual reserve, and invited the conspirators to take Madeira with her in her private room, where Francis had never been before.

"I feel a splendid glow of achievement," said Prince Max, sniffing at his glass. "I am rejoicing in the breadth and ingenuity of our cleverness. I am wondering if I shall be able to resist pinching the little Fugger Jester for myself. But no—that would be unprofessional. He must go with the others. You know, it seems to me to be damn funny that our friend Francis has not said a word—not a single word—about what we have done with his picture."

"I had a good reason for keeping quiet," said Francis. "But I would certainly like to know what is going on, if that is permissible. The Meister has quelled me so completely during the past four months that I don't feel that I have any right to ask questions. I suppose that is what apprenticeship means. Keep your eyes open and your mouth shut. But I'd like to know a little, if I may."

"Tancred, what an old tyrant you must be," said Prince Max. "Cousin, do you think we should explain, just a little?"

"Yes, I do. Though I doubt your ability to explain, or do anything else, just a little, Max. But Mr. Cornish is now in—you shall say in what—farther than he knows, and it would be ill-usage not to tell him what he is letting himself in for."

"Here it is, my dear Cornish. You know that our Führer is a great connoisseur of art? Understandable, as he was himself a painter in his young days, before his mighty destiny declared itself. Because of his determination that the full glory of the German Volk should be made plain to the whole world, as well as to the Volk itself, he wishes to acquire and bring back to Germany whatever German works of art are owned abroad. Repatriation of our heritage, he calls it. That will take some doing, of course. There was a great dispersal of German religious art during the Reformation. Who wanted that ridiculous stuff? Certainly not the Lutherans. But much of it found its way to other countries, and travelled even further toward America, from which it probably will not return. But what is in Europe may be persuaded to return. There was another great dispersal of German art during the eighteenth and early nineteenth centuries, when every young sprig who made the Grand Tour felt obliged to take a few pretty things home with him, and not all of those pretty things were acquired in Italy. Some fine Gothic things went from here. The Führer wants to get it all together, the first-rate and the second-rate—not that the Führer would regard anything authentically German as second-rate—and he is planning a great Führermuseum in Linz to house it."

"But surely Linz is in Austria?"

"Yes, and not a great distance from the Führer's birthplace. By the time the pictures have been assembled, Austria will be glad to have the Führermuseum. Austria is ripe for the picking. Are you beginning to catch on?"

"Yes, but does the Führer really want the kind of thing the Meister and I have been working on? That's very small potatoes, surely? And why send it to England? Why not offer it here?"

"Well—that is a complicated story. First, the Führer wants everything that is German; when it has been acquired, somebody will sort the good from the mediocre. And I may say that you and dear Tancred have lifted these pictures above mediocrity. They are bürger-portraits of considerable interest. How intelligent, how German they look now! Second, the Führer, or I should say his agents, are ready to make deals with foreign dealers. They like to do swaps. For a German picture, a picture of roughly corresponding worth that is not German but now hangs in a German gallery may be exchanged. The Kaiser Friedrich Museum in Berlin and the Alte Pinakothek in Munich have already—under the gentle persuasion of the Führer's artistic advisers—swapped a Ducio di Buoninsegna, a Raphael, some Fra Lippo Lippis, and God knows what else for German paintings that could be made available. There are scores of them in England, you know."

"I suppose there must be."

"And we are just about to ship some more to England for swapping purposes. Things that might have been found in English country houses. Small things, but the Führer's principal agent likes quantity, as well as quality."

"He has an eye for quality, as well," said the Countess, with something like a snort.

"Oh yes, he has, and he has had his eyes on the pictures here at Düsterstein," said Prince Max. "The Führer's principal artistic agent, as you may know, is that very busy man, Reichsmarschall Göring, and he has already visited my cousin to discover whether she would like to present her family collection to the Führermuseum as a token of her fidelity to German ideals. The Reichsmarschall is extremely fond of pictures, and he has an enviable collection of his own. I understand," said Max, turning to the Countess, "that he has asked the Führer to revive in his favour the title that Landgrave Wilhelm III of Hesse gave to his adviser on art—Director-General of the Delights of My Eye."

"What effrontery," said the Countess. "His taste is very vulgar, as one might expect."

"Well, my dear Cornish, there you have it," said Prince Max.

"And you are doing this as a sort of quixotic anti-Hitler thing?" said Francis. "Just to do him in the eye? Surely the risk is immense?"

"We are quixotic, but not so quixotic as all that," said the Prince. "There is a certain recognition for this work, which is, as you say, dangerous. Friendly English firms are most generous. Certain art dealers are involved. They arrange the swaps, and they sell the Italian treasures that go to England in return for the sort of thing we have been dealing with this morning. Such a group of lesser pictures as this may be exchanged for a single canvas—a Tiepolo, even a Raphael. The work is quixotic, certainly, but—not totally selfless. Some money *does* change hands, depending on how well we do."

Francis looked at the Countess, and although he was pretty good at controlling his features, astonishment must have showed. The Countess did not flinch.

"One does not restore a great fortune by shrinking from risks, Mr. Cornish," she said.

That girl did well with Francis's horoscope, said the Lesser Zadkiel. She even hinted at your involvement in his fate, brother. That must have surprised you.

—I am not so easily surprised, said the Daimon Maimas. In the days when people understood about

473

the existence and influence of daimons like myself we were often recognized and called upon. But she did well enough, certainly. She warned Francis of an impending crisis, and against his increasing preoccupation with money.

—He has good reason for it, said the Angel. As he says, everybody exploits him and he is open to exploitation. Look at that gang at Düsterstein! Prince Max assumes that Francis will be delighted to be included in the picture hoax—to give it the least objectionable name—because he regards it as an aristocratic lark, and it honours Francis to be one of the jokers. The Countess thinks, in her heart, that a bourgeois like Francis is lucky to be allowed into an aristocratic secret, and to work for his keep to sustain it. And Saraceni has the genial contempt of the master for the neophyte. But if that scheme were ever uncovered, Francis would suffer most, because he is the only one who has actually forged a picture.

—No, brother, he has forged nothing. He has painted an original picture in a highly individual style, and if any connoisseur misdates it, the more fool he. It is Prince Max and the Countess who are passing it off as what it is not. They are aristocrats, and, as you well know, aristocrats did not always achieve their position by a niggling scrupulosity. As for money, the whole story has not yet been told.

—I bow to your superior knowledge of the case, my dear Maimas. What pleases me is that François Xavier Bouchard, the dwarf tailor of Blairlogie, is at last about to burst upon the world, and be admired, as the Fuggers' Jester, Drollig Hansel. And all because Francis learned to observe, and remember, under the influence of Harry Furniss.

—These are the little jokes that relieve the tedious work of being a Minor Immortal, said the Daimon Maimas.

"Do you suppose that La Nibsmith will take Prince Max's broad hint?" said Saraceni. "You heard what he said when he gave her that book: for astrological notations. He is mad to have her cast his horoscope."

"And won't she?" said Francis.

"Apparently not. He has been begging—in so far as so aristocratic a person can beg—for several months. She is capricious, which is her right. She does not do it professionally, but she is very good. A genuine psychic. Of course, casting horoscopes depends a good deal on the psychic gifts of the astrologer. Germans are just as keen for that sort of thing as Americans. The Führer has an astrologer of his own."

"She doesn't look like my idea of a psychic."

"Psychics often don't—the real ones. They are frequently rather earthy people. Has she cast your horoscope yet?"

"Well—yes, as a matter of fact, she has."

"Have you a good destiny?"

"Odd, apparently. Odder than I would have thought."

"Not odder than *I* would have thought. I chose

you for my apprentice because you were odd, and you have revealed new depths of oddity ever since. That picture you painted while I was in Rome, for instance. It was a portrait, wasn't it?"

"Yes."

"I won't pry. It had the unmistakable quality of a portrait, a feeling between subject and painter, which cannot be faked—not to my eye, that's to say. Where are your preliminary drawings?"

Francis produced them from a portfolio.

"You are a thorough creature, aren't you? Even your preliminaries on the right paper, in the right style. Not your Harry Furniss style. Nevertheless, I'll wager that when you first drew that dwarf, it was in your Harry Furniss manner."

"It was. He was dead, and I did a few sketches while he was being prepared for burial."

"You see? Odd, as I said. How you profited from Harry Furniss's book! Forget nothing; learn the trick of remembering through the hand. I shall be interested to hear what they think of it in London."

"Meister, who are 'they'? Haven't I a right to know what I'm mixed up in, working here with you? There must surely be some risk. Why am I kept in the dark?"

"'They' are a few very distinguished dealers in art, who make all the business arrangements in this little game which, as you say, involves some risk."

"They're swapping these worthless, or at least

trivial, pictures for pictures of greatly superior quality?"

"They are exchanging certain pictures for others, for complicated reasons."

"All right. But is it no more than what Prince Max said? An elaborate hoax on the German Reich?"

"It would be a very bold man who would try to hoax the German Reich."

"Well, somebody seems to be doing it. Is this a government thing? Some sort of Secret Service lark?"

"The British government knows about it, and very likely the American government knows—but only a very few people, who would deny all knowledge if there should be a discovery and a row."

"It's for private gain, then?"

"There is money involved. This work we are doing is not unrequited."

" 'Unrequited'! What a word for such a thing! You mean that you and the Countess and Prince Max are getting damn well paid!"

"For services rendered. The Countess supplies the pictures on which we work. Where else but in such a place as this, where there are two pictures stacked in those innumerable service corridors for every one on the walls, would you find things of the right age, right character, and indeed authentic? I supply a quality of craftsmanship that makes those pictures look rather more desirable to the agents of the great Reichsmarschall than they did in their earlier, neglected state. Prince Max sees that the pictures arrive in England and reach the dealers, which involves substantial risk. Such services do not come cheap, but what we receive is not comparable to what the London dealers receive, because they get fine Italian art for mediocre German art, and they sell it at splendid prices."

"A huge international fraud, in fact."

"If there is fraud, it is not the kind you suggest. If the German experts consider our pictures so desirable that they will exchange Italian pictures of great value for them, are we to say that they do not know what they are doing? No money changes hands—not at that point. The Reich is not anxious that large sums of German money should leave the country even for works of German art; that is the reason for the exchange arrangement. The German experts have a task; it is to form the finest and most complete and most impressive collection of German art in the world. They need both quantity and quality. The work we do here does not aim at quality in the highest reaches—no Dürers, no Grünewalds, no Cranachs. To provide those we should have to resort to faking—from which, of course, I shrink in holy horror. We simply make old, undistinguished pictures into old pictures of some distinction."

"Except for *Drollig Hansel*. He's a fake and he's gone to England."

"My dear man, don't allow yourself to become heated, or you may say things you will wish you had not said. *Drollig Hansel* is a student exercise, undertaken in the style of an earlier day, as a test of skill. The test has been splendidly passed. I am the judge, and I know what I am talking about. If an expert, seeing it among the others, cannot tell that it is modern, what greater proof can you have of my achievement? But you are blameless. You did not paint to deceive, you signed nobody else's name to it, and you did not yourself send it to England."

"That's casuistry."

"Much talk in the art world is casuistry."

Casuistry: the study of Ethics as it relates to questions of conscience. That was how the Church used the word. But in Francis's mind it had a Protestant ring, and it meant quibbling—teetering on the tightrope above a dangerous abyss. His conscience twinged sorely after the Countess received a letter from Prince Max, relating how a newly uncovered picture was causing a small sensation among a score or so of art experts in London.

Pictures of dwarfs are not uncommon, and some of the subjects can be identified. Van Dyck painted Queen Henrietta Maria with her dwarf, Sir Jeffrey Hudson; Bronzino painted the dwarf Morgante in the nude—a front view and a back one so that no detail should be missed; the Prado has the female dwarf Eugenia Martinez Vallego, clothed and nude. The dwarfs of Rizi and Velasquez, who seem to observe royal splendour from a remote, half-comprehending world of their own, are not known by name, but by the pain in their intent regard. Less squeamish ages were delighted by dwarfs, and some of them were used in much the manner that had driven F. X. Bouchard of Blairlogie to put his head in a noose.

The Countess read her cousin's letter to Saraceni and Francis with as much excitement as that reserved lady ever chose to show. The experts had given the painting a little cleaning, and what had they found? That what had looked like the Fuggers' *Firmenzeichen,* their family mark, was perhaps something more; true, it looked like a pitchfork, or a three-branched candlestick with an O beside it, but it could also be a gallows with a noose hanging from it! The experts were delighted by their find, and the puzzle it suggested. Had the dwarf been a hangman, then? That it was indeed Drollig Hansel, known as an obscure figure in history but never before seen, they did not choose to doubt. This was really a find for the Führermuseum, a real whiff from an earlier, spiritually fearless Germany, which did not shrink from realities, even when they were also grotesqueries.

Prince Max's letter was carefully phrased. No inquiring secret police, peeping into the letters that a German aristocrat wrote to his high-born cousin, could have understood anything more than the facts that were stated. But there was rejoicing at Düsterstein.

Francis did not rejoice. His intention to make some record, to offer some comment, on the fate of the dwarf he had known had been unveiled, and he had not expected that to happen. His picture had been a very private affair, an *ex voto* almost, a memorial to a man he had never spoken to, and had come to know only after his death. He could not contain his dismay and torment, and he had to say so to Saraceni.

"Are you really surprised, my dear man? There are very few secrets in this world, as you are quite old enough to have found out. And art is a way of telling the truth."

"That's what Browning said. My aunt was always quoting him."

"Well? Your aunt must have been a wise woman. And Browning a deep psychologist. But don't you see? It is the quality of truth, of depth of feeling, in your picture that has made all these learned gentlemen take notice."

"But it's a cheat!"

"I have carefully explained to you that it is no cheat. It is a revelation of several things about its subject and about you, but it is not a cheat."

If Francis did not rejoice to have his private comment on the incalculability and frequent malignancy of fate acclaimed as a reminder of a long-dead dwarf, he could not help being warmed by the praise he was receiving as a painter, though unidentified. He thought he was being subtle in the way he afforded chances for Saraceni to comment on *Drollig Hansel*, its quality of workmanship, its evocation of a past time, its colour and the sense it gave of being a big picture when it was, by actual measurement, a small one. His subtlety did not deceive the Italian, who laughed at him as fishing for compliments.

"But I am happy to provide the compliments," he said; "why are you not happy to ask for them like a real artist, instead of demurring and hemming like some little old maid who does a few water-colours of her garden?"

"I don't want to over-value the little thing."

"Oh, I see; you don't want to fall into the sin of pride? Well, don't shrink from pride only to fall into hypocrisy. You've had a dog's life, Corniche, brought up half Catholic and half Protestant, in a wretched hole where you got the worst of both those systems of double-dealing."

"Easy, Meister! I have detected a good Catholic in you."

"Perhaps, but when I am working as an artist I banish all that. Catholicism has begotten much great art; Protestantism none at all—not a single painting. But Catholicism has fostered art in the very teeth of Christianity. The Kingdom of Christ, if it ever comes, will contain no art; Christ never showed the least concern with it. His church has inspired much but not because of anything the Master said. Who then was the inspirer? The much-maligned Devil, one supposes. It is he who understands and ministers to man's carnal and intellectual self, and art is carnal and intellectual."

"You work under the wing of the Devil, do you?"

"I must, if I am to work at all. Christ would have had no time for a man like me. Have you

482

noticed how, in the Gospels, He keeps so resolutely clear of anybody who might be suspected of having any brains? Good-hearted simpletons and women who were little better than slaves, those were His followers. No wonder Catholicism had to take a resolute stand in order to include people of intellect and artists; Protestantism has tried to reverse the process. Do you know what I should like, Corniche?"

"A new revelation?"

"Yes, that might come of it. I should like a conference to which Christ would bring all His saints, and the Devil would bring all his scholars and artists, and let them have it out."

"Who would judge the result?"

"That's the sticker. Not God, certainly, as the father of both leaders."

Saraceni did praise *Drollig Hansel*, as both he and Francis now called the picture. He did more. Without declaring it to be so, he included Francis in a closer fellowship with himself, and as they worked he talked untiringly about what he believed to be the philosophy of art. It was a philosophy deformed by that disease so fatal to philosophers—personal experience.

The Countess also became more genial toward Francis. Not that she had ever treated him with anything but courtesy, but now she talked freely about what he and Saraceni were doing, and there were more of those conferences in her private room when Amalie and Miss Nibsmith had retired. The Countess wanted to improve the product she was exporting. If an original like *Drollig Hansel* was so well received, could not Saraceni bring about a greater change in some of the old pictures on which he was working?

"Surely you are not urging me toward fakery, Countess?"

"Certainly not. Just a little more boldness, Meister."

In the course of these talks things leaked out that gave Francis a better idea of what was actually involved in what he could not help considering an elaborate fraud. The Countess and Saraceni were receiving, for the pictures they sent, a full quarter of whatever the dealers could get for the Italian pictures the German museums offered in exchange, and the prices made his eyes start in his head. Where was the money going? Not to Düsterstein; nothing so direct or so dangerous. To Swiss banks, and by no means all to one bank.

"A quarter is not too much," said the Countess. "After all, that is what Bernard Berenson gets for a mere letter of authentication when he writes it for Duveen. We provide the actual works of art and all the authentication they need is the approval of the great German experts who buy them—who must be assumed to know what they are doing."

"Sometimes I wonder if they don't know more than they are telling," said Saraceni.

"They are working under the gleaming eye of the Reichsmarschall," said the Countess, "and he expects them to deliver the goods. And some of the goods—the choicest pieces—are said to find their way into the Reichsmarschall's personal collection, which is large and fine."

"The whole thing sounds crooked as a dog's hind leg," said Francis, falling into the idiom of Blairlogie.

"If that is so, which I do not admit, we are not the leaders in the deception," said the Countess.

"You do not see it as dishonest?"

"If it were a simple matter of business, I would think so," said the Countess, "but it is far from simple. I see it as a matter of natural justice. My family lost everything—well, not quite everything, but a very great deal—in the War, and lost it willingly for Germany. Since 1932 my Germany has been whittled away until I no longer know it, and my task in rebuilding my family's fortunes has been made unbelievably hard. And why? Because I am the wrong kind of aristocrat, which is something much nearer to a democrat than National Socialism can endure. Do you know what an aristocrat is, Mr. Cornish?"

"I know the concept, certainly."

"I know the reality. An aristocrat, when my family rose to prominence, was someone who gained power and wealth through ability, and that meant daring and taking chances, not steering a careful course through a labyrinth of rules that had been made for their own benefit by people without either daring or ability. You know my family's motto? You have seen it often enough."

"*Du sollst sterben ehe ich sterbe*," said Francis.

"Yes, and what does it mean? It is not one of your nineteenth-century, bourgeois mottoes—a mealy-mouthed assertion of a tradesman's idea of splendour. It means: 'Thou shalt perish ere I perish.' And I do not mean to perish. That is why I am doing what I am doing."

"The Countess seems to have decided to march under the banner of the Devil," said Francis to the Meister.

"We all meet the Devil in different forms, and the Countess is sure that she has found him in the Führer."

"A dangerous conclusion for a German citizen."

"The Countess would be surprised if you defined her as a citizen. She told you what she was: an aristocrat, a daring survivor. Certainly not a drivelling eccentric, as P. G. Wodehouse would have it."

"But suppose Hitler is right? Suppose the Reich lasts for a thousand years?"

"As an Italian I am sceptical of claims to last for a thousand years according to any plan; Italy has lasted far longer chiefly by muddle and indirection, and how gloriously she has done it. Of course, we have our own buffoon at present, but Italy has seen many buffoons come and go."

"I gather I am being invited to march under the Countess's banner? The Devil's banner."

"You can do that, Corniche, or you can go back to your frozen country, with its frozen art, and paint winter lakes and wind-blown pine trees, to which the Devil is understandably indifferent."

"You suggest that I shall have missed my chance?"

"You will certainly have missed your chance to learn what I can teach you."

"Really? You forget that now I can mix paint, and prepare grounds on the best principles, and I have painted one picture which seems to have met with a good deal of approval."

Saraceni laid down his brush and applauded gently. "Now that is what I have been hoping to hear for quite a while. Some show of spirit. Some real artist's self-esteem. Have you read and reread Vasari's *Lives of the Painters* as I told you?"

"You know I have."

"Yes, but attentively? If so, you must have been struck by the spirit of those men. Lions, all the best of them, even the gentle Raphael. They may have doubted their own work at bad moments, but they did not allow anyone else to do so. If a patron doubted, they changed patrons, because they knew they had something wholly beyond anybody's power to command—a strong individual talent. You have been hinting and manoeuvring to get me to say that *Drollig Hansel* is a fine painting. And I have. After all, you have been drawing and painting for—what—nineteen years? You have had good masters. *Drollig Hansel* will do, for the present. It's a pretty good painting. It shows that you, nipped by the frosty weather of your homeland, and stifled by the ingenious logic-chopping of Oxford, have at last begun to know yourself and respect what you know. Well—there have been late bloomers before you. But if you think you have learned all I can teach you, think again. Technique—yes, you have a measure of that. The inner conviction—not yet. But now you are in a frame of mind where we can begin on that paramount necessity."

This sounded promising, but Francis had learned to mistrust Saraceni's promises; the Italian not only reproduced faithfully the painting technique of an earlier day, but also the harsh, unappeasable spirit of a Renaissance master toward his apprentice. What new trial could he possibly devise?

"What do you see here?" The Meister stood ten feet away from Francis and unrolled a piece of paper, obviously old.

"It seems to be a careful pen drawing of the head of Christ on the Cross."

"Yes. Now come nearer. You see how it is done? It is calligraphy. A picture rendered in exquisite, tiny Gothic script in such a way that it depicts Christ's agony, while writing out every word—and not one word more—of Christ's Passion as it is recorded in the Gospel of St. John, chapters seventeen to nineteen. What do you think of it?"

"An interesting curiosity."

"A work of art, of craft, of devotion. Done, I suppose, by some seventeenth-century chaplain, or tutor to the Ingelheim family. Take it, and study it closely. Then I want you to do something in the same manner, but your text shall be the Nativity of Our Lord, as recorded in Luke's Gospel, chapter one, and chapter two up to verse thirty-two. I want a Nativity in calligraphy, and I make only one concession to your weakness: you may do it in Italic, rather than Gothic. So sharpen your quills, boil yourself some ink of soot and oak-galls, and go to work."

It was a job of measuring, scheming, and pernickety reckoning that might have brought despair to the heart of Sir Isaac Newton, but at last Francis had his plan, and set himself carefully to work. But what was there here to inspire inner conviction? This was drudgery, pedantry, and gimmickry. His concentration was not helped by an endless flow of reflection and comment from Saraceni, who was touching up a series of conventional seventeenth-century still-life paintings of impossibly opulent flowers, fish and vegetables on kitchen tables, bottles of wine, and dead hares with the glaucous bloom of death on their staring eyes.

"I sense your hatred of me, Corniche. Hate on. Hate greatly. It will help your work. It gives you a good charge of adrenalin. But reflect on this: I ask you to do nothing that I have not done in my day. That is how I have achieved mastery that has not its equal in the world. Mastery of what? Of the techniques of the great painters before 1700. I do not seek to be a painter myself. Nobody would want a painting done today in the manner of, let

489

us say, Goveart Flink, the best pupil of Rembrandt. Yet that is how I truly feel. That is my only honest manner. I do not want to paint like the moderns."

"Your hatred is reserved for the moderns, as mine is for you?"

"Not at all. I do not hate them. The best of them are doing what honest painters have always done, which is to paint the inner vision, or to bring the inner vision to some outer subject. But in an earlier day the inner vision presented itself in a coherent language of mythological or religious terms, and now both mythology and religion are powerless to move the modern mind. So—the search for the inner vision must be direct. The artist solicits and implores something from the realm of what the psychoanalysts, who are the great magicians of our day, call the Unconscious, though it is actually the Most Conscious. And what they fish up—what the Unconscious hangs on the end of the hook the artists drop into the great well in which art has its being—may be very fine, but they express it in a language more or less private. It is not the language of mythology or religion. And the great danger is that such private language is perilously easy to fake. Much easier to fake than the well-understood language of the past. I do not want to make you dizzy with flattery, but your picture of Drollig Hansel whispered something of that very deep, dark well."

"Jesus Christ!"

"No, not at all. As I have told you, Our Blessed Lord wanted something quite different from that dark well, and drew from it like the Master He was."

"But the Moderns—surely one must paint in the manner of one's day?"

"I don't admit any such necessity. If life is a dream, as some philosophers insist, surely the great picture is that which most potently symbolizes the unseizable reality that lies behind the dream. If I—or you—can best express that in terms of mythology or religion, why should we not do so?"

"Because it's a kind of fakery, or a deliberate throw-back, like those Pre-Raphaelites. Even if you are a believer, you cannot believe as the great men of the past believed."

"Very well. Live in the spirit of your time, and that spirit alone, if you must. But for some artists such abandonment to the contemporary leads to despair. Men today, men without religion or mythology, solicit the Unconscious, and usually they ask in vain. So they invent something and I don't need to tell you the difference between invention and inspiration. Supply such inventions and you may come to depise those who admire you, and play games with them. Was that the spirit of Giotto, Titian, Rembrandt? Of course, you may become something rather like a photographer. But remember what Matisse said: 'L'exactitude ce n'est pas la vérité.' "

"Isn't exactitude what you are devilling and

driving me to achieve with this bloody piece of handwriting?"

"Only as a means of training you so that you will be able to set down, as well as lies in your power, what the Unconscious may choose to put on your hook, and offer it to those who have eyes to see."

"You are teaching me to paint reality so well that it might deceive—like that Roman painter who painted flowers, or a jar of honey, or something so truly that bees settled on his pictures. How do you equate that with the kind of reality you are talking about—the reality that rises from the dark well?"

"Don't despise *things*. Every *thing* has a soul that speaks to our soul, and may move it toward love. To understand that is the real materialism. People speak of our age as materialistic, but they are wrong. Men do not believe in matter today any more than they believe in God; scientists have taught them not to believe in anything. Men of the Middle Ages, and most of them in the Renaissance, believed in God and the *things* God had made, and they were happier and more complete than we. Listen, Corniche: modern man wants desperately to believe in something, to have some value that cannot be shaken. This country in which we live is giving fearful proof of what mankind will do in order to have something on which to fasten his yearning for belief, for certainty, for reality."

"I don't like it, and neither do you. Nor does the Countess."

"But we cannot deny it, or change it. These Nazi fanatics are picturesque, so one can take some comfort from that."

Francis thought of the trains, whose journey to the concentration camp in the hills he was recording, and did not find it picturesque. But he said nothing.

Saraceni went on, serenely. "The modern passion for the art of the past is part of this terrible yearning for certainty. The past is at least done with, and anything that we can recover from it is solid goods. Why do rich Americans pay monstrous prices for paintings by Old Masters which they may, or may not, understand and love, if it is not to import into their country the certainty I am talking about? Their public life is a circus, but in the National Gallery at Washington something of God, and something of the comfort of God's splendour, may be entombed. It is a great cathedral, that gallery. And these Nazis are ready to swap splendid Italian masters for acres of German pictures, because they want to make manifest on the walls of their Führermuseum the past of their race, and so give substance to the present of their race, and provide some assurance of the future of their race. It is crazy, but in a crazy world what can you expect?"

"What I can expect, it appears, is that some day I shall finish this idiotic job, or I shall go mad and kill you."

"No, no, Corniche. What you can expect is that when you have finished that idiotic job you will be able to write a splendid hand like the great Cardinal Bembo. And by so doing you will achieve at least something of the outlook upon the world of that great connoisseur, for the hand speaks to the brain as surely as the brain speaks to the hand. You will not kill me. You love me. I am your Meister. You dote upon me."

Francis threw an ink-bottle at Saraceni. It was an empty bottle, and he took care to miss his mark. Then they both laughed.

So the weeks and the months passed and Francis had been at Düsterstein for almost three years, during which he had worked without a holiday as Saraceni's slave, then colleague, then trusted friend. True, he had been back to England twice, for a week each time, meeting the Colonel and— for colour—visiting Williams-Owen. But these jaunts could not be called holidays. He was on easier terms with the Countess, though no one was ever fully at ease with the Countess. Amalie had found her tongue and lost her love for Francis, and he taught her some trigonometry (of which Ruth Nibsmith knew nothing) and the elements of drawing, and a great deal about gin rummy and bridge. Amalie was on the way to becoming a great beauty, and although nothing much was said, it was apparent that Miss Nibsmith's reign must soon give way to a broader education, proba-bly in France.

"You don't care, I suppose," said Francis to Ruth, on one of their afternoon walks. "You're not really a governess—not in the nineteenth-century Brontë sense—and surely you want to do something else."

"So I shall," said Ruth, "but I shall stay here as long as there is work for me to do. Like you."

"Ah, well: I'm learning my craft, you see."

"And practising your other craft. Like me."

"Meaning?"

"Come on, Frank. You're in the profession, aren't you?"

"I'm a professional painter, if that's what you mean."

"Go on with you! You're a snoop, and so am I. The *profession*."

"You've left me behind."

"Frank, nobody at Düsterstein is thick. The Countess has rumbled you, and so has Saraceni, and I rumbled you the first night I noticed you looking out of your open window, counting the cars on the Bummelzug. I was on the ground below, doing the same thing, just for the fun of it. A fine snoop you are! Standing in a window with a light behind you!"

"All right, officer. It's a fair cop. I'll come quietly. So you're in the profession, too?"

"Born to it. My father was in it until he died on the job. Killed, very likely, though nobody really knows."

"And what are you doing here?"

"That's not a question one pro asks another

495

pro. I'm just looking about. Keeping an eye on what you and the Meister are doing, and what the Countess and Prince Max do with that."

"But you've never been in the shell-grotto."

"Don't need to go. I write the Countess's letters, and I know what happens, however much she pretends it's something else."

"Doesn't the Countess rumble *you?*"

"I hope not. It would be awful to think there were two snoops in one's house, wouldn't it? And I'm not very high-powered, you know. Just write the occasional letter home to my mum, who is a pro's widow, and knows how to read them and what to pass on to the big chaps."

"I know it's nosy to ask, but do you get paid?"

"Ha ha; the profession relies to what might be considered a dangerous degree on unpaid help. The old English notion that nobody who is anybody really works for money. No, I work for nothing, on the understanding that if I shape up well I will be in line for a paid job some day. Women don't get on very fast in the profession, unless they are elegant love-goddesses, and then they don't last long. But I don't grumble. I'm acquiring a useful command of Bavarian rural dialect and a peerless knowledge of the borderland between the Reich and Austria."

"Not casting any horoscopes?"

"Plenty, but chiefly of people long dead. Why?"

"It was hinted to me that Prince Max would like to know what you think of his."

"Oh, I know that. But I won't bite. Anyhow, it

would be bad for his character. Max is going to be rather famous."

"How?"

"Even if I were sure I wouldn't tell you."

"Aha, I see in you the iconological figure of Prudence."

"Meaning what?"

"The Meister has me hard at it studying all that sort of thing. So that I can read old pictures. All those symbolic women—Truth with her mirror, Charity suckling her child, Justice with her sword and balances, Temperance with her cup and ewer—scores of them; they are the sign language of a particular kind of art."

"Well, why not? Have you anything better to do?"

"I have a block about that sort of thing. This Renaissance and pre-Renaissance stuff, where you make out the figures of Time, and his daughter Truth, and Luxury, and Fraud, and all those creatures, seems to me to pull a fine painting down to the level of moral teaching, if not actual anecdote. Could a great painter like Bronzino really have been so much of a moralist?"

"I don't see why not. It's just romantic nonsense to suppose that painters have always been rowdies and wenchers. Most of them were daubing away like billy-o in order to get the means to live the bourgeois life."

"Oh well—it's very dull learning iconology and I am beginning to wish something interesting would happen."

"It will, and soon. Just hang on a bit. Some day you will be really famous, Francis."

"Are you being psychic?"

"Me? What put that into your head?"

"Saraceni did. He says you are very much a psychic."

"Saraceni is a mischief-making old nuisance."

"Rather more than that. Sometimes when I listen to him going on about the picture exporting and importing business that he and the Countess are up to, I feel like Faust listening to Mephistopheles."

"Lucky you. Would anybody ever have heard of Faust if it hadn't been for Mephistopheles?"

"All right. But he has in a high degree the trick of making the worse seem the better cause. And he says it's because conventional morality takes no heed of art."

"I thought he said art was the higher morality."

"Now you are beginning to sound like him. Listen, Ruth, aren't we ever going to get together in bed again?"

"Not a hope, unless the Countess goes away on one of her jaunts and takes Amalie with her. In the Countess's house and under her eye I play by the Countess's rules, and I can't be having it off with you when I am supposed to be gently watching over the precious virginity of her granddaughter. Fair's fair, and that's a little too much in the line of eighteenth-century castle intrigue for my taste."

"Okay—I just thought I'd ask. 'Hereafter, in a better world than this—' "

" 'I shall desire more love and knowledge of you.' I'll hold you to that."

"And I'll hold *you* to that."

"Corniche! I want you to go to the Netherlands and kill a man."

"At your service, Meister. Shall I take my dagger or rely on the poisoned chalice?"

"You will rely on the poisoned word. Only that will do the job."

"Then I suppose I'd better know his name."

"His name, unfortunately for him, is Jean-Paul Letztpfennig. I am a great believer in the influence of names on destiny, and Letztpfennig is not a lucky name. Nor is he a lucky man. He wanted a career as a painter, but his stuff was dull and derivative. A failure, indeed, but just at the moment he is attracting a lot of attention."

"Not from me. Never heard of him."

"His notoriety is not mentioned in the German papers, but he is of great interest to Germany. The glassy eye of Reichsmarschall Göring is on him. He wants to sell the Reichsmarschall a ridiculous fake painting."

"If it's ridiculous how did the Reichsmarschall ever cast his glassy eye on it?"

"Because Letztpfennig, who is probably the most left-handed schlemiel in the art world at present, is hawking his fake around, and if it were real it would be the great find of the century.

Nothing less than a major work by Hubertus van Eyck."

"Not Jan van Eyck?"

"No; Hubertus, Jan's brother who died in 1426, quite young. But Hubertus was a very great painter. It was he who designed and painted quite a bit of the magnificent *Adoration of the Lamb*, which is at Ghent. Jan finished it. There aren't many pictures by Hubertus, and the appearance of one now is bound to create a sensation. But it is a fake."

"How do you know?"

"I know because I feel it in my bones. It is my ability to feel things in my bones that lifts me above the general run of art experts. We all have sensitive bones, of course. But I am a painter myself, and I know more about how the great painters of the past worked than even Berenson, because Berenson is not a painter, and his bones keep changing their mind; he has attributed some very remarkable pictures to as many as three painters over a period of twenty years, to the dismay of their owners. When I know a thing I know it forever. And Letztpfennig's van Eyck is a fake."

"You've seen it?"

"I don't have to see it. If Letztpfennig vouches for it, it's a fake. He has made a tiny reputation among gullible people, but I know him through and through. He is the worst kind of scoundrel— an unlucky, muddling scoundrel. And he must be destroyed."

"Meister—"

"Yes?"

"I have never mentioned this, because it seems tactless, but I have been told that you possess the Evil Eye. Why don't you simply destroy Letztpfennig yourself?"

"Oh, what a dreadful world we live in! How spitefully people talk! The Evil Eye! Of course, I know that stupid people say that, merely because one or two people to whom I have taken a dislike have had unfortunate accidents. Only a broken bone, or losing their sight, or something of that sort. Never anything fatal. I am still a Catholic, you know; I would recoil from killing a rival."

"But don't you want me to kill Letztpfennig?"

"I spoke in terms of melodramatic exaggeration, to get your full attention. I only want you to kill him professionally."

"Oh, I see. Nothing serious."

"If he dies of chagrin, that is because he is over-sensitive. Nobody's fault but his own. Psychological suicide. Not uncommon."

"This is just a matter of professional rivalry, is it?"

"Do you suppose I would elevate such an idiot as Letztpfennig to the status of a rival? A rival to me! You must think I hold my abilities in low esteem. No, he must go because he is dangerous."

"Dangerous to the trade of selling dubious pictures to the Reich?"

"How coarsely you judge these things! It is the Lutheran streak in you—a perverse, self-destroying concept of morality. You refuse to see things as they are. I, and several people of whom you know one or two, am carefully securing some Italian art from the German Reich in exchange for pictures they like better. And not one of those pictures has been a fake—only a picture that has been assisted to put its best face foremost. The chain of action is carefully calculated. Everything goes through people with unexceptionable credentials, and we never pitch the note too high—no Dürers, no Cranachs. And now this Flemish buffoon appears with a fake Hubertus van Eyck, and wants gigantic sums either in cash or in paintings the Reich thinks it can spare, and he has the effrontery to haggle, and bring in an American bidder for his picture, with the result that the Dutch government is intervening in the matter, and God alone knows what beans may be spilled."

"Could you give me some facts? I now know the range of your passion; I'd just like to know what Letztpfennig has done, and what you want me to do."

"There is a very nice strain of common sense in you, Corniche. Your family background is in banking, is it not? Not that my experience of bankers puts them above art dealers in matters of probity. But they manage to look and sound so trustworthy, even when they are not. Well—this all began about two years ago when Jean-Paul Letztpfennig let it be known that during a jaunt to Belgium he had come upon a picture in an old country house that he bought because he wanted an old canvas. Idiot! Who wants an old canvas unless he means to fake something with it? Anyhow—he says he cleaned the picture and found it to be a painting of *The Harrowing of Hell*. You know the subject?"

"I know what it is. I've never seen a painting of it."

"They are extremely rare. It was a favourite theme in manuscript illuminations and sometimes in stained glass, but it did not appeal to painters. It is Christ redeeming the souls of the better class of pagans from Hell, where they had presumably languished until His death on the Cross. Well—if it were real and not something Letztpfennig had fudged up himself, it would be interesting, and if it were in the Gothic style it might reasonably go to the Führermuseum, if the German experts passed it. Though those highly intelligent men have so far shown themselves willing to deal only with reputable people like the group with whom I—and you, now that *Drollig Hansel* has given such satisfaction—are associated. But Letztpfennig, like the blockhead he is, asserts that a signature—by which he means a monogram—is on the picture that establishes it as the work of Hubertus van Eyck.

"When that leaked out, there was a sensation, and an immediate request for information and a chance to bid from an American collector. One of the biggest, and when I tell you that his agent and expert is Addison Thresher you will know whom I am talking about. And there were complications, because, as you know, the Reichsmarschall is a keen collector himself, and if there were a Hubertus van Eyck to be had, he wanted it. To be paid for, I need hardly tell you, by paintings from German museums. Great men are above trivialities in such negotiations. He offered, or his agents offered on his behalf, some splendid Italian things, and Letztpfennig was out of his meagre wits trying to decide whether he should grab the American dollars at once, or grab the Italian pictures, for resale in the States.

"That was when the Dutch government stepped in. You know how dearly they love the Reich. Their Ministry of Fine Art said that a great masterpiece by Hubertus van Eyck was a national treasure and could not leave the country. You would have thought that Belgium would have intervened and said that the picture had, after all, been found in Belgium, but nothing was heard from Belgium and that made Addison Thresher suspicious that the picture had never been in Belgium and was probably a fake.

"Not to toil through all the details, the picture is now in the protection of the Dutch Ministry of Fine Art, and all sorts of people have been visiting it, trying to decide whether it is genuine or not. Medland and Horsburgh from the British Museum and National Gallery laboratories in London have seen it, and can't give an opinion unless they are permitted to use X-rays and chemical tests—which the Dutch so far won't allow. Lemaire and Bastogne and Baudoin from Paris and Brussels have hemmed and hawed. Two Dutch experts,

Dr. Schlichte-Martin and Dr. Hausche-Kuypers, are at each other's throats. Addison Thresher is now almost ready to break off all negotiations on grounds that the thing is a fake, and the German experts Frisch and Belmann are outraged because he suggests that they are afraid to speak their minds for fear of being proved wrong.

"They are running out of experts. Of course, they can't have Berenson, ostensibly because his area is confined to Italian art, but really because he is a Jew and the Reichsmarschall would be outraged. Duveen can't get near it or bring anybody to look at it for the same reason. It's the old wrangle between scientific testing and aesthetic sensibility, and Huygens, the judge who is in charge of the matter, is tired of it and wants to have somebody say that the thing is genuine, or that it is dubious and the scientific tests should proceed. So he has sent for me. And I'm not going."

"Why not?"

"Because of the delicacy of the situation in which our group finds itself. It must never for one moment be thought that we want to destroy Letztpfennig, but Letztpfennig must be destroyed or the Germans may become more suspicious than they naturally and quite rightly are, as professionals in art appreciation. We don't want every fool with an old picture horning in on the work we are doing. So I have written to Judge Huygens saying that my health is precarious, but that I shall send my trusted assistant to his aid, and if it proves

505

absolutely necessary, I shall make the journey to The Hague myself. You are going."

"To do what?"

"To decide whether *The Harrowing of Hell* is by Hubertus van Eyck, or not. To show, if you can, that Letztpfennig either painted it himself on an old canvas, or at least over-painted an existing picture, and put in the van Eyck monogram. This is your chance to establish yourself as an art expert. Don't you understand, Corniche? This is one of your great tests, and I am putting it in your way."

"But what is being tested? You are sending me with instructions to declare the picture a fake and to discredit a rival. It doesn't sound like art criticism to me."

"It is a part of art criticism, Corniche. Your North American innocence—to use an absurdly kind word for it—must come to terms with the world in which you have chosen to put your life. It is a cruel world and its morality is not simple. If I had the least feeling that this thing in The Hague was a genuine Hubertus van Eyck I would be on my knees before it, but the chances are ten thousand to one that it's a fake, and the fake must be exposed. Art is very big money, these days, owing to the extraordinary exertions of certain geniuses, of whom Duveen is certainly the greatest. Fakes cannot be endured. Good art must drive out bad."

"But the morality of that—which I understand— won't square with what we have been doing here."

"The morality of the art world is not square, my dear pupil and colleague; it is a polyhedron. But it is a morality, none the less. So—go and win your spurs!"

"And what if I don't?"

"Then I shall come and do what you have failed to do, by one means or another, including even the Evil Eye—if anyone is so foolish as to believe in it, which I don't, as I have made clear—and if you and I have any further association, it will be simply as master and perpetual apprentice. You will have failed and I shall have to find another successor to myself. In this affair you are being tested as well as Letztpfennig."

The Dutch Ministry of Fine Art treated its guests well—indeed, in princely style—and when Francis arrived in The Hague he was put up at the Hotel Des Indes, and ate a splendid meal into which he admitted no scrap of veal. The next morning he presented himself to Judge Huygens, who looked precisely as a judge should, and who took him after an exchange of civilities to a handsome room, where the disputed painting was displayed on an easel. Francis settled to his work, and it was soon clear that the Judge meant to stay in the room all the time he was there. A large, watchful, uniformed attendant was also on guard at the door.

The Harrowing of Hell was a most impressive picture, larger than Francis had expected, and obviously meant for a church. The colours glowed with the extraordinary light and appearance of transparency that the brothers van Eyck were reputed to have perfected and brought to the world of painting in oils; colour had been used at its greatest strength above a light ground, which created the magical glow of even the darkest pigment. In the middle of the picture was the figure of Christ, triumphantly bearing the banner-cross of the Resurrection in His left hand and gesturing toward Adam and Eve, the prophets Enoch and Elijah, and figures of Isaiah, Simeon, and Dismas, the Repentant Thief, with His right hand; He was beckoning them to follow Him through the gates of Hell, which stood open behind Him. On His left, averting their faces from His glory, cringing, gnashing their teeth, and seeking to escape, were Satan and his attendant fiends. The background was a true Dutch sky, flecked with delicate clouds, beneath which was to be seen some parts of a truly Dutch landscape, lying behind the gates of Hell—and Hell obviously employed a brilliant and imaginative metalsmith.

Francis studied the picture for perhaps half an hour. If it were a fake it was a magnificent fake, done by a painter of enviable talent. But there have been magnificent fakes in the history of art. Well, that's enough aesthetic judgement, thought Francis; now we get down to the really inquisitorial inspection. He had brought, in a brief-case, what he thought of as his Little Jiffy Bernard Berenson Art Expert's Set, consisting of a pair of binoculars, a large magnifying glass, and a brush of medium size. He looked at the picture through the binoculars, from the greatest distance the room allowed; then looked at it through the wrong end of the binoculars. Neither magnification nor diminution suggested anything peculiar about the composition. He looked at the picture through his magnifying glass, inch by inch, and then at his request the large attendant stood the picture on its head, and he examined it again from that aspect. With a reassuring nod to the Judge he dabbed at it here and there with his soft brush. He examined the back, tapped the canvas, inspected the workmanship of the stretchers. To the astonishment of Huygens and the guard he crumpled his handkerchief, warmed it with a cigarette-lighter, and held it to the canvas for perhaps ninety seconds. He sniffed the heated area loudly. No: not a whiff of formaldehyde. Then he sat down again and looked at the picture for another hour, occasionally turning away and suddenly rounding on it, as though it might have relaxed some of its pervasive van Eyckishness while his back was turned. He spent a good deal of time peering at the monogram, small but easily enough seen when you knew where to look, hidden in the folds of Isaiah's robe. It might have been many things: Hubert of Ghent? Signatures didn't matter, anyhow; the real signature was the quality of the painting, and try as he might he couldn't find anything wrong with it.

Fakes, as he well knew, tend to declare themselves a generation or two after they have appeared and been accepted as originals. Truth, the daughter of Time, reveals indications of another age, another temper and taste, in a picture which is painted long after the period to which it has been attributed. Paint ages in the wrong way. Fashions in faces change, and the change may be seen when the fashion for a certain conformation of features has passed. But he did not have fifty years to wait. His job was to declare the picture a fake, and to do so as soon as possible.

When at last he said to the Judge that he had seen enough he received a shock. "Several of your fellow-experts are in the city at present," said Huygens. "They are anxious to hear what you have to say, as I am myself. You speak, we know, with the authority and probity of Tancred Saraceni and we have agreed that your opinion shall carry great weight, and indeed will doubtless prove decisive. Will you meet us here tomorrow at eleven o'clock? The painter will be here also. Understandably he expects a triumphant vindication."

"And you, Edelachtbare Heer?"

"I? Oh, my opinion is of no importance. I am simply the director of the investigation. Indeed, it would be improper if anyone holding strong opinions about this sort of painting had been appointed to preside. I do, of course, represent the Netherlands government."

At luncheon, as Francis was treating himself to another veal-free blow-out at the expense of his hosts, he was joined by a smiling American.

"Mind if I sit down? I am Addison Thresher,

and I'm here from the Metropolitan Museum in New York. Also representing one or two other interested parties. There's no harm in our talking; Huygens said it was perfectly all right. What did you think?"

Addison Thresher was an expensively dressed, conservatively dressed, more than ordinarily tastefully dressed man, with silver-rimmed glasses and those American teeth, so disconcerting to the European eye, that always seem to have been furiously brushed not more than an hour ago. His manners were wonderful and he smelled of a costly toilet water. But in his eyes there was a steely glint.

Warily, Francis told him what he thought, which in effect was nothing at all.

"I know," said Thresher; "that's the trouble, isn't it? Not a thing you can quite lay your hand on. The signature is a fake, of course, but that's not important. But there is something about the whole affair I don't like. You've seen the composition before, of course?"

Francis shook his head, his mouth being full.

"Have you ever looked at that late-medieval manuscript of the Cooks and Innkeepers Play, in the Chester group? There's a miniature of the *Harrowing*. Very suggestive. Could van Eyck have seen it? Barely possible. But a faker could know it. There's nothing that hints at the Fra Angelico or the Bronzino of the *Harrowing;* that would have been a dead give-away, for Hubertus van Eyck couldn't have seen either. But there is also a strong feeling of that big wall painting at Mount Athos, and that would be funny, wouldn't it—two minds with but a single thought, and God knows how many centuries between them? The influences, if they are influences, are so damned scholarly. Nothing in any of the work of either of the van Eycks suggests that they were learned in that way. Painters in those days simply weren't."

"Yes, I see what you mean," said Francis, trying to conceal the fact that he was learning fast. "But still—nothing that proves fakery."

"That's what the Germans say. And also what the Dutch say. They want it to be genuine, of course, because it would be a marvellous acquisition for a Dutch gallery. The man from the Mauritshuis is particularly keen. If it proves to be a national treasure they'll never let it out of the country, and they'd love to thwart Göring. They fight about details but they're wholly agreed on that. They'll pay Letztpfennig a goodish price, but not the really big money he would get from the States, or the splendid swaps he could get from the Germans."

"What do you know about Letztpfennig?"

"Nothing to his discredit. Indeed, he is rather an impressive figure. Lectures learnedly on Dutch art, and is probably the best restorer in Europe—except for Saraceni, of course. Knows perhaps a little too much about Old Master painting techniques to be entirely trustworthy in a situation like this. But I mustn't let my suspicions run away with me. It's just that in my bones I sense something wrong, and as long as the scientific boys from London are kept at bay, I have to rely on my bones. Aesthetic sensibility, we call it in the trade, but it comes down to a feeling in the bones."

"Like Berenson."

"Yes, Berenson has wonderfully shrewd bones. But when Joe Duveen is paying you a full twenty-five per cent of the sale price of a picture for an authentication, I wonder if your bones can always be heard above the sweet music of the cash register. It costs a lot of dough to live like Berenson. Of course, it's all academic to me; whatever happens I won't get the picture. But I hate a faker. Bad for business."

Addison Thresher's manners left nothing to be desired. He did not hover over Francis but took himself off, saying that they would meet again in the morning. And what was Francis to do? Go to the Mauritshuis and look at the pictures? He had been there before and he was sick of looking at pictures. Encouraged by his good lunch he went to the Wassenaar, and spent the afternoon at the zoo.

Jean-Paul Letztpfennig's hand, when he gave it to Francis to shake, was unpleasantly damp, and Francis immediately drew out his handkerchief and wiped his own hand somewhat too obviously. Some of the other men in the room were quick to notice. Professor Baudoin, whom Francis had already decided was the nasty one, sucked in his

513

breath audibly. This was much better than when he blew it out, generously, as he did in conversation, for his breath suggested that he was dying from within, and had completed about two-thirds of the job. It was a striking contrast to Addison Thresher, whose breath smelled of the very best caries-defying toothpaste. He was dressed this morning in a completely different outfit, somewhat formal and suggestive of great affairs.

Indeed, great affairs were in hand. Expectancy was in the air, and all the sensitive bones of all the experts must have felt it. Dr. Schlichte-Martin, ample and red-faced, Dr. Hausche-Kuypers, young and merry, were like men playing a game of Snakes and Ladders; if the van Eyck were real, the fat old man advanced and the young jolly one was thrown back, but if it were the other way round, youth rejoiced and age grieved. Frisch and Belmann, the Germans, wore iron-grey suits and iron-grey expressions, for they were losers whatever happened. They rather hoped Letztpfennig would be exploded and regretted their earlier excitement about his find. Lemaire and Bastogne and Baudoin were philosophical, but inclined to negative opinions; the two Frenchmen would have liked the picture to be genuine, but doubted if it could be; the Belgian wanted it to be a fake, for he was a friend of whatever was negative. They were all hedging their bets in the guarded manner of critics the world over.

"Everyone knows everyone else, I believe? Shall we proceed to our business, which may be brief?

Mr. Cornish, will you tell us what your conclusions are?" The Judge was by far the calmest man present. The Judge, and the big guard at the door.

Francis approached his task with inward shrinking, but outward calm. He was inclined to like Letztpfennig, though he wished he could wash the corpse-sweat from his right hand. Letztpfennig was by no means the comic figure of Saraceni's derision. A grey man, with the appearance of a deeply intellectual man, thickly spectacled and possessing a mop of grey hair which might have suggested an artist if the man were not so obviously cast in the mould of a professor. A carefully dressed man, with a white handkerchief peeping from his breast pocket in just the right proportion. A man whose shoes gleamed with loving care. His appearance of calm impressed nobody.

Well, here goes, thought Francis. Thank God I can be both decisive and honest.

"I fear the picture cannot be accepted as genuine," said he.

"That is your opinion?" said Huygens.

"More than simply an opinion, Edelachtbare," said Francis; the occasion he thought deserved the fullest formality. "The picture may indeed be an old picture. The quality of the painting is superb, and it strongly suggests van Eyck. Any painter at any time might be proud to have painted it. But you cannot even attribute it to *alunno di* van Eyck or *amico di* van Eyck; it is probably a century after van Eyck."

"You speak with great certainty," said Professor Baudoin, with unconcealed gloating. "But you are—if you will allow me to speak of it—a very young man, and the certainty of youth is not always appropriate to such matters as this. You will give us reasons, of course."

Indeed I shall, thought Francis. You think Letztpfennig is virtually destroyed and now you want to destroy me because I am young. Well—bugger you, you bad-breathed old nuisance.

"I am sure your colleague will be glad to give his reasons," said Huygens, the peacemaker. "If they are truly convincing, we shall call back the experts from Britain, who will make scientific appraisals."

"I don't think you will need to do that," said Francis. "The picture has been put forward as a van Eyck, and it certainly is not by van Eyck, either Hubertus or Jan. Have any of you gentlemen visited the zoo lately?"

What was this about the zoo? Was the young man trifling with them?

"A detail of the painting tells us all we need to know," Francis continued. "Observe the monkey who hangs by his tail from the bars of Hell, in the upper left-hand corner of the picture. What is he doing there?"

"It is an iconographical detail that one might expect in such a picture," said Letztpfennig somewhat patronizingly toward the young man, glad to defend the monkey. "The chained monkey is an old symbol of the fallen mankind that preceded the coming of Christ. Of souls in Hell, in fact. He belongs with the defeated devils."

"But he is hanging by his tail."

"Since when do monkeys not hang by their tails?"

"They did not do so in Ghent in van Eyck's day. That monkey is a *Cebus capucinus*, a New World monkey. The chained monkey of iconography is the *Macacus rhesus*, the Old World monkey. Such a monkey as that, a monkey with a prehensile tail, was unknown in Europe until the sixteenth century, and I need not remind you that Hubertus van Eyck died in 1426. The painter, whoever he is—or was—wanted to complete his composition with a figure, not too commanding, in that particular spot, so the chained monkey had to be hanging by his tail from the bars of Hell. There are several examples of both *Cebus capucinus* and *Macacus rhesus* informatively labelled in your very good local zoo. That is why I mentioned it."

In the melodrama of the nineteenth century there may frequently be found such stage directions as *Sensation! Astonishment! Tableau!* This was the gratifying effect produced by Francis's judgement. None of the experts tried to suggest that they were well up in the lore of monkeys, but when they were shown the obvious they made haste to declare that it was indeed obvious. This is one of the things experts are frequently called on to do.

As they chattered learnedly, assuring each other that they had had some uneasiness about the monkey, Letztpfennig was understandably undergoing great stress. The big guard brought him a chair, and he sat on it and drew his breath painfully. But he regained his self-possession, rose to his feet, clapped his hands authoritatively, like a professor calling a class to order.

"Gentlemen," said he, "you shall know that I painted this picture. Why did I do so? In part as a protest against the fanatical adoration that is accorded to our Dutch masters of an earlier day, that is so frequently linked with a depreciation of modern painters. It is a bad principle that nothing may be praised without dispraising something else. Nobody nowadays can paint like the Old Masters! That is untrue. *I* have done so, and I know there are many others who could do it as well as I. It is not done, of course, because it is a kind of artistic fancy-dress, an insincerity, an imitation of another man's style. I fully agree that a painter should work in the mode—speaking very generally—of his own time. But that is not because it is a degenerate mode, adopted because he cannot paint as well as his great artistic predecessors.

"Now listen to me patiently, if you please. You have all praised this painting for its skill in colour and design, and its power to lift the heart as only a great picture can do. At one time or another you have all spoken highly of it, and several of you have professed yourselves delighted with it. What delighted you? The magic of a great name? The magic of the past? Or was it the picture before your eyes? Even you, Mr. Thresher, before you found that under no circumstances could you buy this picture for your great client, spoke of it to me in terms that made my heart sing in my breast. The work of a very great master, you said, if not indubitably a van Eyck. Well—? I am the very great master. Do you take back everything you said?"

Thresher said nothing, and none of the other experts were inclined to speak, except Baudoin, who was hissing in Belmann's ear that he had never trusted the *craquelure*.

It was the Judge who spoke, and he spoke like a judge. "We must bear in mind, Mynheer Letztpfennig, that you offered the picture for sale as a genuine van Eyck, and with it you offered a tale about its origins which we now know to be untrue. That cannot be explained away as part of a protest on behalf of the skill of modern painters."

"But how else was I to get attention for my picture? How else was I to make my point? If I had made it known that Jean-Paul Letztpfennig, professor of art, restorer of Old Masters, known as a painter condemned to mediocrity by those who profess to rank artists as if they were schoolboys, had painted a great painting in an old style, how many of you would have crossed your doorstep to see it? Not one! Not one! But as things are you have used words like masterpiece, and transporting beauty. At what were they directed? Toward what you saw, or merely toward what you thought you saw?"

"The Judge is right," said Addison Thresher. "You wanted the top dollar for your picture, not only for its beauty—which I don't deny—but for the glamour of age and a great name. And we fell for it! It's a fine painting, but where can you sell it? I guess it's a draw. Certainly so far as I am concerned, it's a draw."

Of course, it wasn't a draw, and the international press turned it into a sensation. How did they find out what had happened? When eleven men are in a room and something of unusual interest takes place, at least one of them is likely to let something drop which the press seizes on, and the hunt is up. The one who was supposed to have leaked the story was Sluyters, the guard, who was not nearly so impassive as he looked, and who would have been glad to tell what he knew for a consideration. But did nobody else say a word? Certainly Francis didn't until he was back at Düsterstein, but who can answer for Addison Thresher? Did the Judge drop a word to his wife, who may have told an intimate friend in the uttermost confidence? The Germans certainly were not silent when they reported to their superiors, and through them to the Reichsmarschall, who was not known for being close-mouthed. The two Frenchmen and the Belgian would not be inclined toward silence; they had risked little and gained much, for they had been in on a great unmasking which gave the international art world something to talk about for many months.

"Monkey Blows Hoax" was the headline in one form or another, and one paper carried a caricature of Francis instructing the experts, based on a famous painting of the Boy Christ Teaching in the Temple.

"I see that the Letztpfennig file is now closed," said Saraceni, raising his eyes from the *Völkischer Beobachter* he had been reading in the shell-grotto.

"Are they dropping all charges?" said Francis.

"No charges are effective now. He has killed himself."

"Oh God! The poor devil!"

"Do not reproach yourself, Corniche. I told you to kill him, and you killed him. You destroyed him professionally on my instruction and now he has yielded up his life of his own volition. In a very interesting way, too. He lived in Amsterdam in one of those lovely old houses on a canal. You know how they have projecting mounts for cranes hanging over the canal bank, so that in the old days those merchant houses could have goods hauled up to the top floor for storage? Picturesque old things. It seems Letztpfennig hanged himself on his crane, right out over the canal. When he was retrieved by the police they found a note pinned to his coat. Oddly enough, he had worn his overcoat and hat to die in. The note said: 'Let them say what they will now; in the beginning they said it was a great picture.'—My dear man, are you unwell? Perhaps you had better take the day off. You have done quite enough for art, for the present."

That was the making of Francis, said the Daimon Maimas.

—You are not gentle in your methods, brother, said the Lesser Zadkiel.

—Not always, but I am often subtle. It was I, of course, who nudged Francis to visit the zoo, and I made sure he had a good look at the monkeys.

—A bad moment for Letztpfennig.

—Letztpfennig was not my care. And he was not too badly used. He wanted fame and he wanted to be recognized as a great painter. He had both his wishes—posthumously. His death gave a note of pathos to what was, considering all things, a remarkable career. It was the rest of mankind that felt the pathos, as it usually is in pathetic fates. When everything is added up, Letztpfennig did not do too badly. He is a footnote in the history of art. And Francis gained at a stroke a very nice little reputation.

—And that was the fame that Ruth predicted? said the Lesser Zadkiel.

—Oh, by no means. I can do better than that, said the Daimon Maimas.

The downfall of Letzpfennig was of interest to the world, as somebody's downfall always is, but by the autumn of 1938, not long after Francis's twenty-ninth birthday, the Munich Crisis took precedence over all other news, and the apparent triumph of Neville Chamberlain in concluding an agreement with the German Führer gladdened the hearts of millions of innocents who wanted peace and were ready to believe anything that seemed to promise peace. But not everyone trusted that pact; the Countess and Saraceni were two of these. There was uneasiness and change at Düsterstein. Amalie was sent off to a distinguished school in Switzerland, and though Ruth Nibsmith stayed on to help the Countess in secretarial work, she knew that her time in that capacity was short, and before Christmas she had taken affectionate farewells of everyone and returned to England. Saraceni likewise found that he had imperative business in Rome, and could not say how long it would be before he returned—though he assured the Countess that he would certainly return. And the Countess announced that pressing work in Munich, relating to her sales of farm produce, would keep her in that city for several weeks and perhaps for months.

Saraceni and Francis had, between them, in the year past, completed a substantial amount of work, some of which was ambitious. Bigger and bigger pictures were making their way to the wine merchants' cellars—pictures so large the canvases had to be dismounted from their stretchers, and packed around the insides of the big barrels, carefully wrapped to protect them from the wine. The stretchers and the old nails that belonged to the pictures travelled in two large bags of golf clubs, which Prince Max had added to his luggage. These were ambitious pictures of battle scenes, and a number of portraits of minor historical figures, all greatly improved by Saraceni and also by Francis, who was trusted with increasingly significant work. What was to become of Francis during the Meister's long absence? The day before he left, Saraceni told him.

"You have done well, Corniche, and you have done it much quicker than I thought you would. The explosion of Letztpfennig has given you a name—a modest name, but nevertheless a name. Still, before you are ready to appear before the world as *amico di Saraceni* instead of the lesser *alunno di Saraceni* there is an important test I want you to accept now. Quite simply it is this: can you paint as well as Letztpfennig? He was a master, you know, in this lesser realm of art. I can say it, now that you have disposed of him. I am not talking of course of faking, for that is contemptible, but I mean the ability to work truly in the technique and also in the spirit of the past. Unless you can satisfy me of that I shall not feel absolutely certain about you. *Drollig Hansel* was good. What you have done during the past year is good. But when you are not under my eye and subject to my advice and relentless criticism—I know I'm a bastard, but all great teachers must be so—can you really bring it off? So: while I am away I want you to paint an original picture on a large scale—not just big, but big in conception—and I want you to do it not in imitation of anyone, but as you would paint yourself if you were living in the fifteenth or sixteenth century.

Find your subject. Grind your colours. I have found a groundwork for you.

"Look here; it is, as you see, a triptych, an altar-piece of fair size in three panels that hung in the chapel here before it was done over in the great Baroque style. It is a wreck, of course. It has been standing for at least two hundred years in one of the innumerable service corridors of this castle from which we have recovered so many discarded paintings, but it was never very good and now it is rubbish. Clean it, right down to the wood, and go to work. I am expecting something that will tell me just how good you are, when you work independently. You will have plenty of time. I shall return in the spring, or perhaps a little later. But I shall certainly return."

So, shortly before Christmas of 1938, Francis found himself the virtual master of Düsterstein. The family rooms, as well as the great rooms of state, were transformed by dust-sheets and muslin wraps for the chandeliers into the habitations of ghosts. One small room was left for his use, and there he sat and ate his meals when he was not busy in the shell-grotto. He took walks in the grounds, squelching over mossy paths under weeping trees. Another man might have found it melancholy, but Francis welcomed the solitude and the dimness, for he was turned in upon himself and wanted no distraction, no invitation to play. He was seeking his picture.

The philosophy of Saraceni, as distinguished

from the avarice and opportunism of Saraceni, was not something he had learned as Amalie learned her lessons. He had absorbed it, and ingested it, and had made it part of his own wholeness. What was so plainly unworthy in the Meister he regarded with amusement; he was not such a fool as to suppose that great men do not have their foibles, and that such flaws might not be great ones. He had consumed the wheat and discarded the chaff, and the wheat was now bone of his bone. It was his belief, not his lesson.

What did he now believe, at the end of a toilsome and sometimes humiliating apprenticeship? That a great picture must have its foundation in a sustaining myth, which could only be expressed through painting by an artist with an intense vocation. He had learned to accept and cherish his vocation, which was none the less real because it had been reached by such a crooked path. He had worked in the shell-grotto as a man under orders, but now he was to work under no orders but his own, even though he must express himself in a bygone mode of painting. But what was his picture, the masterpiece which would conclude his apprenticeship, to be?

Rooted in a myth, but what myth? In the tangle of mythology, the cosmic bedroom farce and vulgar family wrangles of the gods of Olympus or their diminished effigies as conceived by the Romans? Never! In the finer myth of the Christian world, as seen in a thousand forms in the Age of Faith? Catholicism he certainly possessed, but it was still the sweet Catholicism of Mary-Ben rather than that of the rigorous Church Fathers. In the myth of the greatness of Man, as the Renaissance had asserted, or the myth of Man Diminished and Enchained as it appeared to the Age of Reason? What about Romanticism, the myth of the Inner Man sharply declining to the myth of Egotism? There was even the nineteenth-century myth of Materialism, the exaltation of the World of Things, which had evoked so many great pictures from the Impressionists. But these must be rejected at once, even if they had strongly attracted him (which they did not), because his orders—and he was still under orders—were to paint a picture in the manner of the Old Masters, a picture that would contain some technical instruction even for the ingenious Letztpfennig.

Alone, and only vaguely aware of the Europe that was boiling up toward a war of hitherto unexampled horror almost on his doorstep, Francis found his answer, and it was the only possible, the inescapable answer. He would paint the myth of Francis Cornish.

But how? He was not free to work as a painter might who was not seeking to advance from *alunno* to *amico* in the fierce school of Saraceni. He could not descend, so far as his talent allowed, into the Realm of the Mothers and return with a picture that might evade the understanding of even the most intuitive and sympathetic of observers, but that would perhaps explain itself after twenty years as a prophecy, or a cry of despair. He must have a subject that could be identified as the subjects of the Old Masters are identified, however much these say that is not contained in the obvious subject.

He made and destroyed innumerable sketches, but even as he rejected them he felt that he was moving nearer to his goal. At last a subject began to assert itself, and then to show that it was inescapable, a subject that might be invited to body forth the myth of Francis Cornish. It was at this point that he began to make the preparatory studies and drawings in the old manner, on prepared paper with a silver-point; studies which might, at some distant time, puzzle the experts. His theme, his subject, his myth, was to be contained in a triptych of *The Marriage at Cana*.

It had not been one of the most popular themes of the masters who painted before the High Renaissance, the masters who painted in the mode that preceded the lush depictions of that wedding feast—so improbable in terms of the biblical story—which were, in fact, glorifications of the splendours and luxuries of this world. Francis must work in terms of the austere but not starveling manner of the sunset of the Gothic world. And as he made his drawings he found that this was a manner that would serve him very well; the myth of Francis Cornish was not a Renaissance myth, or a myth of Reason or of self-delighted egotism, or the myth of the World of Things. If he could not speak in the voice of his century he would speak in the final accents of the Gothic voice. And so he worked, not furiously but with concentration and devotion, and when at last his preliminary cartoons were done, and the ruinous old picture on the triptych was scoured and scraped off, and his colours were chosen and prepared down to the last grinding of the lapis lazuli that lay so readily at hand, he began to paint.

It was midsummer 1939 before Saraceni returned, and Francis was growing anxious. He had received a letter in late June from Sir Owen Williams-Owen, saying:

> Your record of your heart's action for the past several months is causing me some concern, and I think it advisable that I examine you again. I suggest that you return to England as soon as you conveniently can, so that I may have another look at you. Your godfather, whom I saw the other day, sends his regards.

That was not hard to interpret, even by a preoccupied painter who had not been paying much attention to the world's news. But he must see the Meister before he left Düsterstein. In late July, Saraceni was with him in the shell-grotto, and Francis, not without a sense of drama, unveiled *The Marriage at Cana*, baked and with Augsburg dust in its *craquelure*.

The Meister followed the familiar routine. He looked at the picture for a quarter of an hour without speaking. Then he went through the inspections with the field-glasses, the large magnifying glass, the poking at the back of the canvas, the sniffing, the rubbing of a corner with a wetted finger—all the ceremonies of expertise. But then he did something which was not usual; he sat down and looked at the picture for a considerable time, grunting now and then with what Francis hoped was satisfaction.

"Well, Corniche," he said at last, "I expected something good from you, but I confess you have astonished me. You know what you have done, of course?"

"I think I do, but I'd be glad if you would reassure me."

"I can understand your bewilderment. Your picture is by no means an exercise in a past manner; those things always betray a certain want of real energy, and this has plenty of energy, the unmistakable impression of here and now. Something unquestionably from the Mothers. Reality of artistic creation, in fact. You have found a reality that is not part of the chronological present. Your here and now are not of our time. You seem not to be trapped, as most of us are, in the psychological world of today. I hate such philosophical pomposities, but your immanence is not tainted by the calendar. One cannot predict with certainty, but this should wear well—which Letztpfennig fakery and fancy-dress painting never does."

"So—am I out of my apprenticeship?"

"So far as this picture goes, you are indeed. Whether you can keep this up, or whether you want to do that, remains to be seen. Offhand, I should say that if you continue to paint in this manner, and let it be known, your goose is cooked. The whole world of criticism would be down on you like hawks attacking a—what? A phoenix? Some very rare bird, certainly."

"So what do I do?"

"Ah, well, that is a question I can answer without hesitation. You get back to England as soon as you can. And I am off to Italy in the morning. Things are growing very uncomfortable, if you haven't noticed."

"What about the picture?"

"If I can arrange it, I shall see that it is sent to you. But it is big, and too stiff to go in a cask, and that may not be easy. But for a while I think it must go into one of the dark service corridors here."

"That isn't quite what I meant. You know how I regard you, Meister. Have I satisfied you? That is what has been gnawing me."

"Satisfied me? I find it very hard to say, because satisfaction is not part of my metier, and I rarely step outside my metier. But here I have no choice, and little time to delay. So, for the present, *a rivederci*—Meister."

PART SIX

Wars are national and international disasters, but everyone in a warring nation fights a war of his own and sometimes it cannot be decided whether he has won or lost. Francis Cornish's war was long and painful, even though he was a non-combatant.

Indeed, being a non-combatant was one of his lesser, if more obvious, troubles. To be an able-bodied man in his thirties, not apparently doing any important work, required frequent explanation, and aroused dislike and suspicion. He had, of course, his letter from Sir Owen Williams-Owen, guaranteeing his troublesome heart and exemption from service, but he could not wear it pinned to his coat; from Uncle Jack, for whom he was working long hours, he had nothing at all, because it was unthinkable, if he should be injured, or challenged, that he should be identified with what he now called, not "the profession", but frankly MI5.

As soon as he returned to England in late July of 1939, Francis became officially—in the sense that he was paid a rather small salary—a counter-intelligence man, which meant that his job was to find out whatever he could about people representing themselves as refugees from Europe, who were in fact German agents. It was not Secret Service in the romantic style; what it meant was that by day he worked with an agency that interviewed refugees and helped them, and at night he hung about in doorways watching who entered and left certain buildings that were under observation. Careful reports of what he learned, which were chiefly timetables, he took as unobtrusively as he could to Uncle Jack, who worked from a small office at the back of a house in Queen Anne's Gate.

It was drudgery, but he managed to give it an individual touch, for which he blessed the name of Harry Furniss and those long hours in Blairlogie, where he had sketched everybody and everything, alive and dead. Once he had seen a man or woman, he could produce a useful likeness, and he was not deceived by disguises. Few people have any aptitude for disguise; they put too much faith in dyed hair, changes of clothes, and peculiar walks; they disguise their fronts, but they neglect to disguise their backs, and Francis, who had learned the lesson from Saraceni, could identify a back when he might be puzzled by a face. So he amused himself by decorating his reports with sketches that were doubtless more useful than he knew, because Uncle Jack was not communicative, and never praised. He was not permitted to use a typewriter, because the sound, late at night, might rouse the suspicion of a landlady; his reports, written in an exquisite, tiny Italic hand, and ornamented with sketches, were little works of art. But Uncle Jack seemed impervious to art, and filed them without comment on their appearance.

What was drudgery for the first months of the war became dangerous misery after the coming of the air raids on London, by day and night in the autumn of 1940, and by night until May of 1941. It was in the great fire-raid of December 29 that Francis lost what had become his chief treasure.

He had rediscovered Ruth Nibsmith, meeting her by chance one October night in a Lyons restaurant where he had gone for a meal before taking up one of his long vigils across the street from a suspected house.

"Le Beau Ténébreux! What a piece of luck! What are you up to? Not that I need to ask; you look the complete snoop. Who are you snooping on?"

"What do you mean, I look a snoop?"

"Oh, my dear—the stained felt hat, the seedy raincoat, the bulge in the pocket where the notebook is kept—of course you're a snoop."

"You only say that because you're a psychic. My disguise is impenetrable. I am The Unknown Civilian, who is catching it so hard these bad days."

"Not half so hard as he'll be catching it before the end of the year—speaking as a psychic."

"You're right, of course. I am doing confidential work. What are you doing?"

"Also confidential." But after some chat it came out that Ruth was in Government Code and Cipher. "Of course, I have the puzzle-solving sort of mind," she said; "I think it was my ability to do the *Times* crossword in half an hour that got me the job. But being a psychic does no harm, either. And that's enough of that." She glanced up at the poster on the wall, which was a picture by Fougasse of Hitler with an enormous ear cocked, and the legend "Careless Talk Costs Lives".

They renewed their friendship, so far as Francis's peculiar assignments and Ruth's occasional night duties allowed, and this meant renewal of their happy hours in bed. Ruth lived in a very small flat in Mecklenburgh Street where the landlady was either indulgent or indifferent and perhaps once a week they contrived a happy hour or so. In wartime London, which had become so grey and stuffy, where laundry was a difficulty and baths were uncertain because of broken water-pipes, it was bliss to strip off their clothes and tumble into the not very clean sheets and lose themselves in a communion where no rules of security had to be remembered and tenderness and kindness were all that mattered. Perhaps it was odd that they never talked of love, or exchanged promises of fidelity; but they felt no need of such words. Without ever saying so, they knew that time was short and the present everything,

538

and a union achieved when chance permitted was a treasure snatched from destruction.

"If a bomb were to blow us up now," said Francis, one night when they had disobeyed the sirens and stayed in the warm bed when they ought to have gone to the nearest chilly shelter, "I would feel I had died at the peak of my life."

"Don't worry, Frank. No bomb is going to get you. Don't you remember your horoscope at Düsterstein? Old age and fame for you, my darling."

"And you?"

She kissed him. "That's Classified Information," she said. "I'm the decoder, not you."

On the night of December 29, when the great fire-raid struck, Francis was on the job, watching a door through which nobody came or went, until it became impossible to keep at his post any longer, and he went to a Tube station, where he lay on the hard pavement with some hundreds of others, unsleeping and in terror. When at last the all-clear sounded he went as far toward Ruth's flat as was possible, for fires were raging and whole streets of houses had disappeared.

She had been rescued, and in a shorter time than he had dared to hope he found her in a hospital. Rather, he found a body swathed in packs of saline solution, a body so heavily sedated that only one hand could be seen, and he sat for several hours, holding it, and praying as he had not prayed since childhood that by holding it he was being of some comfort. But the time came when the ward sister beckoned him away.

"No use now. She's gone. Was she your wife? A friend?"

"A friend."

"Do you want a cup of tea?" It was not much, but it was everything the hospital had to offer. Francis did not want a cup of tea.

So ended the greatest comfort he had ever known, which had lasted, he reckoned, a little less than ten weeks. Nothing during the forty-one years of life and a kind of distinction that remained to him brought anything to equal it.

A hero of romance might have undergone what is called, not very descriptively, a nervous breakdown, or might have thrown away his letter of exemption and pushed his way into the armed services, seeking death or revenge. Francis's heroism was of another sort; he pulled about him a harsh cloak of stoicism, shut the door on love, and drudged on at his tedious work until Uncle Jack, perhaps sensing a great change in him, or finding new worth in him, promoted him to something a little more interesting. He next sat for several months in a small office in a building that did not in the least suggest MI5, and coordinated reports that had been brought in by watchers like himself, and tried to make sense of information that was usually uninformative. Only once, in all this time, did he have any certainty that he had been instrumental in uncovering an enemy agent.

It was not wholly loneliness and drudgery. Early

in 1943 his father turned up, now revealed as MI5's Security Liaison Officer for Canada, and rather a bigwig, for he stayed at Claridge's and could have commanded a car for his use, if he had not preferred to walk. The Wooden Soldier was more wooden than ever, and his monocle was, if possible, more a part of his face than it had been before. He brought news of home.

"Grand'mère and Aunt Mary-Ben won't be long with us, I'm afraid. They're old, of course; the old lady is well over eighty, and Aunt is eighty-five if she's a day. But it isn't age that ails them; it's parsimony and bad food. That miserable Doctor is even older, but he is remarkably bobbish and keeps the old girls ticking. I never liked him. The worst sort of Irishman. Your mother is well, and as beautiful as the first day I saw her, but she's developing some odd tricks; faulty memory—that kind of thing. The surprise of the pack is your young brother Arthur. No university for him; he says you went to two and that's enough for the family. He's been deep in the business already, and very sharp. But he's in the Air Force now; I expect he'll do well.

"And you're doing well, Jack Copplestone tells me."

"I wish he'd tell *me* once in a while. I sometimes think he's forgotten me."

"Not Jack. But you're not the easiest man to place, Frank. Not a swashbuckler, thank God. He'll use you when the right thing turns up. Still, I'll say a word to him. Not as though you had said anything to me, of course. But just to keep the wheels turning.

"You know that both the O'Gorman boys are in the Army? Very junior, mind you, but keen. Unfortunately not very bright—not in a Service way—but full of beans. And of course O'Gorman is up to his neck in what he calls his War Work— selling Victory Bonds and that sort of thing. I suppose somebody has to do it. You know, I think that fat ass is pushing for some kind of official recognition. He's never recovered from that Knight of St. Sylvester fiasco. He wants something nonretractable."

It occurred to Francis that his father could not be very young. He must be at least ten years older than his mother. But Sir Francis Cornish, never having looked young, had not grown to look old, and as he was still part of the profession he must have been good at whatever it was he did. Certainly he looked like a revenant from an Edwardian past, but his step was light, and he was slim without being scrawny.

"You know, Frank, looking back over the years, and the Canadian part of the family, I think I liked the old Senator best of all. If he had had a chance, he might have been a remarkable man."

"I always thought he was remarkable. He certainly became very rich."

"And founded the Trust. You're right, of course; I was thinking of—well, of social advantages. The Cornish Trust—that always surprised me. He thought I was a figure-head, and I suppose I was, really. We lived in different worlds, and it's rum that our worlds should ever have intersected. But they did, to everybody's advantage."

"Grand-père was a man of deep feeling."

"Ah? I suppose so. I never understood much about that, myself. Y'know, Frank, you really must get some decent clothes. You look dreadful. It's still possible to get good clothes, y'know. You've got lots of cash, haven't you?"

"I suppose so. I never think about clothes. They don't seem relevant to what's going on."

"Trust me, my boy, they're always relevant. Even in the profession, you know, protective colouring is of different kinds. If you look like an underling you'll be taken for an underling, because people haven't always time to find out what you really are. So do smarten up. Go to my man, and get him to make you the best suit he can for your coupons. You should wear a school tie, or a college tie. Suppose you get knocked over in one of these raids? When they found you, how would they know who you were?"

"Would it matter?"

"Of course it would. Looking like a lout when you aren't one is just as much affectation as being a dandy. Affectation in death is as ridiculous as affectation in life."

The next day Francis was marched to Savile Row, measured, and promised a suit of dark grey, to be followed by a blue one, in God's and the ration's good time. Sir Francis, having cowed his son, pressed his advantage and gave Francis some decent socks and shirts from his own wardrobe. They were not too bad a fit. To be dressed by one's father when one is thirty-three perhaps suggests unusual compliance of character, but Francis took it humorously; he had been aware for some time that his profession as a lurker had made him look like a lurker, and that something would have to be done about it. The Major provided the necessary shove.

He was well dressed, if still somewhat doubtful in the matter of shoes, when he called on Signora Saraceni at her house in South London. A note from the Meister, smuggled from Paris, had asked him to do so.

The Signora was very English, but perhaps some life in Italy had given her the swooning, fruity manner which she probably thought proper in the wife of an artist. She was confiding.

"Sometimes I wonder if, when this dreadful war is over, Tancred and I will live together again. It will have to be here. I keep my English passport still, you know. I never really liked Rome. And that apartment—well, it really was a bit much, wasn't it? I mean, what domesticity can survive in the middle of so much history? There wasn't a chair that didn't have a lineage, and one really cannot relax perched on a lineage, can one? Not, you must understand, that there was any unkindness between Tancred and me. The war has kept us apart, but before that he visited me every year, and we were lovers. Oh, indeed we were! But I don't suppose Tancred could ever settle happily in this house, and I love it. These chintzes, and this marvellous pickled-wood furniture—isn't it divine? Really, Mr. Cornish, artist though you are, and friend of Tancred's, isn't it divine? From Heal's, every stick of it, and nothing more than a few years old. One ought to live in one's age, don't you think? But I do hope we may live together again."

Her wish was not to be granted. A few weeks later a stray bomb, which was probably meant for the City, wiped out the Signora's street, and the Signora as well, and it was Francis's miserable job to write to the Meister about it, and find a way of reaching him.

"She was the blood of my heart," wrote the Meister in the reply which at last found its way to Francis, "and I truly believe that she would say the same of me. But Art, my dear Cornish, is a cruel obsession, as you may yet learn."

This letter came shortly before Uncle Jack called Francis to him, and at last gave notice that he had never really forgotten about him. Forgetting was not Colonel Copplestone's way.

"You know that we are going to win this war, don't you? Oh yes we are, appearances to the contrary. It will take a while, but it's perfectly clear that we shall win, in so far as anybody wins. The Americans and the Russians will probably be the big winners. And victory will bring some tricky problems, and we shall have to get to work

545

on them now, or be caught unprepared. One of them will be the Art thing.

"It's important, you know. Psychologically. A kind of barometer of psychological and spiritual strength. The losers mustn't seem to be getting away with a lot of spiritual swag, or they'll look too much like winners. So we must be ready to recover a lot of stuff that has gone astray—looted, quite frankly—during the fighting. That's why I'm sending you to South Wales to work with some people who have been keeping an eye on all that. You have a name, you see. That Letztpfennig business gave you a name, but not too big a name, and you must be ready to move as soon as the time is right. Glad to see you've done something about your clothes. You had better do a little more in that direction. Mustn't go to conference tables and sit on commissions looking like a loser, must you?"

Two weeks later Francis was in a quiet place near Cardiff, where what had been a manor-house was now, without attracting too much notice, a part of MI5's curious domain. There, during some of the harshest days of the war, he studied for the coming victory.

It was here, so far from London, that he gained a better idea than ever before of what he was working for, and who he was working with. In London he had been a lowly kind of agent, a snoop, hoofing around dark streets making notes of the journeys and walks and appointments of suspects. He had studied to acquire the knack of invisibility. He learned the psychological hazard of the snoop's trade; anybody one follows for a few days begins to look furtive. He had begun to feel foolish, but it was not for him to ask questions; his job was to lurk in doorways and around corners, to peep into shop windows at the image of the suspect as he passed, to take care that he did not himself attract suspicion, for a few of Uncle Jack's snoops had made themselves ridiculous by reporting on unknown colleagues. In his long hours of waiting he had begun to hate his work, to hate all "systems" and all nationalism. He had begun, indeed, to fall into the state of mind that makes a snoop a possible recruit for the enemy; the lure of becoming a double agent. For what high principle can a man cling to when he has been brought to the lowly employment and personal bankruptcy of a snoop?

In Cardiff he had the job of interviewing many snoops, and weighing them in the balance of his information and judgement. Some of them had been working in MI6, the overseas branch. Again and again Ruth's voice sounded in his head, in a wisdom pieced together from many of their conversations.

"Some of our best agents are very bad boys, Frank, and some of the worst are members of the Homintern—you know, the great international brotherhood of homosexuals. Imagine squealing on somebody you had gone to bed with! But a lot of it's done, and more by the men than the women, I believe. Really, they need more women in the secret-service game: men are such frightful goofs. You can trust a woman—except in love, maybe—because women are proud of what they know, but men are proud of what they can tell. It's a nasty world, and you and I are too innocent ever to get any of the top jobs in the profession."

Yet there he was, in Cardiff, in a job which, if not anywhere near the top, seemed pretty important. Had he sunk so low? Or had Ruth simply spoken from the goodness of her decent heart, without really knowing what she was talking about?

As well as the job, he had to find time for some of the obligations, and the nuisances, of common life. Roderick Glasson wrote to him about once a month, bemoaning the lot of the agriculturist in wartime, and hinting strongly that if more money were not forthcoming which would make possible really big reforms on his estate, all would be lost, and Francis would have his own close-fistedness to blame for bringing the family to ruin. Aunt Prudence wrote less often, but perhaps more pointedly, to report on the growth and progress of Little Charlie, for whom more money was needed if the child were to be brought up in a manner befitting a Cornish. It was in one of these that Aunt Prudence said frankly that it was time Little Charlie had a proper home with parents in it, and should not Francis and Ismay reconsider their position?

This letter was followed in a few days by one from Ismay herself, written from Manchester, saying nothing about Little Charlie, or a proper home, or that she had his address from her mother. But stating plainly that she was very hard up, and did Francis feel like doing anything about it?

So Francis absented himself from his work for a few days, making the roundabout journey, doubly difficult in wartime, from Cardiff to Manchester, and met Ismay again, after almost ten years, over a bad dinner in a good hotel.

"I should judge that this substance had once been whale," he said, turning over the stuff on his plate. But Ismay was not fastidious; she was eating with avidity. She was very thin and, though still a beauty in her own particular way, she was now bony, almost gaunt, and her hair looked as if she might have cut it herself. Her clothes were grubby and of several dark colours, and everything about her spoke of a woman devoted to a cause.

So it was: Ismay was now a full-time zealot, but for what it was hard to tell. Hints that she dropped suggested that she was doing everything in her power to bring about a Revolt of the Workers. Such a revolt, in all the warring countries, would force the conflict to a halt in a matter of weeks, and substitute a Workers' International that would create order and justice in a much-wronged world.

"You don't have to go into detail," said Francis. "As I came through London I was allowed, as a great favour, to look at the file on you at our offices. How you have kept out of jail I don't really know, but my guess is that you are too small fry to worry about."

"Balls!" said Ismay, whose vocabulary had not greatly changed from her student years. "Your lot simply hope that if they leave me at large I'll lead them to people they really want. Catch me!" she said rancorously through a mouthful of whale.

"Well, that's not what we need to talk about," said Francis. "I gather that you have been having some sort of correspondence with your mother, who naturally has no idea what you're up to; she thinks we ought to get together again."

"Fat chance," said Ismay.

"I fully agree. So what have we to talk about?"

"Money. Will you let me have some?"

"But why?"

"Because you've got a lot of it, that's why."

"Charlie used to have some. What's happened to Charlie?"

"Charlie's dead. Spain. Charlie was a fool."

"Did he die for the Loyalists?"

"No, he died because he didn't settle some gambling debts."

"I can't say you surprise me. Charlie never understood the grammar of money."

"The what?"

"I am pretty good at the grammar of money. Money is one of the two or three primary loyalties. You might forgive a man for trifling with a political cause, but not with your money, especially money that Chance has sent your way. That's why I'm not rushing to give you money now.

Chance sent it to me, and I hold it in trust far more than if I had earned it by hard work."

"Come on, Frank. Your family is rich."

"My family are bankers; they understand the high rhetoric of money. I am simply a grammarian, as I said."

"You want me to beg."

"Listen, Ismay, if I am to help you, you must answer a few straight questions in a straight way and shut up about the people's war. What's chewing you? What's all this underdoggery really about? Are you simply revenging yourself on your parents? Why do you hate me? I'm just as much against tyranny as you are, but I see lots of tyranny on your side. Why is a tyranny of workers any better than a tyranny of plutocrats?"

"That's so simple-minded I won't even discuss it. I don't hate you; I merely despise you. Your mind works in clichés. You can't imagine any great cause that doesn't boil down to a personal grievance. You can't think and you have no objectivity. The fact is, Frank, you're simply an artist and you don't give a sweet God-damn who rules as long as you can paint and mess about and stick spangles on an unjust society. My God, you must know what Plato had to say about artists in society?"

"The best thing about Plato was his good style. He liked inventing systems, but he was too fine an artist to trust his systems fully. Now I've come to hate systems. I hate your pet system, and I hate Fascism, and I hate the system that exists.

But I suppose there must be some system and I'll take any system that leaves me alone to get on with my work, and that probably means the least efficient, ramshackle, contradictory system."

"Okay. No use talking. But what about money? I'm still your wife and the cops know it. Do you want me to have to go on the streets?"

"Ismay, you astound me! Don't try that sentimental stuff on me. Why should I care whether you go on the streets or not?"

"You used to say you loved me."

"A bourgeois delusion, surely?"

"What if it was? It was real to you. You haven't forgotten how you used to work up artistic reasons for getting me to strip so that you could stare at me for hours without ever getting down to anything practical?"

"No, I haven't forgotten that. A fine, high-minded ass I was, and a slippery little cockteaser you were, and I dare say the gods laughed fit to bust as they watched us. But time has passed since then."

"I suppose that means you've found another woman."

"For a time. An immeasurably better woman. Unforgettable."

"I'm not going to beg, so don't think it."

"Then what are we doing here?"

"You want me to beg, don't you? You shit, Frank! Like all artists and idealists, a shit at the core! Well, I won't beg."

"It would do no good if you did. I won't give

you a penny, Ismay. And it's no good murmuring about cops, because you deserted me—scarpered. I'll go on supporting Little Charlie, because the poor brat isn't to blame for any of this, but I won't support her like a princess, which seems to be your mother's idea. I'll even go on for a few more years pouring money into that ill-managed mess your father calls an estate. But I won't give you anything."

"Just for the interest of the thing, would you have given me money if I'd grovelled?"

"No. You tried the sentimental trick and I choked you off. Grovelling would have served you no better."

"Will you order some more food? And drink? Not that I'm grovelling, mind you, but I am a guest."

"And we both grew up under a system where a guest is sacred. For the moment I acknowledge that system."

"*Noblesse oblige.* A motto dear to the heart of bourgeois with pretensions to high breeding."

"I know a bit more about high breeding than I did when last we met. *Thou shalt perish ere I perish.* Ever hear that one? And if I fell for your beauty again—and you are still beautiful, my dear wife—I should certainly perish, and deservedly, of stupidity. I have made myself a promise: I shan't die stupid."

In due course the war did end. That is to say, the fighting with fire and explosives ended, and the fighting with diplomacy burst into action. The special task of what was called victory in which Francis was to play a part began to take shape. Something like peace had to be restored in the world of art, that barometer of national good and bad weather, that indefinable afflatus that a modern country must possess for its soul's good. But that would not begin until many other things had been settled, and Francis put in for leave to make a visit to Canada on compassionate grounds. Grand'mère had indeed died in the early days of 1945, and Aunt Mary-Ben, being no longer anybody's Right Bower, had not been long in following her. Indeed, Mary-Tess said, somewhat unfeelingly, that Grand'mère, arriving in Heaven, had needed somebody to manage eternity for her, and had rung the bell for Mary-Ben.

Francis was not surprised, or reluctant, when the family laid on him the task of going to Blairlogie and settling affairs there, and, in effect, ending the McRory family's long connection with the place. His brother Arthur and his cousins Larry and Mick were still abroad in the services, and anyhow they were young for such work; G. V. O'Gorman (a very big man now in the world of finance) certainly could not be spared, and Sir Francis was too grand for an extended errand of that kind. Besides, Sir Francis had had a stroke, and although his condition was not grave, he tended, as his wife phrased it, to look wonky by the end of the day. After all, he was well over seventy, though nobody said quite how much "over" implied.

As for Mary-Jim (all the family had called her Jacko for years) she was now sixty-one, and although she had the ability to look the best possible for her age, her speech and behaviour were disturbing and Francis felt tenderness and affection for her, which was something other than the obligatory, forced worship he had offered her since childhood. If ever he was to speak to her about the Looner, now was the time.

"Mother: I've always wondered about my elder brother—Francis the First, you know. Nobody has ever said anything to me about him. Can't you tell me anything?"

"There's nothing to tell, darling. He was never a thriving child, and he died very young and very sadly."

"What did he die of?"

"Oh—of whatever very tiny babies do die of. Of not living, really."

"He had something wrong with him?"

"Mm? He just died. It was a long time ago, you know."

"But he must have lived for at least a year. What was he like?"

"Oh, a sweet child. Why do you ask?"

"I just wondered. Odd to have a brother one's never known."

"A sweet child. I'm sure if he'd lived you would have loved him very much. But he died as a baby, you see."

Francis got nothing more from his father.

"I don't really remember anything about him, Frank. He died very young. You saw his marker up there in the graveyard."

"Yes, but that suggested he died a Catholic. You've always insisted that I'm a Protestant."

"Of course. All the Cornishes have been Protestants since the Reformation. I forget how he came to be buried there. Does it matter? He was too young to be anything, really."

Is that so, thought Francis. You don't know anything about it. You don't even know that I'm a Catholic by strict theological reckoning. Neither you nor Mother know one damn thing about me, and all the talk about love was a sham. So far as my soul is concerned neither of you ever gave a sweet damn. Only Mary-Ben, and for all her gentle ways she was a fierce old bigot. None of you ever had a thought that wasn't a disgrace to anything it would be decent to call religion. Yet somehow I've drifted into a world where religion, but not orthodoxy, is the fountain of everything that makes sense.

At Blairlogie, to which he made a last journey, taking sandwiches so that he would not have to eat at the dreadful table of "th'old lady", Francis went at once to Dr. Joseph Ambrosius Jerome, now ninety, a tiny figure whose blazing eyes still spoke of an alert intelligence.

"Well, if you must know, Francis—and you once told me you knew about that fellow in the attic—he was an idjit. I was the one who arranged for him to live up there. Your grandfather would have thanked me if I'd killed him, but none o' that for me. My profession is not that of murderer."

"But it was such a wretched existence. Couldn't he have been put some place to be cared for that wasn't so much like a prison?"

"Had you had no education at Oxford? Don't you remember what Plato says? 'If anyone is insane let him not be openly seen in the city, but let the family of such a person watch over him at home in the best manner they know of, and if they are negligent let them pay a fine.' Well—they did their best, but they paid a fine, right enough. That thing in the attic rotted St. Kilda. It cost them all dear in the coin of the spirit, in spite of your grandmother's card mania, and your grandfather keeping himself busy in Ottawa."

"Were they afraid that whatever ailed him might come out again in me?"

"They never said boo to me about it if they did."

"But why not: I had the same parents."

"Had you so?" Dr. J.A. burst into loud laughter. Not the cackle of a nonagenarian, but a robust laugh, though not a particularly merry one.

"Didn't I?"

"You'll not get that out of me. Ask your mother."

"Do you suggest—?"

"I don't suggest anything, and I'm not answering any more questions. But I'll tell you something that few people ever get told. They say it's a wise child that knows its own father, but it's a damn sight wiser child that knows its own mother. There are corners of a mother no son ever penetrates, and damn few daughters. There was a taint in your mother, and so far it hasn't turned up in you or Arthur—not that Arthur isn't such a blockhead that a taint could pass unnoticed—but you've plenty of time yet. You may live to be as old as me, and God grant you manage it with a safe hide. What's bred in the bone will come out in the flesh: never was a truer word spoken. Have a dram, Frank, and don't look so dawny. Whatever became of all that first-rate whisky your grandfather had tucked away in his cellar?"

"There's some there still, and it must be dealt with. I'll send it over to you, shall I?"

"God bless you, dear lad! That stuff'll be proper old man's milk by this time. And at my age I need regular draughts of that very milk."

Clearing out St. Kilda was a weary job, and it took Frank, with two men to fetch and carry and drag loads of stuff to the auctioneer, and to the dump, three weeks to achieve it. He could not live in the house, though Anna Lemenchick was still on the strength as caretaker; he could not face Anna's dreadful food. He stayed at the Hotel Blairlogie, which was miserable, but had no clinging memories. He insisted on dealing with the contents of every room himself: to the auctioneer, all the Louis furniture; to the presbytery, all Aunt's holy pictures and such of her furniture as the priests might use. Francis left the nudes in the portfolio, thinking the priests might appreciate them. To the Public Library went the books and some further prints, and (this was in despair, and rather against the wishes of the librarian) the lesser oil paintings. The Cardinal pictures went to an art dealer in Montreal and fetched a goodish price. Victoria Cameron, now a woman of property, was invited to take anything she wanted, and, characteristically, wanted nothing but a drawing Francis had made, many years ago, of Zadok in top hat and white choker, driving Devinney's hearse. In his own old room he had some things to dispose of, which would not have attracted the attention of anyone else, but which were full of meaning for him.

There was a small collection of old movie magazines, now crumbling and yellow, over which he had once gloated with the ignorant lust of an adolescent boy. The beauty queens of an earlier day showed their knees daringly, and peeped from beneath grotesquely marcelled hair. There were some pictures cut from Christmas Editions of *The Tatler*, the *Bystander*, and *Holly Leaves* that his grandfather had brought home as part of the seasonal celebration, and in these were drawings of coy girls of the twenties in "teddies", or transparent nightgowns, or (very daringly) playing with a dear doggie whose body concealed the breasts and The Particular—but not quite. He saw these now as part of the pathology of Art, the last gasps of the school of erotic painting that had flowered under Boucher and Fragonard. Kitsch, as Saraceni called it.

What he was most anxious to find and destroy was a small bundle of rags—odds and ends of silk and chiffon—in which, in his adolescent days, he had absurdly rigged himself up as a girl, in what he believed was the manner of Julian Eltinge. He now knew, or thought he knew, what that had meant; it was the yearning for a girl companion, and for the mystery and tenderness he thought he might find in such a creature. He had even some intimation that he sought this companion in himself. Browning's lines, written when he was still very young, came to mind:

And then I was a young witch, whose blue eyes,
As she stood naked by the river springs,
Drew down a god. . . .

But even Ruth had not been that young witch, and Ismay, who so completely looked the part, was a sardonic parody of its spirit. Where was the young witch? Would she ever come? It was not as a lover he wished for her, but as something even nearer; as a completion of himself, as a desired, elusive dimension of his spirit.

Thus Francis came to terms, as he thought, with his strange boyhood, in which there had been so much talk of love, and so little to warm the heart. He did not feel lonely in Blairlogie, even as he sat for long evenings in the hotel, rereading—how many times had he read those pages—his favourite parts of Vasari's *Lives of the Most Excellent Painters, Sculptors, and Architects*. He did not feel lonely when he visited the Catholic cemetery, and found the marker for Francis the First, the Looner, the shadow of his boyhood and, if Uncle Doctor was to be believed, still an unexploded bomb in his manhood—the secret, the inadmissible element which, as he now understood, had played so great a part in making him an artist, if indeed he might call himself an artist.

But had not Saraceni, that stern judge, called him Meister, without irony and without offering an explanation?

He could not visit the grave of Zadok. Not even Victoria knew where it was, except that it was in that part of the Protestant cemetery which was called, with Blairlogie harshness, the Potter's Field. But Francis was not by nature a hunter of tombs, and he did not care. He remembered Zadok tenderly, and that was what mattered.

So St. Kilda was put up for sale at auction, as was also Chegwidden Lodge, which had been on rental for several years. A local speculator bought them both, cheap, and there was the end of an old song, as Francis told the family in Toronto, wondering if any of them would understand the reference. From his childhood home he took nothing, except the picture that had hung in his bedroom. No, not the remarkable picture of Christ that opened its eyes when you looked at it, but *Love Locked Out*.

In the manor near Cardiff, in 1946, there was much to be done, many files to be digested and put in order, and hundreds of photographs to be catalogued. Francis needed an assistant who knew what was in the wind, and Aylwin Ross, not long out of the Canadian Navy, was sent to him.

Aylwin Ross was not at all the sort of young man Francis had come to associate with the work of MI5 and MI6. There was no hint of the snoop about him, and he had some trouble concealing his amusement at the cautious, official way in which Francis explained what had to be done.

"I get you, chief," he said. "We've got to know all these pictures well enough to recognize them, even if they reappear somewhat hocussed to deceive the eye, and so far as we can we've got to get them back to the people with the best claim to them. I'm pretty good at recognizing pictures, even from rotten black-and-white photographs like these. And if any ownership is in doubt, as will certainly be the case, we've got to nab as many as we can for the people we're working for."

Francis was shocked. Of course, what Ross said was true, but that wasn't at all the way to phrase it. He protested.

"Oh come on, Frank," said Ross. "We're both Canadians. We don't have to kid each other. Let's make it as simple as we can."

So, when at last the Allied Commission on Art moved into action, and the sector of it in which

Francis and Ross were to work assembled in Munich, that was indeed the way they worked, and Ross had so far loosened Francis from his official persona that he greatly enjoyed himself.

Their part in the Commission's work was a large one, and there were many familiar figures in the splendid room—a section of a palace—before which pictures recovered from the enemy were deployed for identification and reclamation. Francis and Ross were by no means the whole deputation from the United Kingdom. The formidable Alfred Nightingale was there, from the Fitzwilliam Museum in Cambridge, and Oxford was represented by the no less knowledgeable John Frewen. From the National Gallery and the Tate there were, predictably, Catchpoole and Seddon. But Francis and Ross were the experts on what paintings had gone astray in the war years, and what paintings might have vanished beyond recovery in the New World.

Saraceni was there, wearing conspicuously on his left arm a black band which Francis interpreted as mourning for the Signora, although it was fully three years since she had been obliterated in her South London refuge of pickled oak and cheery chintz.

"I shall never forget her," the Meister said, "a woman of the greatest, most tender spirit, even though we did not see eye to eye on matters of taste. While I live I shall not cease to mourn." But grief had in no way clouded his fearful vision—could it really be the Evil Eye?—or diminished the ironic mirth with which he treated the opinions of colleagues who disagreed with his judgements. The chief of these was Professor Baudoin, from Brussels, more evil-smelling than ever and not mellowed by wartime sufferings. From Holland Dr. Schlichte-Martin was present, and with him Hausche-Kuypers, who had been in a resistance group and lost an arm, but was merry as ever, and greeted Francis with a shout.

"Aha, the Giant-Killer! Poor Letztpfennig! How you polished him off!"

"Ah yes, the young man who knows so much about (sniff) monkeys," said Professor Baudoin. "We shall have to keep our eyes open for any zoological problems that evade our mere connoisseur's estimations."

"Who's the old bugger with the charnel-house breath?" whispered Ross. "He's got it in for you, chief; I can see it in his eye."

The German members of the commission were not Frisch and Belmann; their eagerness in the matter of the Führermuseum had discredited them. Germany was represented instead by Professors Knüpfer and Brodersen. From France came Dupanloup and Rudel, and there were men from Norway, Luxembourg, and a number of other interested states. From the U.S. Francis was glad to see Addison Thresher, who would certainly be a voice of reason, as his country had lost no art in the conflict, though what it might have gained it would not be tactful to inquire.

"One of the problems I have had to face is to

find some way of preventing high-ranking Air Force officers from sending home planes packed with art loot. They don't know much about art but they certainly know what they like, and they've heard that hand-painted oils fetch big money. I needn't tell you I haven't solved the problem. Still—it's the nature of fighting men to loot." Thresher was a cheerful cynic.

In all, fourteen states were represented, usually by two experts and a secretary, who was aspiring to be an expert. Ross was one of these. An Englishman, Lieutenant-Colonel Osmotherley, who was not an art expert but a redoubtable administrator, acted as chairman.

"What an array of boffins," said Ross. "I feel totally out of my league."

"You *are* out of your league," said Francis. "So keep your trap shut, at the sessions and everywhere else. Leave everything to me."

"Am I not even to have an opinion?" said Ross.

"Not out loud. Just keep your eyes and ears open."

Ross's cheerful estimate of the Commission's work showed total lack of acquaintance with the way in which such things are done. After a war in which art had not been a first consideration, the experts were determined to assert its importance. After years of serving as air-raid wardens, standing in queues for coffee made of tulip bulbs, watching powerless as the invaders snatched their dearest treasures, being snubbed by Occupation forces, and being in most cases made to feel the weight of their years, they were once again men of importance, to whom their governments turned for expert advice. After wretched food, shortages of tobacco and drink, cold rooms, and no hot water, they were lodged in a hotel which, if not functioning at pre-war standard, was the best place they had known in years. Best of all, they were once again in that world of scholarship, of connoisseurship, of hair-splitting, haggling, wrangling, and quarrelling which was their very own, and in which they moved like wizard-kings. Were they going to hurry, to cut corners, to compromise, to take any steps whatever to hasten the evil day when their work would be done and they would have to go home? As Francis explained to Ross, only a dumb-bell Canadian, fresh out of the Navy, could suppose any such absurd thing.

Of course, he knew long before they went to Munich that Ross was no dumb-bell. He was brilliant; he had, in terms of his years and experience, extraordinary knowledge of art. Best of all, he had flair. His perception was swift and sure. But what especially endeared him to Francis was that Ross was light-hearted, and thought that art was for the delight and enlargement of man, rather than a carefully guarded mystery, a battleground for experts, and a treasure-house to be plundered by the manipulators of taste, the merchants of vogue, the art dealers.

Ross was self-educated in art, but a graduate of a Canadian Western university and later of Oxford (he had been some sort of Commonwealth scholar), where he had studied modern languages. Like many young men from the prairies, he had been drawn toward the Navy, where he was fairly useful, and very ornamental. Ross was that unusual creature, a male beauty, fair but not a Scandinavian blond, fine-skinned, fine-featured, and with a good, though not markedly athletic, figure. There was nothing epicene about him: he was, quite simply, beautiful and knew it. Among the commissioners, and their serious secretaries (most of whom were already gripped by the premature age of the intellectual), he glowed like a rosebush in a forest of evergreens—a rosebush that had not already succumbed to the acid, evergreen soil.

"You preserve my sanity, Aylwin," Francis said one night in the Munich hotel, when he had drunk rather too much. "If I have to listen once again to Schlichte-Martin and Dupanloup hashing it out about whether a canvas is a Rembrandt or simply a Goveart Flink, or if what looks like a Gerard Dou is really a Donner, I may scream and froth and have to be led from the room and plunged in a cold shower. What does it matter? Get the things back to wherever they came from."

"You take it all too seriously," said Ross. "You've simply got to hang on and not care too much. Do you realize that there were over five thousand of these pictures, most of them nothing more than classy crap, in that salt mine at Alt Aussee where so much of the Führermuseum stuff was stashed? And what about all the stuff that has turned up near Marburg? Not to speak of Göring's immense personal loot. We shall have to consider them all, and if we did fifty a day, how many days does that make? Why don't you relax and stop listening? Just look at the pictures, the pictures we do look at. Wonderful! How many *Temptations of St. Anthony* have we seen already? And in every one of them an old geezer nearly dead of starvation is being tempted by a few pesky demons but chiefly by meaty girls over whom he is in no condition to throw a saintly leg. If I were a painter I would show him being offered a lobster *à la* Newburg. That would have tempted him! Temptation works in the place where the weakness is greatest."

"You speak with a banal wisdom beyond your years."

"Always have. Born wise. You weren't born wise, Francis. Not wise and not banal; you were born with a skin too few."

Saraceni was not so greatly taken with Aylwin Ross as was Francis. "He has talent," said he to Francis one day when they met over lunch, "but he is at heart a careerist. And why not? He is not an artist. He creates nothing, preserves nothing. What has he?"

"Insight," said Francis, and told him what Ross had said about St. Anthony's temptations.

"Shrewd," said Saraceni. "Commonplace, but it takes shrewdness to see the wisdom in the commonplace. The temptation gets us at the point of weakness. What is your weak point, Corniche? You'd better take care it isn't Aylwin Ross."

Francis was offended. Of course, he was usually seen in the company of the beauty of the Commission, and he had not quite understood that some of the other commissioners, for reasons best not examined, interpreted this in their own way. In 1947 homosexuality was not so easily accepted as it became later, but for that reason it was much on people's minds.

Because Saraceni was still the Meister in his world, Francis faced what he had said. Of course he liked Ross. Was he not a fellow-Canadian, and one for whom it was not necessary to make apologies to people who saw Canadians as a pseudo-nation of beaver-skinners? Was Ross not witty and merry in a group where wit never arose except as a weapon with which to strike down a rival? Was he not comely among the swag-bellied and the wrinkled? And—Francis did not face this quite honestly—was he not the nearest thing he had ever met to the elusive figure, apparently a girl, who was needed for the completion of himself? To make a friend, and a close and dear friend, of Aylwin Ross was the most natural thing in the world. In this association Francis did not feel himself a pupil, as he was aware that he had always been with Ruth, nor was he a gull, as he had been with the desirable, treacherous Ismay. This was, he told himself, a relationship in which emotion played as little part as it can play in anything, and kinship of mind and friendship were everything.

Nevertheless, he thought he ought to tell Ross what was apparently being said. Ross laughed.

" 'Helter-skelter, hang sorrow, care kill'd a cat, up-tails all, and a louse for the hangman'."

"What's that?"

"Ben Jonson. I did a lot of work on him at one time. Full of excellent good sense, expressed with a trumpeting masculinity. It simply means, screw 'em all! What does it matter what they think? We know it isn't so, don't we?"

Did they? Did they know that? Francis thought he knew it, but Francis's conception of what was being hinted at was to be seen in the bold-eyed, painted youths who hung about in the shadows of the Munich nights. Of the subtler sodomy of the soul he knew nothing. As for Aylwin Ross, he knew only that he often got what he wanted by enchanting those whose lives had been poor in enchantment, and he saw no harm in it. And indeed, could there be any harm in it?

It would have been absurd for the Commission to examine every picture that had changed its ground during the war. Its job was to concentrate on treasures. Francis recognized in the lists that were distributed pictures by Nobody-in-Particular of Nobody Special which were certainly from the Düsterstein studio where he had worked with Saraceni; they were in the Führermuseum group, and nobody wanted them, so they were allowed to stay where they were. Because it was known to a few experts and had caused some sensation in London just before the war, *Drollig Hansel* appeared before the Commission in person—that is to say, exhibited on an easel—and was admired as a pleasing minor work, but as it had no known provenance, and was clearly marked with what looked like the Fugger family *Firmenzeichen*, it was decided that it had better go to Augsburg. This decision sat well with Knüpfer and Brodersen, and was firm evidence of the Commission's desire to be fair.

Francis felt no emotion he could not dissemble when *Drollig Hansel* was on the easel, and he was pleased that Ross thought highly of it.

"There's a kind of controlled *grotesquerie* about it I've never seen before," said he. "Not the rowdy horrors of all those *Temptations* of poor old St. Anthony, but something deeper and colder. Must have been an odd chap that painted it."

"Very likely," said Francis.

It was a different matter, however, when unexpectedly, on a November afternoon, *The Marriage at Cana* was carried in by the porters and put on the easel.

"This picture is something out of series," said Lieutenant-Colonel Osmotherley. "No provenance at all, except that it comes from Göring's personal collection, if you call that robber's cave a collection. But it's thought to be important, and you must make a decision about it."

"The Reichsmarschall knew a good thing when he saw it," said Brodersen, who ought to have

571

known, for the Reichsmarschall had taken all the best things from his own gallery, leaving behind cynical receipts, saying that the pictures had been removed for their own protection. Brodersen had not been a Nazi, and only his reputation, and his unstained Aryanism, had kept him in his appointment.

It *was* a good thing. Seeing it after almost ten years, Francis knew it was a good thing. He said nothing and left the superior experts to say their say, which they did at such length that the light faded and the chairman adjourned the sitting until the following morning.

What the experts said was flattering and alarming to the Calvinist side of Francis's conscience. Could this possibly be a hitherto unknown Mathis Neithart? The vigour and brilliance of the colour, and the calligraphic line, the distortion of some of the figures and the *grotesquerie* (that word again!) supported such an attribution, but there were Italianate, Mannerist features that made it unlikely—indeed impossible. The experts plunged into an orgy of happy haggling, of high-powered knowing-best, that filled a whole day.

Ross simply could not keep his mouth shut.

"I know that I shouldn't speak in such company," he said, smiling at the great men about him. "But if you will be good enough to indulge my amateurish hunch, may I ask if anyone sees a quality in this picture that suggests the *Drollig Hansel* we examined a few weeks ago? Merely a hunch." And he sat down, smiling with a boyish charm that might perhaps have been a little over-done.

This started a dispute in a new direction. There were those who said they had felt something of the kind and had meant to bring it up until Mr. Cornish's secretary anticipated them: there were others who brushed the suggestion aside as absurd. But was there not some whiff of Augsburg about both pictures, said others who fancied such intuitions. Knüpfer and Brodersen did not want to hear anything about Mathis der Maler, who had not been a favourite in Germany for some time because Hindemith's opera about him had made his name unacceptable. Anyhow, elements in the picture put such an attribution out of the question. Strive as he might, Colonel Osmotherley could not push them toward a decision.

What were they looking at?

The picture was a triptych, of which the central panel was five feet square, and the two flanking panels were of the same height, but only three feet wide. What impressed at first sight was the complexity of the composition and its jewel-like richness of colour, so arranged as to throw primary emphasis on the three figures that dominated the central panel, and indeed the whole picture. Two of these were plainly the couple who had been married; they wore fine clothing in the style of the early years of the sixteenth century, and their expressions were serious, indeed elevated; the man was pressing a ring on the fourth finger of his bride's left hand. Their faces seemed to be male and female versions of the same features: a long head, prominent nose, and light eyes that might have been thought at variance with their black hair. The smiling woman who was third of this dominant group must surely be the Mother of Jesus, for she wore a halo—the only halo to be seen in the whole composition; she was offering the bridal pair a splendid cup from which a radiance mounted above the brim.

There were no figures on the right side of this group, but on their left stood a stout old man of a merry, bourgeois appearance, who seemed to be making a sketch of the scene on an ivory tablet, and somewhat behind him, but clearly to be seen, was a woman, smiling like the Virgin, who was holding an astronomical, or perhaps an astrological, chart. Completing this group was a man who might have been a superior groom or huissier, with a smiling, sonsy face, richly liveried; he held a coachman's whip in one hand, but in the other what might have been a scalpel, or small knife; almost concealed behind his back hung a leather bottle; obviously this guest was feeling no thirst. This lesser group—wedding guests? specially favoured friends?—was completed by the figure of a dwarf, in full ceremonial armour, but with no weapon unless the onlooker chose so to define the rope that was coiled around his left arm; with his right hand he was holding out toward the stout artist a bundle of what looked like very sharp pencils, or silver-points.

The startling figure in this otherwise spirited

but not inexplicable composition was a creature floating high on the left above the heads of the bridal pair. Was he an angel? But he had no wings, and although his face was at once sanctified and inhuman, the effect was idiotic; the small head rose almost to a point. From the lips of this creature, or angel, or whatever it was, issued an ornate ribbon, or scroll, on which was written, in Old German script, *Tu autem servasti bonum vinum usque adhuc*. Over the heads of the wedded pair it held, in its left hand, a golden crown, while with its right it seemed to point at the couple who dominated the right wing of the triptych.

The background of this central panel, which also appeared in varied form in the other two panels, was a landscape merging in the farthest distance to a range of sun-tipped mountains.

Compared with this arresting central portion, the flanking wings were subdued, almost in some areas to a treatment in *grisaille*, though here and there were some relieving accents of colour. The wing on the left might seem at first to be readily understood; in it Christ was kneeling amid the six water-pots of stone, his hands extended in blessing. In the foreground, in shadow, were three figures easily identified as disciples: Simon Zelotes, a vigorous man of middle age in whose girdle hung a broad-headed woodsman's axe; St. John, identifiable by his pen and inkhorn hanging at his waist, and by the youthful beauty of his features; and—surely not?—yes, it must be Judas, red-haired and with the purse of the holy community safe under his left hand while with his right he calls the attention of his brethren to figures in the central panel.

But before the eye followed that gesture, what was it to make of the two women with Christ, the one standing in what might almost have been an attitude of anger over the kneeling figure, one hand raised as if in rhetorical condemnation, while the other, reaching bare from a servant's smock, pointed downward at the wine-pots. The other woman, kneeling and seeming almost to protect her Lord, was small, and beneath a curious enveloping cap upon her head her expression was sweet with adoration. Around the head of Christ was a radiance, not strongly emphasized, and otherwise the figure was unremarkable, almost humble.

Following Judas's gesture the eye moves toward the right-hand panel. The figures here might be taken for wedding guests; a knightly figure, one eye obliterated by a bandage, wears a sword but has a warning finger at its lips, as if cautioning to silence; his companion is a lady of great but cold beauty. If any connoisseur were so pernickety as to extend a string from the pointing finger of Judas to its termination in this picture, it would strike a wealthy merchant and his wife, apparently concerned only with themselves; the male figure carries a heavy purse at his girdle. The physician, somewhat apart, stands with his lancet ready in his hand, ready to let blood from any of the marriage group, all of whom are included in the scope of his penetrating, rodent eyes. But if these are wedding guests, surely those others in the background must be beggars at the feast—that rabble of children with twisted, ugly, hungry faces. They are not looking toward the marriage scene, but are concentrated on one of their number who is gouging the eye from a cat with a sharp stone. In this panel the background is markedly desolate, as compared with the landscape elsewhere.

A strange picture, and the experts were happy to sink their learned teeth into it and worry it to some sort of satisfactory interpretation or attribution.

It was in vain that Colonel Osmotherley reminded them that their task was to say what should be done with the picture, and not to decide beyond question who had painted it, or what its curious assemblage of elements might mean. Schlichte-Martin said that he did not think it could ever have been intended for a Christian church; the relegation of the Saviour to a place on a side wing made it wholly unacceptable. Knüpfer wanted to know why the dwarf was in armour; of course, everyone had seen ceremonial armour that had been made for dwarfs, but why was this dwarf wearing it to hold pencils, and had anybody noticed how much the dwarf looked like Drollig Hansel? (Ross nodded vigorously at this.) Everybody was puzzled by the fact that the Virgin had a halo, but her Son did not. And the floating figure? What was anyone to make of that?

Predictably, it was Professor Baudoin who said the disagreeable thing. As the others disputed he glared at the picture from very close range, plied the flashlight and the magnifying glass, rubbed an inch of paint with his spittle, and at last said loudly, "I don't like the *craquelure;* I don't like it at all; much too even; seems to have happened all at once. I recommend that we get the scientific men to work on it. I will lay any money it proves to be a fake."

This brought an opinion—protest, demur, some inclination to agree—from all the experts. But even in his deep discomfort Francis could not miss the glance that Saraceni threw toward Baudoin, from his ill-coordinated blazing eyes. It had an impact like a blow, and Baudoin retreated to his chair as if a fierce gust of hot air had passed him.

When Colonel Osmotherley had quieted the uproar he explained that the Commission had no instructions to act as Baudoin suggested, and it would take a long time to get them, if that were possible. Could the experts not reach some conclusion based simply on what they saw? Giving every consideration to their widely acknowledged ability to see beyond what was given to lesser people, added the Colonel, who had a turn for diplomacy.

It was at this point that Francis, who had been suffering for two days and a half the torments of an inflamed conscience, disputing with a mischievous inclination to let the experts go on and commit themselves to positions from which they could not retreat, felt that he should rise to his feet and make a speech in the manner of the late Letzt-pfennig: "Gentlemen, I cannot tell a lie. I did it with my little paintbox." And then, what? Not hang himself, certainly, with his hat and over-shoes on, as poor Letztpfennig had ridiculously done. But what a sea of explanations, of excuses or denials would follow any such declaration! The only person who could corroborate anything he said was Saraceni, and steadfast as the Meister could be in some things, he might prove alto-gether too supple in such a matter as this.

He had underestimated Saraceni, who now rose to his feet. This was in itself significant, for the experts usually spoke seated.

"Mr. Chairman; Esteemed Colleagues," he be-gan with heavy formality; "please permit me to point out that our attempts to explain the curious nature of this picture in terms of Christian iconog-raphy are bound to fail, because it is not solely—perhaps not even primarily—a Christian picture. Of course, it demands to be called *The Marriage at Cana* because of the words issuing from the mouth of that curious floating figure—*Thou hast kept the good wine until now*. In the Scripture story it is the so-called 'governor of the feast' who says that; here it is this mysterious figure who seems to be addressing the parents—the Knight and his Lady in the right-hand panel. This strange figure holds a unifying crown over the heads of Bride and Groom. Who are they? You will not have missed that they look more like brother and sister than a wedded pair. These facial resemblances are surely crucial to an interpretation of the picture? Look at the face of Christ. Is he not kin to the Bride and Groom? Look at the Knight and his Lady in the right-hand wing; are they not plainly the parents of both the married ones? Look at the old artist; a fat, elderly version of the same face. We cannot pretend that these resemblances come about because the artist can only draw one face; the man with the whip, the astrologer, the dwarf, the old woman in the curious cap, the Judas, all show how adept he was at portraiture and revelation of character. No, no, gentlemen; there is only one way to explain this picture, and I suggest, humbly, that I know what it is.

"Consider where it comes from. You don't know? Of course not, because it has been hidden. But I know. It comes from Schloss Düsterstein, where, as you do know, there is an extraordinary collection of masterworks (or was, until General Göring took the best of them under his protection) upon which I was engaged for some years in repair and restoration work, before the war. But this picture was not among those that were hung. These panels were under wraps in a storage room very near the Chapel, where they had served as the altar-piece until the Chapel was wholly transformed in the Baroque taste by Johann Lys at some time during the first quarter of the seventeenth century. The old altar-piece was replaced by one painted by Lys, or one of his pupils, an inoffensive Madonna and Child with saints, which may still be seen. The old altar-piece had by that time become disagreeable to the taste of the Ingelheim family.

"Why? The picture we see here had grown out of fashion, and it was also, to a strict Christian taste, heretical. Look at it: this is a picture with strong alchemical suggestions. Of course, alchemy and Christianity were never incompatible, but to seventeenth-century theological orthodoxy, which was that of the Counter-Reformation, it was too near a rival to the true Faith.

"I don't know what you may know of alchemy, and you must forgive me if I seem to tell you what is already clear in your minds. But this is plainly a depiction, given a Christian gloss, of what was called The Chymical Wedding. The alchemical uniting of the elements of the soul, that is to say. Look at it: the Bride and Groom look like brother and sister because they are the male and female elements of a single soul, which it was one of the higher aims of alchemy to unite. I won't harass you with alchemical theory, but that unity—that wedding—was not achieved in youth or with ease, and so the Groom, at least, is not a man in his first youth. That such a unity is brought about by the intervention of the highest and purest element in the soul—which is, of course, what Christ has long been, and was to the Middle Ages, and is still in a somewhat altered but not destructively altered sense—is plain enough. Here we see Christ as a beneficent power at the Wedding. But in this picture it is the Holy Mother—what unorthodox but not heretical thinkers sometimes call Mother Nature—who blesses the Marriage of the Soul, the achievement of spiritual union. Am I making myself clear?"

"Clear so far as you go, Maestro," said Professor Nightingale. "But who are these other figures? That creature in the sky, for instance; a very nasty-looking piece of work, like a pinhead in a circus. Who may he be?"

"I cannot tell you, though of course we all know that in Gothic and late-Gothic art—there are lingering elements of Gothicism in this picture—such an angelic figure often represented a relative—big brother, it might be—who had died before The Chymical Wedding was achieved, but whose memory or spiritual influence might have been helpful in bringing it about."

"All very fine, but I don't trust the *craquelure*," said Professor Baudoin.

"Oh for God's sake forget the *craquelure*," said John Frewen.

"With your permission," said Baudoin, "I shall not forget the *craquelure*, and I would thank you, sir, not to snarl at me."

"I do well to snarl," said Frewen, who was a Yorkshireman and hot-tempered. "Do you suppose anybody would trouble to fake such a farrago of forgotten rubbish as this? Alchemy! What's alchemy?"

> " 'That alchemy is a pretty kind of game
> Somewhat like tricks o' the cards,

> *to cheat a man*
> *With charming.'* "

It was the irrepressible Aylwin Ross who spoke.

"No, Mr. Ross, not that!" said Saraceni. "Some alchemists were cheats, of course, as some priests of all faiths are cheats. But others were truly sincere seekers after enlightenment, and are we who have suffered so much during the past five years under the evil alchemy of science to jeer at any sincere belief of the past, whose style of thought and use of words has grown rusty?"

"Mr. Ross, I should remind you that your position here does not extend to expressing opinions," said Colonel Osmotherley.

"I am very sorry," said Ross. "Just a few words from Ben Jonson, that slipped out."

"Ben Jonson was a great cynic, and a great cynic is a great fool," said Saraceni, with unwonted severity. "But, gentlemen, I do not pretend to explain all the elements in this picture. That would give an iconographer work for many days. I merely suggest that we could be looking here at a picture prepared to the taste of Graf Meinhard, who, four and a half centuries ago, was reputed to be an alchemist himself—a friend and patron of Paracelsus—and to do things at Düsterstein in what was the most advanced science of his time. His chapel was not, after all, a public place of worship. May he not have pleased himself in this way?"

The experts, credulous perhaps in a matter not

within the range of their own knowledge, were inclined to agree that this could have been so. Their discussion was long and cloudy. When he thought it had gone on long enough, Saraceni summed it up.

"Might I suggest, Mr. Chairman and Esteemed Colleagues, that we agree that these panels, which certainly came from Düsterstein, be returned to the great collection there, and that we attribute this picture, which we are all agreed is a splendid previously unknown work of art, and a great curiosity as well, to The Alchemical Master, whose name, alas, we cannot determine more exactly?"

And so it was agreed, Professor Baudoin abstaining.

"You saved my bacon," said Francis, catching Saraceni on the great staircase, as they left the session.

"I will confess to being a little pleased with myself," said the Meister. "I hope you listened attentively, Corniche; I did not utter one word of untruth in anything I said, though of course I was not officious in stripping Truth naked, as so many painters have done. You never knew I studied theology for a few years in my youth? I recommend it to every ambitious young man."

"I'm grateful forever," said Francis. "I really didn't want to confess. Not because of fear. It was something else that I can't just put a name to."

"Justifiable pride, I should say," said Saraceni. "It is a very fine picture, wholly unique in its approach to a biblical subject. Yet a masterpiece of religious art, if one means religion in the true sense. I forgive you, by the way, for giving Judas my features, if not my hair. The Masters must find their models somewhere. I did not call you Meister idly or mockingly, you know. You have made up your soul in that picture, Francis, and I do not joke when I call you The Alchemical Master."

"I don't know anything about alchemy, and there are things in that picture I don't pretend to explain. I just painted what demanded to be painted."

"You may not have a scholar's understanding of alchemy, but plainly you have lived alchemy; transformation of base elements and some sort of union of important elements has worked alchemically in your life. But you do know painting as a great technical skill, and such skills arouse splendid things in their possessors. What you do not understand in the picture will probably explain itself to you, now that you have dredged it up from the depths of your soul. You still believe in the soul, don't you?"

"I've tried not to, but I can't escape it. A Catholic soul in Protestant chains, but I suppose it's better than emptiness,"

"I assure you that it is."

"Meister—I shall always call you Meister, though you say I've graduated from *alunno* to *amico di Saraceni*—you have been very good to me, and you have not spared the rod."

"He that spareth his rod, hateth his son. I am proud to be your father in art. So do something for me: I ask it as a father. Watch Ross."

Nothing more could be said, because of a commotion that broke out on the great staircase behind them. Professor Baudoin had misjudged his step, fallen on the marble, and broken his hip.

—*That was Saraceni's Evil Eye, I suppose, said the Lesser Zadkiel.*

—*Nobody becomes as great a man as Saraceni without extraordinary spiritual energy, and it isn't all benevolent, said the Daimon Maimas. The Masters and Sibyls turn up in lucky people's lives, and I am glad I could put such good ones in Francis's path.*

—*Lucky people? I suppose so. Not everybody finds Masters and Sibyls.*

—*No, and at the present time—I mean Francis's time, of course, because you and I have no truck with Time ourselves, brother—many people who are lucky enough to come into the path of a Master or a Sibyl want to argue and have their trivial say, and prattle as if all knowledge were relative and open to argument. Those who find a Master should yield to the Master until they have outgrown him.*

—*If Francis has really made up his soul, as Saraceni said, what lies ahead of him? Hasn't he achieved the great end of life?*

—*You are testing me, brother, but you won't catch me that way. Having got his soul under his eye, so to speak, Francis must now begin to understand it and be worthy of it, and that task will keep him busy for a while yet. Making up the soul isn't an end; it's the new beginning in the middle of life.*

—Yes, it will take some time.

—You are fond of that foolish word time. Time in his outward life will run much faster for him now, but in the inward life it will slow down. So we can get on much faster with this record, or film, or tape, or whatever fashionable word Francis's contemporaries would apply to it, because his external life occupies less of his attention. Onward, brother!

What was Francis now in the world of MI5? Not one of the great ones, who inspire novelists to write about danger and violence and unexplained deaths. His work with the Allied Commission on Art continued when the conferees in Europe were completed, because the decisions of the conferees created all sorts of problems that had to be settled diplomatically, with much bargaining, much soothing of ruffled national pride, and a few arbitrary judgements in which he played a significant if not a leading role. He had a liaison association with the British Council. But only Uncle Jack knew that he was expected to keep a watchful eye on some people who were important in the world of art but who had other loyalties that did not jibe with those of the Allied cause.

It was this secret aspect of his work that gave him the air of Civil Servant, a conventional man, a clubman who might turn up anywhere in the art world, the country-house world, the fashionable world, and sometimes even close to the Court. Anywhere, in fact, where there were clever people who did not think him clever, or quite one of themselves—not a Cambridge man—and who therefore sometimes talked less discreetly when he was present than they would otherwise have done. He was thought to be rather a dull dog who somehow managed to have a finger in the art pie. But he was also a useful man who could arrange things.

For instance, he arranged that Aylwin Ross should receive favours that might not otherwise come his way and Ross, being what he was, showed gratitude but not for long, because he thought the favours the natural outcome of his own brilliant abilities. It was through Francis that Ross gained a good appointment in the Courtauld Institute, and began his rapid climb toward influence as a critic and creator of taste.

Saraceni had warned Francis to watch Ross, so watch him he did, and saw nothing but a brilliant, attractive young man whose career it was a pleasure to advance. He would have watched Ross at closer range if Ross had not been so busy with his concerns and a little inclined to patronize Francis.

"I really think you misjudge Ross," he said to Saraceni on one of his yearly visits to the crammed, cluttered flat in Rome. "He is coming on like a house on fire; soon he will be a very big figure in the critical world. But you hint as though he were somehow dishonest."

"No, no; not dishonest," said the Meister. "Probably he is all you say. But my dear Corniche, I mean that he is not an artist, not a creator; he is a politician of art. He turns with the wind, and you stand like a rock against the wind—except when it is Ross's wind. You are a little too fond of Ross, and you don't understand how."

"If you suggest that I am in love with him, you are totally mistaken."

"You don't want to snuggle up with Ross and whisper secrets on the pillow—or I don't suppose you do. That might not be so dangerous, because lovers are egotists and may quarrel. No: I think you see in Ross the golden youth you never were, the free spirit you never were, the lucky man you think you never were. There is some grey in your hair. Youth has flown for you. Do not try to be young again through Ross. Do not fall for the charm of that sort of youth. People who are young in the way Ross is young never grow old, and never to grow old is a very, very evil fate, though the twaddle of our time says otherwise. Remember what that angel, or whatever it was, says in the great painting you have made: *Thou has kept the good wine until now*. Do not pour out the good wine on the altar of Aylwin Ross."

Ross met Francis on an autumn day, walking along Pall Mall.

" 'Thou look'st like Antichrist in that lewd hat,' " said he, in greeting.

"Jonson, I suppose. What's wrong with my hat?"

"It is the epitome of what you have become, my dear Frank. It is an Anthony Eden hat. Sedate, gloomy, and out of fashion. Come with me to Locke's and we'll get you a decent hat. A hat that speaks to the world of the Inner Cornish, the picture-restorer—but of the highest repute."

"I haven't restored a picture for years."

"But I have! I most certainly and indubitably have! I'm restoring it to its proper place in the world of Art. And it's a picture you know, so why don't you take me to Scott's for lunch, and I'll tell you all about it."

Over the sole Mornay at Scott's Ross told his news with exuberance extraordinary even for him.

"You remember that picture we saw at Munich? *The Marriage at Cana?* You remember what happened to it?"

"It went back to Schloss Düsterstein, didn't it?"

"Yes, but not to oblivion. No indeed. I was tremendously taken with that picture—that triptych, I should say. And don't you remember that I spoke about a link between it and the *Drollig Hansel* we had seen earlier? The picture that was clearly marked as having belonged to the Fuggers of Augsburg? I've proved the link."

"Proved it?"

"The way we prove things in our game, Frank.

590

By the most careful examination of brushwork, quality of paint, colours, and of course a great deal of flair backed up with expertise. The full Berenson bit. Short of all that really rather inconclusive scientific stuff, I've proved it."

"Aha. A nice footnote."

"If I weren't eating your lunch, I'd kill you. Footnote! It makes clearer the whole affair of that unknown painter Saraceni called The Alchemical Master. Now look: this is obviously a man who loves to deal in puzzles and hints to the observant. That device in the corner of *Drollig Hansel* could have been the Fuggers' family trademark, or it could have been a gallows. A hangman, you see? A dwarf hangman. And who turns up in *The Marriage at Cana* but the same dwarf hangman, and this time he is holding his rope! And he is glorious in his dress armour!

"That bothered me for years, until at last I was able to get a grant—never do anything without a grant, Frank—to go to Düsterstein and persuade the old Countess to let me see *The Marriage*. She's tremendously chuffed with it now, you know. It hangs in the best gallery. I stayed for three days— she was very hospitable (lonely I suppose, poor old duck)—and I've cracked the code."

"Cracked what code?"

"What *The Marriage* is really about, of course. The Alchemical Master cloaked it all in alchemical mystery, and for a very good reason, but it's not really an alchemical picture. It's political."

"You astonish me. Go on."

"What do you know about The Interim of Augsburg?"

"Not a thing."

"It's not on everybody's tongue, but it was important when that picture was painted. It was a scheme to reconcile the Catholics and the Protestants in 1548. It was a compromise that led up to the Council of Trent. The Catholics made certain concessions to the Protestants, the biggest one being communion in both kinds, if you know what that means."

"Don't insult me, you prairie Protestant. It means the laity receive both the bread and the wine at Communion."

"Good boy. So—the Marriage at Cana, where Christ certainly gave everybody the wine, the best they'd ever had. But look who's the principal figure in the picture: Mother Church, personified as the Virgin Mary, offering the Cup. So that's one-up for the Catholics because they are graciously yielding something very precious to the Protestants. The married couple are the Catholic and Protestant factions united in amity."

"There's a hole in your explanation. Mary may be yielding the Cup to the Protestants, but she certainly isn't giving it to the Catholics, and they haven't got it yet."

"I thought of that, but I don't think it really matters. The ostensible point of the picture is not to shout its message to every chance visitor to the Düsterstein Chapel, but to offer an altar-piece representing the Marriage at Cana."

"Well—what about the other figures?"

"Some can be identified. The old man with the writing-tablet is obviously Johann Agricola, one of the framers of the Interim of Augsburg. Who is holding his spare writing materials? Who but Drollig Hansel, the hangman with his rope, but he is in parade armour and thus dressed for a celebration, which he assists by holding the pens. Symbolic of the cessation of persecution, do you see? The Knight and the Lady in the right-hand wing of the triptych are surely Graf Meinhard and his wife—the donors of the picture, just where you would expect to find them. Even Paracelsus is there—that shrewd little chap with the scalpel."

"And what about all the others?"

"I don't see that they really matter. The significant thing is that the picture celebrates the Interim of Augsburg, by linking it with the Marriage at Cana. The message of the angel, about the good wine, obviously refers to the Protestant-Catholic reconciliation. Those women quarrelling over Christ—Protestant preaching versus Catholic faith, obviously. And The Alchemical Master has laid out the whole squabble so that the picture, if necessary, could be explained in a number of different ways."

"What did the Gräfin say to all this?"

"Just smiled, and said I astonished her."

"Yes, I see. But Aylwin, I really do think you ought to be careful. It's ingenious, but a historian could probably blow it full of holes. For instance, why would the Ingelheims want such a thing?

They were never Protestants, surely?"

"Perhaps not avowedly so. But they were—or Graf Meinhard was—alchemists, and they chose a painter with this obvious alchemical squint. Graf Meinhard probably had something up his sleeve, but that's not my affair. I shall simply write about the picture."

"Write about it?"

"I'm doing a large-scale article for *Apollo*. Don't miss it."

Francis certainly did not miss it. He worried for many weeks before the article appeared. Obviously he should tell Aylwin the history of *The Marriage at Cana*. But why "obviously"? Because conscience required it? Yes, but if conscience were given a foremost place in the matter, it would be Ross's duty, as a matter of conscience, to denounce Francis as a faker, who had sat in silence while *The Marriage* was praised by the Munich experts. Conscience would involve the Gräfin, who, if she were really as innocent as she seemed about *The Marriage*, was certainly not innocent in the matter of *Drollig Hansel*. And if the Gräfin were involved, what about all those other pictures that had been so stealthily prepared by Saraceni and palmed off on the collectors for the Führer-museum? This was not a time to expose impostures practised on the Third Reich by Anglo-Franco-American entrepreneurs, which had involved the loss to Germany of genuine and splendid pictures; Germany, as the loser, was in the wrong, and must be firmly kept in the wrong for a time, to satisfy public indignation. Francis's dilemma had a bewildering array of horns.

And there was the matter of Ross himself. He counted on his article about *The Marriage* to provide a fine step upward in his career. Was Francis to hold him back by a confession which, if it were to be made at all, should have been made years earlier?

Finally, Francis had to admit, there was sheer pride in having brought off a splendid hoax. Had not Ruth Nibsmith warned him about the strong Mercurial element in his nature? Mercury, who added so much that was uplifting and delightful in the world, was also the god of thieves and crooks and hoaxers. The division between art and deviousness and—yes, it had to be admitted—crime was sometimes as thin as a cigarette paper. Beset by conscience on the one hand, he enjoyed a deep, chuckling satisfaction on the other. He was no Letztpfennig, to be brought down to ruin by a monkey: his picture, though anonymously, was to be given wide exposure and an interesting ambience by a rising young expert in the Mercurial world of connoisseurship. Francis decided to keep mum.

The article, when it did appear, was everything he could have wished. It was soberly, indeed elegantly written, without any of the gee-whiz enthusiasm Ross had shown when he told Francis what he was about to do. It was modest in tone: this very fine picture, hitherto unknown, had at last come to light, and except for *Drollig Hansel* it was the only example from the brush of The Alchemical Master, whoever he might be. He must have been known to the Fuggers, and to Graf Meinhard, and these facts and the quality of the painting put it with the best of the Augsburg group, of whom Holbein had been the finest master. Was The Alchemical Master a pupil or associate of Holbein? It was more than likely, for Holbein had delighted in pictures that offered concealed messages to those who had the historical knowledge and the flair to read them. Fuller explication of the iconographic intricacies of the masterpiece Ross was happy to leave to scholars of greater insight than himself.

It was a fine article, and it caused a sensation among those who cared about such things, which meant several hundred thousand professional critics, connoisseurs, and that large body of people who could never hope to own a great picture, but who cared deeply for great pictures. Perhaps best of all, it offered a fine colour reproduction of the triptych as a whole, and a detailed picture of each of its three parts. *The Marriage at Cana*, now dated and explicated, became art history, and Francis (the Mercurial Francis, not the possessor of the tormented Catholic-Protestant conscience) was overjoyed.

The Countess refused all subsequent requests to examine the picture. She was, she said, too old and too busy with her great farm to oblige the curious. Did she smell a rat? Nobody ever knew. *Thou shalt perish ere I perish.*

The article destroyed Francis forever as a painter. Clearly he could not go on in the style which he had, with so much pain and under the whip of Saraceni, made his own. The danger was too great. But with the perversity of his Mercurial aspect, he now found himself eager to paint again. He had done nothing since the end of the war except amuse himself with a few drawings in the Old Master manner and executed with his Old Master technique. After Ross's article appeared he enlarged his portfolio of sketches in this style that had been preliminary studies for *The Marriage at Cana;* created them, so to speak, after the fact. They had to be kept locked up. Now he wanted to paint. The obvious thing—he had grown fond of Ross's word "obvious"—was to learn to paint in a contemporary style. He bought new, ready-made paints and canvases prepared by an artist's supplier, and remembering his early enthusiasm for Picasso he set to work to find a style related to that of the greatest of modern painters, but which would be the true style of Francis Cornish.

That could never have been easy but it became wholly impossible after Picasso made a statement to Giovanni Papini, which was included in an interview that appeared in *Libro Nero* in 1952. The Master said:

In art the mass of people no longer seeks consolation and exaltation, but those who are refined, rich, unoccupied, who are distillers of quintessences, seek what is new, strange, original, extravagant, scandalous. I myself, since Cubism and before, have satisfied these masters and critics with all the changing oddities which passed through my head, and the less they understood me, the more they admired me. By amusing myself with all these games, with all these absurdities, puzzles, rebuses, arabesques, I became famous and that very quickly. And fame for a painter means sales, gains, fortune, riches. And today, as you know, I am celebrated, I am rich. But when I am alone with myself, I have not the courage to think of myself as an artist in the great and ancient sense of the term. Giotto, Titian, Rembrandt were great painters. I am only a public entertainer who has understood his times and exploited as best he could the imbecility, the vanity, the cupidity of his contemporaries. Mine is a bitter confession, more painful than it may appear, but it has the merit of being sincere.

He lost no time in bringing this interview to the attention of Ross. He had to translate it, because Ross had only a smattering of tourist-Italian; he was always meaning to learn the language properly, so that he could read things like *Libro Nero*, but he never did so.

"What do you make of that?" said Francis.

"I make nothing whatever of it," said Ross.

"You know how artists are; they have bad days and fits of self-doubt and self-accusation when they think their work is rubbish, and abase themselves before the artists of the past. Often they are trying to coax whoever they are talking to into contradicting them—giving them new assurance. I suppose Papini, whoever he may be, caught Pablo on a bad day, and took all that rubbish for his real opinion."

"Papini is a rather well-regarded philosopher and critic. He doesn't write to create sensations and I am certain he would have asked Picasso to reread and consider such a statement as this before he published it. You can't brush it aside as a passing comment, made in a fit of depression."

"Yes I can. And I do. Listen, Frank: when you want opinions about an artist's work you don't ask the artists for them. You ask somebody who knows about art. A critic, in fact."

"Oh, come on! Do you really think artists are inspired simpletons who don't know what they're doing?"

"Artists have tunnel vision. They see what they are doing themselves, and they are plagued by all sorts of self-doubt and misgivings. Only the critic can stand aloof and see what's really going on. Only the critic is in a position to make a considered and sometimes a final judgement."

"So Picasso doesn't know what he's talking about when he talks about Picasso?"

"You've put your finger on it. He is talking about Picasso the man—troubled, influenced by ups and down in his health, his love-life, his bank account, his feelings about Spain—everything that makes the man. When I talk about Picasso I talk about the genius who painted *Les Demoiselles d'Avignon*, the master of every genre, the Surrealist, the visionary who painted the prophetic *Guernica*—one of the greatest things to come out of this rotten era—*The Charnel House*, the whole bloody lot. And about that Picasso, the mere man Picasso knows bugger-all, because he is sitting inside himself and has too close a view of himself. About the artist Picasso I know more than Pablo Picasso does."

"I envy your assurance."

"You're not a critic. You're not even a painter. You're a craftsman, a creation of that old scamp Saraceni. And you ought to understand this, Frank, because it's part of the truth. A very big part of it. Too much rides on the reputation of Picasso to allow any rubbish like that interview to rock the boat."

"Money, you mean? Fashion in taste?"

"Don't be cynical about fashion in taste. Among other things, art is very big business."

"But what about what he says about seeking consolation and exaltation in art?"

"That was the fashion of an earlier day. That was probably true about the Age of Faith, which has been bleeding badly ever since the Renaissance, and which got its death blow with the revolutions in America and France. The Age of Faith took a deadly disease from the Reformation.

Ever see a really great picture inspired by Protestantism? But the passing of the Age of Faith didn't mean the death of art, which is the only immortal, everlasting thing."

"But he says in so many words that he was serving fashion, pleasing the crowd, devising absurdities and puzzles."

"Don't you hear what I'm telling you? What he *says* is rubbish. It's what he *does* that counts."

Francis could not win the argument, but he was not convinced, and it was his determination that consolation and exaltation must somewhere and somehow be the chief care of the artists that pushed him to his decision to return to Canada, where art was still not big business, where art was indeed little considered, and where therefore art might be persuaded to remain true to the path he was convinced was the right one.

He could not embark on this great missionary journey, this return to his roots, quickly or easily. First of all he had to detach himself from MI5, and to his surprise Uncle Jack was not willing to release him without argument.

"My dear boy, perhaps you feel that you've been neglected—not pushed ahead in the profession as you might have been. But you don't understand how we work—how we are compelled to work. We get a trustworthy, first-rate man in a key job, and we leave him there. You are just what we need in this art connection. Knowledgeable, respected, but not too visible; able to go anywhere without making too much of a stir; a Canadian and therefore supposed to be a bit dumb by people who value a glittering cleverness above everything else. You've got enough money not to be always nagging me for extras. I'd describe you as ideal for what you are doing. You've provided quite enough useful tips about dangerous people to have fully earned your passage in this work. And now you want to throw it up."

"Nice of you to say all that. But where does it lead?"

"I can't possibly promise that it leads anywhere other than where you are at present. Doesn't that satisfy you? Your father never worried about where things led."

"For him it led to a knighthood."

"Do you want a knighthood? What would you get it for? Most of the chaps you are keeping an eye on are pestering for knighthoods for themselves. A thing like that would tip off every clever rogue that you were something more than you seemed."

"Well, I'm grateful for everything, but in fact I am certain that I am something more than I seem, and I want to go home, and be what I am in my own country."

That would have been that, if another upheaval—not a blow or a misfortune, but a disturbing change of circumstances—had not shaken Francis profoundly.

Saraceni died, and as his wife had died in the Blitz, and his daughter had died from a less dramatic cause, Francis discovered that he was the Meister's sole heir.

That meant going to Rome and spending long hours with Italian lawyers and civil servants who explained to him the complexities of inheriting a large private collection of art—not all of it art of the highest quality but every bit of it of museum quality—in a country that had been virtually beggared by a war it had never really wanted.

The Italian lawyers were rueful, and very courteous, but firm that the law must be served in every respect. Serving the law in Italy, as in every civilized country, was an extremely expensive business, but Saraceni had left plenty of money to take care of that and leave some over. What the Italian lawyers could not control, though they tried, was whatever Saraceni had deposited in numbered accounts in Switzerland.

This was what shocked Francis, for he had never thought of the Meister as a very rich man. But the Meister must have made some remarkably good deals with the people who paid him and Prince Max and the Gräfin for the pictures that had made their way to England from Düsterstein. When he made himself known to the quiet men at the banks, and established his undoubted right to Saraceni's wealth, Francis could not believe the record of millions in good hard currency that were his. He came of a banking family and money in substantial sums was not strange to him. But until now his income had reached him from Canada without any necessity for him to think about the capital sums that generated it. Money, to him, meant a lump that appeared in his account every quarter, a lump from which he allotted sums for the miserable estate in Cornwall that never fulfilled the promises that were made for it by Uncle Roderick, and an increasing sum for the maintenance of Little Charlie, who was now almost grown up and appeared to eat money, so great were the demands made on her behalf by Aunt Prudence. Francis, who thought of himself as "careful", sighed and sometimes cursed whenever he signed these cheques, and although he never spent anything like the remainder of his income, he considered himself as a man financially somewhat straitened.

It was a two-year job to shake himself loose from MI5 and make the best he could of Saraceni's estate, but at last it was done, and he returned to the land of his birth.

The land of his birth had not stood still in the years since Francis had left it to go to Oxford. The war had taught it something about its place in the world, and about the exploitative attitude taken by great countries toward small countries— small in population and influence, however gigantic they might be in physical dimension. Canada the wide-eyed farm boy was becoming streetwise, though not truly wise. Large numbers of immigrants from every part of Europe saw a future for themselves in Canada, and their attitude was understandably exploitative and somewhat patronizing. Nevertheless, they could not wholly abandon the sort of intelligence they had gained as a birthright in Europe, and in some respects the Canadian surface became observably smoother. Perhaps the most significant change, in the long term, was that of which Ruth Nibsmith—intuitive as always—had spoken at Düsterstein; the little country with the big body, which had always been introverted in its psychology—an introversion that had shown itself in a Loyalist bias, a refusal to be liberated by the military force of its mighty neighbour from what the mighty neighbour assumed was an intolerable colonial yoke—was striving now to assume the extraversion of that mighty neighbour. Because Canada could not really understand the American extraversion, it imitated the obvious elements in it, and the effect was often tawdry. Canada had lost its way, had suffered what anthropologists call Loss of Soul. But when the Soul was such a doubting, flickering, shy entity, who would regret its loss when there were big, obvious, and immediate gains to be had?

Thus Francis returned to a homeland he did not know. His real homeland, compounded of the best of Victoria Cameron and Zadok Hoyle, of the broad adventurous spirit of Grand-père, of the sentimental goodness of Aunt Mary-Ben, was nowhere to be found in the city of Toronto. Like many another, Francis thought his homeland was the world of childhood, and it had fled.

What he did find in Toronto was a new version

of the Cornish and McRory family, with Gerald Vincent O'Gorman a very big man in the financial community and a power of great but undefined influence in the Conservative Party. If the Tories ever came to power, Gerry was a sure bet for a seat in the Senate, an appointment safer and richer than a knighthood of St. Sylvester, and something which would, in his opinion and his wife's, make him the true successor to Grand-père. Gerry was Chairman of the Board of the Cornish Trust, which was now very big business; the President, succeeding Sir Francis (who had died while Francis was deep in financial affairs in Rome, and could not return to Canada), was a Tory senator of unimpeachable dullness and respectability, and he gave Gerry no trouble. Gerry's sons Larry and Michael were high in the Trust and they were as friendly to Francis as he would allow them to be. But he missed his younger brother Arthur, who, with his wife, had been killed in a car crash, leaving their son Arthur to the care of the O'Gormans, who did their best, but confided Arthur chiefly to men and women Trust officers. Francis didn't want any help with his money; his fortune from Saraceni was the first money he had ever possessed—apart from the miserable stipend paid him by MI5—that was not controlled and managed by the family, and he was determined not to reveal its extent or let any part of it be ruled by another hand.

"Frank, you must do as you think best, but for God's sake don't get skinned," said Larry.

"Don't worry," said Francis. "I've been skinned enough in my time to know my way around."

As soon as it could be managed he settled a modest—in the light of his wealth, a mingy—sum on Little Charlie, and informed Uncle Roderick and Aunt Prudence that the girl was to be maintained out of the interest on it until she was twenty-five, when she could take over the management of it herself. He also informed them that under his new circumstances—which he did not explain—he could no longer provide anything more than a very small annual sum for the maintenance of the estate, and he left unanswered the wailing, beseeching letters that followed. He thought it was good of him to give them anything at all.

He then settled himself to the task of devoting his very large income (for he never thought of touching his correspondingly larger capital) to the encouragement of art in Canada, and the experience was like that of a man who bites into a peach and breaks a tooth on the stone.

It was not that the Canadian painters whom he very quickly sought out were disagreeable, but they were strongly independent. More accurately, the good ones were independent and the ones who responded with glee to the appearance of a possible patron were not good. Francis could not get rid of his money because he would not divorce it from his advice, and the painters did not want advice. He tried to band some of them together to do work that consoled and exalted, and his words fell on politely deaf ears.

"You seem to want to create a new Pre-Raphaelite Brotherhood," said one of the best, a large man of Ukrainian antecedents named George Bogdanovich. "You can't get away with it, y'know. Buy some pictures. Sure, we're glad to sell pictures. But don't try to be a big influence. Just leave us alone. We know what we're doing."

What they were doing was respectable enough, but it did not appeal to Francis. They were utterly in love with the Canadian landscape, and tried to come to terms with it in a variety of ways, some of which, Francis knew, were admirable, and a handful splendid.

"But no people ever appear in your pictures," he said, again and again.

"Don't want 'em," said Bogdanovich, answering for all. "The people stink. Most of 'em, anyway. We paint the country, and maybe after a while the people will learn about the country from the pictures, and stink a little less. Got to begin with the country. That's consolation and exaltation. We have to do it our own way."

There could be no quarrelling with that. There were painters, of course, who followed the newest, fashionable trends. Without being pressed, they would explain that they dipped deep into their own Unconscious—a word that was new to Francis in this context—and drew up conceptions that were expressed in pictures that might be gaudy and rather messy rearrangements of what they saw, or felt; some were carefully wrought arrangements of colours, usually dingy. These messages

from the Unconscious were deemed to be infi-
nitely precious, evoking in sensitive viewers some
hint of an Unconscious deeper than any they
could explore unaided. But Francis was not impressed. What had Ruth said? "You can't talk to
the Mothers by getting them on the phone. They
have an unlisted number." These delvers clearly
did not have the number. It was such fakers of a
chthonic inner vision whom Francis grew to detest
above all others.

So Francis had to content himself with buying
pictures that he thought good, but did not much
like. Without being quite sure how it happened he
found that he was taking pictures from painters
who lived in inaccessible places, and keeping them
in his Toronto dwelling, where from time to time
he was able to sell them and remit the money to
the painter. He took no fee, but in a way he was a
dealer. The world of collectors, not large in Canada, understood that he knew a good picture
when he saw one, and his recommendation was a
guarantee of quality. But this did not satisfy him,
though in a desultory way it occupied him.

His satisfaction came from the pictures that had
been in Saraceni's collection, which he was able to
sneak into Canada by not altogether blameless
means, and store in his Toronto headquarters.

These headquarters were on the top floor of an
apartment house he owned in a decent, though
not a fashionable, part of Toronto. He had bought
it, years before, on the advice of his cousin Larry,
who had told him that he ought to diversify his

holdings, and get some good real estate. There were three apartments on the top floor of the dull building, product of an unadventurous period of architecture, and Francis spread his possessions among all three. To begin, this top floor looked like a richly if oddly furnished large single apartment, but as time went on the rooms became more and more cluttered, and the space in which Francis lived grew smaller and smaller.

"God, what a magpie's nest," said Aylwin Ross, the first time he visited it. "'Blind Fortune still bestows her gifts on such as cannot use them.' Jonson, not me, but apt, I'm sure you will admit. Where in God's name did all this stuff come from?"

"Inherited," said Francis.

"From Saraceni. You don't have to tell me."

"In part. Much of it I have bought."

"With the ghost of Saraceni looking over your shoulder," said Ross. "Frank, how do you endure it?"

Frank endured it because he never thought of it as a permanent state. He was always meaning to go through his possessions carefully, banishing some to storage, perhaps selling some others, and arriving at last at a dwelling space over-furnished and over-decorated, perhaps, but recognizable as a human habitation. Meanwhile he lived in something like an antique dealer's warehouse, to which he was continually adding the contents of new crates, cartons, and parcels. It was fortunate that his apartment house possessed a freight elevator, as well as the shuddering, murmurous bronze cage in which visitors ascended to what Ross named The Old Curiosity Shop.

Ross was a frequent visitor, for he had taken to returning to Canada several times a year, to give a lecture here, offer advice to an aspiring municipal or provincial gallery there, and contribute articles to Canadian periodicals on the state of art and the dizzy ascent of art prices in the international salerooms. He brought Francis the gossip of the art world—the sort of thing that could not be printed—and stories about its personalities, some of whom were people Francis had watched on behalf of Uncle Jack. Not that Francis ever mentioned his real London work to Ross; he was as close-mouthed as ever about that, and he was expert in deflecting delicate inquiries that might give a hint as to the extent of his fortune. But it could not be concealed that he was rich, and very rich, for such eccentricity as he was developing could not be sustained by less than a large fortune. He bought pictures at Christie's and Sotheby's at high prices, and although he did so through an agent, Ross was the kind of man who could ferret out who the real buyer was. What Ross did not know was that such heavy purchasing was Francis's way of assuaging the great yearning he felt to paint himself. More than once he tried to find a new style, and every time he gave it up in disgust. The Mothers would not speak to him in a contemporary voice.

Ross's preoccupation with the art world of Canada, which might have puzzled a less astute person, was no mystery to Francis. Ross wanted to be the Director of the National Gallery in Ottawa, and to secure such an appointment it was well to lay his plans some years ahead of the event.

"I really am a Canadian, you know," he said; "a Canadian in my bones, and I want to do something important here. I want to raise the Gallery to a level of world importance, which it isn't now. Of course, it has some fine things. The collection of eighteenth-century drawings is enviable, and there are other good individual holdings. But not enough. Not nearly enough. The buying has usually been unexceptionable in terms of a budget that is simply derisory; but there is far too much that has merely been donated, and we know what that can mean, in a country without many real connoisseurs. It's hard to turn down donations, or to stick 'em in the cellar when you've got 'em. Too many feelings to be hurt. But the time must come. There must be some ruthless weeding and some major buying.—Look here, Frank, what are you going to do with the best of what you have?"

"I haven't really thought about it," said Francis, which was a lie.

"My dear man, the time to think about it is now."

And so, after much haggling about choices, Francis gave his six finest Canadian pictures to the Gallery, and Ross let it leak out in the proper places that it was he who had secured this benefaction, and from whom it came, although Francis tried his best to keep the gift anonymous.

"If it gets out every gallery in the country will be after me," he said.

"Do you blame them? Come on, Frank, get wise to yourself. If you're not a benefactor, what in God's name are you? When are you going to give the Gallery some of that fine Italian stuff?"

"Give away? But why? Why is it assumed that someone who has fine things is under an obligation to give them away?"

In the course of time, and quite a short time as such things go, the Director of the National Gallery had to be replaced, and who was a more obvious candidate for the post than Aylwin Ross?

True to Canadian style in such matters, the committee that was empowered to recommend a successor to the relevant Minister of the Crown fretted and agonized before they did so. Would Ross, now a man with a wide and brilliant reputation, think of accepting such a post? Should not some worthy but relatively unknown scholar from a Canadian university, who for rather vague reasons was thought to deserve something from his country, be appointed instead? Were there not rumours about Ross's private life? Would Ross want more money than the job at present paid? It was possible for Francis to exercise some influence with certain members of the committee, and he did so, but with caution lest the other members of the committee, who hated him for his knowledge and his wealth, should discover that he was interfering. But at last, when the committee had enjoyed as much of this obligatory Gethsemane as could be endured, the recommendation was made to the Minister, the Minister wrote to Ross, Ross asked for a month in which to consider whether he could see his way clear to making the inevitable sacrifice of an international career as a critic, and in the end he agreed to make the sacrifice—at a substantially increased stipend.

The Minister announced the appointment, and as things happened it was the last appointment he did announce, for the Government of which he was a member fell, and after the hubbub and pow-wow incidental to a General Election had been completed, a new Ministry was formed, and the Minister to whom Ross was to be responsible proved to be a woman. What could be more suitable? Among a large number of Canadians it was assumed that women were good at art and culture. After all, in pioneer days, such things, embodied chiefly in quilts and hooked rugs, had lain entirely in their hands, and there was a great deal of pioneer opinion still operative in a fossilized state in the political world.

Ross had not paid much attention to the election. He said himself that he was in no way a political man. He had not heeded, if indeed he heard, the vehement promises made by the political party that now formed the Government to cut expenditures, to lance the boil of a swollen Civil Service, and above all to get rid of what the politicians assured the voters were "frills". But expenditures, especially when so many of them are baby bonuses, mothers' allowances, medical subventions, or pensions to the old and the disabled, are not easy to reduce; indeed, the clamour of the deserving and the needy is always mounting and always for more. Nor is it really possible to reduce the Civil Service without offending multitudes of voters, for all Civil Servants, and especially those on the humbler levels, come not from families but from tribes, engorged with tribal loyalty. This leaves only frills to provide showy economies. And when a country has a National Gallery already full of pictures, as any fool who visits it on a wet day may plainly see, are not more pictures frills, and frills of a peculiarly dispensable, elitist, and effete nature?

Nothing of this struck in upon the consciousness of Aylwin Ross, who was jaunting from one side of Canada to the other, and back again by a different path, explaining to interested groups that it was time Canada had a National Gallery worthy of it, that its present Gallery was not even in the second rank of excellence, and that something decisive must be done, and done at once. His eloquence was much admired. We cannot take our place in the world as a nation of millions of hockey-watchers and a few score hockey-players, he said. He quoted from Ben Jonson: "Whosoever loves not picture is injurious to truth, and all the wisdom of poetry. Picture is the invention of Heaven, the most ancient, and most akin to Nature." (He did not continue the passage, in which

Jonson says flatly that painting is inferior to poetry; the art of the quoter is to know when to stop.) His splendid voice, in which the Canadian accent was softened but not obliterated, was in itself a guarantee of his sincerity. His great good looks enchanted the women and not a few of the men. This was a Canadian presence of a kind to which they were not accustomed. And how he could joke, and drink, and tell good stories of the art world at the receptions that followed his public addresses. Ross's popularity grew like a pumpkin, and was as bright and shiny. When he had completed his great tour, by which time the new Ministry was comfortably in the saddle, Ross exploded his firework.

A firework that misfires can be like a bomb. Ross let it be known, in an unwise press conference, that it lay in his power, at a stroke, to lift the National Gallery to a new level, and set it well on the way to recognition as a collection of world importance. He had, by long negotiation and a lightning trip to Europe, succeeded in pledging all the Gallery's allocation for acquisitions for the forthcoming year, and in addition a sum that would gobble it up for six years to come. He had agreed to purchase six pictures, six pictures of world importance, from a great private collection in Europe. He had got them at bargain rates, by dint of keen negotiation and, it was hinted in the gentlest terms, by personal charm.

Who was the owner? Ross let it be teased out of him that the owner was Amalie von Ingelheim, who had recently inherited the collection from her grandmother, and as the Gräfin—for so Ross incorrectly but impressively called her—had need of money (her husband, Prince Max, was taking over a large cosmetic empire with its headquarters in New York), she was letting some of her private treasures out into the world, where they had never been seen before. For a few paltry millions Canada could put itself on the map as a country possessing a notable national collection.

Comparatively few people know what a million dollars actually is. To the majority it is a gaseous concept, swelling or decreasing as the occasion suggests. In the minds of politicians, perhaps more than anywhere, the notion of a million dollars has this accordion-like ability to expand or contract; if they are disposing of it, the million is a pleasing sum, reflecting warmly upon themselves; if somebody else wants it, it becomes a figure of inordinate size, not to be compassed by the rational mind. When the politicians learned that one of their functionaries, an understrapper holding a minor post in a *cul de sac,* had promised several millions abroad, for the acquirement of pictures—*pictures,* for God's sake—they burst into flames of indignation, and none were more indignant than those of the party, now Her Majesty's Loyal Opposition, who had appointed Ross just before they fell from power.

The Minister was under the gun. She did not like Ross, whom she had met two or three times, and her Assistant Deputy Minister, who dealt directly with Ross, was another woman who liked him even less. He had quoted Jonson to her, and she had assumed that he was talking about Samuel Johnson, and had made a goat of herself. (Or so it seemed to her, for Ross, who was used to this misunderstanding, paid little attention.) The Assistant Deputy Minister was a feminist, and certain that Ross's deferential manner toward women was mockery. She had her suspicions that Ross was a homosexual—so handsome a man, and unmarried—and she detailed a trusted henchman (one of the Palace Eunuchs of her Department) to get the goods on Ross if he could, by any means short of making him a proposition in a Parliamentary lavatory. Ross, in his dealings with this lady, was unquestionably tactless; in the words of his favourite author, he was "plagued with an itching leprosy of wit", and he could not dissemble it in his dealings with politicians and Civil Servants.

The Minister relied on the advice of her Deputy, who relied on the advice of her assistant (who was not quite her lover but would have been if they were not both so busy and so tired), and her path was clear. A Civil Servant under her Ministry had behaved with unwarrantable freedom, making deals involving money not yet allocated, and without a word to her. She made a statement in the House repudiating the purchases, and assuring the Commons that no one was more zealous in cutting down unwarrantable expenditures than she. Piously, she said that she yielded to no one in her love of art in all its forms, but there were times when even she had to regard art as a frill. When grave financial problems confronted the country, she knew where her priorities lay. She went no further, but it was assumed that these priorities lay in the Maritimes, or on the Prairies, where money problems are endemic.

Without an election, the press was in need of a political punching-bag, and Ross provided one for at least two weeks. The most conservative insisted that he be humbled, made to understand the facts of Canadian life, taught a sharp lesson: the more extreme papers demanded that his appointment be revoked, and hinted that he ought to go back to Europe, where he obviously belonged, having learned that decent people didn't blaspheme against hockey.

The righteous uproar was almost over when Ross appeared one night in the Old Curiosity Shop. Looking at him, in his painfully reduced state, Francis knew that he loved him. But what was there to say?

"The Ark of the Lord seems to have fallen into the hands of the Philistines" was what he did say.

"I have never met this kind of thing before. They hate me. I think they wish me dead," said Ross.

"Oh, not at all. Politicians get far worse abuse all the time. It will blow over."

"Yes, and I will be left discredited in the eyes of my staff and perpetually school-marmed by the Minister, who will grudge me every penny that goes to the Gallery. I'll be nothing more than a caretaker, looking after a cat-and-dog collection and without any hope of improving it."

"Well, Aylwin, I don't want to be stuffy, but you really shouldn't have spent money you didn't have in your grip. And the Minister—you know that as a woman she has to show herself tougher than any of the men; she can't afford a single feminine weakness. The Prime Minister reserves all those for himself."

"She's out to get me, you know. Wants to prove me a fairy."

"Well—are you? I've never known."

"Not more than most men, I suppose. I've had affairs with women."

"Well, why don't you make a pass at the Minister? That would answer her question."

"Grotesque suggestion! She smells of drug-store perfume and cough-drops! No, there's only one thing that will put me right."

"And that is—?"

"If only I could get one of those pictures for the Gallery. Just one would raise enough interest in the international art world to show the Minister I wasn't completely a fool."

"Yes, but how could you do that?" But even as he spoke, Francis knew.

"If I could get a private benefactor to give one to the Gallery, it would do an immense amount to put me right, and eventually it would put me totally right. If I could get the one I want, that's to say."

"Benefactors are very elusive creatures."

"Yes, but not unknown. Frank—will you?"

"Will I what?"

"You know damn well what. Will you stump up for one of those pictures?"

"With art prices what they are at present? You flatter me!"

"No I don't. I know what you have been paying in London in the past two or three years. You could do it."

"Even if I could, which I don't for a moment admit, why would I?"

"Haven't you any patriotism?"

"It is variable. I take off my hat when our flag goes by—heraldic eyesore though it is."

"For friendship?"

"From what I've seen of the world the worst thing that can happen to friendship is to put a price on it."

"Frank, you're making me beg. All right, damn it, I'll beg.—Will you?"

Never in his life, which had not been sparing of discomfort, had Francis been so cornered. Ross looked so wretched, so beaten, and so beautiful in his wretchedness. In the biblical phrase, his bowels yearned toward Ross. But his compassion was not the whole of Francis's complex of emotions. The more money he had, the more he loved money. And—he couldn't explain it but he felt it—having relinquished his work as an artist, so much of what was deepest in him was now caught up with possessions, and therefore with money.

To give a picture to the nation—very fine in the saying, and so dangerous in the doing. Be known as a benefactor and everybody wants something, often to sustain mediocrity. Yet—there was Ross, the last of his loves, and miserable. He had loved Ismay with his whole heart—and like a fool. He had loved Ruth like a man, and Ruth had died with hundreds of thousands of others, a victim of the world's cruel stupidity. He loved Ross, not because he wanted Ross physically, but for his daring youth, which the years had not touched, for his defiance of conventions that Francis knew had kept himself in chains, had made him the sustainer of a failing estate and the supporter of a child who was not his own, had held him back from claiming a great painting as his work. Yes, he must yield, whatever the hurt to his purse, which was now almost his soul. Almost; not wholly.

And so Francis was about to say yes, and would have done if Ross had been able to hold his tongue. But his fatal urge toward speech stepped between Ross and his success.

"The gift could be anonymous, you know."

"Of course. I would insist on that."

"Then you agree.—Frank, I love you!"

The words startled Francis more than any blow. Oh God, this was putting a price on friendship, and no doubt about it!

"I haven't agreed yet."

"Oh yes you have! Frank, this will put everything right! Now, about price—let me get in touch with Prince Max tomorrow!"

"Prince Max?"

"Yes. Even you, drinker of cheap schlock though you are, must know about Prince Max, head of the great Maximilian wine-importers in New York? He's acting on behalf of his wife. She was Amalie von Ingelheim and she inherited the whole collection from the old Gräfin."

"Amalie von Ingelheim. I didn't know she'd married Max! I know her—knew her."

"Yes, she remembers you. Calls you Le Beau Ténébreux. Said you taught her to play skat when she was a kid."

"Why is she selling?"

"Because she's a girl with a head on her shoulders. She and Max are a thriving pair of aristocratic survivors. They even look alike, though he must be a good deal older than she is. She's had a good career already as a model, but you know those careers don't run much more than eighteen months. She's been on the covers of the two biggest fashion magazines, and there's no place else to go. She and Prince Max are buying a cosmetic business—a really good one—and she'll make herself a hugely rich, international beauty."

"And the pictures?"

"She says she never gave a damn about the pictures."

"So? Little Amalie has certainly grown up—in a way."

"Yes, but she's not without heart. She'll listen

623

to reason. And if I tell her you are the buyer, everything will work out well. That's to say, as cheaply as we have any right to expect—from aristocratic survivors. The picture could be here and in the Gallery before Christmas. What a gift to the nation!"

"There are six pictures, I believe. I've never seen any report that said which pictures. I can guess which ones might make a big price in the market. Is it the little Raphael?"

"No, not that one."

"The Bronzino portrait?"

"No. Nor the Grunewald. Since the row here other buyers have appeared and five are gone. But she's holding the one I want."

Ruth had told Francis he had plenty of intuition. It had been slow in acting, but it worked now with full force.

"Which picture?"

"Not the greatest name, but the very picture we need, because it has mystery, you see, and historical importance, and it's virtually unique because only one other picture from the same hand is known to exist. It's a picture that I dearly love, because it did more than anything else to establish me in my present place as an expert. You've seen it! A prize! *The Marriage at Cana*, by the so-called Alchemical Master!"

Intuition was now working furiously. "Why has she kept it? Aylwin, did you tell her you might still be able to arrange to buy it?"

"I may have dropped a hint to Max. You know how one talks in these deals."

"Did you hint that I might put up the money?"

"Certainly your name came into it. And as you're an old friend they have agreed to hold it for a month or so."

"In other words, you have once again spent some money that you didn't have assured. My money."

"Come on, Frank, you know what these situations are like. Don't talk like a banker."

"I won't buy it."

"Frank—listen—I simply did what had to be done. Buying art on this level is extremely sensitive business. When I had Max and Amalie in the right mood I had to move quickly. You'll see it all quite differently tomorrow."

"No, I won't. I will never buy that picture."

"But why? Is it the money? Oh, Frank, don't say it's the money!"

"No, I give you my word it isn't the money."

"Then why?"

"I have personal reasons that I can't explain. The Raphael, the Bronzino, two or three others—yes, I would have done it for you. But not *The Marriage at Cana*."

"Why, why, why! You've got to tell me. You owe it to me to tell me!"

"Anything I owed you, Aylwin, has been paid in full with six excellent modern paintings. I won't buy that picture, and that's flat."

"You shit, Frank!"

"Oh come, I should have thought that under these circumstances you could have found a quotation from Ben Jonson."

"All right! 'Turd in your teeth'."

"Pretty good. Nothing else?"

" 'May dogs defile thy walls,
And wasps and hornets breed beneath thy roof,
This seat of falsehood and this cave of cozen-
age!' "

And Ross flung out of the room. To Francis it seemed that he was laughing at his own apt quotation, but in truth he was weeping. The two grimaces are not so far apart.

Francis washed his hands and retired to the narrow space he had kept for his bed. Before he went to sleep he looked long at a picture that puzzled those of his friends who had seen it, and that still hung over his bed's head. It was not a great picture. It was a cheapish print of *Love Locked Out* and to him at present it was more poignant than any of his heaped-up master-works.

Of course Francis did the only possible thing. He couldn't under any circumstances have allowed the friend he loved to be taken in by a picture he knew to be a fake, and his own fake at that, to place it in the principal gallery of the country to which they were both supposed to owe their first allegiance, said the Lesser Zadkiel.

—I disagree totally, said the Daimon Maimas. He could certainly have done it, and what he called

626

*his Mercurius influence—myself really—urged him
to do it. I reminded him of what Letztpfenning
had said. What is being sold, a great picture or the
magic of the past? Is it a work of grave beauty that is
being purchased, or such a work given its real worth
by the seal of four centuries? I was disgusted with
Francis. Indeed, I nearly deserted him at that instant.*

—Can you do that?

*—You know I can. And when a man's daimon
leaves him, he is finished. You remember that when
Mark Antony was playing the fool with that Egyp-
tian woman his daimon left him in disgust. That was
because of a stupid love, as well.*

*—Francis's love for Ross was not stupid, brother.
I thought it had a flavour of nobility, because it
asked nothing.*

—It made him betray what was best of himself.

*—Questionable, brother. Love, or worldly gratifi-
cation? Love, or vanity? Love, or a wry joke on the
world of art that seemed to have no place for him? If
poor Darcourt, who longs to know the truth about
Francis, knew what we know, he would rank Francis
very high.*

*—Darcourt is a Christian priest, and Christianity
cost Francis dear. It gave him that double conscience we have seen plaguing him throughout his life.
Darcourt would have said he did the right thing. I do
not.*

—Yet you did not reject him.

*—I was disgusted with him. I hate to leave a job
uncompleted. I was told to make Francis a great
man, and he went directly contrary to my urging.*

627

—Perhaps he was indeed a great man.

—Not the great man I would have made.

—You are not the final judge, brother.

—Nor was I wholly defeated, brother. Greatness is achieved in more than one way. Watch what follows.

The suicide of Aylwin Ross caused the usual curiosity, the flow of easy pity, the satisfaction at having been witness at second hand to something that newspapers describe as a tragedy, in the public at large. The world of connoisseurship mourned him as a fine talent brought untimely to an end. In Canada it was assumed that he had been unable to bear public disgrace, and there were expressions of regret, mingling guilt with covert contempt that a man had broken under stress, when he should have taken his medicine like a little soldier. There was some speculation of the easy psychological kind that he had killed himself in order to make his enemies and detractors feel cheap, and although some of them did feel cheap they were angry with themselves for having been manipulated in such a way. In Parliament the Minister spoke briefly of Ross as a man who had meant well, but who was not a realist in public affairs; nevertheless, the Honourable Members were charged to think of him as a great Canadian. And the Honourable Members, who are accustomed to such work, obediently did so for a full minute. A memorial service was mounted at the National Gallery and the dead savant was accorded the usual public honours: poetry was spoken, some Bach was played, and the Deputy Minister read a carefully worded tribute, written by a minor poet from the pool of governmental speech-writers; it said many splendid things, but admitted nothing. It enjoined the National Gallery staff, and the nation, never to forget Aylwin Ross in its upward journey toward prudent, economical greatness.

As for Francis, who had suffered no nervous breakdown when Ruth was killed, he allowed himself such a collapse of the spirit now and he toughed it out by himself in his cave of cozenage, living on beer and baked beans, cold from the can. Perhaps because he sought no professional help in dealing with his misery, he was as much himself in a few weeks as he would ever be again.

His final years were productive, in their way, and he had his satisfactions. These were years when it was fashionable to speak of the Century of the Common Man, but Francis saw little real evidence that it was so, and as he remembered his years at Carlyle Rural, spent with the Common Child, he was neither surprised nor regretful. People who met him casually thought him a misanthrope, but he had friends, drawn chiefly from the academic community. Extensive and curious knowledge of European life during the few centuries that most appealed to him established a kinship between Francis and Professor Clement Hollier, who sought historical truths in what many historians chose to overlook. Professor the Reverend Simon Darcourt (the splendour of his title amused Francis) became a great friend because he and Francis were fellow enthusiasts for rare books, manuscripts, old calligraphy, caricatures, and a ragbag of half a dozen other things about which he was not always deeply informed, but that came within the net of his swelling collections. It was Darcourt who revived Francis's sleeping love of music—better music than had ever been known to Mary-Ben—and they were often seen at concerts together.

There were evenings when these cronies gathered in the Old Curiosity Shop and while Hollier sat almost silent, Francis listened as Darcourt poured out a stream of lively, amusing, endearing talk, like wine bubbling out of the bottles that Darcourt always remembered to bring, for Francis was tight about hospitality. It amused him that Darcourt, something of a connoisseur, favoured vintages that bore the distinguished label of Prince Max on which the motto "Thou shalt perish ere I perish" was of course assumed to refer to the wine.

Another friend, not so close but valued, was Professor Urquhart McVarish, whose appeal to Francis (though McVarish never guessed it) was that in him there was something of the Mercurial spirit he felt so strongly in himself, though he kept it hidden, whereas McVarish let it rip, and boasted, and lied and cheated, with a vigour

Francis found amusing and refreshing. It was Darcourt who persuaded Francis to read the works of Ben Jonson in a fine First Folio, and because of that Francis often addressed McVarish as Sir Epicure Mammon—a reference McVarish never troubled to check, and assumed to be complimentary. Indeed, in Jonson Francis discovered a spirit he would never have divined from the carefully chosen quotations of Aylwin Ross—a spirit apparently harsh, but inwardly tender, much like Francis himself.

McVarish had the Mercurial trait of thievery, as well; his method was the tried-and-true one of borrowing something which somehow he never remembered to return, and after the disappearance of a valued old gramophone record— Sir Harry Lauder singing "Stop Your Tickling, Jock"—Francis had to take care that only lesser objects got out of his hands to this merry, amoral Scot. But McVarish never felt the need to do anything in return for what arose from his friendship with Francis. It was Hollier and Darcourt who contrived to have Francis elected an honorary member of the Senior Common Room at the College of St. John and the Holy Ghost in the University of Toronto—Francis's old college, affectionately known as Spook. This was the reason why Francis put Spook down for a handsome inheritance in his will—the will that he now delighted to revise, daub with codicils, and play with.

The will cost him much thought, and some

anxiety. He had the document acknowledging that what he had done about Little Charlie was all that the child could expect; but he prudently, though not very agreeably, had his London lawyers secure a document from Ismay, who was still pursuing The Workers' Cause in the Midlands, guaranteeing that Little Charlie was not the child of his loins, and that neither Ismay nor Little Charlie could make any claim on his estate. This was not easy, because Ismay was still in law his wife, but Francis provided his lawyers with the names of one or two members of the profession who knew a good deal about Ismay, and could make things uncomfortable for her if she did not toe the line.

He was still enough of a McRory to feel that he must remember relatives in his will, and he arranged bequests—mean, in the light of his great wealth—to Larry and Michael. Something better, but by no means lavish, was left to his nephew Arthur, son of his brother Arthur. Now and then Francis felt some guilt about this young Arthur, some stirring of a parental instinct that was never really strong. But what has a man in his sixties to say to a boy? Francis had an un-evolved Canadian idea that an uncle ought to teach a boy to shoot, or fish, or make a wigwam out of birch bark, and such ideas filled him with dismay. The notion that the boy could be interested in art never entered his head. So to Arthur he remained a taciturn, rather smelly, un-Cornish old party who turned up now and then at family affairs, and who was always good at Christmas and birthdays for a handsome money gift. But although Francis was convinced that a boy must necessarily be interested only in what he himself thought of as boyish things, he saw a glint in Arthur's eye which persuaded him, as the years passed and the boy became a man and an innovative, imaginative figure in the Cornish Trust, to name Arthur as his executor. With his three cronies, of course, to guide the supposedly Philistine young man in the disposal of his now unwieldy accumulation of art. For a collection it could no longer be called.

Once a week, if he remembered, he visited his mother, now in her mid-eighties, beautiful and frail, and with all her wits, if she chose to use them. They were both old people and it was possible for Francis to admit that he had never been on close terms with her, but that now he was past the obligatory, unquestioning love that had been required of him earlier, he quite liked her. She had once taken refuge in her useful vagueness when he asked about the first Francis, whom he still thought of as the Looner, but he thought he might sound her out about those flirtations, which had so embarrassed him as a boy, and which his father had brushed aside as insignificant.

"Mother, you have never told me anything about your youth. Were you and Father very much in love?"

"Franko, what an odd question! No: I wouldn't say we were much in love, but he understood me wonderfully, and we were the greatest friends."

633

"But were you never in love?"

"Oh—dozens of times. But I never took it very seriously, you know. How can one? It's such a troublesome feeling if you let it go too far. I knew lots of men, but I never gave your father cause for anxiety. He was always Number One, and he knew it. He was rather a strange man, you know. He rode his life on a very easy rein."

"I'm awfully glad to hear that."

"Once, before your father came along, I was desperately in love, the way young girls are. He was the most beautiful man I have ever seen. Beauty is such a disturbing thing, isn't it? I was so young, and he was an actor, and I never met him—only saw him on the stage, but that was the love that really hurt."

"There were a lot of very handsome actors then. It was the fashion. Do you remember which one he was?"

"Oh, indeed I do. I think I've got a picture postcard of him somewhere still, in a play called *Monsieur Beaucaire*. His name was Lewis Waller. What a perfect man!"

So much, then, for Dr. J.A. and his scientific malice about an unspecified taint. This cool, ancient, beautiful flirt had loved once, and with abandonment, and the fruit of that passion was the Looner!

What a punishment! What a slap in the face for a Catholic girl from the God she had been taught to worship! No wonder she had put all passion from her, and had become, like Venus in the

634

Bronzino *Allegory,* someone to whom love was a toy. Francis thought a great deal about it, and formed some highly philosophical conclusions. They were utterly mistaken, of course, because he knew nothing of the well-intentioned, maternally solicitous meddlings of Marie-Louise. Nobody ever knows the whole of anything. But if he had known, his compassion would doubtless have extended to his grandmother, as it now embraced more fully than ever before his mother, Zadok Hoyle, and that poor wretch, the Looner.

Thus it was that when Francis came to die, he had pretty well made up his accounts with all the principal figures in his life, and although he seemed to the world, and even to his few close friends, an eccentric and crabbed spirit, there was a quality of completeness about him that bound those friends tighter than would have been the case if he had been filled with one-sided, know-nothing sweet-ness and easy acceptance.

The end of his life, though not of his fame, came on a September night, following a Sunday that had been close and humid as Toronto often is in September. As it was his birthday he had made himself go out to dinner, although he was not hungry, and afterward he lay on a sofa in the Old Curiosity Shop, hoping that a breeze from the window would help him to breathe more easily. The sofa had been Saraceni's, and it was beauti-ful, but it was not well suited to lying; it was for some reclining beauty of the early nineteenth century, who saw herself in the image of Madame Récamier. But Francis could not make himself go to bed, and so when he felt the first shock of his quietus he was fully clothed, and in a position that was neither sitting nor lying. And after that shock, he knew he could not move.

Indeed, he knew he would never move again.

So this was it? Death, whom he had seen so often represented in art, usually as a figure of cruel menace, was there in the Old Curiosity Shop, and Francis was surprised to understand that he had no fear, though his breathing was now laborious and increasingly so. Well, one had always understood that there must be some struggle.

His vision was clouding, but his mind was clear; uncommonly clear. The reflection drifted through his consciousness that this was very different from what Ross must have felt, dying of a surfeit of sleeping-pills washed down with gin. How different was it from the last hours of Ruth? Who could say what that burned body enveloped of an active, certainly courageous and wise mind? But death, though people prate about its universality, is doubtless individual in the way it comes to everyone.

His feeling was going, but another sort of feeling was taking its place. Was this the famous cliché of all one's life passing before one's eyes that drowning men are supposed to experience? It was not all of his life. Rather it was a sense of the completeness of his life, and an understanding— oh, this was luck, this was mercy!—of the fact that his life had not been such a formless muddle, not quite such a rum start, as he had come to believe. He was humble in the recognition that he had not done too badly, and that even things that he had often wished otherwise—the crushing of the wretched Letztpfennig, for instance—were part of a pattern not of his making, and the fulfilling of a destiny that was surely as much Letztpfennig's as it was his own. Even his denial of Ross, which he had so often looked back on as a denial of love itself—death to the soul!— had been brought about as much by Ross as by any fault in himself. Ross was dear, as dear as Ruth, in another way, but something else was dearer and had to be protected. That was his one masterwork, *The Marriage at Cana,* now in a position of honour in a great gallery in the States, gloated over by lovers of art and by countless students who had university degrees in Fine Art, guaranteeing the infallibility of their knowledge and taste. If that bomb ever exploded, it would not explode in Canada, and ruin a friend.

No: that was hypocrisy, and he had no time now for hypocrisy. Surely Death had given a hint of His coming a week ago when he had carefully bundled up the preliminary studies, and those he had done after the fact, for *The Marriage at Cana,* and labelled them in careful Italic "My Drawings in Old Master style, for the National Gallery". Some day, somebody would tumble to it.

Discover who The Alchemical Master had been—that was a certainty and it would give the wiseacres a great deal to chatter about, anatomize, and discuss in articles and even books. Lives would be written of The Alchemical Master, but would they ever come close to the truth, or even the facts? In the picture in which, Saraceni had said, he had made up his soul, both as it had been and as it was yet to be, the figure of Love was indeed the two figures at the very centre, but it was love of the ideal wholeness that was shown there, and not the real loves of his life. Would they read his allegory, as he had once read the great allegory of Bronzino? In that picture, so dear to him, Time and his daughter Truth were unveiling the spectacle of what love was, as some day Time and Truth would unveil *The Marriage at Cana*. And when that day came there would be, to begin with, a great deal of harsh talk about deceit and fakery. But had not Bronzino said much that was relevant about deceit and fakery in the wonderfully painted figure of Fraude, the sweet-faced girl offering the honeycomb and the scorpion, whose lower parts were depicted as the chthonic dragon's claws and swingeing serpent tail? This was Fraude not simply as a cheat, but as a figure from the deep world of the Mothers, whence came all beauty, and also all that was fearful to timid souls seeking only the light, and determined that Love must be solely a thing of light. How lucky he was to have known Fraude, and to have tasted her enlarging, poisoned kiss! Had he, at the end, found the allegory of his own life? Oh, blessing on the angel in *The Marriage at*

Cana who declared, so mysteriously, "Thou hast kept the best wine till the last."

Francis was laughing now, but laughter was such an effort that there came another shock, and he dropped deeper into the gulf that was enclosing him.

Where was this? Unknown, yet familiar, more the true abode of his spirit than he had ever known before; a place never visited, but from which intimations had come that were the most precious gifts of his life.

It must be—it was—the Realm of the Mothers. How lucky he was, at the last, to taste this transporting wine!

After that, nothing, for to any outward observer it would have seemed that Francis had stood on the threshold of death some time before, and now he had taken the last step.

So you stood by him to the end, brother, said the Lesser Zadkiel.

—The end is not yet. Though he had sometimes defied me, I obey my orders still, said the Daimon Maimas.

—Your orders were to make him a great, or at least a remarkable man?

—Yes, and posthumously he will be seen as both great and remarkable. Oh, he was a great man, my Francis. He didn't die stupid.

—You had your work cut out for you.

—It is always so. People are such muddlers and meddlers. Father Devlin and Aunt Mary-Ben with

their drippings of holy water, and their single-barrelled compassion. Victoria Cameron with her terrible stoicism masked as religion. That Doctor with his shallow science. All ignorant people determined that their notions were absolutes.

—Yet I suppose you would say they were bred in the bone.

—They! How can you talk so, brother? Of course, we know that it is all metaphor, you and I. Indeed, we are metaphors ourselves. But the metaphors that shaped the life of Francis Cornish were Saturn, the resolute, and Mercury, the maker, the humorist, the trickster. It was my task to see that these, the Great Ones, were bred in the bone, and came out in the flesh. And my task is not yet finished.

"I've been thinking."

Arthur had returned from his two-day absence, and, having eaten grapefruit, porridge with cream, and bacon and eggs, had now moved into the coda of his usual breakfast and was busy with toast and marmalade.

"I'm not at all surprised. You think quite often. What now?" said Maria.

"That life of Uncle Frank. I was wrong. We'd better tell Simon to go ahead."

"No more worry about possible scandal?"

"No. Suppose a few drawings turn up at the National Gallery that look like Old Masters but are really by Uncle Frank? That doesn't make him a faker. He was an art student once, in the days when a lot of them copied Old Master drawings and even drew that way themselves, just to find out how it was done. Not faking at all. The Gallery people will spot them at once, though of course Darcourt mightn't. Nothing will come of it, you mark my words. Simon's a literary type, not an art critic. So let's give him the go-ahead, and get on with the real work of the Foundation. We ought to get some applications soon from needy geniuses."

"I have a few on my desk already."

"You call Simon, darling, and tell him I'm sorry I was arbitrary. Could he come in tonight? We could look at your letters and get on with the real job. Being patrons."

"The modern Medici?"

"No immodesty, please. But it should be sport."

"Blow your whistle, Arthur, and let the sport begin."

The publishers hope that this
Large Print Book has brought
you pleasurable reading.
Each title is designed to make
the text as easy to see as possible.
G.K. Hall Large Print Books
are available from your library and
your local bookstore. Or, you can
receive information by mail on
upcoming and current Large Print Books
and order directly from the publishers.
Just send your name and address to:

G.K. Hall & Co.
70 Lincoln Street
Boston, Mass. 02111

or call, toll-free:

1-800-343-2806

A note on the text
Large print edition designed by
Janet Zietowski.
Composed in 16 pt Plantin
on a Xyvision 300/Linotron 202N
by Henry Elliott
of G.K. Hall & Co.